Praise for Scions

"A semi-historical with sassy demigods, and a secret world on the brink of war, Scions has everything teen readers could want."

— Aprilynne Pike, #1 NYT bestselling
author of the Wings series

"This page-turner is Josephine Angelini's best yet!"

— Beth Revis, NYT bestselling author of
Across the Universe

"Josephine Angelini's series gives the Trojan War a captivating makeover for the modern age."

— Katharine McGee, NYT bestselling
author of American Royals

"Electrifying, action-packed story-telling with sworn enemies to lovers, Greek Gods, and an ending that's going to have you reaching for the next book."

— Aileen Erin, USA Today bestsell
author of the Alpha Girl s

SCIONS

A STARCROSED NOVEL

JOSEPHINE ANGELINI

SUNGRAZER PUBLISHING
LOS ANGELES

For my Pony

The Four Houses

House of Atreus

Upper East Side and Central Park

Elara Atreus - Head of House

Polyduces (Duce) Atreus

Daphne Atreus - Heir to House

House of Thebes

Washington Square, The Village and Alphabet City

Paris Delos - Head of House

Jordana Lycian

Tantalus Delos - Heir to House

Castor Delos

Pallas Delos

Ajax Delos

Antigone Lycian

Pandora Delos

House of Athens

Downtown, the Waterfront and Tribeca

Bellerophon Attica - Head of House

Ladon Attica

Daedelus Attica - Heir to House

Nilus Attica

Lelix Attica

House of Rome

Upper East and Harlem

Melia Tiber - Head of House

Leda Tiber - Heir to House

Adonis Tiber

CHAPTER 1

I've always hated the first day of school. I don't know for certain that it would be easier if we didn't move so much, but I have this feeling that if I could stay put in one school for long enough maybe the other kids would get used to the way I look. Maybe they'd even start to accept me.

But probably not. I guess it doesn't really matter anymore. I'm a senior this year. All I have to do is survive until graduation. One day at a time, right? I know that's a mantra from Alcoholics Anonymous, but as far as odious afflictions go, it's been my experience that high school should have a twelve-step recovery program of its own. There'd probably be fewer alcoholics if it did.

Manhattan is a big change from Massachusetts. I don't exactly blend in here, but at least I'm not as conspicuous as I was in Wellesley, or Duxbury before that, or any of the scores of places we've lived over the years. Since we moved here two weeks ago, I've been taking walks around the city while wearing different faces—faces that won't cause any problems. I've been able to wander, explore, and blend in. Couldn't do that before. Strangers get noticed in small towns, but in big cities everyone's a stranger. Or just plain strange. There're a lot of strange people in New York. I've discovered I'm fond of strange.

I've loved it here, even though New York City is probably the most dangerous place for me to be. I feel the tang of inspiration everywhere I go. Even the dirtiest wall can become the birthplace of a truly original thought. Like my newest discovery, which I've stumbled upon: a graffiti artist who's been leaving tags—which is a mural with the artist's name in it—on the side of some seriously expensive real estate. The tags are unique. More like works of guerrilla art than vandalism. They pull at me, even though I haven't been able to make out the name of the artist yet. Graffiti font can be hard to decipher.

I'm not the type to get gushy over art. I've never had an eye for paintings or an ear for music or anything like that, but these tags are different. I've been sneaking out to look for them. I'm invested. It feels good to look forward to something. It's been a while since I gave a shit about anything.

I change my face when I go tag hunting so I can have some privacy. Time away from being me, but the honeymoon is officially over. I can't wear a different face to my first day of school, although simply looking like someone else would solve most of my problems. I can't for two reasons. First, because my human father has no idea what I am, and it would be quite a shock to him to find some unfamiliar face hovering over my name in the yearbook. Second, and more importantly, I must wear my face for the majority of every day or Aphrodite will remove love itself from the world. But I'll explain that later.

Today, and every day from now on, I have to wear my true face to school. The Face.

I see the other kids streaming into the exclusive private school across the street from Central Park and swallow, my hand still on the door handle. I'm stuck here for a moment, reluctant to open the car door, and wishing like crazy that this time it'll be different. Wishing I'll make even one friend this time.

My driver looks at me in the rearview mirror, worried, and I push open the door of the black town car before he gets into trouble with my father for my tardiness. I look down at my button-down oxford shirt, green and blue kilt, white tights, and burgundy leather penny loafers as I hurry across the street and into the school. I worry that my oxford isn't loose enough and that my kilt isn't long enough to hide my figure. I hunch my shoulders and scowl.

Keep your face down, I coach myself. *Don't smile.*

As I start weaving my way through the crowded halls, I can feel eyes landing all over me; eyes lingering, peering closer, and searching for some kind of imperfection.

I think most of the time people stare because they can't believe it. They stare because they want to be sure that I am as flawless as their first glance hinted, and once they confirm that, they can let it go for the most part.

It's only the people who are missing something in themselves, the people who are the most shallow, who can't let it go. They come after me, coveting me like a thing. And there's no lack of shallow kids in the kinds of schools my dad sends me to. I've begged to go to public, but he'd never allow it. What would all his high-powered partners think about me mingling with the serfs of the middle class? They'd probably never develop another luxury building with him again.

I try to concentrate on the map I got in my orientation packet. I hear the conversations of the other students around me die down as I pass, and the whispers that rise up like a hissing tide behind my back. *Just ignore them.*

I read the numbers on the lockers to my right, counting my way down the row, and realize that my locker is buried behind a cluster of large, noisy boys. Jocks for sure, each of them flooded with testosterone and the strange goat-like urge to butt their heads into things. I can feel static tingling in my fingertips, and I push down the fight-or-flight response. The last thing I need to do is accidentally kill someone in the hallway on my first day of school.

But I stop and almost turn around to flee when the jocks see me and break apart.

"Is this yours?" asks a tall boy with sandy-colored hair. He steps back and gestures to my locker.

I nod and deepen my scowl, my head bent. I dart between the tall sandy-haired boy and a shorter, thicker boy with dark hair. Another boy joins them, closing me in.

"You're new here," says the sandy-haired boy confidently. I can already tell he's the alpha, staking his claim. There's one of him in every school. "What's your name?"

"Daphne," I say, fumbling with the combination lock. My hands are shaking.

"I'm Flynn," he replies, his voice dropping. He's moving closer to me, but I doubt he's aware of that. I doubt any of them are aware of the fact that they've surrounded me. Cutting off my exit. Like a pack of wild dogs.

Lightning thrills under my skin, responding to the male threat. I try to calm down. I remind myself that they can't help it. They want to see my face—they need to see it—so they're coming closer. I wonder if I should try something different this time. Maybe if I let them see me they'll get what they want and give me some space. I tuck my hair behind my ear with my pinky, straighten up to my full height of five feet ten inches tall, and look Flynn full in the face.

His gray eyes go hazy and he sways closer to me, reaching, wanting, his self-restraint spiraling to nothing. Bad idea. I should have kept my head down.

"Flynn!"

His shoulders tense and he turns. Behind him I see a pretty brunette glaring at us. A well-dressed and expensively accessorized clique of It Girls surrounds her, each of them wearing looks of varying shades of jealousy and outrage. Except for one girl in the back, African American with a face full of freckles, who seems amused. She wears her natural hair cut in steep layers around her head with a face-framing fringe of curly bangs. She hasn't been brainwashed by the lame restrictions of high-school hierarchy. Hope flickers inside me.

"Who's this?" Kayla asks Flynn. Like I'm not even here. She takes his hand possessively.

"I'm Daphne," I reply. I don't bother trying to smile at Kayla. We aren't going to be friends. I hope she doesn't try to do the whole "hostess of the school" thing—showing me around, pretending to be helpful and welcoming until she finds a good place to stick her knife.

Kayla looks me up and down and turns away without saying a word. Good. She's not even going to pretend to be civil. Her honesty is refreshing. The bell rings and the It Girls haul the rest of the boys away from me like they're saving them from the plague.

I know that by the end of the day Kayla and her prep school mafia will have spread some vicious rumor about me trying to have sex with their boyfriends against the lockers or something equally absurd, and the whole school will turn against me. This must be some sort of record. Usually, I make it through an entire week before the lies start about me sleeping with teachers, somebody's father, or half the football team. It's like I'm stuck in an '80s movie where the cheerleaders are all bitches. *It's 1993. Catch up.*

One more year of this bullshit and I'm free. I shouldn't care. I shouldn't even have the energy to care at this point, but my throat closes off with tears anyway. I pull myself together. I've cried about this enough times and I refuse to do it again. I look down at my map to find my homeroom.

It's a small school. I think there are only about seventy or eighty kids in my grade, but even so I don't see any of the jocks or the It Girls in my first three classes. I'm in the Advanced Placement track with all the geeks.

I'm comfortable around geeks, especially the math and science kind. The girls are too busy thinking deep thoughts to care how I look and the boys are too freaked out by anything female to even acknowledge me. I would try to be friends with any of them, but I know that as soon as they find out my GPA crushes theirs they'll all hate me too. Jocks and It Girls have nothing on geeks when it comes to competitiveness.

I'm early to fourth period. AP Social Studies. I have my book out on my desk, pretending to read, while the rest of the students take their seats. I feel someone standing over me. It's the It Girl with the freckles. She shifts from foot to foot. It feels like she wants to say something to me.

"Hi," I say guardedly. There's something in her eyes. Something almost like caring.

She opens her mouth but suddenly stops herself. She walks past me and takes her seat, a worried frown on her face. Class begins. The lecture is short and the round table discussion is long, more like a debate, really. There are twelve kids in this class, and they throw themselves into the topic with relish. I stay out of it and just listen. I learn that Freckles' name is Harlow. I can't help but like her.

I see Harlow again at lunch and I smile at her. She almost smiles back, but it gets stuck halfway across her lips. Her eyes unfocus with conflicting thoughts and her almost-smile slinks back down into a fretful frown.

I sit alone. Several boys ask if they can eat lunch with me and I tell them no. I don't say it nicely, either.

At my last school I tried to date once. Sweet kid. He asked me to junior prom and for some idiotic reason I said yes. By the end of the day he'd already been in three fights and his nose was broken. I went to the nurse's office while they waited for the ambulance to come take him to the hospital and told him to forget it. It totally broke his heart but better that than his neck. As long as I say no to everyone no one fights over me. Enough wars have been started over me.

Well, not me, not really. Just my face. My curse.

Lunch ends and I glance at my syllabus. Phys Ed. Oh joy. I

trudge to the girls' locker room, wondering if the people who decided on the class order are purposely trying to make the students barf. Who schedules Phys Ed right after lunch? Not that gym class is any kind of workout for me. In fact, it's insufferable. I'm always so paranoid that I'll move a little too quickly or lift something that's a little too heavy for a girl my age, and I'll be found out.

Rule number one for my kind: don't EVER let humans discover that demigods exist.

As I pull open the door to the girls' locker room, I hear a whispered "It's her," and my heart falls. I underestimated Kayla. I didn't think she'd resort to a physical attack, not yet anyway. I should have suspected this from the way she didn't even try the "hostess of the school" passive/aggressive route. This girl isn't passive about anything. She's just aggressive. My uncle Deuce is going to strangle me for letting a bunch of humans get the drop on me.

Kayla and the It Girls don't know this, but I can see them all moving in on me. They're so slow it's pathetic. Before they can grab me I already know what my choice has to be. I have to let them get me or they'll see how fast I can move and they'll know that there's something seriously strange about me. And Kayla is the type to dig. She won't let it go until she finds out what I am.

And then I'll have to kill her.

They grab me and pull me back into the showers. I fight the instinct to electrocute them. It isn't easy. I go sort of limp in their arms, knowing that if I don't struggle I won't miscalculate my strength and accidentally break anyone's arm.

There's a chair set up, waiting. Kayla's put some thought into this. They throw me down into the chair and she stands in front of me. Smug. There's a glint in her eye that tells me she enjoys this a bit too much. I've seen the look before. That twisted kid in my sixth-grade class had the same look in his eyes when he stuffed a firecracker into a toad's mouth and watched it explode. He was one of those skinny, wimpy-looking bullies—the kind who gets by not on size but on sheer cruelty. Kayla's like him, I realize. She's not the prettiest (that would be Harlow) she's just willing to do things that the other girls aren't.

She has a pair of scissors in her hand. I'm worried now. I'm not afraid of pain, but what if she tries to cut me, and realizes that no matter how hard she tries she can't even penetrate my skin?

"Please stop," I say, my lower lip trembling. It's not an act. I don't want to have to kill. Not again.

"I haven't even started yet," Kayla says. "Harlow," she calls over her shoulder.

Harlow comes forward, her lips pursed together resentfully. I look up at her, pleading. She doesn't want to do this, and I can tell from the looks on their faces that about half of the It Girls don't either, but Harlow is the only one with strength to stand up to Kayla. I shake my head at her, hoping the real Harlow shows up and tells Kayla to go to hell. Harlow grabs a lock of my long hair and Kayla hands her the scissors. They're going to cut my hair.

"Don't, Harlow," I plead, tears blurring my eyes. They don't understand. Without my hair, I'll have no way to hide my face. I'll be exposed and it'll just get worse.

Harlow's forehead puckers, her face drawing together with hopelessness. I realize that she wanted to tell me in Social Studies that this was going to happen, but she stopped herself. I wonder what Kayla has on her.

"Do it," Kayla snarls.

A dark look crosses Harlow's face, a tiny spark of rebellion, and then disappears. She obeys. As Harlow hacks through my hair, I glare at Kayla. Angry tears are spilling down my face even though I try to blink them back. It's so humiliating to cry in front of them, but I can't help it. I hate Kayla. I hate her because she's taking my hair and leaving me exposed, yes, but I hate her even more for Harlow. For a second there I thought maybe, eventually, Harlow and I could have been something like friends.

"Not brave enough to do it yourself, Kayla? Have to get some other girl to do it for you in case I talk?" I say to her.

Her satisfied expression falls for a moment. She knows that everyone heard that, and that it will stick with them long after today. Resentment will brew in the ranks. Kayla has no choice but to take the scissors away from Harlow and do it herself. Good. Get your hands dirty, I say to her with my eyes. Show them what you are.

"You're not going to talk," Kayla says through gritted teeth. She takes the front lock of my hair, the one right over my eyes, and I feel her cut it down practically to the scalp. "Or next time, I'll cut more than your pretty blonde hair."

Kayla sprinkles my hair on the grimy tile of the shower. It glistens as she drops it, like she's making it rain gold thread from her hand.

"Stay away from my boyfriend," she says.

My chest is so tight with tears I don't trust myself to speak aloud. As if Flynn, the poster child for overprivileged and overconfident average, is any kind of temptation for me. I nod contritely, like she's broken me, just to get this over with.

Kayla smirks and motions with her head for everyone to leave. They file out silently, some of them overwhelmed by what they witnessed. I lower my wet eyes. I don't want to see their expressions. I'm too ashamed I'm crying.

When they're gone, I stand and go to the mirror. I can hear the girls at their lockers in the next room, getting ready for gym class. I look in the mirror. A big section of hair is missing from the side of my head and, of course, there is the shorn part over my forehead.

I can't go back to class with my hair like this. The teachers will know something bad happened to me, even if I deny it, and eventually they'll figure out what happened in the showers of the girls' locker room. Kayla won't get into trouble. Evil chicks never do. But the others will, and I'll have made enemies out of all of the It Girls, even the nicer ones who went along with this but didn't really want to. Then Kayla will have what she really wanted—an army of spiteful little monsters, all of them looking for any way to make my life even more miserable. Kayla may not be book smart enough to be in AP classes, but I realize a few hours too late that she is a genius when it comes to malice.

I have to get out of here. Go home. Try to fix my hair before anyone sees. I'll get in trouble tomorrow for skipping class—I'm sure Kayla's aware of that—but there's no help for it.

I run.

CHAPTER 2

I'm fast enough that no one can see me, although they would be able to feel the rush of air as I blow past them. Luckily everyone is inside their classrooms and I don't cause a disturbance. I race through the empty hallways, vault over the metal detector at the entrance to the school, and I'm out on the streets.

This is the tricky part. Central Park West isn't the easiest place to navigate at Scion speed. There are too many people, and a collision is almost inevitable. If I were to collide with humans at this speed I could kill them. I only have a few blocks to go from school to home. I hurl myself over the bumper-to-bumper traffic, my arms and legs reaching and striding like I'm running on air before I touch down on the opposite sidewalk. I leapfrog over the pedestrians and the stone wall before their eyes can focus on me, and smack down on the packed earth of Central Park.

Trees rush past, blurring. In seconds I've cut diagonally through the park and I'm at West 59th at the bottom of Central

Park. I see my building and slow down to a walk. I can make it the last block at a normal pace.

People stare. They tilt their heads down as I pass, trying to see my face under the curtain of my remaining hair, like they always do. And they notice the hack job. Some even notice the red tear streaks on my cheeks. I push past them all, even the kindly ones who only want to help. I know from experience that if I give in and accept anyone's compassion, I'll have a stalker the next day. That's the worst part of my curse. Needing to act like such a bitch all the time.

Rich, the doorman at my building has spotted me, and waves. Now I can't alter my face to avoid the stares. I should have thought of changing my face before I slowed to a walk. As I come through the front door Rich notices my hair. His face is aghast. I put my finger to my lips as I rush to the elevator, my big doe eyes begging him not to tell. It's unfair, really. I don't like manipulating people, but right now I have no choice.

I get inside our huge penthouse apartment and hurry past my stepmother's tacky gilded furniture, crystal chandeliers, and silk upholstered walls. I swear, my stepmother thinks she's Marie Antoinette or something—if Marie Antoinette had a Texas drawl and an obscenely obvious boob job. I used to feel bad for her. It isn't easy following in the footsteps of my mother who, like me, had The Face. But then Rebecca, my stepmother, sent me to finishing school. Any goodwill I had toward her went right out the window with that stunt.

I get to my room and rush straight to the bathroom. I have scissors under my sink and take them out. I don't have many options with my hair so short in front. I have to cut it all almost to the scalp. I think about shaving it, but then stop myself. A bald girl will attract even more attention than one with severely short hair. When I'm done, I realize I have the same pixie haircut as Mia Farrow in *Rosemary's Baby*.

It looks good. Great, even. In fact, I probably look better with short hair because you can see all of my face and the fragile-looking curve of my neck. I look ethereal.

I am so screwed.

Frustration strangles me. I can't get away from myself. It's like I'm trapped inside a movie that I've been totally miscast for. I'm not a fragile doll, or a man-stealer, or a bitch, or a temptress, or any of the things people think I am when they look at me.

I look down at the heart-shaped charm around my neck. It's half of a powerful relic, handed down an unbroken line of mothers and daughters for 3,300 years. I have one half, and my mother, Elara, has the other. It can alter my appearance at will and make me look like any woman in the world, but it can't make me comfortable in my own skin.

I dig out the makeup kit my stepmother gave me three Christmases ago. I peel off the plastic and open it. I glob on the black eyeliner, mascara, and shadow. I've never put on makeup before, so I just wing it. When I'm done inking out my eyes and whiting out the red of my full lips, I turn to my closet. It's stuffed with very understated clothes in the finest materials—lots of merino wool kilts, cashmere sweaters, and tailored couture blazers for private school in Massachusetts.

I hack off the hem of one of my kilts, cut the neck off a soft T-shirt, and rip holes in a pair of black tights. My stepmother has a pair of black leather boots with tough-looking silver buckles on them. I get dressed and take the boots from her closet. I take a black leather jacket while I'm at it and turn to look at myself in her full-length mirror. I'm still me, but at least now my outside looks as angry as I feel inside.

I want to see some graffiti. I want something clever and dangerous in my life. Something that hovers right on the edge of dirty. I leave the apartment and go outside with my head held high. Well, higher at least.

The last time I saw one of those special tags, it was downtown around Greenwich Village. I head west and hop on the A train, planning to get off at Spring Street.

I don't like the subway. Someone always tries to chat me up or, worse, rub up against me. I stand with my back against the end of the car, glaring at anyone who comes too close. I think the eyeliner and the boots are working. People actually leave me alone for once.

Out of the corner of my eye, I see one of those special graffiti murals at the deserted end of the Washington Square station. I race to get off the train before the doors close. My heart starts pounding as I stride toward it.

It's gorgeous.

Big and bold, it's a portrait of a beautiful young woman. I slow down as I get closer. Her hands are bound and her head is shaved like a medieval martyr. She's even wearing a crown of thorns, sticking cruelly into her otherwise smooth brow. She's crying black tears. I stare at her face.

It's me.

This is impossible. There's no way this artist would have had time to make this mural since I cut my hair and painted my eyes. I just stepped out of the apartment ten minutes ago. *Who did this?*

I look in the bottom right-hand corner of the mural for his tag, which is always a 3-D rendering of a pile of jacks. For the first time I'm close enough to one of his works that I can see the letter A in front of it. A-jacks.

Ajax.

That's a name from The Iliad. It's a Scion name. *How did I never put that together before?* I thought the pile of jacks looked so cool, like a kid playing; I guess I never tried to think about it. There is no Ajax in my House. He could be my enemy. My skin sparkles with lightning. I don't know if it's fear I feel or something else. Something like hunger.

I can't help it. I touch the curve of her lip—my lip—which looks too rounded and real to be made of something flat. I come away with blood-red fingertips.

The paint is still wet. I have to get out of here, now.

The mural is on the downtown platform. I run to the stairs to go around to the uptown side. As I'm striding up the steps, I hear whispers. Sobs.

My vision blurs with rage. Not anger, or frustration, but a white-hot hatred that takes my breath away.

The Furies are here.

I scramble blindly through the turnstile with the Furies' shrieks for vengeance in my ears.

Oh gods, no.

The other Houses don't know that my House still exists. They think we went extinct, and that's how we've managed to survive, although barely. Right now, this other Scion is feeling the Furies as I am and knows there is a Scion from an enemy House in this subway. But he or she does not know which House. My only hope is that I'm not caught. I can't get caught—or killed. Then my House will be discovered.

Two trains are pulling into the station, side by side on opposite tracks. One train is going uptown, and the other is going downtown. I throw myself onto the uptown train and watch the doors, willing them to hurry up and close. At the very edge of my sight, I can see the Furies. They blink in and out of view as I turn to look at them. I've never really known if they entered the real world when a Scion felt them, or if they only lived, ghostlike, on the margins of a Scion's mind.

Their long black hair is matted with ashes and their faces are streaked with gore as they weep tears of blood. They whisper the names of the dead and call to me, begging me to murder my enemy and avenge my House. I back up against the windows opposite the door and spin around.

In the other train, looking at me through the window, is the most beautiful boy I've ever seen. He has golden hair and bright blue eyes. His skin seems to glow softly, like he carries light inside him. One of his paint-stained hands is clutching his chest, like he just got punched, and the other is pressed flat against the glass of the window. I raise my own hand and press it against my window, mirroring him. He looks so confused. Stunned. Like he's just seen the same ghost I have.

This must be him. My enemy.

"Ajax," I whisper. The screams of the Furies rise to a fever pitch.

I watch as his hand balls into a fist and smashes at the plexiglass. The trains begin to pull out of the station in opposite directions and he and I are both running now inside our cars to stay level with each other. Our eyes locked, our purposes clear. We want this fight. We want this more than anything.

I get to the end of my car first, throw open the door, and using the bar over the doorframe, I swing myself onto the top of my train. Now that I can't see him for a moment, it dawns on me that this is a terrible idea. I left the apartment with no weapons, but he might be carrying.

I run in the other direction, trying to add my speed to the speed of my train to get me away from him, when I hear a thump behind me. I spin around.

Ajax has jumped onto my train and he's striding toward me. He seems fearless of falling and he moves so smoothly it's like he's slicing the wind.

"Who are you!?" he shouts over the shrieks of the Furies and the thunder of the train.

I don't do witty banter. Instead, I step toward him.

He lurches back to dodge my first punch and I see his surprised expression as he watches my fist come much closer than he apparently thought it would. He has to overcorrect and falls back, landing solidly on the train's roof.

When he looks up at me, I shiver. I can feel the Furies running their torn fingers down my spine. I can feel their hate bleeding into my nerves, white-hot and stinging.

I don't know why I pause. I don't know why I use every last drop of restraint I have in my body to take a step back. But I do. I fight the ugly, animal urge to kill, and I don't know why. Maybe he's too beautiful to kill.

Ajax is quick to recover. He pops up to his feet and I have to throw myself at him. There's a flurry of exchanges. Too fast for me to think. I just fall into the rhythm of violence that's been pounded into me since I was a child. We do our brutal dance while another train passes. And in the flashing lights of the subway cars, he's gone.

I turn in time to see he's made the leap to the other train. He's speeding away from me. I run toward him across the top of my train until I reach the end. I could jump, but it's too late. I see him on his knees on top of the last car on his train.

He's clutching at his chest like it aches, just like I'm doing with mine.

CHAPTER 3

"Y ou're not concentrating!" Deuce hollers at me.

I dab at my nose, sniffing back blood. My uncle Polydeuces—Deuce for short—is sixty-six years old, but he can still hit like he's got rocks for hands. Probably because at this point, his hands are more knuckle than finger. In fact, pretty much everything about my Uncle Deuce looks like a knuckle. His nose, his ears, even his forehead has that gnarly look to it. The guy's completely busted. And probably the best fight trainer ever.

"How many times to do I have to tell you? Keep your damn elbows in. This ain't ballet."

"Yeah? Then why the tutu?" I tease, grinning as I tip my chin up at his chiton.

Uncle Deuce likes to fight old school, and that means he wears the traditional Greek version of a toga, wrapped around his lower body when he trains. To him, fighting is sacred, and my insistence on wearing modern gear is an insult. He puts up with me though, and despite his best efforts I can tell he likes me.

Before Deuce can respond to my tutu joke, I feint, bob my head, and jab at his face as I take a step back—a gutsy move to throw while you're backing up, but it does the trick. Deuce's head snaps back when I connect, and he grins at me.

"The Heir to the House of Atreus decided to show up this morning. I guess I can wake up now."

Uncle Deuce shoots in to take me to the mat. Nimble old buzzard. I let him have my right ankle, bear down on his hand to give me the leverage that I need, and send a spinning back kick to his temple with my left foot. He dodges it, but he gets the point.

"You could have clipped me with that, but your mind is else-where." he says, circling me with his wiry shoulders hunched and his head weaving behind his raised fists.

I'm ticked off because he's right. I'm not really here. The only thing I've been able to think about since yesterday is *him*.

What I can't get out of my head aren't his heaping muscles or his flashy face. It's those paint-stained hands. The push and pull of a dozen different wants rise up in me at the thought of them. Mostly, I want to kill him. Mostly, but not entirely.

"Aaannd she gone again," Deuce drawls. He unclenches his fists and faces me, hands on hips. "Where's your head at?"

"I don't know," I lie. I know where my head is. It's at the end of a subway platform, imagining a boy as he turns a dirty wall into art. His canvas is dank, and it stinks, but he knows how to make anything beautiful.

He's my enemy. I hate him. Ajax. The Furies fill Scions with rage at even the mention of a rival House, and simply thinking his name makes me angry. But still, I want to see him. It doesn't make sense. Now, more than ever, I should be focused on my training, but I'm not. At any moment Ajax could tell his family that he saw an unknown enemy Scion on the A train and they could come after me, but even though I'm in danger, I can't focus. I'm obsessing about where he is, what he's doing. Like I used to obsess about my mother after she left me.

It's almost like I miss him. There's—what is this? Longing? This is insane. I have to clear my head.

"Time out," I say. I grab my water bottle and drink.

I wonder what House he's from. The Village is Theban turf. The House of Thebes are Apollo's children. Apollo—the god of all the arts among other things. But he's a graffiti artist and accustomed to breaking laws, so I can't be one hundred percent sure he's from the House of Thebes. Violating the inter-House agreement by not keeping to the carefully mapped-out territories is a huge deal for my kind, but Ajax looks like a rebel. He might be from another House.

At least, I'm praying he is even though I pretty much know that he isn't, because if he's Theban, I may as well shoot myself right now. Not that bullets can harm me—or blades, or any kind of weapon at all as long as I wear the Cestus of Aphrodite around my neck—but you don't need a weapon to kill someone. The point is, if he's Theban, I'm dead. There are too many of them, and they're too well organized. They don't call themselves the Hundred Cousins for nothing. They're a frigging army. Lightning thrills under my skin. I want to fight, but not with my uncle. I want a real fight with Ajax. Bare skin. Sweat. Blood.

I wonder which House Ajax is. He's blond and sun-kissed even in autumn, just like a son of Apollo should be, but sometimes the archetypes get mixed up in the Houses. Black hair and blue eyes doesn't necessarily mean that a Scion is a son of Poseidon from the House of Athens, and auburn hair and green eyes doesn't always mean that individual is one of Aphrodite's offspring from the House of Rome.

I'm chasing my own tail. He's an artist, he's blond, and he was in the Village. Of course he's Theban.

Could he even be a Delos? Ajax Delos. More lightning crackles up my spine just saying the name in my head and I shiver. The Delos are the ruling family of the whole House. They're closely guarded and very powerful. It's rumored they have more talents than the rest of us. Not a stretch to imagine, considering the god Apollo was a jack-of-all-trades where the Greek gods are concerned. There are about a million talents attributed to Apollo, and a lot of them have to do with fighting.

And beauty. Ajax certainly has the looks. Honestly, it's late autumn—how dare he have a tan? Like his skin had been dusted with gold...

I'm thinking about him again. Worse, I'm daydreaming about him again. I knock the water bottle against my forehead in a futile attempt to dislodge him from my brain.

"I realize you're going through a lot right now with moving and everything," Deuce says gruffly. "I actually like your new haircut, very practical, but I know it's not something teen girls up and do unless they've got... personal reasons." I cringe, knowing what's coming. "You're not having... lady problems, are you?"

I moan, looking heavenward for strength. "I'm fine, Deuce."

He sighs gratefully. "Thank gods. I thought maybe you needed to talk." He shudders like someone just walked over his grave. We grin at each other.

I'm the Heir to the House of Atreus. The daughter of Zeus. Deuce is the bearer of the Aegis of Zeus. It's his duty to train me and protect me with his life, but we both know he'd do it even if he hadn't inherited the job. Deuce trained my mother, and before her, he trained his sister—my mother's mother—but I've always known I'm special to him. He's the only person who's ever really cared about me, even if he is a giant grouch. And even if he does hold me at arm's length.

Guilt dries my mouth. I should tell him that I've been spotted. I should've told him as soon as I got home last evening. If Ajax tells his family about me, Deuce and I are in serious danger. There's so few of my House left. Deuce and I are basically alone, except for my mother, Elara, but she's gods-knows-where.

In my House, the Head of the House and the Heir can never be together once the Heir is of childbearing age, for safety's sake. Like that thing where the President and Vice President aren't allowed to fly on the same plane.

There must always be at least one of us wearing this cursed Face for most of the time, no matter how much pain it brings us, or Aphrodite will remove love itself from the world. All because Aphrodite loved her sister Helen so much that she couldn't bear to go a single day without seeing her face. I wish I knew what that kind of love felt like. To love or to be loved so much that you couldn't go a single day without seeing that person.

I got my period and haven't seen my mom since. Not that she was ever really there for me before that.

Deuce is the only one I've ever been able to count on, and not telling him the whole truth puts him in danger. Basically, I am an asshole for not telling him.

"Deuce?" I begin.

"What?"

I stop. What if Ajax doesn't turn me in to his family? Deuce would hunt him, wait for the right moment, and Ajax would have to face him alone. My uncle may be an old coot, but with the Aegis of Zeus—a shield that strikes panic into anyone who looks at it—he's one of the deadliest Scions in the world. In single combat, Deuce would certainly win.

And if anyone is going to kill Ajax, it's me.

He's mine.

"Nothing," I say.

"Are you on drugs?" Deuce asks matter-of-factly.

I laugh. "Not yet."

I grab my bag and head for the door, but before I can get past him, Deuce reaches out and gives me an awkward one-arm hug. He even pats my shoulder a few times.

Gods. He must be really worried about me.

I clean up quickly in his cramped bathroom and change into my school uniform.

Deuce rented an apartment in the same building my father moved us into, gutted it, and turned most of it into a fight cage. He sleeps on a cot in the back. A little too Spartan for most people's tastes, but Deuce doesn't go for the comforts of home. Considering he lost his brothers, sister, wife, and four children in the Scion wars before I was born, I can't say I blame him. To him "home" is just a place where you find out people you love have been murdered.

Losing all those people made him especially protective of me, even if it also broke him in a way that means he can never fully love me. My father puts up with Deuce's constant presence in my life partly because my mother insisted on it when I was young, and then I insisted on it after my mother left.

Deuce and my father tolerate each other, probably because at this point my father has figured out that he doesn't have a choice in the matter. Deuce baffles him, but my father knows my family comes from what he calls "old money" and because of that he can excuse Deuce's lifestyle by thinking of it as eccentric, rather than crazy. My stepmother on the other hand straight up hates Deuce. She thinks he's an embarrassment.

I put on makeup before I go. The uniform is non-negotiable, so I can't do the whole "get the hell away from me" look that I adopted yesterday, but there's no way I'm going to school with a naked face. The truth is, I look better without make-up, so I don't have any other option now that my hair is gone. I pile on the eyeliner and mascara, poke myself in the eye a few times, and wonder how anyone tolerates the stuff.

I shout a goodbye to Deuce as I leave his apartment and go downstairs to an idling town car. My father is waiting next to it. He doesn't look happy.

"What have you done to your hair?" he asks, his face stiff with anger.

"I cut it." He starts to argue with me, and I talk over him. "I don't have to check with you before I cut my hair. It's my hair. I cut it. End of story."

That shuts him up, but it also makes him angrier. "Where were you?" he asks.

"Uncle Deuce's," I reply.

"And where were you yesterday when you were supposed to be in school?"

I close my mouth and stare at him, tightlipped.

"Who were you with?" he asks in a cold, calm way.

"No one." My voice is high and defensive. Almost whiney. I hate that, so I drop my voice and continue icily. "I was alone."

It almost slips out of me. The thing that's been hanging between us since my mom left and he started seeing her in me. No. That's not exactly it. Every day I grow—not into a face like hers—but into the exact face that bewitched him and then ditched him. The face he'd still do anything to possess. It is, in fact, The Face that launched a thousand ships—the exact same face as Helen of Troy, daughter of Zeus, and Aphrodite's beloved sister.

Literally, nobody could let this chick go, not even a goddess. So here I am, over three thousand years later, suffering for it.

I cross my arms and turn my head so he can't look at me.

"Well, you can't just skip school because you want alone time," he says authoritatively. Remembering to play Dad again.

I glare at him, hoping to end this. The driver is staring. He senses something isn't right between my father and me. I need this whole episode to be over. Having to say that I don't like anyone is really bothering me because the opposite is true. I like plenty of people, but none of them like me back. Obsession, possessiveness, fixation—that's what I get from others on a good day, but apart from Deuce, no one truly likes me. I think of Harlow and how she almost liked me, and I have to clear my throat. Biologically, clearing the throat stops tears. I hate that I know that.

"You're going to be late," my father says, like he wasn't the one keeping me here. Trapping me. Blocking my way. He's looking down at me. His eyes are tracing the line of my neck and the top of my button down.

"Can I go now?" I ask, my face hot.

Slowly, he steps away from the door so I can get into the car.

I dive into the back seat, holding my breath until the car pulls away. He can't have been looking at my breasts. My dad's not a pervert. He wouldn't do that. That's not what happened.

I get to school before the first bell, but I don't even bother going to my homeroom class. I go directly to the principal's office.

I get a lecture, but it's a confused one. The principal eyes my haircut and tells me that the gym teacher found a lot of shorn blonde hair in the showers. I can tell she honestly doesn't know what to make of all this. She asks me why I've moved from school to school, never spending more than a year or two in any one of them. She has no idea what to do with me. I can see the uncertainty in her eyes. She's asking herself, is this girl a serial troublemaker, or a serial victim?

There's no solution in this for me, so I sidestep her questions. I can tell she's a nice person, but she simply can't help me. The principal reluctantly gives me detention. I nod, smile, and go to my first class. It's not her fault.

I keep my head up. Make eye contact. I'm done hiding. It never helped anyway. People stare at me all day. Whispers follow me wherever I go. I think of Ajax and wonder if he goes through this, too. I've never known another Scion my age, but for the first time, I want to. I want to know if he knows what this feels like.

He grabbed his chest just like I did on top of the train. Maybe he feels everything just like I do. For a moment it comforts me to think that he does. Then I hear the Furies whispering in my head, and hatred flares up inside me. My lightning crackles through me at the thought of him and I have to breathe in and out, slowly, so the sparks don't come spilling out of my skin like stars.

I feel like I'm thirsty for him. I want to kill him so badly I catch myself wringing my hands into fists under my desk.

I see Harlow at lunch. I sense her looking at me, but she immediately turns her head, looking away. I watch for her eyes, hoping that maybe she'll look over again, but I notice there's something wrong. She's sitting alone, like I am. The popular girls are a few tables away with their backs to her.

I notice Harlow's too-straight shoulders, and how the very edges of her lips are pinching together. She's eating her lunch like nothing is wrong, and to someone who'd never been shunned she'd look like the picture of cool. But I know better. I was born with a giant red A on my chest.

Selfishly, I hope that she's being shunned because she stood up for me. Maybe after yesterday, she told Kayla off. Maybe she really does want to be my friend.

I grab my tray and stand up. It's a long shot, but I don't care. Carrying all my stuff—books, bags, food, everything—I'm going to go over there and ask her if I can sit with her.

I've taken one step when I see a balled-up piece of paper leave Kayla's hand and arc toward Harlow's head.

Physically, I could stop it. I could race over to Harlow at Scion speed and intercept the projectile, but then I'd have to kill everyone in this room. While that might sound a ridiculous over-reaction, it is very much the lesser of two evils. Because if humans knew that Scions existed, they'd start hunting us down. And if it ever got to the point that there was only one Scion House left, then the gods will be released from their prison on Olympus, and they'll come back. When they do, they will finish the war they started at Troy, and probably Western Civilization along with it.

Not even I hate high school that much.

My shoulders slump and my feet go numb as I let the piece of paper hit Harlow in the face. She's stunned for a moment. Obviously, no one has ever thrown anything at her before, but Harlow's a strong girl. It'll take more than that to intimidate her. She picks the wad of paper up off the floor, opens it, and reads it. Her skin goes red. Tears fill her eyes.

Hoots and hollers echo through the large room. Everyone is taunting Harlow, repeating some phrase I can't get straight in my head. Heartbroken, she stands up and bolts for the door.

I fumble after her, still carrying my stupid lunch tray like a bozo. I've got a bag over each shoulder and the straps snag onto the backs of chairs as I pass them. I overturn half the cafeteria with a clatter, making an ass of myself as I try to make my way to her. The bell rings and a flood of sniggering dickheads block my path. I can hear her sobbing as she runs down the hallway.

I stare after her, feeling clumsy and useless. How odd. I can catch a bullet in my hand, but I can't catch one crying girl.

My last three classes are just background noise. Harlow doesn't show up for Social Studies, and I assume she's skipped school. Then I report to detention, which for some inscrutable reason is held in the chemistry lab (is it a wise choice to let delinquents loiter around Bunsen burners?) and see Harlow sitting in the front row. I can tell she's never been in detention before, like I can tell she's never been ostracized before, because if she had been, she'd know better.

I go right over to her.

"You don't want to sit here," I whisper urgently.

She looks up, debating whether she should talk to me. "Why not?" she finally responds. "I always sit here. This is my regular seat in chemistry class."

"This was your seat when you were popular," I remind her quietly. "But now you don't want to sit in a place where the entire class can throw things at you when the teacher isn't looking."

She looks scared for a moment. Two boys pull open the door and she nods, following me to the back of the class before they can bogart the safe seats in the corner. Harlow and I settle in next to each other. I shoot her a half smile—one that's easy to ignore if she feels like it. She smiles back bigger, and I let my smile spread all the way across my face.

The teacher comes in and informs us that there is to be no talking. Harlow and I take out our books and start our homework. When the hour is over, Harlow and I walk side by side out of the school. I'm anxious. I don't want to just walk away, but I don't know what to say.

"I've never really understood the concept of detention," Harlow says, breaking the ice for me. "What's so menacing about having to spend another period at school, doing what you'd be doing at home anyway?"

I laugh. "Right? How are we supposed to know we're being punished if they can't paddle us like they do in Catholic school?"

"Wow. Dark," Harlow responds, cringing. I feel foolish for making such an off-color joke for a second, but then she grins at me. "I like dark," she says appreciatively.

I'm fidgeting, and when you're as tall as I am, fidgeting makes you look goofy. I try to remind myself to stand up straight, but Harlow is shorter than me because she's normal size and I'm Amazon tall. I feel like I have to crouch a bit so I'm not looming over her. I compromise and settle for a cocked hip and one slumped shoulder. *I am ridiculous.*

"Which way are you going?" I ask.

"Not in the direction of home," she responds.

I can tell there's something meaningful behind that comment, and I freeze up. I don't have enough experience socializing with girls my age to know if asking her something personal about her family is out of line or if it's expected. I must have a pained expression on my face because Harlow nudges my arm playfully and continues.

"It's nothing like that. My parents aren't going to freak out and lock me in my room for getting detention. They'll just be really sad."

"That's even worse," I say.

She gives me a quizzical little smile. "Want to go shopping?"

"Right now?" I ask, stunned.

She looks me over. "You need some clothes to go with your new style."

"Okay," I say, trying not to sound too eager. I trail after her, quite sure I look like a giant puppy dog, but I can't help it. I've never been invited to just hang out before. By a girl. No strings attached.

"I'm sorry about your hair," she says, looking down at the ground as we walk.

"It wasn't your fault," I say immediately.

"I should have warned you," Harlow continues. Then she sighs. "Fat lot of good keeping my mouth shut did me anyway."

"What did she have on you?"

Harlow looks over at me, surprised. "How did you know that?"

I give her a bitter smile. "You think this is the first time I've ever been hazed? I could write a freaking handbook on high-school bitch politics."

She pauses and considers it. "My dad's gay," Harlow says boldly, but she glances over at me uncertainly. My face doesn't flinch, and her guard drops some more. "He came out to my mom and I two months ago. Kayla threatened to tell the whole school if I didn't back her plan to..." she trails off and gestures to my head.

"Does it look that bad?" I joke, rubbing my short, spiky hair. Harlow laughs.

"You're gorgeous. With or without hair," she says without one drop of envy in her voice. My being so takes nothing away from her, and because she knows that, for the first time I like the compliment.

"But Kayla outed your dad anyway."

Harlow doesn't answer right away. "I felt horrible about what we did. What I did to you." She breaks off. "I wanted to go to the principal and tell her the whole story. But Kayla found out, and she..."

"Got revenge," I finish for her. We walk along quietly for a bit. I finally realize what all the kids were chanting in the cafeteria. Fag Hag. Lightning thrills through me I'm so angry. "Thank you anyway."

"Don't thank me," Harlow says, wrinkling her freckled nose. "That's too—sincere."

"Very uncool," I agree, nodding. "Hold on a sec while I pretend nothing matters to me."

Harlow looks me over, eyes narrowed appraisingly. "We're going to get along just fine," she decides. "Ooh, I love this shop!"

She hauls me into a swanky little boutique. "So does my dad, which explains a lot."

I pick up a pair of ruby slippers on display under a blue-and-white-checked dress and hold them up. "Ya think?" I say raising my eyebrows suggestively. She gets my "friend of Dorothy" reference right away, nodding and smiling appreciatively. I'm glad. She could have been offended, but she's better at reading people than that. She knows there's no judgment in my joke.

I feel relaxed, around a human no less, which is a first for me. Harlow starts pulling clothes off the racks (she calls them "pieces," not clothes) and her eyes go Zen with concentration. Fighters and yogis get the same look when they're training—looking both at a thing and through it. I know not to interrupt a general when she's studying the battlefield.

"Yeah, this will work great on you," she mumbles, laying a pair of leather pants over my shoulder because our arms have already been overloaded. "And this... wait, let me see your cleavage." She pulls my sweater-vest down a bit. I giggle and turn red. "A high, round C-cup. Perfect," she says. "I'm going to love dressing you. It's like having a human holodeck. Go, go, go," she says, shooing me into a dressing room.

I try on a dozen outfits. Harlow and the store owner—an elegant Korean woman named Hye-Su who looks like she's thirty but is probably fifty—tell me exactly what I need for my new tough-girl look, and they give me pointers on how to mix and match. I tell them I'm going for the biggest "f-you" I can manage stylistically, and they squeal like seven-year-olds at a slumber party.

"Elite? Ford?" Hye-Su asks me when I step out of the dressing room in a simple black sheath.

"I-I don't drive?" I stammer. I have no idea what she's talking about, but I think it's cars.

"Daphne's too modest to be a model," Harlow says.

She digs in her bag and pulls out a Polaroid camera. I turn my back to her before she can snap a picture.

"Please don't." I say.

There's no way Harlow can understand this, but the more pictures there are of me floating around, the more my House is put in danger. One of the biggest problems with having The Face is that I'm going to have to share it with my daughter someday. How will she ever be able to explain how her *exact* face got into a decades-old picture? My line of mothers and grandmothers have had to avoid all sculptures, paintings, and photographs for over three thousand years, and it hasn't been easy—especially when we have the kind of face that others feel compelled to immortalize. Pictures are inevitable. But the fewer there are of me, the safer it is all around.

Harlow gives me a pleading look. "Daphne, don't take this the wrong way, but you're a fashion idiot. You have no idea how clever some of these outfits are, and I really want this for my scrapbook. Can't I take just a couple of shots?"

I can see this means a lot to Harlow. Shopping isn't just fun for her, it's a way to express herself. I don't get the shopping bit of this equation, but I do get the self-expression bit.

"Neck down only," I say. Harlow shakes her head at me, but she does as I ask.

I don't have a clue about fashion, but I feel like I'm part of a creative process for both of these savvy women. It's not about the way I look, it's about their vision.

Hye-Su tries to give me a huge discount on the clothes, but I pull out my dad's Amex Onyx, and I kindly refuse her offer.

"Come again soon. Even if it's just to try on and take neck-down pictures of everything," she says, and walks Harlow and me to the door.

We get outside and Harlow and I exchange numbers and say goodbye, promising to sit together the next day.

I have a friend.

Chapter 4

I look at my new clothes, fanned out across my bed. The comfort and camaraderie of just a few hours ago has been replaced with restlessness.

The sun set long ago. My quiet room feels too alert, like the furniture is staring at me. The lights of Manhattan bead the darkness outside my window. I try to imagine which light is shining on him right now. What he's doing under it.

It's been building in me, getting worse every hour since yesterday. I've been ignoring it, but I can't anymore. It's been over twenty-four hours since I've seen him, and the whisper has turned into a scream.

All the pretty clothes in the world won't scratch this itch for me. I need to find Ajax, or see some evidence of him at least, or I'm going to start howling at the moon. My hand is on the doorknob before I stop myself.

"What the hell am I thinking?" I mumble to the overly alert furniture.

If I go out there looking for him, I'm asking for a fight. I'll eventually be dragging Deuce into it, too, because if anything were to happen to me, he'd avenge me. And if anything were to happen to Ajax, his family would avenge him. That's the thing about being a Scion. Nothing you ever do is about you alone. We take our families with us wherever we go.

It starts with one fight. Soon both Houses are dragged into it. If only one of the four Scion Houses is left, the gods will be freed from their prison on Olympus, and... actually I don't know specifically what they'll do. But they are vengeful gods, and they've been imprisoned for a very long time.

I've been standing here with my hand on the knob for five minutes now. Without making a conscious choice, I turn it and slip out of the apartment. It appears I can't go a whole day without seeing his face.

My stepmother is watching TV while she's talking on the phone, and my father is in his office working. I don't even need Scion speed to sneak out. I could pretty much walk out the front door, waving at Rebecca as I went, and she wouldn't notice.

Rich, the door guy, is another story. He'd tell my dad that I left the building at ten o'clock on a school night, so I make sure the person he sees leaving the building isn't me.

But I wear the Cestus of Aphrodite as a charm around my neck, passed down through my family by our first mother, Helen of Troy. She was Aphrodite's favorite sister. It's because of Aphrodite that I have Helen's Face and her Cestus.

A cestus is a girdle, and one of the ways a girdle was worn in ancient Greece was as lingerie. As such, it functioned as a tool of seduction. But seduction is a tricky thing. What does it for one person definitely doesn't do it for another. In order to fulfill its purpose, the Cestus of Aphrodite adapts.

Here's the thing about true love. If there are seven billion people on the planet, there are seven billion different ways to see it. There is no such thing as the most beautiful woman in the world. What looks like love for one person doesn't for another. Aphrodite, the Goddess of Love, could become any woman because any woman could be the most beautiful woman in the world to someone.

I've always loved that about Aphrodite. Even though she'd picked her favorite, she knew that every face was worthy of adoration.

I can't do men, though. I don't know if it's prohibited by the Cestus, or if I just have a mental block against it. It's probably me. I think I might freak out if I felt a dangly set of man-tackle between my legs. I just can't go there.

I use the Cestus to change my appearance and stroll out of the building easily. Getting back in will be harder. If you aren't a resident, you need to sign in and leave an ID to get upstairs after ten o'clock at night. I guess I can always climb up the outside of the building and break in my own window.

I stuff my hands into my new black jacket and tip my chin into the collar, strolling casually down the street. I'm not looking for a fight. I'm really not. But I do need more information. I need to know more about who Ajax is and where he lives if I'm going to avoid him. The best way to do that is to try to figure out where all of his tags are. Maybe I can come up with some kind of map of his territory and use that to triangulate where he lives. He's bound to live somewhere near his artwork, but not too close, because only an idiot would tag his immediate neighborhood.

I head downtown toward the Village, even though that means I have to leave my territory. Every major city in the world is divided up for the Scions. Humans don't know it, but we've always had our separate, agreed-upon territories. But with the whole world to choose from, for some reason we've always ended up living in the same city at once. There was a time when Rome was where the Scions gathered. Then Paris. Then London. Now it's New York.

Scions are like the Hatfields and the McCoys, I guess. We need our enemy right over the fence so we can keep an eye on each other. Either that or it's the Fates driving us together again and again. But I don't like that theory. I don't like to think that everything I do is controlled by someone or something else. I hate the Fates. Probably because they haven't been kind to me.

I stay aboveground, looking along the way. The first tag of his I saw was on the side of a building. I had no idea how he pulled it off—must have been seven stories up—and that's part of why it caught my attention. Now I get it, of course, but at first I couldn't figure out how a human got up there.

I jostle my way through some foot traffic outside a club. The boom sizzle of bass and hi-hat escapes as the door to the club swings open for me. I shake my head at the bouncer who's trying to wave me inside and I hustle to cross the street, away from the commotion.

"What am I doing?" I say out loud to myself.

I know it's wrong. Dangerous. Stupid.

But I have to see something of his tonight or I'm going to lose it.

I run all the way to the Washington Square stop of the A train. In a few minutes I'm standing in front of the mural I saw earlier. There's no doubt in my mind that it's me. Not another version of The Face, but me.

It's not just the shorn hair or the inky black eyeliner running down her teary cheeks. It isn't what she's wearing—even though she's in the same kilt I'm wearing right now. It's the thing behind the features that I recognize. I've spent my whole life sharing a face with my ancestors, but whatever it is that makes me me, and not just the latest version of Helen of Troy to roll off the assembly line, this guy knew what it was and he painted it.

I'm crying and I have no idea why. I want to rip the thing down. Burn it. Anything to get rid of it so I don't feel so wide open. How dare he put my insides up on a wall in a subway station for anyone to judge? How dare he know what my insides look like to begin with? I hate him.

People are coming on and off the trains around me. They're starting to stare at me as I cry and kick the wall. A few of them whisper, "That's her," as they realize that I'm abusing my own image. The sound of their shocked voices brings me around before I do something that will give me away as a Scion, like punching a hole in the concrete or using my lightning to sear the picture away.

I look around the tracks for what I need—discarded spray paint cans. I can see a few of them, knocked down the rail line by passing trains.

I jump onto the tracks, hearing people on the platform gasp. They have no idea that touching the third rail is actually kind of fun for me, but I avoid it because I could short the whole system. I spot one paint can that isn't crushed beyond use, and I notice there's a piece of paper under it. It's sooty from the subway dust, but there's no doubting that this is high quality stationary. It has a velvety feel, and it's folded into an origami swan. His tag is on the wing—an A followed by a pile of jacks.

I see a light coming toward me. People are panicking on the platform, calling for me to get out of there.

"I'm okay," I yell at this one guy who's preparing to jump down and come get me. He's in a fancy suit and tie and he's wearing great shoes, but he doesn't seem to care if he trashes the whole outfit trying to save me. Not that I've ever needed saving, but I'm touched.

"Hey, kid!" he's yelling as he throws down his stuff and dives for the edge.

"Stay there," I say, my eyes reaching into the guy and working on his heart. I can tell he's a good person, so I don't mind using the Cestus of Aphrodite to influence his emotions in order to make him stay put. Humans are more susceptible to the persuasion of the Cestus than Scions, but messing with a heart is never a sure thing. He follows my suggestion, thank goddess, and moves back from the edge.

I step into an arched nook in the concrete wall as the train screeches into the station. The gust and rumble of the train try to shake me loose from my hidey-hole, but I'm too solid for that. I stand on one leg and brace my other foot against the opposite plinth of the arch, unfolding Ajax's swan as the train's wheels squeal to a stop beside me.

A nub of a pencil drops out of the origami folds, and I catch it before it hits the ground. The train has brought enough light for me to read by.

I've dreamed about you my whole life, but I never

imagined you were real. I should have known
what you were, but it honestly never occurred
to me. I don't know if I should be happy or
sad that you're one of us.

It doesn't make any sense for us to meet again, but
I saw you and I can't unsee you now. All I can
think about is that you're here, somewhere in
the city. It makes me want to burn down
every building between us until all that's left is
you and me.

I think the less I know about you, the safer you'll
be, but I can't shake this feeling that there's a
reason I've been drawing you since I was old
enough to hold a crayon. I need to hear from
you.

Tell me you hate me.

Tell me to go to hell.

Anything.

Just write me back.

Ajax

I stare at his handwriting. Strong, angular, masculine—but it also
lies in a lovely way on the page. Every word is sculpted. Every para-
graph is plotted out like poetry. And the way he writes his name is
so... personal. Like you can almost hear his voice whispering it to
you, or see his hands cupping the word and giving it to you like a
gift.

The train pulls away from the station and I tear my eyes away from his name. My breath is rasping in and out of me with fury, frustration, and something else I can't quite place. Happiness? Excitement? I really don't know what I feel anymore. I see that nice guy on the platform, looking for me frantically. I wave to him to let him know I'm fine, and then I use the Cestus to make him care less about me. I just think what I want him to feel while I look at him and it happens. My mom taught me that using the Cestus was effortless for us. The trouble is not using it sometimes.

He shuffles off, confused about why he just missed his train. It's not that he's forgotten the whole bit about me jumping onto the tracks. The Cestus doesn't wipe a memory, but it can do something more insidious than that. The Cestus influences feelings. It can make a person not care, and they just stop thinking about whatever it is that's happening. Indifference really is the ultimate brainwash.

Even though the Cestus is working on the guy, I still have to hide. The drawback to the Cestus is that it's very short-term. If that guy sees me here, still on the tracks, he'll get worried again. That's why I can't use the Cestus on people I see every day. I can make them not want me, or not hate me in the moment, but when they see me again their true feelings come back to them twice as strong. I could keep influencing them again and again, but it's so exhausting to manipulate people like that. And I hate doing it, so I only use it in emergencies like this.

I press myself into the nook to hide from the Good Samaritan, and that's when I notice that the arch I'm in is actually a doorway. You can't really see the door unless you're practically making out with it, like I am at the moment. I press my shoulder against it and, using my Scion strength, I push until I hear the gritty sound of rock scraping against rock. I open the door into an abandoned service tunnel.

I see a rusted spiral stairway that leads down, and shadows beyond. I hear water dripping, and the rumble of a far-off train. Rust dust falls. The hiss of a whisper breaks the silence.

"Who's there?" I shout, whipping my head around to the source of the whisper. I see nothing but deep darkness.

The air smells earthy and metallic. I can feel the weight of eyes on me, but I can't see from where. I hold out my hand and summon a spark of lightning. I can just barely hear the shuffling of many feet. The back of my neck tingles with creeping fear. My hand glows blue with electric fire and I hold it aloft as I look around me, trying to stay calm.

Stairs. Pipes. Nothing else for as far as the dome of my icy light can reach.

Whatever it is that lives in these tunnels is not entirely human or there's no way it could have moved fast enough to elude me.

My mother used to tell me stories of mythical monsters still living among us. The chimera and the hydra aren't dead, she said. In fact, they've had babies. A lot of babies. Elara is not a fanciful woman, and she never believed anything as surely as she believed that there are more monsters in the modern world than there were in the ancient one. She said that they just got better at hiding themselves—and better at selecting dumbasses like me who stick their heads down abandoned subway service lines for no good reason. It's easy for a monster to hide its kill if the carnage can be blamed on something as messy as a train strike.

I hear another train heading for the station. I extinguish my lightning and yank the door closed before anything primeval can eat me. I wait in the nook until the train leaves and then I hop out of the tracks with the half-full paint can. The guy's gone, as are all the other people who knew I jumped onto the tracks. I'm alone in the station.

I stand in front of the mural, thinking. I'm sure Ajax grew up on all the Greek myths, just like I did.

I shake the can and spray green paint over the mural, covering the image of my face. I'm not going to leave him my name, not in words, but maybe he can figure it out on his own. I'm no artist, but I manage to paint a pretty good laurel leaf hanging from the limb of a tree that has a suspiciously feminine shape to its trunk. Daphne was a nymph who turned into the first laurel tree to escape the unwanted affections of Apollo. Let's see if he figures it out.

I put his origami swan into my pocket and dash out of the station—not wholly satisfied with the night's excursion, but calm enough now to actually get some sleep.

🦋

"Where were you last night?" Harlow asks, practically shrieking into the phone.

I sit up and look around my room. It's still dark out. "Harlow, what time is it?"

"Crack of dawn," she says enthusiastically. "I called you last night and you weren't there. Your parents let you go out on school nights?" she asks.

"Not exactly. Um... Harlow, who did you talk to when you called?"

"Your stepmom." Harlow waits a beat. "You frisky little minx. You snuck out to meet someone, didn't you?"

"No!" I say. My voice is so shrill and defensive even I don't believe myself. But at least there's a chance my dad doesn't know I snuck out. If he does know I'm in so much trouble.

"Who is he... or she?" she demands. "I know it can't be any of the Larrys or Marys at our school. That place is an utter toolshed."

"It's not that. Really." I have no choice but to tell Harlow some of it, or she's never going to shut up about this. "I snuck out to look for graffiti. There's this artist who puts up these mind-blowing tags, and I'm trying to find his territory. That's it."

"Suurre," she drawls, not buying my story. "He's hot, isn't he?"

"I don't know him," I say.

"Then how do you know it's a him?"

I'm busted. "Ugh." I groan. She starts laughing at me and I have to chuckle along with her. "I think his name is Ajax," I feel a flare of anger when I say his name and I can't keep it totally out of my voice. "And it's not what you think."

"Ouch. Touchy."

"Sorry." I pause and let the brush of the Furies pass. "I'm looking for him, but not because I like him." Actually, it's exactly the opposite. I'm looking for him because I want to rip his head off. "I can't explain, so please don't ask, but this is really important to me."

Harlow is silent for a moment, thinking. "Okay," she says seriously. "What's your plan?"

I tell her. She agrees that my triangulation method could work, except for one small thing.

"You were wandering around, looking for tags, in the dark," she points out. "Maybe try during daylight?"

I laugh. She really can't understand what I've been feeling—bloodlust is completely outside her range of experience—but I notice that just talking with her about it, even in an oblique way, has helped me. I feel calmer. "Light might be a good thing," I admit.

"I'll come with you today after school and we'll look together."

Actually... that sounds good to me. I say goodbye to Harlow and get out of bed. I'm up before my dad and my stepmom. If my dad knew I snuck out last night, he'd be waiting for me in the kitchen to tell me that I could turn right around and spend the rest of the day in my room. So far so good.

I go down a floor, and Deuce tosses me around the fight cage for a bit. I'm more focused today, mainly because I know that after school I'm going to go tag hunting with Harlow. Deuce is happier with my effort. He doesn't pat me on the back or anything, but I know he's pleased.

I don't tell him about Harlow and how I finally have a friend. Deuce always gets so angsty when I talk about the humans in my life, partly because up until now I've always been either ostracized or stalked by them, and partly because humans and Scions don't mix too well.

It's not a love/hate thing. It's a love/love/die thing. Scions can't marry other Scions because of two huge glitches. We're either in the same House and therefore related, or we're in different Houses and the Furies make us want to kill each other. So we marry humans and, usually, we're completely infatuated with them when we do. Most Scions have a huge soft spot in their hearts for humans and can't keep away from them. Sort of like the gods, actually. The gods couldn't keep their hands off of humans either, as my entire existence can prove.

Zeus fathered tons of Scions, but my line, the House of Atreus, is the only one of his that escaped his wife Hera's wrath and survived until now. Hera used to concoct the worst punishments for the women Zeus raped and the children that the women bore him. Not at all fair, but nothing about being a Scion is in my experience.

You'd think generations of marrying humans would have diluted the "god" part of our demigod powers, but it hasn't. The gods are immortal, and so is their blood. A demigod doesn't have a quarter-god for a child—he or she has a demigod—so basically that means we're all stuck with this demigod thing no matter how many generations pass.

And it means that Deuce always freaks out when I talk about humans too much because all he can think of is his wife. He loved her more than anything. She died completely by accident, too. Knocked down in the middle of a fight between two Scions who never intended to hurt her. Irony is a huge part of every Scion's life. When we're at our most miserable the Fates throw in the added kicker of irony, just to make sure we know that the universe is actually trying to screw us.

So, I want to tell Deuce about Harlow, but I can't. He'd worry too much about her if I did. Humans are fragile, but spunky. They tend to throw their delicate bodies around like the strength in their hearts could make up for the strength their bodies lack. Sometimes it does. Mostly, though, it doesn't. Deuce has been telling me since I was a kid to stay away from humans. Make babies with them and continue the line of the House of Atreus—

that's a must—but don't love a human or let them into our world. They almost always end up prematurely dead.

"See, that's how you prepare your body for a fight with the Hundred Cousins," he says approvingly after our last bout. The Hundred Cousins are a cult inside the House of Thebes.

Guilt swamps me. "Why are you so focused on them lately?" I ask. "Is there something about the House of Thebes you're not telling me?"

Deuce unwinds the wrap on one of his hands slowly. "They're the reason we hide, Daphne. Their House has always had the Oracle, and because of that, they know the future."

He's silent for a while, but I can tell he's not done talking yet, he's just trying to manage the Furies that always come when we talk about our enemies. I manage my own emotions and wait for him to be ready.

"There was a prophecy made twenty-five years ago when Tantalus Delos, the Heir to the House of Thebes, was born. The other Scions, the rest of us, we don't know what it said, but afterward his father, Paris, the Head of the House... he changed."

"Changed how?" I ask curiously.

"Before the prophecy, the House of Thebes operated like normal. Like the House of Rome, and Athens. But afterwards... well. Paris and Tantalus too, now that he's grown, they don't want to keep all four Houses alive and separate to keep the gods from coming back. They don't want what we want. It's why we're hiding—not just to protect the secret of you and your mother's face, and the Cestus, like the House of Atreus has always done. The Hundred Cousins want to destroy every other House. We can't let it happen."

I stay silent, though it makes me a traitor.

After our lesson, I clean up and, standing in front of a mirror, I hate how pure I look. I should look as deceitful as I am.

I try some of Harlow's accessory suggestions. I still have to wear my stupid uniform, but there's no saying that I can't turn my schoolgirl kilt into something edgier with the right white top, some boots, and a bit of punk rock bling.

My driver notices my new style. He doesn't say anything, but his eyes widen and, trust me, that's a huge thing. He's a veteran of some desert war, not sure which. All I know is that bombs have gone off and that man hasn't blinked. If he did a double take at what I'm wearing, I'm going to have a rough day. I brace myself for school, but I don't go back upstairs to change. I'm done hiding.

When I get to my locker, Flynn is already there. His locker is to my left, and it seems to me like he's just standing there, fiddling with his stuff. Waiting.

"Daphne," Flynn says, like he can't stop himself from rolling my name around his mouth, even though I know my own name and don't need to be reminded by him.

I have two choices. I can ignore him completely or I can nod quickly and acknowledge him. Here's the problem with both options. If I ignore him, I'll make him angry, and it will turn into something he feels like he has to win. But if I acknowledge him, he could interpret it as encouragement. There's no right response and I hate acting like a snob, so I nod at him—no smile—and busy myself with my books.

"I like your bracelets," he says quietly.

"Thank you," I reply, not making eye contact.

He's shy. *Oh, goddess.* The only time an alpha gets shy is when he's smitten. I close my locker door, turning to my right so he gets my back as I walk away.

"Wait," he says.

He doesn't touch me, but his voice is just the right combination of rough and vulnerable to make me stop. He's really feeling something, and I can't ignore that, even though I probably should. I'm such a softie. I turn, making sure that my cursed face is a perfect blank when he sees it.

"I'm sorry about your hair," he says, his chest swelling with charged breaths. "I know how it happened, and I'm sorry. Kayla totally misunderstood. About us."

"Don't sweat it," I say. There's no emotion in my voice at all. There is no *us* between Flynn and me. I walk away and try to leave him exactly as I found him.

I see frigging Kayla coming up behind me.

I weave through the hall traffic fast—maybe too fast. It's like I'm running away from a crime. I hear Kayla and Flynn arguing with each other in my wake. I can't win. No matter what I do, no matter how I try to smooth things over, my actions will always be misinterpreted.

Everywhere I go I start a war.

I get stares all day—guys staring at my legs, at my breasts, at my ass. I keep my head up and ignore it when they whisper whatever dirty nonsense they think up. I've heard it all before. Some of it so filthy you just want to run home and wash out your brain. By third period, it gets so ridiculous I'm actually laughing. Do boys seriously think I'm going to take my shirt off because they say they want to see my tits? And why would a guy think profanity would entice a girl to begin with? Has any woman in the world, ever been turned on by harassment?

Flynn passes me in the halls between every class. It's not coincidence. I guess he's figured out my schedule and he's rearranging his just to see me. By the time I meet Harlow at lunch, I'm starting to get worried. I know Flynn is searching for me, but he isn't smiling when he sees me. Something dark is bubbling in that kid.

"Well, you were right about one thing," I say to Harlow as I sit.

"What's that?"

"The guys in this place are a pack of Larrys."

She laughs. "So," Harlow says, "tell me about Ajax."

My teeth are set on edge at the sound of his name, and for a brief moment I envy that she can say it without feeling the Furies. I can't say "Ajax" without wanting to blow up a car. It occurs to me that Harlow can keep a clear head about him even when I can't. Huh. Deuce always believed that humans could be just as useful as Scions in our inter-House feuds—even if they weren't any good in an actual fight.

"Are you serious about helping me find him?" I ask.

She tilts up a corner of her red-lacquered lips in a sly smile. "I'm dying to meet your foxy little felon."

I take out Ajax's origami swan and put it on the table between us. "He left this in a subway station for me," I say.

"How do you know it's for you?" she asks, eyeing it. "Your name's not on it."

"Because it was near a mural he made of me."

"Back up," she says, holding up a hand. "He painted you?"

"Yeah," I reply, lowering my eyes. I blush and grin and hate myself all at the same time. "And it was amazing."

"Was?"

"I painted over it."

Harlow studies me for a moment and then her freckled nose wrinkles with sympathy. "You really hate looking the way you do, don't you?" she asks. Like yesterday, there's no judgment in what she says. She's just watching. Processing.

"Harlow," I say, smiling at her with relief, "people hate me before they even meet me."

She smiles back at me. Her pert face reminds me of Tinker Bell for a second and I imagine her in a glittery green gown and wings.

"My dad always says that every head, no matter how smart, is attached to an asshole by a few feet of tubing," she says. "And most people are full of crap, not ideas."

My laugh rings out around the room. Every boy hears it and scowls with jealousy, wishing he'd been the one to make it happen. I lean closer to Harlow.

"It's a letter," I say, regarding the origami.

"What does it say?" she asks.

I can tell she wants me to offer to let her read it, and even though I want to share it with her I know I can't. How would I explain the bit about Ajax wanting to burn down the whole city to get to me?

"He just said that he wants me to write him back," I reply.

Come to think of it, reading his note and seeing his art does not fill me with the Furies. I don't know why. Maybe the Furies predate a time when most Scions could read and write? Or maybe there is something sacred about art and writing in general that protects them from rage. I could write him back, and he could write me back... and then what?

"Why write? Why didn't he just leave his phone number?"

"It's complicated," I reply. "We don't get along."

"You don't get along, but he paints amazing pictures of you and leaves you intricately folded paper swans?" Harlow looks at me skeptically. "What does he do for girls he hates? Buy them yachts?"

"I know this is really strange but trust me. He and I do not want to meet face to face. If we do, something bad will happen."

"Okay. That's odd." She waits for me to fill in the blanks, which, of course, I don't. "You don't want to meet him, but you still want to find out where he lives?"

"Yes."

"Kind of stalkerish, don't you think?" she asks, wrinkling her nose.

"I want to know where he lives so I can avoid him." I lean across the table and look at Harlow intently. "The last thing I want is to accidentally run into him."

Harlow face relaxes into a taunting smile. "Keep telling yourself that." She picks up her sandwich and inspects a dubious layer of lunchmeat while she thinks. "Okay, I'll help. I haven't stalked anyone in years, and I don't want to get too rusty. He'd better be hot, though."

"So hot," I say, frowning down at the swan in my hand.

"Who's hot?" asks a defensive voice behind me. I turn and see Flynn, flanked by the two wingmen who were with him when he accosted me at my locker on the first day of school.

The thick, dark one is called Parkman—I think that's his last name—and the reedy one is named David. They're just background noise, though. Flynn is the decider among them. He looks down at the swan in my hand, and his face freezes.

"Who gave you that?" he asks. Like he's accusing me of something.

I put it away quickly. I don't want Flynn looking at anything Ajax gave me.

"It's none of your business," I remind him carefully. I'm polite. I know that if I'm standoffish, he might start something with me right here in the cafeteria.

Flynn's eyes seem to be stuck on me for a moment. He knows I'm right, but he can't let it go. He finally looks away and keeps walking. After the guys are out of earshot, Harlow turns back to me and lowers her voice.

"That was weird," she says, eyebrows raised. "It's like he thinks he's your boyfriend."

"Super weird," I agree, trying to look like I have no idea what's going on inside Flynn's head. Like I've never seen this kind of irrational possessiveness before.

⁕

"Harlow... seriously? Get off my face."

"Sorry," Harlow whispers. "But I can't reach the stupid ledge. How the heck did he get up here, anyway?"

Ajax left a tag on the side of a water tower atop an old brownstone in Greenwich Village. It's his A-Jacks symbol, done in woodland shades of brown and green. There's a crown of laurels around the A, which is pretty damn presumptuous of him, I think. I huffily wonder what it is he thinks he's won from me, exactly.

Harlow and I are on the roof of the building and I'm giving her a boost. She's trying to scramble up to the water tower but it's inaccessible. For humans, anyway.

"I can see something. I think it's another origami swan," Harlow says, straining.

I could have snagged Ajax's message and been home by now, but I can't use my Scion powers to get to it. Not with Harlow along. I'm sort of frustrated, and sort of not. She came along with me like she promised, and she was the one who spotted the tag, so I can't get too mad at her. But even still. She's standing on my freaking neck right now.

"Will you just stick out your hand and reach for it?" I snap.

The Furies have been whispering to me all afternoon, which means that members of the House of Thebes are all around me. I'm in their territory, and I can feel the shadow of a threat closing in. It's been a struggle to keep my temper while we waited for it to get dark enough to climb up here. I remind myself that Harlow is being an amazing friend right now and change my tone.

"My arms are killing me," I lie.

"I'm trying," she says. "But I'm not crazy strong and flexible like you."

I had to do a few things that weren't strictly "normal" for a girl my age in order to get Harlow and me up here. There was one moment when I had to haul myself up onto a ledge one-handed. Luckily, Harlow didn't see that one.

I pretend to strain and pant under Harlow, even though she weighs less than some shields Deuce has made me train with.

"Hurry!" I complain. "I can't hold you." Actually, I could do this all night—except for the foot-in-face part. Gods know what she's stepped in today while we tromped around the Village.

"Got it!" she says, and I put her down. She slips and clatters loudly across the roof tiles. I grab her and steady her before she can fall.

"*Shh*!" I hiss. She and I hold still and listen, clutching each other. We're in all black, standing on top of an apartment, and the last thing we need it to have someone call the police. We wait, but don't hear anything. Harlow's eyes meet mine and sparkle in the dark.

"This is so much fun," she whispers.

I make a face at her. "You're going to end up in an orange jumpsuit someday."

She stifles a giggle and points at me.

"What?"

"You've got my boot-print on your forehead."

She wipes it off and we scramble down, helping each other and trying not to squeal excitedly. This *is* fun. We run a few blocks and dart into a café on the corner of Bleeker and MacDougal before I look at the folded piece of paper in my hand.

"It's a butterfly," I say blankly. I can see Ajax's symbol, drawn in red and purple ink on one wing. He's altered the design, so it fills the wing like the scrawling shapes of a butterfly's adornments.

"Beautiful," Harlow whispers.

I nod, frowning, and open the letter carefully, my fingers suddenly clumsy.

Daphne,

I don't think I need to point out how ironic your
name is. I've thought about chasing you, but I

think you would turn into something far
more dangerous than a tree if I caught you.

By the way, you didn't leave me much. I asked you
to write me and all I got was one cryptic clue.
It's safer, I guess. But the thing is, I don't
want you to run away.

I don't want you to go where I can't catch you.

Last night when I was sorting through my paints I
kept wondering what color would suit you
best. I can't get it out of my head. Red? Blue?
Green?

Don't tell me where you go to school. Don't give
me your phone number. Don't give me your
address. Tell me something real about you,
something that has nothing to do with the
pile of family bullshit you and I have to deal
with every day.

Tell me your favorite color, Daphne, and I'll paint
the sky with it.

Ajax

A waitress has come and gone. A cup of coffee is steaming in front
of me. The letter leaves my hand. My eyes are looking in, not out,
but I know that Harlow has taken it. I don't resist her. There's
nothing in that letter that would give us away.

I stop my thoughts right there. Ajax and I are not an *us*.

"Oh... wow." Harlow sighs as she reads. "Who is this guy?"

Harlow stares at me, nonplussed. "This guy makes you origami swans and butterflies. He paints you. He climbs up the side of a water tower to leave a note asking you what your favorite color is, and you've said yourself that he's unbelievably hot. I'm happy if a guy calls me the next day after I've made out with him, so unless Ajax is a total psycho, you're going to have to explain why you aren't sucking face with him right now."

"I told you," I say. "Our families don't get along."

"And what's all that crap about you turning into a tree?" Harlow asks, ignoring my answer. "And why the hell would you run from him?" She's in full rant mode now.

"It's an old Greek myth," I say calmly. "The god Apollo's first love was a sworn virgin huntress named Daphne, and she ran from him. When he was just about to catch her, she begged her father, who was a river spirit, to help her. He turned Daphne into a tree so Apollo couldn't... well... rape her, basically. She was the first laurel tree and Apollo declared the laurel sacred to him. That's why it's the greatest honor to be crowned with laurel leaves. It's the ultimate prize."

"So, Daphne is the laurel." She studies me carefully. "The ultimate prize."

"To some," I say. "To people who think everything is a game, I guess." I try to stay neutral, but my tone is bitter. Harlow can't see just how messed up this whole situation is. She doesn't know that Ajax is a direct descendent of Apollo. I feel duped, somehow. Like the Fates are maneuvering me in a direction I don't want to go.

"How do both of you know all of this Greek stuff?" she asks. "I saw the laurel wreath surrounding the A on his tag."

I look down at the sugar bowl on the table, but I don't really see it. "It's just the way we were raised. We both come from really old families."

"Really old families that hate each other."

"Exactly."

Harlow looks me over. "Okay," she finally says, shrugging. "It's totally weird, and I don't understand it, but you haven't judged me for my nontraditional family, so I'm not going to judge you for yours."

She pulls out a detailed map of lower Manhattan. Harlow adds another red X to a cluster, marking the spot of the water tower. Even after one afternoon of tag hunting, Ajax's pattern is pretty obvious. "He seems to keep to the Village. There's only one place where he hasn't tagged at all."

"Washington Square Park," I mumble, looking at the map.

"Right. NYU's Main Building is right there, and security is really tight. It could be that he hasn't tagged there because he'd get caught if he did." Harlow leans back in her chair and crosses her arms. "But that area's also loaded with old money, and you did say that he came from an old family."

"That's it," I say with certainty. "That's where he lives." I don't know how I know it, but I do. Maybe it's the Furies trying to goad me into a fight. There's nothing those bloodthirsty ghouls love more than watching Scions kill each other.

"Should be pretty easy for you to avoid," Harlow says pointedly as she folds up the map. Harlow and I look at each other over the table, slow smiles spreading across our faces. "You are going to avoid him, aren't you?"

"That's the plan," I say through a grin.

"Uh-huh." She kicks my foot under the table.

Tal

I watch The Face and her human companion finish their coffee and fold up their maps and letters. The companion gets into a cab and leaves. I stay on my target.

The Face pauses on the street corner. Her skin catches the glow of a streetlamp overhead as she tilts her head sideways in quiet contemplation. The light seems to bend around her beauty as if it, too, wants to hold her. She makes a sudden decision and breaks into a run so quickly it would seem to a human as if she'd disappeared. I take off after her, easily keeping pace.

Vaulting over rooftops, slipping silently from shadow to shadow, I follow without her discovering me. The only time she's come close to sensing my presence was when the Underthings in the subway tunnels nearly gave me away with their hissing and scuttling. That was partly my fault, though. The monsters in the sub-world are skittish by nature. I had been away from my target while she moved and had not prepared the Underthings in New York City for my intrusion into their bizarre and secret world. It was sloppy of me.

The Face comes to her destination—the water tower the boy painted. She easily swings herself onto the platform and stands in front of his frenetic piece of street art. She picks up a discarded spray can and shakes it, thinking. After a moment she writes ALL OF THEM before she departs.

I follow her back to her apartment building, and finally leave her when she goes inside.

I never set out to be what I am now. I was not created to creep in subway tunnels or follow young Scions as they chase each other around the city. I was created to protect. And, yes, I was created, not born, to protect my island. Crete. If the gods are released from Olympus they will ravage it. Humans do their share of damage, to be sure, but only a god could destroy my land utterly. Sink it, like they did Atlantis.

Because of this, my mandate is clear. Olympus must remain locked, and the gods imprisoned there by Zeus's vow on the River Styx. The vow states that when there is only one Scion House left, the gods may return to fight the Scions for dominion over the Earth.

It's a simple pact, one that was made to put an end to the Trojan War, that horrendous war where humans fought, Scions fought, gods fought, and nearly pulled heaven and earth themselves apart. The pact had to be made or everyone was going to lose. And yet, in a game where every player is a cheat, it's hard for me to understand the rules no matter how clearly they are spelled out.

I understand that the gods want the day of reckoning with the Scions to be when the Houses have gutted each other, and there is only one Scion House left, weakening the Scions. I can also understand that the Fates want the day of reckoning to be when the Houses have joined, and there is only one Scion House left, making the Scions stronger than the gods ever were. The Fates want the children to overthrow their parents, and as the Fates favored the gods over the Titans, so they favor the Scions over the gods.

I believe that the Fates are the biggest cheats in this game, for there is something they gave the Scions that they did not give the gods. The Scions can blend.

This is a thing humans do. Something I can't quite understand. They blend with others, but it is not impurity. It is closer to perfection.

I am one thing. I have always been one thing with one purpose. For thousands of years I've tried to understand how mixing does not make something muddy. It makes it better. Stronger. Long after my creation it was discovered that carbon mixed with tin at high heat becomes steel. Steel is strong, and like steel, every generation the Scions get stronger because they blend.

The Fates have decreed that the strongest of this mixing of Scion blood will be the Tyrant. She will have the powers of all the gods in her blood. The Tyrant is the only one who can send Zeus and all the Olympians to Tartarus—like the gods did to the Titans.

This is Fated. This will happen. But when? When must be later. Always later. Or I have failed in my one purpose. The gods will not sink into Tartarus without a fight, and they do not care about this world, or my island. My home. My one reason for being. If the gods return, the whole world will burn and Crete will fall.

The Scions do not want this, either. They want to keep the Houses separate. They do not want the world they love to burn. Well, most of them do not.

But as long as the Four Scion Houses stay separate, the Tyrant cannot come into being and the gods will not return. There will be no war to end all wars. There will be no war to end my island. This is good for the humans and the Scions. And for me.

Interbreeding between the Houses cannot be permitted. Usually, the curse of the Furies keeps love from blooming. The Furies are powerful. They set the Houses against each other in a blind rage. Sometimes, they set a House against itself when one becomes a kin-killer. The blood lust spirals out of control and decimates a family. Like it did with the House of Atreus.

And yet, something seems to eclipse the sway of the Furies. How it happens still baffles me. How can love come from hatred? I don't understand, but it happens.

Sometimes, enemies swim through the haze of clannishness that tries to drown their better selves and they see a person opposite them, instead of the insignia on the shields or the banner flying the opposing House colors. And they fall in love.

I do not understand it. I am one thing.

But they want to blend.

When the Furies fail to keep the Houses separate in this manor, I step in. The threat of these inter-House unions will continue until the Fates get what they want, and what they want is to start anew. My old island will surely be sunk. The second Atlantis. I exist to make sure this does not happen.

Helen of Troy started the first war and I have no doubt that one of her progeny will start the next. They can't help it. Scions flock to the bright flame of their beauty like bumbling moths. So, I have always kept a close guard.

I have watched the House of Atreus long enough to know how miserable the plight of The Face is. How lonely it is to be the latest version of Helen of Troy. Everyone harbors a secret hatred for the most beautiful girl in the room, and she's the most beautiful girl in the world. The whole world secretly hates her.

This newest Face, Daphne, has reached the critical age. She is seventeen. The same age Helen of Troy was when she started the Trojan War. The Fates love nothing more than symmetry—a perfect circle that ends where it begins and begins with what is usually a catastrophic ending. For three and a half thousand years I have watched each Face when she reached her seventeenth year to make sure that the Fates' plan is stalled indefinitely.

But this time I find myself nearly too late. She is barely into her seventeenth year, and she has already snared the attention of a son of Apollo. I have no doubt that he, like his father-god, will chase Daphne.

It's my job to make sure he doesn't catch her.

Once The Face is in her apartment for the night, I go to the boy's house. He could be a problem. He is Ajax, the youngest son of Paris Delos, Head of the House of Thebes. His older brother, Castor, who is not the Heir but should be for all the effort he puts into his House, watches Ajax very closely. Castor is smart and ruthless when it comes to defending his family. The boy has been getting into a lot of trouble lately, both in school and with the police. Artists who are beloved by the Muses, as Ajax is, always have it hard. They are gifted in such a way that leaves them excluded, even from other Scions.

And now there is the girl. She is his enemy, but he hasn't told his brother about her. Ajax doesn't understand why just yet, but I do. He wants the girl for himself. Whether it's to kill her or love her, I can't tell yet. I'm going to have to keep a close eye on both of them, it seems.

I climb a tree in Washington Square Park until I can see into the window that belongs to Ajax. He's in his room, painting the walls so he doesn't climb them, I suppose. Like the girl, he seems to bend the light around him, and although he is nearly as attractive as the girl in his own way, it is his artistic fire that creates a bubble around him rather than his beauty. The Muses are speaking to him—or maybe it's through him. I've never been sure how it feels to be beloved by one of the Twelve, but it looks like pleasure and pain put together. Ajax paints most of the night away, and finally pulls off his clothes and collapses into bed just before dawn.

A riot of colors and vibrant, angry shapes coat the walls in what is an otherwise austere setting. Apart from his tousled, narrow bed the boy has books stacked in toppling piles on the floor, art supplies, canvases, and an easel. All his things are pooled in the middle of the room and tarps skirt all four walls. I've known monks who've had more possessions. Despite the fact that his family has amassed untold wealth over the centuries, the boy lives like a pauper. Every ounce of his thought and time seem to go into his art. If he ever poured that passion into a girl, I'm not sure even the Furies could keep him from her. I may have to kill him, but it's far too soon to tell.

She might just kill him and save me the trouble. It's happened like that many times before.

More often than not, star-crossed lovers are their own worst enemies.

CHAPTER 5

"Have you seen the new guy?" Harlow asks excitedly.

I smile, happy to see it's Harlow joining me at my locker and not Flynn. It's been a Flynn-free morning so far, and I'm wondering if that's good or bad. He could be trying to "punish" me with his absence.

I check my watch. "It's eight o'clock in the morning. How do you know there's someone new in school already?"

"He's gorgeous," she continues, ignoring my question. "His name is Tal."

"Tal?" I ask, closing my locker door. "That's unusual."

"Probably short for something." Harlow backs away from me, heading to her homeroom.

This school has a rotating schedule, where seven classes do a round robin of six hours. At the top of the rotation, class A starts the day and class G is dropped. The next day class G occupies the first hour, followed by A-E and class F is dropped, and so on.

In one way, I can see the sense to have a rotating schedule. It means that every student gets seven subjects instead of six and no subject is permanently stuck in the learning dead zone just after lunch, when all the blood in your body leaves your brain to digest your food. It also means that I still have no idea where the heck I'm supposed to be after homeroom. I pull out my schedule.

I'm standing in the empty hallway, trying to remember which freaking class got dropped the day before, when I hear someone speak behind me.

"Is today a C day?" asks a pleasantly pitched male voice.

I turn and see a stunning guy. He's exceptionally tall and broad shouldered. His coppery-colored skin is just a few shades lighter than his burnished hair and his big, golden eyes glow a few shades paler than his skin. Every part of this specimen looks like it was color-coordinated and sculpted to perfection. Not good. He looks like a Scion.

"They explained it to me in the office, but I'm still wicked lost," he continues, ignoring the fact that I'm staring at him.

"I think it's a C day," I say, narrowing my eyes at him distrustfully. "But I'm new, too."

"My name's Tal." He steals a glance at my schedule. "I think we both have Calculus right now. Look."

I look at our schedules and nod at him coldly. He's demigod gorgeous. But I don't feel the Furies around him, so he can't be a Scion from another House. And I know everyone in my House because there's only three of us left. He must be a human even if he is crazy pretty. I feel like a jerk now for being rude to him.

"It's this way. Are you from Massachusetts?" I ask politely, leading him down the hallway to our class. He smiles brightly, practically twinkling in the sunlight streaming in the windows. If he's not a demigod, he certainly does a great impression of one.

"Yeah," he says. "Well, not originally, but for long enough now. What gave me away?"

"Wicked?" I say, raising an eyebrow. "I'm from there too."

He smiles. "I can say "park the car" like a normal person, but for some reason I just can't stop myself from saying wicked."

"Me neither. This is our class."

He opens the door for me like its second nature to him, and another warning bell goes off in my head. It could be that he was raised to be polite, but there's still something a bit off about it. Who opens doors for girls anymore? I don't know who this Tal guy is, but he isn't a normal teenager.

"Thanks," I say, narrowing my eyes at him distrustfully again.

I have three more classes with Tal, and only one without. When I get to lunch I see Harlow already waiting for me at our little table. Tal is standing over her, chatting her up. His hands are on the back of the chair next to her, and he's leaning into it. He looks completely at ease, something no normal kid would be on his first day in a new school.

Harlow laughs at something he says. He's a charmer. I know from experience that Harlow's a tough crowd, but whatever it is he's dishing, she's eating it up. I can't tell from his posture if he's hitting on her or not, but there's something about the way he's holding the back of the chair that tells me he's just stopping by our table, and he's not going to sit. Which is good.

"Hey, Daphne," Harlow says cheerfully. "This is Tal."

"Yeah, we've met," Tal says.

"Oh." Harlow looks troubled.

"We're in a few classes together," I say breezily, barely acknowledging him as I take my seat.

"Oh," Harlow says again, her frown deepening.

Crap. She's starting to worry about Tal and me and how much time we'll spend together in classes without her as the semester continues. I want him to go away immediately.

"Tal," Flynn calls out.

Tal waves Flynn over, like they've been buddies for years. Who the hell is this guy? He's already got half the school wrapped around his finger.

"Hey," Tal says to Flynn, smiling his radiant smile.

"What's up?" Flynn asks when he gets to our table. He is pointedly not looking at me. "You coming?"

"Yeah. Just saying hi," Tal says, oblivious to Flynn's agitation.

I scoot my chair closer to Harlow. "How was your morning?" I ask her, shutting out the two males who have descended on us. I don't want either of them here. Harlow doesn't take my hint and looks up at Tal.

"You can have lunch with us if you want," she says with a delicate shrug.

"I'd like that," Tal says, smiling warmly at her. He turns to Flynn. "Maybe we could all eat together?"

Flynn finally looks at me and his face falls. He wants to say yes. He wants to sit next to me. I look at Harlow, begging her with my eyes. *Gods no.*

"Flynn!" Frigging Kayla. "Are you coming?" she scolds.

"Yeah," Flynn answers, annoyed. "Let's go, man."

"See ya," Tal says to Harlow.

Harlow tips her chin up at Tal, her pixie face full of mischief.

When the guys are seated at the popular table, Harlow turns to me.

"Thank you," she says.

I have no idea what she's talking about. "For what?", I ask.

"For farting in front of him."

I'm still lost.

"He didn't even look at you," she explains. "Just me. What did you do?"

"Nothing! Of course he was looking at you," I say. "You're adorable."

She narrows her eyes at me. "You can tell me. You farted while you were talking to him, didn't you?"

"I swear I didn't," I say through a laugh. "He just likes you."

I'm happy she's getting attention from a guy. She's been through a lot, and I know that her confidence could use a boost right now. But I'm worried, too.

"Look, Tal's really cute," I start to say.

She shoots me a look. "Don't even try to warn me off of him."

"Fine," I say, holding up my hands. We eat in silence for a few minutes.

"Okay," she says, sighing, like she already knows she's going to regret this. "What did you hear about him?"

I actually don't know what to say. How can I tell her about my suspicions without telling her about my world? "He just seems a little too... perfect."

"Seriously?" she says, trying not to smile. "Too perfect? Coming from you?"

Unless I'm willing to tell Harlow that there is a slight possibility he is a member of an ancient family that's half Greek god, I've got to drop it.

"Just be careful," I say.

Harlow looks across the room, her eyes locked on Tal. "Careful I don't hump his leg in public? Maaaybee."

"Well, look at that," Deuce pants. He's wet with sweat and sucking wind, but he's grinning like he hasn't enjoyed himself this much in ages. "It hasn't forgotten how to fight."

"No, It hasn't," I say, grinning back at him. I actually love it when he calls me It. He used to call me Thing and It when I was a little girl—like I was some big scary monster he would have to battle to the death.

"Are you staying for dinner?" he asks.

"I can't," I reply.

"Okay," he says. I can tell he's a little disappointed.

It's Friday night, and I usually hang out with him on the weekends. I've never had friends, so I've never had Friday night plans before. The only time I've ever had anything scheduled for the weekend is when my stepmonster Rebecca makes me attend some dumb function, like she's doing tomorrow night. She's throwing a cocktail party for some of the investors in my dad's next big development. *Oh joy.*

"Are you meeting friends?" he asks with quiet disapproval. I still haven't told him about Harlow, but I think he's getting suspicious anyway. I think he knows I've been sneaking out, but I have no idea how. Maybe I'm just paranoid.

"No," I reply honestly. Harlow did invite me out, but I told her I couldn't.

Tonight, I have to go to Washington Square Park. I'm not

going to hang out long, I just want to see if I can tell where he lives. I want to see if I can feel which window is his. The guilt I feel about going to see Ajax makes me want to come clean in at least one way to Deuce.

"I did meet a nice girl at school, though," I say. "Her name's Harlow. We've been spending a little time together."

"How'd you meet her?" he asks, totally unsurprised. So, the old buzzard does know I've been sneaking out.

"Detention," I say, and then wish I hadn't. Deuce gives me a look, and I try to explain. "She's not a troublemaker. She was in detention for sticking up for me. Harlow's a good person." I'm giving my uncle the abridged version, but it's the spirit of the truth at least.

Deuce nods and looks down at the floor. He's sad. "She sounds brave," he says, probably envisioning her tragic death that will come as a result of her befriending a Scion.

Now I wish I hadn't told him. But it's always like this when I talk to Deuce. I always end up saying too much, even if I've only said one or two sentences.

"I'm being careful," I say.

"You've always been careful around humans, but that doesn't mean it's safe for them to be around you. Remember what happened in Virginia."

I freeze. Deuce and I stare at each other.

"That boy wasn't my friend," I say through clenched teeth. "I did what I had to do."

Deuce doesn't look away. "I know he wasn't your friend. That's exactly my point. Before you get any closer to this girl, I want you to consider how much harder it would be to kill someone you do care about if she manages to find out about you."

I break eye contact first. I gather my things and leave Deuce's place angry. And I stay angry the whole time I'm changing clothes and sneaking out.

I've already been through the whole "my life is so unfair" phase. I've thrown tantrums and screamed and shot lightning into the sky. I've cried and begged and bargained. And when all the yelling was done, and every tear shed, not one thing about my life had changed. I don't throw tantrums anymore.

I walk, changing my face with the Cestus as I go. Right now, I get a few hours of actually believing that I'm someone else. This girl I become has a mediocre life. Decent parents she only hates a little, and a touch of hormonal acne that she thinks makes her look like an alien once a month when she gets her period. Her on-again, off-again boyfriend just dumped her. It's okay, though. She doesn't love him, and it gives her an excuse to cry. She doesn't know why she needs to cry but crying soothes an unnamed ache in her for a while before crying starts to hurt in its own right. Like an ice cube pressed to a burn. It starts off being heaven, and then, held there for too long, does its own kind of damage.

I snap out of it and realize I'm standing in Washington Square Park, allowing my face to become its own again. I'm not too sure how I got here or what time it is. I must have been walking around the city for a few hours now. I circle the park, trying to see into the residential windows.

The Furies whisper.

I stop and look up. A light goes on in a window and brightens momentarily when the curtains are parted. The light goes out.

The Furies howl.

I whirl to see Ajax standing about ten paces away from me.

He's wearing battered jeans and a tissue-thin T-shirt that has a few holes around the wide, stretched-out neck. He's splattered with paint and his blond hair is messily pushed around his head in a dozen different ways. He's barefoot and beautiful and real. Somehow, I'd forgotten he was actual flesh and blood, and not just the heavy object in my mind that the rest of my thoughts had begun to orbit.

"Go home, Daphne!" His voice breaks as he looks away, shaking with effort to stay where he is. "Now!"

Our breaths fill the frigid air like smoke. The Three Furies tear at their hair and wail, their pale bodies fizzing in and out of my sight like static. Rage claws its way up my throat, hot like a sob.

Ajax runs and I chase him. I want him dead.

He leads me uptown. We blur through the streets, moving too fast in the sparkling dark of New York City for any human to pin eyes on us. He leaps cabs and vaults over pedestrians, his lithe limbs negotiating the air in elegant arcs. I can see the muscles of his back ebbing and flowing under his thin shirt. I watch his hands cup the wind and his bare feet tuck under him as he leaps. I've never seen anyone, man or woman, move with such power and grace. The shapes he makes when he's in midair—the way his body curves and the wind seems to hug him—it's like watching a dancer underwater.

But I'm faster than he is. And I'm gaining on him.

In seconds we've run all the way up Fifth Avenue to Central Park, and for a moment I wonder if he knows where I live. If he's showing me how exposed I am by leading me home? He suddenly throws himself over the railing and into the heart of the park.

We pass a lake, through more trees, over rocks, and across a street that cuts through the park. He's definitely not leading me home, but he is leading me somewhere. His strength is flagging. He leaps, and I catch his ankle. He feels strangely light in my hand as I pull him to me, and then, suddenly, he becomes far too heavy.

He doesn't just feel like he weighs a ton, he literally weighs a ton, and I have no idea how that's possible. Ajax lands on me, nearly knocking me senseless as he crushes me into the stiff, cold ground.

"We're on neutral ground," he pants in my ear. I try to gather my wits as I struggle under his impossible weight. His lips are pressed against my neck, and I can't seem to think. He catches my hands and grinds them into the ground over my head.

I flail under him, forgetting all of my training. I'm just reacting now, and I know it, but I can't help it. He's between my legs. It's a standard position in wresting and dealing with it is something I've practiced a million times, but with him I have no idea what to do. His chest is so heavy I can't breathe. I try to summon a bolt, but everything starts to go blurry. I thrash under him, frantic to drag in a breath. The Cestus around my neck protects me from weapons, but not from suffocation.

"Calm down, or I won't be able to stop!" he begs. It slowly dawns on me that he's not trying to kill me. He's just trying to get me to hold still.

"Can't... breathe."

I feel his weight lighten a bit and I inhale. The white spots dancing in front of my eyes begin to shrink and I catch a glimpse of our surroundings. The tiered seats of a Greek amphitheater rise above us. Ajax and I are on an outdoor stage.

"Where are we?" I ask.

"Delacorte Theater," he says. He pulls back a bit and looks

down on me. "Amphitheaters are sacred ground—well, the ones blessed by Dionysus. They're the only places the different Houses can meet in relative peace. It's where we have inter-House meetings." His weight eases even more. "How can you not know that?"

I listen for the Furies, and only hear a faint whisper. I still want to kill him, but I'm not blinded by rage. His face is inches from mine. I can feel heat pouring out of him as if he has a furnace in his core. He smells like sunshine.

"Get off me," I snarl.

"No," he says. A faint smile tilts up one side of his lips. "I'm comfortable here."

"Really?" I let a current run under my skin, and he jumps back, gasping.

He moves away from me and crouches on his knees, ready to jump up and fight me if he has to. He shakes out his numbed hands.

"You're a bolt-thrower," he says, eyes wide. "I thought they were all gone."

Okay, that was a really big mistake. Uncle Deuce drilled it into me that I shouldn't give away any of my talents unless it's necessary. The less your opponent knows about your abilities, the better chance you have of winning a real fight. But I wanted to wipe that cocky smile off Ajax's face. *Stupid.* I sit up and rub the back of my head while I think about what to do. My fingers come back bloody.

"Not gone. But one of them is leaking," I say. He sees my fingers and his brow wrinkles with concern.

"Sorry," he says. For a moment he looks sheepish and sweet.

"Dionysus, huh?" I say, looking around at the marble

columns. I know Dionysus was not really an Olympian. He was born mortal and, therefore, he was not banished from earth with the rest of the gods in the Pact. "Why would the party god do something like that for us?"

Ajax shrugs. "There's a consecrated amphitheater in most major cities. New York. London. Paris. Rome. Maybe he likes a good DJ, doesn't want us Scions getting into a fight and ruining a good party."

I laugh. "The end of the world is kind of a buzz kill," I add.

"Then he'd have to go back to Olympus and eat nothing but ambrosia for all of eternity," Ajax says, grimacing at the thought.

We stare at each other for a bit, smiling. Then he averts his eyes and takes a deep breath, his stomach fluttering unevenly. The Furies are quieted, but not absent. Bloodlust is building in Ajax. "We should go."

"Yes." I know he's right. But I don't want to leave him just yet.

"Don't come to my house again. My brothers will kill you. The Village is Theban territory." He stops himself and softens his tone. "I still can't believe you're real."

I'm used to being stared at, but this is different. He's not really looking at my face. It's like he's watching the air around me, the breath filling my lungs, and possibly even the thoughts swirling in my head. Like he sees me, really sees me, and maybe he sees through me a bit, too.

"I'll write you," he says, then stands suddenly. "And this time, write me back," he adds with a teasing grin.

He runs off and disappears in the trees. It takes everything in me not to chase after him. I make myself count to a hundred before I trust myself enough to stand up and go home.

I take my time as I walk the length of Central Park to our apartment building on the southwest end. The park is amazing at night. It's like being in the middle of a deep forest, and not in the middle of Manhattan. It feels magical, and now that the adrenaline rush from my encounter with Ajax has passed, I am pleasantly exhausted enough to let my thoughts wander.

Ajax could have killed me, but he didn't. He should have killed me. I broke a law among the Four Houses—I invaded his territory. Every major city has clear territories staked out so Scions don't accidentally run into each other and start killing one another in front of humans. It's a necessary precaution for us to stay hidden. When my clueless father decided to move me to New York, my mother and uncle only allowed it on the condition that we lived around Central Park—my House's territory. My father agreed, probably because you can't get much better than a Park Avenue address. I am not supposed to leave my territory, even though I've been doing it since day one of my time here in New York.

Ajax had every right to kill me for breaking one of our laws, but he controlled himself, and led me to neutral territory. I didn't know about the amphitheater being neutral. Deuce and my mom, Elara, didn't see any reason to tell me about it. Probably because the amphitheater is used for meetings between the Houses, and my House is supposed to be extinct, so it's not like we'd ever be going to any inter-House meetings anyway.

My House. Descended from Zeus. Zeus the bolt-thrower. I wonder if Ajax has already put it together and guessed that I'm Daphne Atreus. I know that a Scion's talent doesn't necessarily mean he or she is a part of any one House. But a bolt-thrower? That talent just screams Zeus.

That's something he would have to tell his family. When he does, the Hundred Cousins will come looking for me... and Deuce. *How could I be so stupid?*

I look up and see the night doorman in front of my building. I stop dead, remembering that I snuck out. He sees me. Luckily, it isn't Rich. It's some guy I don't know yet, probably because I'm not supposed to be out at this hour. I stuff my hands into my pockets and try to dart past him.

"Miss? Are you okay?" he asks.

I shoot him the stink eye and notice the scared look on his face. My hand flies to the cut on the back of my head. It's healed, but I realize I'm covered in blood. I could seriously punch myself in the face right now. It's like seeing Ajax has entirely switched off my brain and my idiocy has reached critical mass.

"I'm fine," I say. I force myself to laugh. "It's fake blood. Doing a student film. NYU?"

He relaxes a bit and laughs with me. "It looks so real," he says. Just a hint of doubt creeps into his tone at the end.

"Right?" I exclaim excitedly, grinning in a way that a girl with a gash on her head definitely wouldn't.

I sell the lie with a little help from the Cestus. The doorman lets me get into the elevator without any more hassle. I have to crawl out the hallway window and climb around the outside of my building to get to my bedroom, but I manage it without my father ever knowing I've ever left. I drink a ton of water and wash off the blood.

My last thoughts before sleep are of Ajax. I dream of killing him.

CHAPTER 6

"Just do me this one favor first," I plead.

"But why won't you come with me?" Harlow pleads back. "I can't just walk up to Ajax's front door and hand him a letter."

"Why not? I'd totally do it for you."

"Yeah, but you won't let me say who it's from," she whines. "He has no idea who I am."

Normally whining bothers me, but Harlow manages to do it in a cute way. Maybe it's the freckles.

"He'll know it's from me," I say convincingly.

"What if he doesn't answer the door? What if it's his mom? What do I say?"

"Say your name's Harlow. Just don't tell her the letter's from me."

Harlow sighs, giving in. "All right. But when I get back, we go shopping at Hye-Su's."

"Promise," I say. I turn and hail a cab for her. "And then you can tell me all about the party last night."

I wait for Harlow at a café near Hye-Su's boutique while she goes to Ajax's for me. My leg is bouncing up and down and it's not just from the caffeine in my double cappuccino.

I couldn't write everything I wanted in my letter to Ajax, just in case Harlow read it, but I still wrote more than I should have. I basically begged him not to tell his family about our "electrifying" encounter last night. There's no reason for him to do as I ask, but for Deuce's sake, I had to try.

I also told him I dreamt about him, but that my dream had been a nightmare. I know that sounds terrible, and will probably push him away, which is why I wrote it.

A part of me is sad about that.

It takes Harlow forever to return, and when she does, she's freaking out.

"Oh my god!" she yells.

"What happened?" I ask, worried. Her face is flushed scarlet.

"Do you want me to start with the part where he answered the door without a shirt on, or do you want me to skip to the part where he drew you this amazing flip-book in about five seconds?" She gives me a little handmade book and plops down into the chair across from me. "My god, he has got to be the sexiest man on the face of the earth! Except for maybe Tal."

I wave a hand in her face to snap her out of it. "Were his brothers home? What about his parents? Did you get a look at any of them?"

"Just his little sister. Her name was Dora or something. Cute kid. She has a serious case of hero worship for Ajax, by the way. Followed him around like a puppy." Harlow stops and holds up a hand, like she can't take it anymore. "He was babysitting. How adorable is that?"

I always pictured the Delos family as this mass of hulking, bloodthirsty men who deserved a thumping. I never really stopped to think about them having little sisters who would cry if they got hurt. Or killed.

"He wants to see you again tonight. He said you'd know the place." She smiles. "He said he'd wait all night until you showed up."

What does he think will happen if I meet him tonight? That we'll suddenly not want to kill each other and go catch a movie?

"You look strangely upset about something that sounds unbelievably romantic, you know."

"Did he say anything else?"

"Probably," Harlow replies, shrugging dismissively. "Like I could concentrate on what was coming out of his mouth when I couldn't stop staring at those lips."

The server comes to our table and Harlow orders a coffee and biscotti. I take the opportunity to look through the flip-book Ajax made for me.

The little ink drawings show a stick figure cartoon of our chase from the night before. It ends with the boy stick figure being electrocuted by bolts from the sky, and then him standing alone, his heart beating and growing bigger and bigger with every *lub-dub*.

I know they're just stick figures, but somehow they have personality, too. The black lines that make up the girl's body seem to pulse with strength, and the angle of the boy's basic circle for a head makes it seem as if he's full of stormy confusion.

The last page simply says, "I won't tell."

"Won't tell what?" Harlow asks. Her shrewd eyes are narrowed at me over her coffee cup.

I shove the flip-book into my bag. "That we met last night."

"Aannd," she says impatiently.

All this talk about Ajax is making me angry and I'm tired of being angry. I don't want to hate him anymore, but I don't think I have any choice. I need to change the subject. "What happened at the party? I still can't believe that you went to Flynn's."

"Tal asked me to meet him there. No way was I missing that. He was sweet to me all night," she says with a hint of censure in her eyes.

"I'm sorry I didn't go with you, but I'm not as brave as you are. Kayla's already cut all my hair off. That bloodsucker would start in on my fingers if she saw me anywhere near Flynn again."

"It's okay. I totally understand," she says, looking down, still feeling guilty about cutting my hair. I nudge her playfully and ask for more details as we pay the bill and walk.

"He didn't kiss me, but I have a feeling he's going to soon," she begins, and then launches into a diatribe about how Tal spent more time with her than with anyone else at the party. How he got her drinks, and kept asking her if she needed anything, and basically treated her like they were already a couple.

Somehow, Harlow and I manage to try on outfits at Hye-Su's for three hours, and I don't think she stops talking about Tal for more than five minutes put together. I listen and nod and vehemently support everything she says, like a good friend should. Like I always dreamed a friend would, back when I didn't have one.

I'm happy, just plain old happy, for a regular afternoon. Harlow and I walk to her house. Her parents are at work, so we share a pack of Twizzlers and drink way too much Diet Coke while we sit on her kitchen counter. Eventually, though, I have to leave her place and go home.

The second I walk through the door, my stepmonster is on me. Rebecca's big fake boobs are propped up extra high, and her usual cloud of sickly sweet perfume has passed through noxious and entered into weaponized territory. Someone's feeling especially insecure tonight, and I can tell from the look on her face that she's about to take it out on me.

"Where have you been?" she demands, waving her still-wet manicured tips like she's about to flap herself airborne.

"Shopping with a girlfriend," I reply, lifting my bags. "I needed a dress for tonight."

That shuts her up for a second. One of my stepmonster's biggest complaints about me is that I take no interest in the things she finds important, like clothes and cosmetology. She reels back on her tacky silver heels for a moment, regroups, and dives back in, her spray-tanned cleavage all aquiver.

"You know, Daphne, one of these days you're going to have to step up your responsibilities around here." She cocks a hip, and really hits her lecturing groove. "You father is a very important man, and the people who go into business with him are privileged. Do you understand?"

I make a concerted effort to not roll my eyes and remind her that I have an extensive vocabulary. "I understand, Rebecca," I say calmly.

"I can't do all this by myself," she says, throwing her hands out wide to include the staff of three permanent housekeepers and the dozen or so people she hired to decorate, cater, and serve a single cocktail party.

"It is a lot. Handling all this help," I say, nodding my head sympathetically. Her face goes blank. She's trying to figure out if I'm being sarcastic or not. Sometimes I feel bad for Rebecca. Then there are times like this when I don't.

She swallows hard, and a lost look widens her eyes. I've hurt her. I glance away, feeling ashamed of myself. I've known for a while now that I have a ruthless streak in me. I'm still not sure if it's something I was born with or something I learned. I hope I learned it and, someday, I hope I'll have the kind of life where it'll be safe enough for me to unlearn it.

"What's going on?" my dad asks, entering the room. He's holding a martini glass. Early start, I guess.

Rebecca throws up her hands. "She won't do anything to help me."

"I was getting a dress," I say defensively. "If I'd stayed here and tried to help, I'd have just be in your way and you know it, Rebecca. Sorry I didn't give you the opportunity to be disappointed in my poor hostessing skills."

Her face turns bright red. "This is exactly what I'm talking about, Mitch," she says, turning to my father. "She thinks she's just too good for me."

My father stays silent. I can almost hear him thinking, *She is too good for you*. And so can Rebecca.

Now I feel bad.

"I'm sorry," I say, trying to make peace. "I know this party means a lot to you, and I went shopping to find a dress so I would look nice."

"See?" my father says, trying to avoid an argument. "She didn't mean it. You didn't mean it. Problem solved."

Rebecca shuts up, even though I can tell she still has a ton to say. Right now she's walking a fine line. If she pisses off my dad too much she's going to end up getting traded in for a younger version of herself, and she knows it.

"Can I see the dress?" my dad asks. He's trying to sound casual, but there's an edge to his tone. His eyes run over my body and then narrow in anger. Like he's mad at me for having a woman's body.

He snatches the bag out of my hand and digs through the tissue paper and the other items until he finds the dress. He inspects it carefully and I can hear his blood pressure rising. He's picturing me in it, picturing other men looking at me in it. "Don't you think it's a bit... provocative?" He nearly chokes on the word.

I shrug. "It looks very conservative on," I say in a neutral tone. I don't want to aggravate him anymore.

"Let me see you in it," he orders.

"At the party," I say, taking everything out of his hands and putting it all back into the bags. I feel strange. I'm hot all over, like I'm embarrassed. I cross my arms over my chest and slump.

"Put it on," he says, a warning in his voice.

"Mitch," Rebecca snaps. Her voice is deeper and more forceful than I've ever heard it before.

Rebecca stares down my dad. He finally backs off, and Rebecca turns to me. I swear she looks almost protective. "Go to your room, Daphne."

I rush out, giving Rebecca a curious second glance. I'm grateful she spoke up for me, but also worried that she had to. My dad's getting worse. Not even Rebecca can ignore the fact that he's weird around me anymore.

I close my bedroom door and sit on the edge of my bed. I'm not sure what to do about my father. I don't know how much longer I should live with him, but I know he's never going to just let me go. When we moved here he was talking about me applying to Columbia University so I could live at home next year and still go to college. He doesn't want me more than a few blocks away from him, not even to go to school.

My bedroom phone rings.

"Hey," I say when I pick up, expecting it to be Harlow or Deuce. No one else ever calls this line.

"I waited hours before calling you, even though I've been thinking about you all day. How's that for willpower?"

The Furies wail at the sound of his voice.

"How'd you get my number?" I whisper, though I'm pretty sure my dad can't hear me in here.

"Did you get my message?"

"I can't meet you."

"No, you're right, this is crazy and stupid and dangerous. Meet me anyway."

I laugh despite the Furies. How is that even possible?

"My dad is throwing a party tonight for some investors. My stepmother will have a fit if I bail."

I wait a few moments, but it takes a while for Ajax to respond.

"Please don't tell me your father is Mitch James."

"How did you know that?"

"Get out of the building!" Ajax says urgently. For a moment, my brain can't process his words. "My father is one of his investors. He's on his way there right now with two of my brothers. You have to run. Now! I'll meet you in the park," Ajax says, and he hangs up.

I open my bedroom door carefully and look down the hallway. I can hear Rebecca's voice. There's no way I can get past her without being noticed—unless I don't look like myself.

The college girls Rebecca hired to cocktail waitress are all wearing little black dresses under their waist-tie aprons. I go to my closet and pull out the simple black sheath I bought on my first shopping trip with Harlow. I put it on quickly and use the Cestus to change my appearance.

Looking like a pert brunette with a bit of an overbite, I sneak out of my room. As soon as I'm a few steps away from my door I take on the purposeful stride of a server. I pick up a tray and maneuver my way to the front door. Rebecca is yelling at the chef when I pass her. I manage to get out the front door without anyone stopping me, and race down the stairwell to Uncle Deuce's apartment.

I let myself into his place and drop my disguise, but he isn't home. I grab a notepad and leave a message telling him to stay away from the apartment building. I yank a jacket off the coatrack and bolt out the door.

If the Delos family is in the process of coming up, they'll use the elevator. I take the stairs. For just a moment, somewhere around the tenth floor, I feel a whisper of the Furies as Ajax's father and brothers pass by me on their way up.

If I'm close enough to feel them, they can feel me.

I'm too late. They know an enemy Scion is in the building. My only chance is to beat them out the door and to the neutral ground of the Delacorte Theater. There, the Furies are lessened enough that the Delos might not be able to sense me from afar. Right now I'm too terrified to feel the Furies. I've heard a lot about Paris Delos and his two oldest sons, Tantalus and Castor. If they catch me, I'm dead.

I get to the ground level and run like hell. Thank gods Rich is holding the door open for some old lady. I vault over her stooped back and the gust of wind I create nearly blows the brittle thing halfway across the street before Rich can latch on to her. I stifle the urge to slow down and apologize and make it to the amphitheater in seconds.

Ajax is already there, waiting for me. When he sees me his face relaxes and he exhales a deep breath. "Were you followed?"

I close my eyes and concentrate. "I don't think so," I say, and open my eyes. *Huh.* "I just noticed something. I think the Furies are quieter with my eyes closed."

We both close our eyes.

It's difficult to stand in front of him with my eyes closed. I feel so exposed. "Say something," I say through a nervous laugh. "You're freaking me out."

"This is really weird, isn't it?" he agrees. We lapse into a tense silence. The Furies aren't completely gone, and it's taking a huge amount of self-control to stay where I am. But they are lessened.

"Okay, I'll go first," I say. "Thank you."

"Have you told your family about me?" he asks in return.

"My family is basically just my uncle Deuce and I. My mom and I have to stay separate..." I sigh, mentally kicking myself. "I shouldn't have told you any of that."

"I swore I'd never tell anyone about you, Daphne, and I meant it," he says sincerely. "Daphne Atreus, right? Daughter of Elara?"

"Yes." In our world, the children always take the surname of their Scion parent, whether that parent is male or female. My human father's last name of "James" has no meaning to Ajax, even if that is what's on my ID card.

"How old are you?" he asks.

"Seventeen."

"My father thinks he killed Elara twenty years ago."

It's a good thing he didn't, I add silently to myself. For humans and Scions alike. There's more to my family curse than simply sharing an identical face with my mother and her mother before her, but the other Houses are completely in dark about this. Thanks to the Cestus, they don't even know about the shared face bit.

I hear Ajax swear under his breath. "What is it?" I ask, confused.

"Everyone thinks he did. All the other Houses think your House is extinct and they all come and go through your territory, even though they're technically not supposed to. You're not safe, Daphne."

"Yeah, I noticed," I say dryly. "I had to run my ass off tonight."

"My oldest brother, Tantalus, wants all the other Houses gone. He won't stop until you're all dead." His voice shakes momentarily.

"I've heard. It's a big part of the reason my family has been *playing* dead." I think of Deuce telling me about Tantalus Delos and the Hundred Cousins, and how they're on some kind of fanatical mission to destroy the other Scions. I also think about what a traitor I am. "But aren't you one of the Hundred Cousins?" I ask.

"No," he says, his voice grating. "I love my father and my

brother, but I don't agree with them." I can hear his breathing speeding up and he's making small, frustrated noises, like he's struggling with himself. I realize he must have opened his eyes. I open mine and see him looking at me.

"Because you want to kill me yourself?" I say, half-jokingly.

His face gets serious, and I get a sense that Ajax isn't all origami swans and cartoon flip books. He's just as much a fighter as his famous brothers.

"You're mine," he says.

"Really?" I ask. My voice is low and dangerous.

"You are," he continues. His tone suddenly lightens. "But I don't want to kill you." He cracks a smile, diffusing the tension. "At least, not entirely."

I actually laugh.

"I want to sort of kill you," he says, drawing out the joke.

"I guess I want to sort of kill you, too," I admit.

"I guess that means I'm yours, then," he says.

"Guess so."

"It's official," he says. "No one can kill you but me."

"And no one can kill you but me," I say, sealing the deal. His smile is slow to grow and lovely to watch.

"We just might end up living forever," he says. He suddenly takes a deep breath and looks away. I see his fists clench. The Furies won't let us stay here with each other much longer without a fight. "Were you going someplace?"

"No," I reply, momentarily taken off guard. I look down at my dress and realize that I'm a tad done up for the park. "I had to wear this—" I start to say but he cuts me off.

"I meant do you have a place to go to? A friend's house?"

"Uh... I could go to Harlow's?" I say uncertainly. I've never just showed up at her house before, but I don't think she'd mind.

"You should go." I turn to leave but he stops me. "Wait."

I breathe a laugh. "Do you really think me staying is a good idea?"

"Quick. Tell me a story."

I laugh again, surprised. It's like every other thing he says throws me. "A story?"

"Anything. Just start talking. Tell me something totally random about yourself."

"Right. Okay." Grasping on to the first thought that comes into my head, I think of the lake we ran by on our way here. "I can't swim."

He looks at me, stunned just enough for a moment that all the anger is knocked out of him. "How can you not know how to swim?"

"I sink in water."

"No one sinks in water."

"I do. It's a family trait, or something. My mom, her mom, none of us have ever been able to swim."

"You don't find that strange? Creepy?" he says, delighted.

"Says the demigod who paints pictures of a girl he's never met."

He looks down, serious. We haven't talked about this in person yet, but he told me in his first letter that he has had visions of me all his life. I don't know what that means, or how it could be possible, but the thought of it makes me feel something feather-light and warm inside.

"How did you know I cut my hair?" I ask, truly curious about how this... whatever it is between us... works.

"I don't know," he replies quietly. "It's like a dream image that flashes in my mind when I least expect it, really bright and clear. I'd always pictured you with long hair, and then the other day I saw you with a shaved head. You were crying."

We settle back into silence and the Furies start whispering to us again.

"I got hazed by a group of girls on my first day at school," I say quickly, answering the question he didn't ask out loud but wanted to. "They cut my hair."

"And you had to let them," Ajax says. He understands, and not just about me having to hide my Scion strength.

I nod, frowning. I've never really thought about what it would be like for a male Scion. He can't fight back either. For a girl that's not such a big deal, but for a guy it's social suicide. Everyone would think he's a coward. I wonder what it must be like to have to live with that.

"Okay, now it's your turn," I say, pushing down my tangled emotions. "Tell me something totally random about yourself."

"I have a third nipple," he answers, like it's the first thing that came to him.

A surprised laugh jumps out of me. "You're lying!"

"I'm not. Look," he says, lifting up his shirt.

Wow. I blush and glance away.

"Look," he repeats insistently, pointing to a small, dark bump about three inches under his left nipple.

"I'm looking." I try to act as clinical as I can while inspecting his impressive torso. Tan. Smooth. Lush as fruit. "That's a mole," I say turning away quickly.

He grabs my shoulder and positions me so he's facing the light. "It's a mini-nipple. A triple nipple. The little nipple that couldn't."

"Okay, yes, I guess maybe it might be," I say, pulling away. "Now will you please stop saying the word nipple?"

He studies me, amused.

We fall into silence. "I should go," I say.

"No. Stay a little longer," he pleads.

I can see him struggling. His hands are clenching, and his eyes fever bright.

"Thanks again." I reply, conflicted, as he takes a step toward me.

I fight the urge, and turn to run.

I have to slow down to human speed when I reach the stairs of Harlow's brownstone. I don't dare turn to look back to see if Ajax has chased me. But I can feel him nearby.

The door swings open, and Harlow pops through it and grabs my arm. Years of training to act normal in front of humans kicks in, but I know that if Harlow had taken even one second longer to answer the door Ajax and I would be fighting right now in front of her.

"You are never going to believe who's here!" she says in an ecstatic whisper. As she grabs my arm to haul me inside, she notices Ajax across the street behind me. "Ajax!" she calls to him. She widens her eyes at me meaningfully.

Ajax shoves his hands into his pockets to hide his clenched fists.

"Hi Daphne," says a male voice. I turn and see Tal behind Harlow. I must really be distracted because I didn't hear him coming down the hallway.

Ajax turns abruptly and goes before he loses control. All my anger unwinds and disappears as Ajax sprints back to his territory. The pressure and heat of it is replaced with a dull nothing. I feel better and worse now that he's gone. I wish I could feel one emotion at a time.

"Everything okay?" Harlow whispers to me.

"Yeah," I say, waving it off. I look at Tal and then back at Harlow pointedly to change the conversation.

"How about a soda?" Harlow asks, already dragging me toward the kitchen. I shrug, undecided, and she turns to Tal. "We'll be right back," she says. He takes the hint and leaves us for a bit of girl talk.

Harlow rounds on me, her face glowing with barely contained glee. "He showed up on my doorstep, like, ten minutes before you did!"

"No way," I say, my jaw dropping. "Just like that?"

"Nice dress by the way," she adds with a teasing smile.

"It's a long story—" I begin and stop myself when I see her bust out laughing. I laugh with her, acknowledging that I am a tad overdressed.

I opt for water instead of soda and wait as Harlow pours it for me. Her judgment is addled by that pretty smile of Tal's—if it wasn't, she would be more bothered by this. A guy she's known for four days just shows up on her doorstep, out of the blue. And I can't point this fact out to her, that there's something strange about Tal and I'm frustrated that I can't say anything to her about it. Hopefully she'll wake up tomorrow with her brain intact again and she'll see that something's not quite right.

We go down a level in her five-story brownstone to the family room. Tal is down there playing pool by himself waiting for us.

"Where are your parents?" I ask Harlow when it finally occurs to me that we're alone.

"Date night." Her Kewpie-doll lips twist cynically. "I don't know why they bother anymore. It's not like going to a fancy restaurant is going to save their marriage."

"Do they still enjoy each other's company?" Tal asks as he lines up a shot.

"Oh yeah," Harlow replies emphatically. "They've always gotten along really well."

"Then that's why they go out together," he says, and sinks his shot.

Harlow's face softens as she watches him. "I never really thought of it that way before."

Tal looks up at her, and I can tell from the neutral look on his face that he's not catching how hard Harlow's crushing on him right now. Which is crazy because she couldn't look more love-struck if cartoon hearts were spinning around her head.

"How'd you and Ajax meet, Daphne?" Tal asks. "He doesn't go to our school, does he?"

"You know him?" I ask.

"No, I heard Claire say his name."

"I met him on the subway," I reply.

"What school does he go to?"

"Don't know," I answer, looking down at my shot.

"Are you two...?"

"No," I say flatly.

Harlow groans. "Give them a minute. Daphne's just stubborn." She tosses me a saucy look.

"Hey, didn't your stepmonster have a party you were supposed to be at tonight?" Harlow asks, remembering.

"I ditched," I say.

"Thus, the dress. Yikes. Think you'll be in trouble?" Harlow asks.

"Oh yeah," I say with certainty. "Not like it would be any different from any other day."

"What do you mean?" Tal asks.

"My dad doesn't like me going out."

"Like, at night?" Harlow asks, not getting it.

"Like, ever," I say. There's more emotion in my voice than I expected. I sound bitter. An uncomfortable moment follows. I probably said too much. Tal's eyes narrow as he considers me. I try to laugh it off like it's not a big deal.

Tal's eyes stay on me as I finish our game. He doesn't say much, but I can tell he's still thinking about what I said.

We hang out for another couple of hours, watching movies, eating popcorn. Tal is a sci-fi geek. He likes those movies where something huge invades Earth and destroys all of humanity's favorite landmarks in a series of eye-blinding explosions. Thankfully, he's not one of those pushy movie buffs who insist on silence while the hero says something pithy and then single-handedly saves Earth. He has no problem ignoring the movie and chatting with Harlow and me as we crack jokes and moan about homework. We have fun. There's no doubt about it, Tal is a likable guy.

Harlow's parents come home. Tal and I meet Mr. and Mrs. Tate. They're stylish and good-looking. Harlow gets her freckles from her dad. He's darker than she is, but his eyes are green. I wonder for a moment if he's Brazilian. Her mom is multiethnic as well, and she wears her hair in a giant mane of natural tight ringlets. It's gorgeous. As the Tates chat with us in the kitchen I can see how comfortable they are with each other. Whatever happens with them, I can tell Harlow's parents will remain friends through it. This may be an unconventional family, but there is no doubt that something about it works. Tal was right about that.

Tal tells Mr. Tate he has an interest in architecture, which is Mr. Tate's profession, and they hit it off right away. I tell Harlow I have to go. I leave her and Tal chatting away with her folks. She's so happy she barely notices.

It's late. The party will be over and the Delos will be gone. I run home to face my father, knowing full well that I will probably end up grounded for life.

Tal

After Daphne leaves, I finish up with Harlow's parents, confident that I've ingratiated myself with them, and go to Washington Square Park to find out what the Delos family thinks of tonight's happenings.

It was a close call. Daphne nearly didn't make it out in time before Paris, Castor, and Pallas Delos arrived at her father's apartment. I can't be sure, but I think that they may have gotten close enough to Daphne to have felt the Furies as they passed each other. From that, the Delos will know that a member of an enemy House had been in the building, and that he or she got away in a hurry. Luckily, Daphne is fast. Even I lost her as she made her escape.

It appears she went to meet Ajax, rather than go directly to Harlow's to hide. I thought she would certainly go to her friend first. I have underestimated how much trust has formed between Ajax and Daphne. Things are moving faster between them than I thought, and this troubles me.

Still, she might kill him yet. She may be waiting for the right time and place to face him, as is traditional if she hopes to have a Triumph, although I don't think the House of Atreus throws a Triumph anymore when they kill an enemy. The Delos certainly do. Tantalus rekindled that tradition of having a hero's parade for a murderer as part of his forming of the Hundred Cousins. I suppose it makes the killers feel more like heroes.

It could just happen by accident, no matter how kindly they feel toward each other. The Furies never lessen, and if the afflicted Scions manage to resist killing each other in that first, fiery encounter, the effect of the Furies becomes more insidious. Over time, the afflicted Scions grow careless and convince themselves they have it under control, but the more contact Ajax and Daphne have with each other, the more dangerous it will become. Hubris. Forever the downfall of their kind. One slip, and one of them will be dead. In this way the Furies have pushed children to kill their own parents, mothers to murder their own babies, and more than once I've watched the look-alike daughters of Helen of Troy kill their star-crossed lovers only to curse themselves the moment after.

That wouldn't be the preferred option. I'd much rather that the House of Atreus and the House Thebes stay ignorant of this unfortunate connection between Daphne and Ajax, and that the other Houses stay ignorant of the existence of the House of Atreus in general. Of course, I would step in before I would allow this to cause open war between the Houses. Unfortunately, I shall have to kill the Delos boy. Atreus must be spared. Although, I must confess I don't like that option.

I'll do what I must, but it is not my goal to kill him. The prophecy says that only when all four Houses are one, the gods will be freed. It does not make it clear if that means the four Houses will be joining together, or if there will be only one House left standing after an inter-House war. Prophecies tend to be irritatingly vague in this manner, and each Scion seems to interpret the prophecy in the manner that suits his or her purpose. Like I said, everyone in this game cheats, and sometimes they cheat themselves with what they choose to believe.

Personally, I don't care much about how humans see only what they want to see. All I care is that the prophecy—inevitable though it may be—is fulfilled at the latest date possible.

I arrive at the Delos' handsome brownstone and break in. They have an alarm system, but they rarely bother to set it when they are at home. Like most Scions, the Delos are conditioned to have a bit too much faith in their supercharged senses. They are comfortable knowing that a full human is too noisy to break in without being detected, and that an enemy Scion would awaken the Furies and alert them. As if there were only two kinds of threats left in the world. The Scions have forgotten that there are beings like me, and hardly bother to lock their doors anymore. I have found this very useful over the past few centuries.

I shrink down and follow the voices, hiding myself in the shadows of a nearby room. Why the Delos family always chooses to crowd into the kitchen to talk about serious matters, I'll never know. There are much more secure places in the house to have these kinds of conversations, but for some unfathomable reason they always seem to end up in the kitchen when something important is happening.

"We should at least try to find out for sure which House it was," Castor says passionately. I have caught them in mid-argument. Paris looks at his second son with a fondness that borders on favoritism.

"It would make no difference, Castor," Paris answers. "Athens would deny it, and Rome would only counter that they have more right to the abandoned Atreus territory than any of us."

"It couldn't have been Rome," Castor replies. Paris nods in agreement. It's obvious to me why Castor is his father's favorite. At twenty-five, he is not Paris' firstborn, nor is he as pretty as his younger brothers, Pallas and Ajax, but Castor has the mind of a leader.

"Why not Rome?" asks Pallas.

Pallas is only ten months younger than his brother Castor, but he has so little sense you would think ten years separated them. The House of Rome is descended from Aphrodite. All of their members have some sort of control over emotions, and most of them are taught the trick of quieting the rage that comes with the Furies. Not all of them can manage it—it is quite hard to learn how to do, I understand.

"Someone from Rome would have tempered our anger in order to avoid a fight, like they do when we go to inter-House meetings," Castor answers his brother calmly.

"They wouldn't dare venture out of their territory otherwise," Paris says darkly.

The House of Rome is not known for its strength of arms,

but rather its strength at diplomacy and deception. The last thing a Roman wants is to come head to head with a Theban—or worse, a brute of an Athenian—in a physical fight.

"What I felt wasn't tempered," Castor continues. "We need to speak to Athens. Find out why they were there."

"Probably not a good idea," Ajax says quietly.

"Why not?" Castor asks. His intelligent eyes rest kindly on his youngest brother. As Paris favors Castor, so Castor favors Ajax, and no wonder. Ajax has far more maturity than his seventeen years warrant.

"They would have the right to ask us why *we* were there," Ajax answers with just the right amount of indignation in his tone. "Our business is none of their business."

Clever boy. His father and brothers scowl and nod at the justness of his statement. Ajax pretends to be insulted by the thought of explaining himself to Athenians along with them, but I can see his eyes darting around as he gauges whether or not his ruse worked. He's protecting Daphne from them. That suits my needs at the moment, but it troubles me as well. It is very rare for a Scion to betray his House in this way.

"You weren't home when I arrived. Where were you?" Paris asks Ajax.

"Ran out to the store for a sec," he lies.

"You're supposed to be grounded."

"It's not a prison. I came right back."

Paris regards his son for a moment. The three young men then watch their father stride out of the room. Ajax sits stock-still, holding his breath.

"Keep pushing it." Castor says to Ajax.

"I can't step out of the house for a moment?" Ajax asks

bitterly.

"Quit getting arrested, kid." Pallas says.

"I couldn't run away." Ajax replies defensively. "Half the artists tagging that night were watching me work when the cops showed up. What was I supposed to do—take off and disappear in front of them?"

Pallas and Castor exchange a look. It's obvious they both feel sympathy for their younger brother.

"Maybe you should stop tagging," Castor says.

Ajax's face tilts down, his expression echoing a difficult thought. "I can't. Not yet."

"Jax," Pallas begins, like he's gearing up to give his brother a lecture.

"I will—," Ajax interrupts. "But not just yet. There's one more thing I have to do."

"What's that?" Castor asks.

Ajax smiles. "I promised someone I'd paint the sky."

After a long silence. "Such a dork," says Pallas, and they all laugh.

I watch the sons of Paris talk some more, eat something cold right out of the refrigerator, and shove each other around as they knit among themselves the baffling fabric of brotherhood. Part teasing, part competitive, their bond is not a simple thing to describe. It's rare, what I'm watching. I could count the number of times I've witnessed its equal over the course of my long years.

If only I could get the Atreus heir to focus more on the humans in her school. Maybe she could turn her love to one of them, and the Delos family would be spared.

That would be the wisest course of action, for I can already tell that if Ajax were to die now in the bright blush of his youth, the brothers who love him so dearly would avenge him no matter how long it took, or how many Scion souls they sent to Hades. This is counterproductive.

I retire to my subterranean lair, near the monster Ladon. I listen to an exchange between him and his brother, Daedelus the Heir to the House of Athens. Ladon is the eldest son of Bellerophon, Head of the House of Athens—but not his Heir. Ladon is a monster, scaly-skinned and hulking like the dragon he was named after, and he lives beneath the ground in the subway tunnels of New York City, as do I.

Ladon may be disowned by Bellerophon but Daedelus, his younger brother and the Heir to the House, keeps him informed out of love or duty or some combination of both I have not yet deciphered. It is because of this bond that I keep a close eye on Ladon and have made my subterranean home here in New York close enough to his that I may hear him when he has visitors. I have found that it is always a good idea to know the major movements of all the Houses when I am watching The Face in her seventeenth year.

Tonight, they do not discuss anything important, and it makes me wonder why Daedelus would trouble himself to come below like this where the water flows up into the oldest tunnels of the city's subway lines. They speak for no reason. They talk of little things, like the human news of the day. I don't understand why.

Here, too, are brothers together, and yet all my kind are gone. I know that there is something special in this, so I will try to spare all those that I can.

Yes. I will distract Daphne with plenty of friends and devoted boys to love her. That is the safest course of action.

CHAPTER 7

"Don't let your emotions dictate your strategy," Deuce says calmly. He takes his foot off my neck and pulls me to my feet. "If you can lose your head over something as silly as getting grounded, what do you think it's going to be like when you have the Furies screaming at you?"

I don't rub my neck even though it hurts. "Again," I say.

"No. You're done for the day." Deuce turns his back on me and starts unwinding the sparring straps that are wrapped around his hands.

"Again," I repeat, trailing after him. Looking for a fight.

"Why? You're not listening, you're not concentrating, you're just lashing out at me like a two-year-old." Deuce says.

"Wouldn't you be angry?" I say, hating the helpless sound in my voice. "He took the phone out of my room. He's having me followed. I'm not just grounded, I'm—I'm," I stammer, trying to come up for a word for what I am. "I'm imprisoned. He's gone crazy, Deuce, and you know it." I force myself to say it. "He's been looking at me—in a not so... right way."

Deuce lets out a sigh, a worried frown adding more wrinkles to his face. "I called your mother."

"What?" I say, shocked. "Why'd you do that?"

I haven't seen my mom in years, and the last time we were together I told her I was better off never seeing her again. She'd agreed with me. That had stung a bit more than I'd thought it would.

"I'll let her explain," Deuce says uncomfortably. He starts to fidget.

"What aren't you telling me?" I ask.

"What aren't *you* telling *me*?"

I look away first. I hate lying to him, but there's no point in telling him about Ajax now. Before my phone was removed from my room, I dialed Ajax and told him not to call me again, and hung up. So, that's it.

"You're bleeding pretty bad from your bottom lip. Let's get you some honey." As we walk to the kitchen, Deuce snakes one of his wiry arms around my shoulders and gives me a quick hug before letting me go.

I pour some honey down the back of my throat and feel it working its magic on my body. My wounds close and my swelling bumps sink back into my skin seconds after I swallow. Honey heals humans too, I've heard, but nothing like what it does for Scions. I don't need honey to heal small injuries. It's just faster and sweeter this way. I'll take whatever sweetness I can get at this point.

I leave Deuce's. The beefy ape my father has tailing me shoves himself off the wall of the hallway and falls into step a few paces behind me.

"I'm just going back to my room," I tell him. He doesn't say anything, doesn't look me in the eye. I don't even know his name, although I've asked him for it several times. My dad's gotten so deranged he won't even let my bodyguards/jailers talk to me anymore. If he could blindfold them, he probably would.

I slam my bedroom door in the guy's face. Childish, I know, and I regret it as soon as I do it. I wonder if he knows how messed up this situation is. I wonder if he can see how strange it is that a father would be this possessive of his own daughter. I wonder if he goes home to someone and tells that person how effed up this job is.

I peel off my workout clothes and shower, flop into bed, shut off the lights, and then I see it. A triangle of white paper wedged into the window beside my bed.

I scramble up onto my knees and look around my bedroom, but fear is the second thing I feel. The first thing is happiness, and that's why I'm afraid. It means I've got something to lose.

I don't think my father has put video cameras in my room. Strangely, I hadn't thought about that when I was undressing, but now that I see Ajax's letter, I do. I stretch my senses out and seek all of the sources of electricity in my room. The glittering circuit of the light sockets and the zing of the copper wires in the walls are all laid bare to me. I can feel the flow and swell of it all around me. Not even the smallest micro camera could hide from me. When every outlet and battery is accounted for, I'm comforted to know that my father hasn't completely lost his mind.

I open the window to get the letter and pull it back into bed with me. It's a simple triangle. Nothing fancy this time, just my name written on one side and his on the other. I flip the triangle over and over, seeing our names joined by an object but facing in opposite directions.

I unfold the letter and read:

> I made you a promise. Meet me at the subway
>   station next Saturday night.
> -A

I know which station he means—it has to be the one where we first saw each other—but I don't know what promise he's talking about. Unless he's talking about our promise to kill each other.

Half of my mouth tics up in a smile. Does he really think he can take me? As if any son of Apollo has ever been a challenge for a daughter of Zeus. I'd ruin him. Anyway, I don't think that's what he means. If it was, why would he wait a whole week?

I stretch out in bed, still staring at his note. I'm not reading, really, just looking at his handwriting and imagining him writing it. He's a southpaw. I know from fighting him. I picture him curling his wrist over the words so as not to smudge the ink. Lefties always look so contorted when they write, but there's also something protective about their posture. Like they're about to hug the page. I hold what he's held as I fall asleep.

"You have to come," Harlow says.

"Why? I'm not into basketball," I reply.

"Doesn't matter. First game of the season everyone has to attend. If you don't go, you get detention."

"Seriously?" I grimace at the flyer taped to the wall next to Harlow's locker. It is informing me that I am required to have school spirit in a few hours. "That's blackmail."

"Keeps the bleachers full," Harlow replies with a shrug. She shuffles books out of her bag and into her locker. "We don't have to stay for the whole game."

I contemplate sitting in a sweaty gymnasium, surrounded by people who hate me, watching a bunch of mouth breathers bounce a ball. At least with football there's the possibility of seeing some blood or broken bones. But basketball? They don't even hit each other. What's the point?

"Torture," I mumble.

"It'll be fun," Tal says optimistically. "Here, let me carry those." He takes Harlow's books for her, and she pops her eyes at me meaningfully as we turn into the streams of kids going to class.

We pass by Kayla at her locker and Tal smiles and waves at her.

"What are you doing after the game?" he asks her as we breeze by.

"Flynn's captain, so we're going out with the team," she answers. She opens her mouth, closes it, then opens it again and calls after us. "You can come," she offers. "You can all come."

"Great," Tal answers. "We will."

"We will?" Harlow says doubtfully after we're too far away for Kayla to hear.

"Sure," Tal says. "It's silly to hold a grudge. The people in this school are really nice. You'd enjoy their company if you gave them a chance."

I'm too dumbfounded to say anything. I have no intention of going out with Kayla and Flynn, and I'm sure Harlow won't want to go either. What I can't figure is how he got Kayla to invite us in the first place.

We go our separate ways for our morning classes and meet up again for lunch. By the time I scrounge up something decent to eat and find Harlow, I notice she's sitting with Tal. And Kayla. And Flynn. I don't know what to do. I hover outside the vicinity of the table and try to catch Harlow's eye. She sees me and waves me over. I approach slowly.

"What's going on?" I ask, giving Harlow a disbelieving look.

"Sit," Tal urges cheerfully.

"No thanks," I reply. "What's going on?" I repeat, glaring at Harlow.

"Just lunch," Harlow says nervously. She smiles up at me hopefully.

I look at Kayla. She has a glassy sheen to her eyes, but she doesn't seem openly hostile. Flynn isn't even looking at me. In fact, he's making a big deal about not looking at me. I wonder if Harlow really believes these are her friends.

"Not hungry," I say, even though my lunch tray is piled high. I dump it on my way out the door, feeling guilty about wasting food but too sick to consider eating it.

I hear Tal say, "She'll be fine," as I walk out of the lunchroom.

I see Harlow waiting for me by my locker at the end of the day.

"Say you're not mad at me," she says.

"Aren't you angry at them?" I ask indignantly. "Think about what she did to you. She outed your dad."

Harlow looks down at her shuffling feet. "I know." She blows her bangs out of her eyes in frustration. "But Tal put it in this really smart way. It's like, not being friends with her when she was only telling the truth is really me being ashamed of my father."

I think it through, and it takes me a second to grasp what he was getting at. "That's utter garbage. The issue isn't that your father is gay, and you were trying to hide it because you're ashamed of him. The issue is that you told Kayla something in confidence, and she used that to get you to do this." I point at my shorn head. "Remember?"

Harlow frowns, picking through her thoughts and combing out all the tangles. "You're right," she decides, her face growing more and more disgusted. "She blackmailed me."

"Right," I say, watching her carefully. It's like she's fighting her way out of a fog.

"It just sounded like forgiving her was the better thing to do."

"And maybe it is. Tal is probably giving you good advice. Maybe you should forgive her," I admit grudgingly. "But that doesn't mean it's smart to hang out with her again. She's not a good friend."

Harlow nods, her eyes clearing. We exit the school and I see the goon my father has tailing me waiting right outside the door.

"Who's that guy?" Harlow asks, narrowing her eyes at him.

"Bodyguard," I mumble. She stares at me for a moment. I shrug. "My dad."

"Your dad put a bodyguard on you?" she repeats disbelievingly. "Are you in danger?"

"Only of going out and enjoying myself," I say.

I wave to Harlow and turn, my bodyguard falling in two steps behind me.

I notice other kids staring. I drop my head and watch my feet, one black boot kicking in front of the other. I focus on the rhythm of it rather than the heat crawling up my cheeks. I slide into the back seat of the town car. The goon gets into the front seat. I don't look out the window.

My dad's still at work when I get home, but Rebecca is there. She's sitting at the island in the center of the kitchen, flipping through a magazine. My unplugged phone is next to her elbow. Something's off. I can feel it. I don't know what she's up to, so I stay where I am, several steps away from her.

"Is that for me?" I say.

She doesn't look up. "Yes," she says. "Your mother insisted." She turns a page.

"My mother?" I repeat, confused.

"Uh-huh," she replies, still looking at her magazine. "Your mother. She said that she wanted a way to contact you at all times, privately. I guess she thinks you need your own line to do that." Rebecca looks up at me and I can practically feel the heat of her anger radiating out of her eyes. "I wonder if she knows about the tail your father's put on you. You didn't happen to tell her, did you?"

I shake my head. "I haven't even spoken to her in... since I came to New York." Actually, way longer. But I don't want her to know that.

"Good. Because that would upset her. Then she'd know that things aren't exactly *normal* around here."

I resist the urge to squirm. "May I have my phone back now?"

Rebecca nods and I come forward, but just when I'm about to grab it, she slams her hand down over it and looks me in the eye.

"One more year," she says, speaking dangerously low. "One more year of this and then you leave for college."

I don't say anything. If I do, I know it'll be obvious that she's hurt me. Instead, I just focus on keeping my face neutral. Blank. Rebecca finally lifts her hand and I take my phone. I snatch it up and practically run from the kitchen.

I pass by the goon on my way to my bedroom. I wonder how much of that he heard. His face is impassive. It occurs to me that maybe he doesn't speak English. Or maybe he just doesn't care.

Once I'm safely in my bedroom I plug it into the wall and get a dial tone. Good thing I memorized Harlow's number.

I call her and tell her I'll meet her at the game. I know Ajax's number, too. I didn't intentionally memorize it, but it stuck in my head regardless. I only had to see it once to know it backward and forward. I start dialing his number and stop. I hang up. Slow. Like I'm watching someone drive farther and farther away until I can't see the car anymore. I can't involve him in this. In my life. What would he say about my leering father and the bodyguards? What would he think of me if he knew?

I hear my dad come home and I go out to tell him that I'm going to a basketball game.

"No," he answers immediately. "You're grounded."

"It's mandatory," I reply. "Call the school and ask for yourself. If I don't go, I get detention."

My dad looks caught. He tries to think of some reason to make me stay home.

"She's got to go," Rebecca says, her irritation grating around the edges of her voice.

"Who's going to be there?" he asks.

"Everyone. The whole school is required to go," I say, rolling my eyes.

"I'll call the principal and explain," he says, trying to put an end to the conversation.

"Why?" I ask him honestly, because at this point, I'm not sure even he knows.

"You disobeyed me and went out without my permission. You were supposed to be here for Rebecca's cocktail party."

"Don't drag me into this," Rebecca says. My dad glares at her, but she won't help him on this. "It's a school function, Mitch. She has to go."

He looks back at me. "Go to your room."

"Do you even hear what you're saying anymore? Do you know how irrational you've become?" I ask. I see the goon in the corner avert his eyes. I laugh and gesture to him. "Even he knows this is messed up."

"Go to your room!" He's furious. And I don't care.

"No." I cock my head to the side.

He takes a step toward me, an arm raised. I really think he's going to hit me. The goon makes an instinctive move to intervene, like he knows he should protect me, but he stops when he remembers that my dad cuts his paycheck. It's Rebecca who steps in.

One of her spray-tanned arms shoots out—fast and instinctual, like a mom sticking out her arm to brace the child in the passenger seat if she has to step on the brakes too hard. Then she stands and blocks my dad's path with her whole body.

"If you touch her, I'll call the police," she says quietly. She turns to look me full in the face. "Get out," she says.

I grab the essentials—shoes, keys, wallet. I stumble out the door, goon in tow. My heart's pounding, thumping slow and deep. I can hear it in my ears and feel the pressure of my blood inside my body, thick as slush.

I walk to school. The goon stays a few steps behind me. A couple of times I hear him take a breath like he's about to say something, but he never does. I'm glad. I don't want to hear his voice. He knows. I feel nauseated and I don't want anyone to see. But he saw. He saw the whole thing. That means I can't pretend it didn't happen.

That's twice now Rebecca has protected me. She hates me even more for it, though. Because I saw—I know—and she doesn't want witnesses any more than I do.

Someone hisses obscenities at me as I pass. I tug down on my skirt. Is it too short? There must be something I'm doing. It has to be me. Maybe if I'm different around my father he'll stop all this. I just want him to go back to being normal.

I lift my head and see people streaming into the school. Faces are painted. Everyone's wearing school colors—blue and white—except me. I didn't get the memo.

I mill around outside for a bit, looking for Harlow, telling myself to shake it off. I'm upset and it's getting worse, turning into anger. My head feels buzzy and hot, like I can't pop my ears. My lightning crackles just below the surface of my skin, making the gold dusting of hairs on my arms stand up with static. I feel someone touch my shoulder. I spin around and grab the hand. I register how tiny and soft it is and pull up short of delivering a back fist.

"Harlow," I say breathlessly.

"Sorry," Harlow replies in a cowed voice. This is the first time she's seen a glimpse of what's really inside me. It was only a second, but it scared her.

"No, I'm sorry. I got into a huge fight with my dad tonight," I say, trying to explain away what she saw. "I'm a little touchy right now."

"What was the fight about?" she asks, steering me into the line headed toward the gymnasium.

I explain the bones of the argument, downplaying the stranger aspects of my father's behavior. Even still, Harlow can't help but notice that something odd is going on.

"He's your father. He doesn't own you," she says.

I glance a few feet back to the goon. He's keeping his distance, but he hasn't gone away. "Yeah. I've had about enough of it," I say under my breath.

When we get into the gymnasium, Harlow starts scanning the bleachers. The hopeful look on her pixie face can only be for one person. Tal.

"I don't know if he's here yet," she mumbles distractedly. She squeezes my hand. "There he is," she says, lighting up. Harlow drags me to Tal. My feet slow when I notice who he's with.

I don't get it. I really don't understand why Tal is pushing this issue, but he's sitting with Kayla and waving us over like it's totally normal.

"Seriously?" I say. "Harlow. You have to have a talk with him."

"I will," she promises. "But let's just play nice for right now. I'll explain to him later."

I keep my mouth shut as we climb the bleachers and slide into seats next to him, putting myself as far away from Kayla as possible. The game starts, but I hardly notice. I clap when other people clap and stand up when I see people's butts in front of my face. The air is close and hot and it feels like there's no oxygen in here.

I keep looking over the court to the other school's spectators and scanning the faces there. The bleachers on the other side of the gym are filled with people in red. It looks like a wildfire climbing the side of a hill. The smell of sweat and adrenaline hangs in a humid funk around me.

The clash of colors, red and blue, tilts dangerously from left to right as Harlow excitedly hauls me up, clapping and cheering. I feel nauseated and hot. The flushed faces around me start to warp into something sinister and the cheering seems to turn into jeering.

I look again into the sea of red and that's when I see him. His golden curls are like a bright crown, marking him and setting him apart. His eyes lock with mine, and he stands up. I realize I'm standing, too. No one else is. It's just Ajax and me facing each other.

"Daphne. Sit down."

Who's talking to me? I fight through the fog in my head and look down to see Tal, looking back at me. People are staring. I sort of care, but not really. I glance back across the gymnasium. Ajax has disappeared. I make a move to go chase him and realize someone's got my arm.

"Daphne," Tal repeats. "You've got plenty of friends right here."

I look down at him, Harlow, and Kayla and see them through a haze. I land in my seat with a jolt, like I've missed a step on a staircase. I'm not angry. Ajax left and took the Furies with him, but even still I know I'm not entirely in control of myself. I fight my way through the droning in my head and see Harlow talking at me.

"Game's over," she says, overemphasizing her words like I'm new to English. Didn't we just get here?

"Okay," I say, because there doesn't seem like any other option. But it's not okay. Something very strange just happened to me.

"Daphne?" Tal is standing next to Harlow, looking concerned. "You look pale. You should have some water."

"Yeah," I say briskly, and take a long draft of the bottle he hands me.

I stand to join them. I follow them out of the gym, vaguely aware that we're still with Kayla. Her presence doesn't bother me anymore. I guess it should, but I can't quite get my head around why it should.

As we walk a few blocks to the postgame party I'm vaguely aware of my bodyguard following me in the car. I don't care, though. I find myself laughing with Harlow and Kayla. I can't quite remember what Kayla said, but the way she said it was so charming. She's a charismatic person, really animated, but she listens, too. She's a spotlight. When she listens to you it's like you're funnier and more interesting just because she's paying attention.

I get it now. I get why she's the queen bee. Something about her being the queen bee bothers me. The thought sticks in my head and repeats over and over.

I realize there's music blaring and people holding blue plastic cups all around me. The edges of people stop smearing with every move they make, and I realize I have a blue cup in my hand and I'm talking to Flynn. He's looking at me wistfully, like I'm a really good movie and he's sitting in the dark with a forgotten bucket of popcorn on his lap, his heart gone gooey in the glow of an imagined life.

But I'm not a movie. And I don't have a happy ending. I squeeze my eyes shut and run a hand through my hair, feeling how short it is, and it hits me all at once. Kayla jumping me in the showers. Flynn hounding me like I'm prey.

Flynn's still talking, living inside the movie of me with no idea who I really am. These aren't my friends, but they believe they are.

"I think I'm going to try to do both this year," he's saying. He looks down for a moment, frowning. "My dad says that you have to focus if you want to get really good at something, but I don't want to be known for just one thing, you know? I want to be, like, good at everything."

This is important to him. I can see that, even if I'm not exactly sure what it is he's talking about. Whatever it is he's deciding, he's discussing it with me like I'm his closest confidante. I can't find it in me to be cruel to him.

Tal appears at my elbow.

"We're gonna go," Tal says, saving me. Kayla and Harlow are

with him. I look at Kayla for a spark of possessiveness, but I see nothing. She's bobbing her head to the beat and sipping on her blue cup, her gaze skimming the crowd contentedly.

"What time is it? I have to go, too."

"I'll walk you home," Flynn offers. My head cranks around to Kayla, but she's not even paying attention.

"Uh—I'm good," I reply.

"Why don't you let Flynn walk you home," Tal suggests.

My arm feels heavy. I turn to Flynn. "Okay," I say. Flynn beams at me, and I stare back at him, trying to figure out why he's so happy.

Oh yeah. He's going to walk me home. We start off together, and a huge guy dressed in black falls into step behind us. My bodyguard. Wait a second...

"Hold on," I say, stopping. I shake my head to clear it and turn to Flynn. "I gotta go with him." I back away from Flynn's crumbling smile.

I follow the goon, and slide into the backseat of a black sedan parked a few steps away. I see the bodyguard glancing up in the rearview mirror repeatedly as he drives me home. That's the only thing that betrays how nervous he is. He's nervous for me, I realize.

I can hear my dad yelling before I even unlock the door to our apartment. I brace myself and go inside.

Deuce is there, blocking my dad's path to me.

"You think you can just come and go as you please?" my dad yells at me. "You think you can spend the night out like a little slut and I won't notice? I know where you were! You were with another man!"

The bodyguard steps in front of me as my dad lunges.

"You can't just walk back in here like you own this place," he rages. "I own it! I own you, Elara!"

He thinks I'm my mother. He's come completely unhinged. I look at Rebecca. She's sitting on the couch, frozen, a hand covering her mouth. My dad is struggling with Deuce, still going on about how he knows I'm unfaithful and manipulative and how he won't stand for it anymore. Deuce has had enough of this. He hits my dad once across the jaw and my dad goes limp. Deuce transfers him into the bodyguard's arms with a mild look of disgust on his face.

"He needs to lie down and sleep it off for a while," he tells the bodyguard. The bodyguard disappears down the hallway carrying my unconscious father. When they're gone, Deuce turns to Rebecca. "Daphne's going to stay with me for the next few days," he tells her.

"She can stay with you forever," Rebecca replies. Even shocked as she is, she manages to sneer at me.

Deuce bites back whatever it is he wants to say to her. "You explain it to him. I'm not getting into another argument about his rightful custody of Daphne, or any of that bullshit. Got it?" Deuce says. Rebecca wisely holds her tongue. He looks over at me and his eyes soften. "Get your stuff," he says quietly.

It seems to take forever for me to unstick my feet, but once I start moving I run to my room and start blindly throwing things into a duffel bag. I don't know what I'm grabbing. My head is chattering with ugly words and my hands are shaking.

I stumble along behind Deuce, past the stony-faced bodyguard and Rebecca's open disgust. Her eyes are screaming accusations. I did something. I must have.

"He wasn't like this when I met him," she whispers as I pass.

Is she right? I grapple with my memory, combing through it to find what I did. My stomach crawls with cramps.

We get to Deuce's apartment. He unfolds a cot for me and sets it up in an empty room. The room smells like fresh paint even though Deuce has lived here for a few weeks now. He hasn't been in this room, not even to open the door. I stand under the single bare bulb blaring overhead, holding my bag tight to my sour stomach. Deuce comes back with a sheet, a pillow, and a blanket. He lays them on the cot and stands next to me for a moment.

"Do you want to talk?" he asks.

"No," I whisper.

He nods. "It's like this sometimes—with the fathers of The Face. Not all of them. It takes a rare person to see past it, I guess."

I look over at him. "So, who?"

"Someone who doesn't covet. Someone who cares more about what's inside a person than outside. Someone who lives more for others than for himself." Deuce drops his head and laughs bitterly. "So, not your dad. And I'm sorry about that. For you."

I scrub my face with my hands. "Why did my mom agree to marry him? Why didn't she tell her mother to pick someone else?"

In my family, The Face has no say in who she marries. Our husbands are chosen for us, usually by our mothers. We aren't allowed to decide for ourselves, because the last time The Face chose to be with the man she loved, she started the Trojan War. I've always known this, but I try not to think about it because it means that eventually my mom will find me a husband and I'll just have to marry him.

"My sister was not very good at understanding people. Neither of us were," Deuce says, smiling at me ruefully. "I'm sorry, kid. I'll make sure your mother picks someone... unlike your father, for you."

We sit for a while. The room's too cold. The walls too bare. He eventually leaves me alone, closing the door behind him.

I sit on the edge of the cot, my duffel bag tucked into my lap like a teddy bear. I can hear the quiet around me. It presses painfully against my ears now that the shouting is done.

The next morning, I go back up to my father's apartment to get the rest of my stuff. Both my dad and Rebecca are gone. As I'm packing, my room phone rings. I snatch up the receiver before the first ring even finishes.

"I think your team won."

Even though the Furies rise up in me at the sound of Ajax's voice, I still smile. I went to a basketball game last night, like everyone else from my school. Isn't that normal?

"That's because your team sucks," I reply.

"They're horrible," he agrees.

"I wish I could see you," I say.

"We have a date tomorrow remember?" he says. I don't reply right away, and he continues. "Don't even think about standing me up. I spent the last few days getting ready."

"I don't want to stand you up, but things have gotten really complicated around here," I say. "My father's been acting... strange."

"Define strange."

"I'm staying with my uncle for a while."

There is a long, uncomfortable pause. "What did your father do to you?"

"Nothing."

"Then why are you staying with your uncle?"

"My dad's just... confused." There's another long pause. I finally just bite the bullet. "I look a lot like my mother. Lately he's been looking at me... like I'm her."

Ajax finally says, "Are you safe?"

"I guess," I reply.

"I wish I were there with you right now."

"Me too." I grimace to myself, fighting the Furies. "Except that would probably involve bloodshed. And my uncle just painted."

He gives a weak laugh. There's another long pause. "Please say you'll be at the subway station tomorrow."

I can feel the air in the room crowding in close, watching me, waiting for my answer.

"I'll be there."

CHAPTER 8

"For a moment there, I didn't think we'd ever see you again," Harlow says, her eyes sparkling over the rim of her latte. "I thought your dad was going to ship you off to a convent."

"He might have, if he were Catholic, but my father doesn't believe in anything. Except money." I take another bite of my omelet, unwilling to tell Harlow the whole story, but wishing I could.

Tal looks around the café. "Didn't you have an escort last night?" he asks.

"You mean the goon? He's gone," I say. Tal frowns, although I can't imagine why he should be upset.

"Where'd he go?" Tal presses.

"My dad's out of the picture, and so are his goons. We had a disagreement, and I'm staying with my uncle for a while," I admit.

Tal nods, but he still looks troubled. "Did you call Flynn?" he asks.

"Why would I call Flynn?" I blurt out.

"You two seemed to hit it off last night," Tal replies. Perplexed, I narrow my eyes at him. He flashes me a smile. "I just figured, now that you have a little room to breathe, maybe you'd like to go out on a date."

"Not with him," I say. I drop my eyes and ride the jumbled tide of excitement that rises with the thought of my date tonight. I've actually never been on a date before—not a successful one.

"Are you going to see Ajax?" Harlow asks. I don't reply, but my lower lip quivers as I suppress a smile. Harlow throws her napkin at me. "Shut up. You're so hooking up. Where're you going?"

"No idea," I answer. "Seriously," I continue off her disbelieving look. "I don't know what he's got planned."

"Are you sure that's a good idea? Going to a place you don't know with some guy you don't know?" Tal asks.

"No. It's probably a terrible idea. But I'm doing it anyway," I say. Tal searches for a rebuttal.

"What are you going to wear?" Harlow asks.

"I don't know," I reply, rolling my eyes in frustration. "I have no idea how to dress for a date." I grimace and think, considering the situation I should probably wear armor. "It'll have to be something really easy to move in."

Harlow wags her eyebrows at me.

"We'll probably take a walk," I finish, throwing her napkin back at her. "Filthy buzzard."

"Hye-Su's," she says with a grin. "We'll go right after breakfast."

"I just don't see why you won't date Flynn," Tal bursts out. "He's remarkably healthy. He's your age. He's considered desirable by many others."

I shoot Harlow a look, but she doesn't seem to notice Tal's odd choice of words.

"I'm not interested in Flynn," I say as politely as I can.

"But why not? He likes you. You'd make the perfect couple," Tal persists. He lets out a frustrated breath. "Why can't you just like him back?"

I don't have a response for that, so I change the subject. Tal is snippy for the rest of breakfast, and he leaves right after we split the bill, saying, "Be careful tonight, Daphne." I've never seen him look so serious, and when he raises an eyebrow at me, I get the feeling he knows.

"Call me later?" Harlow calls after him. He doesn't seem to hear her.

"He's just distracted," I say, but I honestly have no idea what's wrong with him. Or what he's up to.

In fact, I have no idea what Tal is doing in the picture at all, and for some reason I've been blithely overlooking his mysterious appearance in my life when I should be suspicious of him. I haven't even told Deuce about him, but Tal has somehow managed to insinuate himself into every hour of my day. I realize I know nothing about this guy.

"Do you know where Tal lives?" I ask.

"I think he lives downtown somewhere," Harlow answers.

"Why do you think that?"

"I don't know," she says hazily. "Just stuff he's said. Like, I'm going down for the night."

"Going 'down' for the night? No one says that," I respond.

"He says a lot of things that no one says," Harlow replies with a shrug.

"Well, I'm going to find out where he lives." I stand up to set out after him.

"No!" Harlow grabs my arm.

"Why not?"

"He wouldn't like it." She frowns and looks at the ground as if she's misplaced something and she's trying to remember where she last saw it. "It's ... not right to follow people without them knowing it."

I raise an eyebrow at her. This, from a girl who helped me stalk a graffiti artist and figure out where he lived?

"Um, when is the real Harlow going to show up? Because I'd like my friend back now," I snap.

She has a blank look on her face for just a moment, and then she smirks to herself, shakes her head and meets my eye. "Okay. Did you see which way he went?" she asks.

There's my girl.

I grin as I cock my head, indicating Tal's path, and she and I fall into step next to each other to follow it.

We shade Tal carefully, never getting too close, and eventually follow him down into the subway station at Lincoln Center. It's crowded today, but he isn't hard for us to spot.

We see him go all the way to the end of the track. He waits for an arriving train with his hands in his pockets. Looking bored. A gust of hot air blasts us all in the face, and I see Tal's profile in the flashing bright-dim-bright of the light bouncing off the shiny metal of the cars as they slow.

And then he's simply not there.

"Where'd he go?" Harlow asks, her confusion echoing my own.

The train comes to a full stop and the doors open.

"Where'd he go?" she repeats, her head swiveling around as a mass of humanity surges out between the doors and a competing swell pushes its way in. The doors close with a *ding-dong*, and then the train pulls out of the station.

"Did you see him?" Harlow asks, incredulous.

I shake my head. I didn't see him, which can only mean one thing. He's faster than I am. It feels like cold fingers are tracing up the back of my neck. Like animal eyes are watching me.

"It was really crowded. We must have just lost him," I say.

Harlow gives me a dubious look, but after a moment she has to accept it. What else can she think? That he disappeared into thin air?

I'm such an idiot. I don't know what he is, but I know now he isn't human. I realize that I should never have involved Harlow in this hunt. I have to get her away from Tal. How could I have been so blind for so long?

"Let's get out of here," I say, brushing it off. Like it's no biggie. "There's a much easier way to find out where he lives."

"How?" Harlow says, excited.

"We ask him." I force myself to smile. "And maybe we should give up on the cloak-and-dagger stuff. Apparently, we're not very good at it."

She doesn't look satisfied. I tug on her arm, acting as if I've grown tired of this game, and after a few more suspicious looks thrown into the dark corners of the station, Harlow lets me lead her out of the subway and back up into the light.

Tal

I vault onto the top of the train and lie flat so Daphne and Harlow can't see me. I can see the fear in Daphne's face after I move so quickly I seem to disappear. She knows now. She may not know exactly what I am, but she knows enough to fear me.

As the train pulls out of the station I wonder if that's a good thing or not. I had hoped to remain undiscovered while I pulled the two star-crossed lovers apart, as I did with Elara and her love a generation ago.

But Daphne is proving more difficult than I'd like. I have been able to cast a spell over her friends and, briefly her as well, but she seems to be fighting through the magic I learned from Medea. Flynn and Kayla are easily persuaded and therefore easy for me to ensorcel, but Daphne and now, Harlow, seem bent on thinking for themselves. Magic may not hold when I need it most. I'll have to find a backup plan.

There is one more thing I can do. I don't like the idea of involving more humans in this struggle, but it's either that or I have to kill the Delos boy outright. I jump off the downtown train and onto an uptown one as it passes and go back the way I just came.

I hop off and go aboveground to walk the few blocks to Daphne's apartment. An aging woman wearing too much perfume opens the door. Her eyes drift up and down my form and her pupils dilate. She unconsciously adopts an S shaped posture that displays her figure.

"Yes?" she asks, her voice dropping low.

"I'd like to speak with Daphne's father," I say. The woman purses her lips in annoyance and stands up straight. All traces of her unbecoming coquetry vanish at the mention of Daphne's name.

"About what?" she replies.

"Who's there? Is it Daphne?" asks a hopeful male voice. The middle-aged man looks a bit wild around the eyes when he comes to the door. The woman named Rebecca steps back.

"No. I'm a friend of Daphne's, though," I reply. "I'd like to talk to you about her."

His face darkens with a scowl as he considers me. "What do you want?"

"To protect her," I say, and I can say it honestly. This step I'm taking is to protect the diminished House of Atreus. They would never survive a war with the House of Thebes. "She's seeing a boy tonight, and I don't think he's good for her. I think he's very dangerous, in fact. Do you have any way to locate her?"

I can see a vein standing out on her father's temple. He strides to the wall and pulls the receiver off the hook.

"As a matter of fact, I do," he replies calmly. He makes a phone call. "Where is she now?" he asks into the phone. He waits while he listens to the response. "Don't let her out of your sight."

CHAPTER 9

I take my time as I walk all the way downtown to the West 4th subway station in the Village. Night begins to fall. Cool air hits my face, and just like that, I'm no longer waiting. I'm on the edge of something still, and not quite in it, but the frustration's gone. It's like I'm looking out across a huge distance, and I can see for miles. I feel at peace, and don't want it to end—this almost-with-him feeling where nothing's ruined yet. I slow to a stroll, cocooning myself in this perfect moment.

When I get to the station, I'm smiling so wide I'm practically causing a stampede. Men and women bump into things, tripping over their own feet as they stare at me. I don't care. I meet their eyes and smile back, knowing that everyone I pass is going to fall in love, even just a little bit, tonight. I want to share this glowing bubble in my chest. I want to give everyone this touch-less hug.

I'm scanning the crowd for him and waiting for the telltale flare of rage that heralds the coming of the Furies. Trains come and go. People pass. It dawns on me that maybe he isn't coming.

Maybe he's rethought this whole insane thing and decided I'm not worth it. The glowing bubble darkens and deflates. Then I smell spray paint.

I scan the grubby concrete underfoot and see red—both the color and the feeling. Spray-painted on the floor in Ajax's jagged, purposeful script, it says...

CHASE ME

Then I hear the Furies' whispers rise to wailing and see their ashen bodies blinking in and out of the corners of my eyes.

I look up and see him standing halfway up the exit stairs. He's even more paint-covered than usual. His clothes are misted with a dozen different colors and his shirt is so disheveled it looks like it's trying to twist off his body. His blond curls are a chaotic tangle, and his face is flushed with sun and wind. He smiles at me. And then he runs.

It's like my ribs are attached to a string in his hands. He tugs, and I'm dragged along behind him. My head is full of heartbeats and my legs are aching to move. I leap up the grubby stairs and into the sparkling night. I can hear myself laughing.

Ajax heads straight for Fifth Avenue. He has to fight to stay in front of me. His lithe body is leaping and reaching, always just a few agonizing inches out of my grasp. He pushes himself as hard as he can and manages to get almost a full block ahead of me, but the effort nearly makes him stumble and lose his footing. At the last minute he reaches for something dangling from a lamppost— a cord—and he pulls down on it hard.

There's an avalanche of color and texture. Silken banners unfurl from an arch of wires strung over the sidewalk. Twelve feet long and six feet wide, the dropping banners begin to obscure my view of him as they scroll down in between us like curtains falling at the end of a play. I push through one after another and notice that the many shades of reds give way to every kind of orange, and then gradually lighten into yellow. I'm running through a rainbow.

People gasp at first, and then they start to cheer as they realize that they must be part of an art installation, or maybe even some gay pride display.

The successions of curtains end, and I have to stop to scan for him. I've lost the thread of anger that was pulling me toward him. He's brought me up to 34th Street, out of his territory and into mine.

I spot him waiting for me at the entrance to the Empire State building. He's holding a bunch of rainbow-colored Mylar balloons. The look on his face is so hopeful and so open that the Furies' voices muffle. I forget to be angry. I forget who we are. As soon as we make eye contact, he leaves the balloons behind and darts through the revolving doors. The ribbons on the balloons are attached to a basket that's keeping them anchored. Inside the basket is a ticket for the observation deck at the top of the building. I pull the ticket out of the basket and the balloons are set free. They arch into the sky—a rainbow that rises into the sky rather than descending down to earth.

Entering the building is like stepping into a new set of rules, and our breakneck courtship slows to a crawl. There are too many people and not enough space for Ajax and me to chase each other here. I see him waiting in front of an elevator. There's a sign in front of the elevators that says, "Observation Deck Closed."

His elevator dings and the doors open. A herd of excited

tourists clomp out. I catch snippets of their conversation, but I'm too focused on my quarry to give it much thought.

Two guards have remained in the elevator to make sure no one else gets on. Ajax turns into a blur in the corner of my eye. As his elevator closes, I see his face peek out at the top of the doors. He's got to be clinging to the ceiling somehow, but I can't see how he's managing it. He winks at me. *Cheeky*. The Furies wail.

My elevator opens and people spill out. They're all chattering in hushed undertones. I dart in between the closing doors too quickly for the remaining guards to see, climb the wall, and press into the corner to keep myself anchored to the ceiling of the car. It's a risky move. My hands slip with sweat, but I tell myself that if Ajax managed it, so can I.

As soon as we get to the observation deck I can tell that something isn't right. There are security guards everywhere. I dart out of the closing elevator doors and slink into the shadows. I see Ajax slip across the floor on his knees. He slides like he's on ice, puts down a hand to stop himself, and spins to face me. We're both close to the ground and our eyes meet across the expanse of dark, waxed floor. He grins at me and sinks into a shadow.

Again, the Furies hiss in my ear. Blood for blood, they say. I look down and count silently to myself, fighting for control.

When I look up again, I notice a tight knot of confused people are repeating one question. "How could anyone get up there?"

Interesting. I head toward the doors that lead outside to the famous wraparound viewing platform that's been in about a hundred movies. A giddy laugh is building in my chest. What the heck did Ajax do out there?

"I want all those cameras pointing in the right direction by morning!" someone yells at someone else. "There has to be footage of the vandal moving one of them, at least."

There are too many people. I have to wait almost half an hour. I can still feel the Furies, but not as strongly. I know Ajax is still up here somewhere, but he's far enough away that I'm not enraged. I look around at the turnstiles, metal detectors, and the gift shop. This space doesn't seem quite large enough for the Furies to feel so distant. I have no idea where Ajax is anymore, but I'm not going anywhere until I see what's out there on the viewing platform.

The crowd starts to thin out as underlings scurry to fulfill orders. I see my chance and slip outside.

I look out at the view first, because—wow. Manhattan really is a beautiful city and seeing it from the top of the Empire State Building is bucket list-worthy. Then I turn around.

The observation deck isn't actually at the top of the building. There's still quite a bit of spire up there, and on it Ajax has painted a mural of me in every color of the rainbow.

In the mural I'm smiling, on the cusp of a laugh, and I'm just about to turn away. What strikes me the most about it is that it's not just a picture of a face. It's a picture of a feeling. It's someone experiencing a moment of joy and it doesn't really matter if the face is attractive or not. What matters is how relatable the subject is. How openhearted. How human. Even I like her, and I've never really liked myself much.

"I told you I'd paint the sky. This was as close as I could get," Ajax says. He's floating next to the mural and looking down at me with shy pride.

"You're flying," I say stupidly.

He laughs.

I've never seen a flyer before. They're extremely rare, always have been. It looks like he's suspended in water. His arms are flung out and his clothes billow around him as if coaxed by something more viscous than air. A moment ago, I thought the mural was the most beautiful thing I'd ever seen. Now it comes in second. My breath—and so much more—is taken.

"Meet me at the amphitheater," he says. And I see him shudder and look away. The Furies have him again.

They manage to penetrate my shock and awe and they take ahold of me, too. I'm leaping for him, bounding twenty feet in the air, before I can stop myself.

"Daphne, don't!" he yells. "I can't support you!"

He darts away from me, and I grab an armful of nothing. I'm falling, thinking, that was dumb.

I manage to grab onto the curving fence that's meant to keep people from jumping off the building. I slam into it and slide, slowing my descent. Then I duck under the overhang underneath it. I cling to the side of the Empire State Building with the wind snatching at me.

Guards have heard us, and they start pouring out onto the platform. I tuck myself as far under the overhang as I can. I listen to them searching. They eventually give up, deciding that what they heard was impossible. I listen to them conjure up reasonable-sounding excuses, all of which are utter nonsense.

I can't stop smiling.

Chapter 10

The people finally go back inside. Following them and trying to take the elevator or stairs might get me caught, but I figure it's safe enough to make my way down the outside of the building. The masonry is old but sturdy, and there are plenty of places to hang on to. I'm lucky Ajax didn't decide to paint the top of a glass skyscraper. That would have sucked.

The dismount is an issue. Street level is packed with people. I stay four stories up and circle the base of the building, looking for a way down at the rear of the building where there's far less foot traffic. I see someone familiar. My dad's goon, just standing there in the dark. Looks like he's brought a few buddies. They're all cut from the same cloth—necks as thick as their heads, shoulders wide enough to get stuck in doorways. Their eyes scan the streets with practiced calm.

How did they find me? There's no way they followed me. I go back to the entrance side of the building. There's a row of news vans broadcasting identical reporters saying identical things about the unknown street artist who defaced the Empire State Building. With my face.

Damn.

Okay—so it's a mural of my face in profile. And it's kind of blurred because I'm in motion. And my eyes are almost closed because I'm laughing. But someone who knows me will know it's me, and my dad definitely knows what I look like, so that explains the goons.

There's no safe place to climb down. I have no choice but to jump from where I am—four stories up. I coil up my muscles and spring out, aiming for the other side of the street.

I land hard. I smack down on the pavement with more noise than I'd hoped, and I feel one of my ankles break. All eyes are focused on the other side of the street but the people nearest to me see me hit the ground. I stand up and try to pass it off as a stumble. I can see their bewildered faces as they help me up. I put weight on my ankle and have to bite down on my lower lip to keep from screaming.

A nice couple—German tourists, I think—take my arms and try to help me, but I shake them off with assurances that I'm fine. Just clumsy. Wasn't looking where I was going. Please don't worry. Have a nice stay in New York.

I extricate myself from the situation, but not before drawing more attention than I would like. I want to run to Delacorte Theater to see Ajax, but my ankle is worse than I'd thought. I have to settle for walking until it heals. I stop at a street vendor and wolf down a bacon-wrapped hot dog and a pretzel. My ankle knits itself up as I stand there chewing and swallowing the calories it needs. It's still a little stiff when I get there, but it's healed enough that I don't limp.

Ajax is pacing back and forth across the center of the stage, raking a hand through his hair. I stop at the edge of the round and watch him until he notices me. Relief breaks across his face, but it doesn't completely erase the worried frown. Despite the location, the Furies whisper in my ear. I clench my jaw and shut them out.

Not now. Please, not now.

"What happened?" he asks as he rushes to me. "What took you so long?"

"I can't fly?" I answer, turning my palms up.

"I know but..." he breaks off with a strangled sound and attacks his hair with his hands again. He takes a steadying breath. Fighting the Furies. "It was a bad idea. I shouldn't have done it."

"No. You shouldn't have," I say quietly. I count in my head. *One, two, three, four, five. Quiet, Furies.* I want—no I need to look at him. I come toward him until I'm so close I can feel his body heat. "And I shouldn't have loved it as much as I did."

He reaches for me with just his fingertips. They graze the front of my throat and trail downward.

"This is what I needed to paint," he says. "This line right here."

His fingers come to rest under my collarbones, and he splays his huge hand out until it spans across the very top of my chest. Like he's pressing against the place where my breath and my heart are trying to fly out of me. The blood roars in my ears until they ache. I'm reaching for him. He takes a jerky step back, squeezing his eyes shut.

"Don't," he says. He takes another step back, stops, and then springs forward and pulls me against him. The Furies wail and gnash their teeth.

Ajax is suddenly ripped out of my arms. I'm knocked over,

more from shock than force, and watch aghast as three humans huddle up over Ajax and rain punches and kicks down on him. He's not fighting back. He's barely even protecting himself.

"Run, Daphne!" he screams.

In the flurry of violence, I can barely see faces. They're like animal masks, snarling and distorted. But I recognize these men. They're my dad's goons. They must have spotted me when I broke my ankle and followed me here.

"Stop!" I yell as I get back on my feet. For a moment, imperious affront takes ahold of me. How dare they? Ajax is mine. I stride toward them, but Ajax sees me and holds out a hand, motioning for me to stay back.

"Run!" he says, shielding himself for a moment so he can look me in the eye. *You can't reveal yourself or we'll have to kill them.*

I watch helplessly as Ajax absorbs blow after blow. His face is bloody, and he's got an elbow pinned to his side to protect what are by now surely broken ribs. Still, the goons show no sign of stopping.

"You'll kill him!" I scream, but they keep going. They're wearing themselves out beating him. I don't think they'll stop until he's dead. "Ajax!"

He manages to roll, throw off a few tackles, and get to his feet. He starts to run, but he's slow. I don't know if it's because he doesn't want to show his speed or because he's taken such a beating at this point that he can't go any faster. Two of the goons chase after him, and one of them stays back with me. The one who had been my personal guard. I try to get past him, but he blocks me.

"Why are you doing this!?" I say, my voice breaking with tears.

"Orders," he replies stonily.

"Please stop," I beg. He looks at the ground like he's ashamed of himself. "Whatever my father's paying you, it isn't worth it—" I want to say his name and I realize I don't know it.

He looks at his fists. His knuckles are bleeding and swollen.

I hear a loud pop.

It takes a moment because I've never heard this sound before. In movies, gunshots make a deep, booming sound, but in real life a gunshot sounds like a firecracker. And not even a big firecracker. It's almost silly, really, that quick, crackling snap.

Nameless looks startled. His head spins around and his face falls as both he and I register what that sound means.

I push past him. I'm running now, but I can't feel my feet.

I see figures by the lake. As I approach, they scatter. I hear Nameless calling out. His voice gets more distant as he chases after the others. Or maybe he's just running away—I can't tell anymore. They're not important. I let them go.

I don't see Ajax anywhere on the shore. I scan faster and faster with my Scion eyes. Then I look out at the water and notice a ripple. A gush of bubbles roils the surface. "Ajax!" I scream.

For the first time in my life, I'm glad that the women in my family don't float. Floating is for staying on top of the water, and that's not where Ajax is. He is sinking to the bottom of the lake.

I step into the water and walk down into the dark. My feet stick to the bottom of the lake as if held there by magnets. Atreus women sink like rocks. We might look thin and delicate, but really our bodies are denser than mercury.

The cold shrinks my chest as I take one dragging step at a time. As the water closes over my head the silence is filled with my inner screaming. Terror—thick and sticky—slows every thought. Slippery weeds tangle around my legs and arms. They brush my face and clog my eyes. Still, I walk forward. I can't see anything, but I feel Ajax. I hear the Furies calling me, urging me onward through my fear. *Never stop until you have his throat in your hands. Never stop until one of you is dead.* So that means he isn't dead. Yet.

I feel the heat of him, even in this cold place. I grab a fistful of his clothes and skin and pull him to me. He isn't moving.

My lungs are burning. They suck at my throat, trying to get me to open my mouth and inhale a choking death. I fight against the dragging water, the tangling weeds, and the hammering of my body as I tow Ajax back to the shore.

When I break the surface, I gasp and sputter. I throw Ajax down on his back. He isn't breathing. Isn't moving.

No. This isn't how it ends. We made a deal. No one can kill him but me.

I hit his chest. I pound on it until I see him spasm. He's choking, so I turn him on his side. Water and blood gushes out of his mouth. He writhes and turns his face to the ground and vomits up black water.

I say his name over and over. He puts a hand to his stomach and presses down on the bullet hole there. He's still coughing and panting.

"Let me see," I say. I move his hand. Blood rushes out of the hole. I rip his shirt right down the front and start tearing it into long strips. "I have to get you out of here."

"Daphne," he says, his voice like a creaky moan. So weak it breaks my heart.

"*Shh,*" I say as I struggle to wrap the strips of cloth around his middle. The bullet is still in there. I don't know what to do. And my father's goons could come back at any moment.

Ajax groans as I tie off the bandage tightly. I scrounge through my brain, trying to think of where to take him. I can't take him to my place—Deuce will kill him. And if I take him to his home, his brothers will kill me.

"They're gone," Ajax says. His pale face is turned up, eyes closed, a beatific smile on his face. "The Furies... they're gone."

I pause, my hands still on his bare chest, and wait for the rage. It doesn't come. His hands come up to catch mine, and he pulls my fingers up to his lips. His lips graze the back of my hand. His eyes flutter close, and his hand drops away.

"Ajax?" I say, giving him a little shake. He doesn't respond. I put my ear to his chest and hear his heart still beating, but only faintly.

He'll die if I don't do something.

I pick him up and throw him over my shoulder. I know it's suicide, but somehow I have to get him downtown to his family. Apollo is the god of healing. There must be a healer somewhere in that gob of cousins. I sprint south through the park, but I can't hit my usual speed. I wonder how I'm going to carry him through the streets. I keep going.

The trees seem to move in the dark. I must be more drained than I think. I shake my head to clear it. The wind stirs, sighing actual words. This can't be just fatigue.

My spine tingles and I halt. I'm not alone.

"Who's there?" I call out. I hear laughter—bright and airy, like a young girl's.

"Where are you going, Daughter of Zeus?" asks a high, singsong voice behind me.

I spin around and see the leaves of a bush shiver as if someone had just passed.

"Who are you?" I say loudly, hiding my fear behind bluster. Whoever it is knows I'm a Scion.

"Leave the beauteous boy with us, Sister of Aphrodite," sighs another voice in front of me. I turn again, and again, seeking the speaker. I see only big, stately oak trees.

A laugh flutters through the branches to my right. "Yes! Leave him. We'll take much better care of him than you can, Cursed One."

"Such a gentle boy," says a rustling voice on my left. "He will be much better off without you."

"For war and death will forever follow you and your daughters," sings the first voice again.

"Bearers of The Face," hisses something right in front of me.

I plant my feet and get ready for a fight. "Show yourself," I say, trying to keep my voice from shaking. "Come out and let me see you."

For a moment I think there's something wrong with my eyes. The bark of the oak tree in front of me seems to crawl. Then it comes toward me, taking shape. A slender brown girl with green hair steps forward on bare, delicate feet. She's smiling at me, her golden eyes glowing softly, and her skin shining in the moonlight like polished mahogany.

"Give us the Son of Apollo," she says quietly. "We will mend him and give him back to the Muses."

"They cherish him so. They will reward us," says another voice.

I look to my left and right. Two more girls have appeared out of the wood.

"Dryads," I say, swallowing my surprise. "I thought your kind had gone."

The girl shakes her long, green hair. "There are more of our kind, both above and below the ground, than you and your kind know, Child of Thunder and Lightning."

"Give us the Lovely One," pleads the dryad on my left. She reaches for him, and I jerk away.

"No," I reply, fiercely sure of one thing only. "He's mine."

The dryad in front of me narrows her glowing eyes, as if searching for something inside of me. "Yes," she says. "There is an oath between you."

"Sealed by the Fates," hisses the dryad on my right.

"More blood is to come of it," whispers another sadly.

The dryads start to retreat toward their trees. "It is sealed. They are sworn. The Fates strive for the final fight," they say in unison.

"What fight?" I ask.

The leader stops and looks at me. Her eyes have no center. "The final fight, when the children must usurp their parents," she answers.

"Like Zeus did with Cronus," whispers a tree.

"And Cronus did with his father, the Sky," whispers another.

"The Scions must defeat the gods. The Fates will it so, to complete another Cycle," says the third.

The leader gives me a smile that sends a chill through me and turns back to her tree. I don't understand any of this, but I can't let them go.

"Wait! Can you help him?" I beg. "Please."

The leader pauses. Her face is troubled.

"Please," I repeat. "Everything he touched he made more beautiful. He doesn't deserve to die."

The dryad frowns as if deliberating, and finally waves a

hand. A leaf appears in her palm, and she holds it out to me. "Draw the metal out," she says. "Draw the metal out and cover the gouge."

I take the leaf. It's filled with golden sap.

"Save his life, and then leave him, Cursed One," she says regretfully. "Your union will bear no fruit. Only death."

The dryads melt back into the trunks of their trees and the night air goes still and quiet.

I lay down Ajax on his back, move the makeshift bandage off his wound, and pour the sap over it. The sap sinks into the hole as if sucked in.

A moment later I see twitching under Ajax's skin, and then fresh blood wells up. There's more movement under his skin until, finally, I see the slug of metal inch its way out of the hole and roll off his stomach onto the ground. I cover his wound with the leaf and rewrap it tightly with the bandage.

I wait, wondering if I've done something wrong, but as time passes his breathing becomes easier and I can hear his heartbeat getting stronger.

"Ajax?" I whisper. His eyes open. He doesn't say anything, he just looks at me.

I put my hand over his heart and it starts to speed up. "How're you feeling?"

"What happened?" He reaches up and touches my bottom lip with the side of his thumb. "The Furies..."

I don't feel them either. "They're gone." I say, just as puzzled.

He considers. "You saved my life."

"Blood for blood," I say, thinking. If killing is what started the Furies, maybe saving a life ends them?

I'm painfully aware of my hands on his chest, and that an

entirely inappropriate blush is spreading across my face. Get it together. This is not the time to get swoony.

"I have to get you home," I say.

He shakes his head from side to side with surety. "No," he says as he props himself up on an elbow.

"What are you doing?" I say, trying to make him lie down again.

Ajax sucks air between his teeth and gingerly touches his ribs. "They're definitely broken," he says, and then he peeks under the bandage. Did you do this?" he asks.

"I had a little help," I say. That's an understatement. "Dryads. Apparently, you're very valuable."

"That's good to know." Ajax is in too much pain to ask more questions. He discards the bloody bandage and hauls himself to his feet.

"You really shouldn't," I say.

"I really have to. If I don't get home soon my brothers are going to come looking for me."

When we get to the edge of the park, I take off my wet jacket and give it to him. He's still shirtless, soaked, and badly bruised, but at least my jacket covers him up. Mostly. The jacket is cut perfectly for me, but not for his muscled chest and shoulders. He looks like a bear wearing a toddler's onesie.

Getting him back downtown isn't going to be easy. Luckily, it's so late at night it's almost early, and the few pedestrians who are still out are either too drunk to notice us or are themselves limping home after experiencing their own series of unfortunate events.

The only bad part about the hour is that it's in the middle of a shift change for the cab drivers. There isn't an on-duty taxi on all of Manhattan right now.

I spot a 24-hour deli and leave Ajax on a bench outside in the relative cover of darkness while I run in to buy a jar of honey, a couple of cinnamon buns, and some chamomile tea.

I rejoin him at the bench and hover over him nervously while I unscrew the honey jar.

"Sit. I'm okay. I just need some food," he says. He's lying, but I sit anyway. "So, dryads, huh?" he continues as he dips his bun into the jar of honey.

"They were going to trade you to the Muses for a favor." I watch him while he eats. Even in this small motion his hands are so careful, his movements precise and elegant. I watch his wrists, fascinated by how fluid all of his gestures are, and see his hands shaking from shock. He's hiding it well, but I have to get him home soon. I scan the street for a cab. Nothing yet.

"The Muses?" he asks. He lifts an eyebrow and the cut running through it knits up while he chews. Seeing him healing, I relax a little and sip my tea. "Twelve gorgeous women wanted me, and you didn't hand me over?"

"I was protecting your virtue."

"For something better, I hope." The laugh we're sharing peters out as we stare at each other. "I like your laugh," he says.

He just glossed right over it. I know it's childish, but I can't let it go. "I'm assuming your virtue *is* present and accounted for, right?" I ask, immediately regretting it.

He smiles slowly, taking his time. "I've been waiting for this girl. She took forever to show up." He leans a little closer to me.

"So inconsiderate." I lean a little closer to him.

"Terribly. Total lack of regard for the pining and loneliness she's caused me." He leans even closer. "And then, when she did show up, she nearly got me killed."

"The nerve." We're so close I can see golden hairs dusting his skin. "Are you sure she's worth it?"

"Definitely."

I'm close enough to see how pale he is, and how dark his bruises are. He's shaking, too.

"Ajax—"

"Don't say it."

"My father just tried to have you killed." I can't look at him any longer, so I look at his eloquent hands. "All because of my face."

He touches my chin to tilt my face up until I meet his eyes. "It's a nice face. But I don't think you can blame it for this."

"Yes, I can. All of this stuff with my father and why he attacked you is because my face... does things to men. There's something the other Scions don't know about the House of Atreus. Something we've hidden since the beginning." I shake my head. "It's better if I just show you."

I use the Cestus to change my face. Ajax jerks back and his jaw drops when I turn into the first face that pops into my head—a younger version of Hye-Su.

"Holy shit," he whispers.

"My true face is cursed," I say, changing back into myself. "It's my mother's face, and her mother's face, and so on all the way back to the Trojan War and the first woman to wear it. Helen."

"The Face that launched a thousand ships," he recites quietly.

"The Face that started a long and bloody war that lasted ten years and ended in the total destruction of an entire culture. My line, the House of Atreus, passes this," I point to my face, "from mother to daughter exactly. And we pass down this along with it." I touch the pendant I'm wearing. "It's the Cestus of Aphrodite."

"Aphrodite was Helen's half-sister," Ajax mumbles, recalling his god genealogy correctly.

"They were very close. The Cestus protected Helen when Troy fell. She passed it, and its adornments, down to her daughter. Two necklaces. One for the mother, one for the daughter. It makes us impervious to weapons, and it allows us to be any woman in the world. That's how we've survived and how we hid the secret from the rest of the Scion Houses."

"And the secret is?"

"That it's all our fault," I whisper. "The Furies. The blood debt. The constant revenge killings between the Scion Houses. It all started at Troy, and it started because of this." I gesture again to my face. "It's the reason our kind has been killing each other for thirty-three hundred years, and no matter what I do, everywhere I go people will kill to possess it. I've even driven my own father crazy. I thought having me followed was bad enough, but now he's having his men shoot any guy who gets near me. Shoot *you*. All because of my face."

He leans back, considering everything I've told him. "You aren't your face, Daphne," he says simply. "You're not Helen of Troy. You're Daphne. And none of this is your fault." He says to me.

"But my father," I say. "Sometimes he gets confused. He thinks I'm my mother, and he—" I can't even say what my father wants. Ajax grabs my hand. Tears jump into my eyes. I'm so ashamed.

"It's not your fault." He tilts his face down so he can meet my eyes. "Don't you ever blame yourself for that."

I swallow until the urge to cry goes away. And just like that, I feel clean. I lean forward and kiss him.

He tastes like honey and his mouth is soft and firm. I feel his hands, one on my neck and one against my waist. He pulls me to him in stages, like he wants to let me know he'll stop whenever I want him to.

I know what lightning feels like. This thrill is sharper, and so sweet I could burst into pieces, like my chest is an egg full of light. I want to touch him. I slide my hands under the jacket. He winces when I graze his ribs and I pull back.

"Sorry," I say, covering my mouth with a hand.

He suddenly tilts forward, holding his side and rocking slightly with pain.

"I need to get you home," I say. I stand and help him to his feet.

"This is as far as you go," he says firmly. "We're just about to enter Theban territory."

"You can barely put one foot in front of the other," I say. He starts to argue, but I don't let him. "You can't win this. I'm going with you."

"Daphne," he says.

Gods, I love how he says my name.

"Look. The taxis are coming on duty again," I say, ignoring his protests. I hail one at the curb and go back to help Ajax get inside. By the time we get to Washington Square Park he's tried to stop the driver about four times.

"I'll tell you as soon as I feel even a hint of the Furies," I assure him.

"Then it'll be too late," he replies, shaking his head.

I make the driver take us all the way to his doorstep and I get out with him.

"Are you crazy?" he says. But at this point he can't stand up on his own. I have to practically carry him to his door.

"First inkling of anger, and I'm out, I swear," I say. "But I don't feel anything. Honestly."

His eyes blur with pain before he can argue more. I change my face back into young Hye-Su's and knock on his door.

"Without the Furies, they'll think I'm a human," I tell him with more confidence than I feel.

This better work or I'm dead.

"You gotta go. Now," Ajax says, but it comes out a moan.

The door flies open. Standing in the doorway is a very large blond man. I shrink back instinctively. He's tall and thick, and with that aura of badass that only a soldier who's been in a fire-fight can pull off. This is the kind of guy you'd walk lightly around on a good day. Angry, he's flat-out terrifying.

"Hey, Caz," Ajax gasps apologetically.

Caz. Castor Delos. Oh my gods, what am I doing here?

He gives his little brother a look that could melt lead. "Should I ask what happened?" he asks Ajax.

"Later," Ajax replies. He gestures at me and shakes his head as if to say, "not in front of her," and Castor nods.

I let go of Ajax and wait awkwardly on the top step while Castor takes him inside. Before the door closes, Ajax catches my eye.

"I had a great time," he says.

"You had a terrible time," I retort, incredulous.

I hear Ajax's laugh on the other side of the door.

Best date ever.

CHAPTER 11

There's no point trying to sneak in on my Uncle Deuce. When I get back home (home is now Deuce's cavernous and nearly empty apartment), he's drinking cocoa at the round, Formica-topped kitchen table that he's had since the seventies. It's made every move with him since I can remember.

"Hey," I say. I even wave.

"Where's your coat?" he asks.

"I gave it to a boy," I reply. No point in beating around the bush.

He thinks about that. "Isn't it supposed to be the other way around?

"Probably." I stare at him, waiting. "Aren't you going to lecture me?"

"Nope." He shrugs and gets up, putting his cup in the sink. Now that I'm home, he's going to bed.

I follow him. "You don't care?"

He lets out a groan before turning and facing me. "Just keep it short, make a clean break, and don't let the human know what you really are."

I bite my tongue about the "human" bit. Of course he'd think I was seeing a human. How could I possibly be seeing another Scion? We'd have eaten each other by now. Deuce turns back around and heads down the hallway toward his bedroom.

"So, just to get this straight—I can date?"

"It's your life. For now, anyway. Just try not to make a mess of it." He pauses before shutting his door. "And call next time. I hate waiting up."

I go to my room, wondering what I'm going to do with all this freedom. I try to lie down, but I feel too light and floaty to fall asleep. Two things keep circling my mind. The fact that my father's goons have apparently been given orders to kill, and that Ajax kissed me.

Well, I kissed him. But he definitely kissed me back. Which isn't supposed to be possible because of the Furies.

I sit up and throw off my blankets. I've never heard of anyone escaping the Furies. While I have a working theory about why Ajax and I were spared, I wonder if there's any historical evidence. I get out of bed and go to Deuce's sparsely populated bookshelf. I pull down a copy of Edith Hamilton's *Mythology* and look up Erinyes in the Index. Of course, Edith doesn't call them the Furies. She uses their proper name. Good old Edith.

Birth of: The Erinyes were made from the blood of Heaven when Cronus, Titan and son of Heaven, wounded his father the Sky and would have killed him at the urgings of his mother, the Earth. The Erinyes were born of a family blood feud, of a child trying to kill one parent because the other parent ordered him to. They were meant to chase the wrongdoer, to punish Cronus for spilling family blood, and they could never be banished from the earth.

So, what happened? Why are Ajax and I suddenly off the hook?

I go back to the index to reread where the Erinyes come into the picture for the Scions. I know this bit by heart, but I go through it anyway in case I missed something.

The Orestes Cycle: Euripides really fleshes out The Furies here. After the Trojan War, Orestes kills his mother, Clytemnestra, for killing his father, Agamemnon, whom she killed to avenge her daughter (and Orestes' sister) Iphigenia, who Agamemnon killed to make the winds blow so his thousand ships could go get Helen back from Troy. Agamemnon was from the House of Atreus. *So, yeah, the Furies, like Helen, started with my family. Hooray for us.*

What Edith doesn't mention is how the blame spread. All four of the Scion Houses—Atreus, Thebes, Athens, and Rome—are descended from the gods, and the gods are related. Once we started killing each other at Troy, we were killing what the Furies considered to be our brothers and sisters and they chased us for it, compelling us to pay the blood debt by killing the killers. Who are also our relatives. Which starts the Cycle all over again. *Just like Orestes. We're damned if we do and damned if we don't.*

Edith has our Houses clearly outlined (even the House of Rome, although Edith just called them the descendants of Aeneas, who was the founder of Rome and a Son of Aphrodite) but there isn't a peep about the Furies still chasing us to this day. She also has no information on why Ajax and I have been released. I put her back on the shelf. Maybe my first guess was the best one.

If the Furies demand payment for a blood debt, then it could be that saving a life is what pays it. I didn't feel the Furies when Castor opened the door last night. I think I've paid my debt to his House.

Deuce is asleep, so I can use the kitchen phone. I desperately want to call Ajax, but he's got to be sleeping. I call Harlow but she doesn't answer. Then I realize I don't need anything right now. I'm not hungry or angry or anxious. I'm alone but not lonely.

I can't recall many moments in my life that were enough, just as they were. Even moments when I've been happy have felt slightly skewed. I try to find the place inside that had never joined up before, the sense that I was a too-small jacket that didn't quite span across the cold strip running down the middle of me. But it's gone. I fit inside myself for the first time, and nothing is missing. The middle of me is warm.

I go to my empty, paint–fume-filled bedroom and fall asleep.

When I wake, Deuce's phone is ringing. I go to it and answer.

"Your face is on top of the Empire State Building!" Harlow squeals.

"I admit nothing," I say. "Gotta go."

In the living room I turn on Deuce's ancient television. It's the kind that's built like its own piece of furniture, only gets four channels, and I think it has actual tubes in it. My uncle calls it a "set." I can practically hear it wheezing when I switch it on.

When the picture finally appears, an artfully trussed up collection of silicone and hair extensions is yodeling about how much she loves her blender. I change to one of the other three channels and finally find the news. It isn't the top story, so that's good. I guess they don't want to encourage anyone else to do what literally no one else in the world could do.

They're no longer running pictures of the mural, either. The reporter says that the police have no leads on who committed the "act of vandalism," and I breathe a little easier. Ajax is still going to catch hell from his family, but at least he won't go to jail. I hope, anyway.

I make myself a bowl of cereal and eat it at the Formica table, staring at the gold flecks suspended in a moment for decades. Some of their glitter has been lost to the scuffing and yellowing of years, but I like to watch them swirling and folding over each other in their frozen dance.

I hear a knock at Deuce's front door, and I freeze on instinct.

"Daphne?" It's my dad.

I go through a moment when I wonder if I can pretend last night didn't happen. But that's ridiculous. He sent men to kill my date, and as far as he knows they succeeded, and there's a dead teenaged boy at the bottom of the lake in Central Park. That's not something you can brush under the carpet, even if they don't expect anyone to find a body. But dealing with my dad would require a rather stellar bit of acting that I'm not sure I can pull off.

I sit silently at the small table and wonder how I would react if I were a normal girl and my boyfriend had been shot in front of me.

Like trying on different hats, all of which make me look a little silly, I imagine myself pretending to scream and cry (too after-school special), or threaten with icy unflappability to go to the police (too cigarette-smoking dame from a Hitchcock film).

What would I really do if my father had had someone killed? I guess it would depend on who I would be if I'd never killed anyone. I don't know how the imaginary person I'm supposed to be would behave. I just want this to stop. I want my dad to be my dad again.

Eventually, my father walks away.

I feel like an idiot.

I haven't heard from Ajax all day. I called the number I know —the phone line in his room—but got a recording saying my call couldn't be completed. A few hours ago I felt so stable, so complete. Where did that girl go? I want to be her again, and I hate to think that I'm only capable of being her if I get bi-hourly exposure to Ajax.

It's strange to feel like I need someone. I'm not going to say I've never needed anyone before—that's absurd—but in a general sense, barring my infant years, it's very near the truth. I don't think I'll actually die if he doesn't call me, but it certainly feels like I will. And who says they'll die if they don't hear from a boy? An idiot. So, I feel like an idiot.

By afternoon, I realize I'm going to lose this battle with myself. I don't care if needing Ajax is all in my head. And why do people say it's all in your head like that makes it easier to get over? If missing him hurt anyplace else—say, in my pinkie toe—I could just chop it off, but my head is the one part of my body I can't remove or escape or take a ten-minute break from because even when I'm sleeping, I'm still in there. And so is he.

I run down to the lobby of my building too fast to be seen and change my face when I have to slow down enough to maneuver my way out the doors without killing anyone. A moose of a man wearing all black marks me, but since I look like an African American girl, his eyes skip away and go back to scanning the streets.

I don't recognize him. I'm pretty sure I won't be seeing any of the men from last night again. Attempted murder definitely warrants a personnel change.

It's when I see Ajax's front door that I realize from now on every second in my life that doesn't include him is between. Things still happen and time still exists, but it's like the montage in a movie where they blast the music and fold the days together. *Placeholder*.

I wait until I pass under the relative obscurity of a shadow and turn myself into the young version of Hye-Su. I knock. I'm smiling just knowing he's somewhere on the other side of that door. Sound is sharper. Colors brighter. Real time has picked up again because I know he's near me. I don't feel the Furies, even though I'm standing at the front door of my enemy. They really are gone.

I hear bare feet slapping against the marble floor inside and the door gets yanked open by a little girl. She's missing a front tooth and her bangs are crooked. She grins at me and tugs on her grubby t-shirt. There's a glob of glitter and blackened glue on the back of her hand.

"Who are you?" she demands.

"Hye-Su," I say. "Who are you?"

"Dora. I'm not supposed to let anybody in," she says, and then sticks a glittery finger in her mouth to prod at the gap in her baby teeth.

I laugh. "Why not?"

"Cuz everyone's gone bananas!" she replies delightedly, and then she runs away, giggling like a lunatic. She's left the front door wide open. After a few minutes of standing there, I edge inside.

"Hello?" I call out.

I hear the slap of Dora's bare feet as she bangs down a flight of steps I can't see. Adult voices are somewhere far off. I shut the door behind me and stand in the entryway, waiting for someone to show up. No one does.

The entryway is grand and stately. There are marble busts on columns, and friezes along the wall depicting battle scenes from ancient Greece. There's even a small bronze statue of a perfect young man, a kouros, which looks almost alive. The face is vaguely familiar, but that's nothing new. All the modern Scions are just recycled faces from the past. Different haircut, same cookie cutter. No idea what that means or why it is, but you get used to strange when you can shoot lightning bolts out of your fingers.

I peek into the parlor room next to the entryway and spot some seriously uncomfortable-looking furniture. It's one of those rooms that no one ever uses so all the oldest, lumpiest antiques get piled in there.

"Dora?" I try again, but apparently she's forgotten all about me.

The Delos family brownstone, like all the other homes on Washington Square, is tall and relatively narrow. I go up three flights of stairs, passing by what looks like a rec room and then a study before I reach the level of what I hope are the bedrooms. Down the hallway I see a brightly painted door that stands out from the otherwise subdued and tasteful palette.

I don't get nervous until after I've knocked.

"Go away, Dora," says a sleepy and annoyed voice.

I crack the door open and peek inside. The smell of turpentine and oil paint hits me in a wave, making my eyes water. I almost can't find Ajax in the riot of color.

Every wall, even the ceiling, is covered in murals or layers of onionskin sketches for future works, which are taped up on top of each other. The floors around the walls are covered in bunched-up tarps. In the center of the room is a mattress that rests on the floor with no frame or headboard. Piles of books and sketchpads teeter precariously at its corners. There's no real furniture in Ajax's room apart from what looks to be an antique easel and stool set up by a window. The bed is a tangle of black sheets and tanned skin. My stomach flutters.

Ajax groans as he rolls over and throws the pillow off his head in frustration. "I said, go away!" he says. He sees me and freezes.

His eyes are still blank like he doesn't recognize who I am. Then I get it. "Oh, sorry. This must be weird," I say sheepishly, and change my face back to my own.

"Are you insane?" he whispers. "Get in here and shut the door!"

I hurry to do as he says, but I stay near the door, not fully entering the room. This is his bedroom, where he sleeps and does other stuff. Like, naked stuff. He sits up and looks at me with a bemused smile on his face. "Come here," he says.

The floor is a jumble of drop cloths and paint supplies. There's no place to go but his bed. I look down and see little traces of lightning running across the surface of my skin and do my best to get it together. But he isn't wearing a shirt.

"I had to make sure you were okay," I say from my spot near the door. "You didn't answer when I called."

"No phone," he replies, gesturing at the empty wall socket. "My father's a bit angry." It's clear by his tone that "a bit" is an understatement.

"The police don't know it was you."

"My dad does." He looks away, frowning. "And he recognized your face. It was like he was looking at a ghost. He grilled me about it."

I nod and glance at my feet. "What did you tell him?"

"That I made you up."

"Did he believe you?"

"I don't know. He was so stunned he forgot he was angry and started talking about his youngest brother, Perseus, and how he was murdered."

"By someone who looked like me?" There's a cold feeling in the pit of my stomach.

"By Elara. Your mother. That's why my dad killed her—or at least thinks he did." He's silent for a while.

I can't deny it, though I wish I could. "She's never told me about why your dad came after her. Or about Perseus." I look away. "But she's never told me much of anything."

I can see motes dancing in the slanted rays of late-day light coming in through his windows. They almost sparkle around him. He even makes dust look good.

"Come here," he repeats, more softly this time.

I come to the edge of his bed and sit down, pulling my knees up to my chest. "How's your wound?"

"Gone. Thanks to you."

"Thanks to a bunch of dryads who thought you were too pretty to die," I correct, grinning at him.

"How did you know they were there? I thought dryads were extinct."

"They said there were more of their kind than of ours."

Ajax bites his lower lip in thought. "I don't want to owe anyone my life without understanding what's expected in return," he says.

I nod in agreement. "Maybe the dryads know why the Furies are gone for us now, too."

"I was hoping you would know," he says.

I shake my head. "What did you tell your family?" I ask, watching him pull his lower lip through his teeth.

"That I got jumped by humans I didn't want to kill." He raises a bare shoulder in a shrug.

"How badly are you grounded?" I ask, stalling for more time with him. Ajax smiles ruefully in response.

He's slow to take my hand. Almost like he's expecting something to stop him. A stream of tingles flows up my arm to the back of my neck and down again in a delicious wave. His eyes are lowered. I stare at the shadow of his lashes on his cheek.

"The guys who shot me, you sure they were your father's?" he asks.

I nod, ashamed. "He's become completely unhinged about me." I focus on the weight of his hand covering mine, rather than what I'm saying. "It's like I can be any woman in the world, but I don't know how to be my father's daughter."

"Yeah well, when you figure it out, let me know." He looks around his room at the screaming walls. "My dad says art is supposed to be beautiful. Balanced. 'How can a son of Apollo make something so chaotic and ugly?'"

"I was just thinking I've never seen anything more beautiful."

Ajax looks at me. "Ditto."

For a moment I'm worried he's going to kiss me again. Last night it was okay. There's only so much you can do sitting on a bench in the middle of the city, but here in his room, alone? I don't know if I can deal with that yet. Even just holding his hand is making me shaky.

But he doesn't try. And now I'm wondering why not.

We both hear someone come down the hallway and stand outside Ajax's door. I change my face back to the young version of Hye-Su's as someone simultaneously taps and cracks open the door.

"Knock, knock?" a young woman asks. She's a beautiful girl, probably just a few years older than me. Something about the way she moves screams "human" to me. "Oh, sorry," she says when she sees me. She gives me a worried look. "Are you supposed to be up here?"

"Not really, I guess." I say looking at Ajax.

The pretty girl with auburn hair frowns slightly, as if she's debating what to do about me. "Are you staying for dinner?"

"No, she should probably go," Ajax says to me.

"Will you be eating in your room?"

"Downstairs."

"You sure?" the auburn-haired girl asks kindly. "Your father is still wicked mad."

"You from Boston?" I ask, catching the "wicked."

"Providence," she replies. "You?"

"No. I've just been around people from Boston too long," I lie. She closes the door and I allow my face to go back to my own.

"That's Noel. She just started working here. Really talented chef," Ajax explains.

"She's gorgeous," I say.

"Yeah, my brother Castor noticed," he replies, grinning.

"Must be difficult to keep a human who comes into your home all the time in the dark about what you are."

Ajax shrugs. "How does *your* family do it?"

"We don't have staff," I reply. "My father does, but not my uncle. We don't have anyone, really."

Ajax looks troubled. "You have each other," he says.

It's better he knows right off the bat that my family isn't exactly a Norman Rockwell painting. But I feel embarrassed. Like I'm poor where he's rich. Everywhere he goes he's got people who care. I've got one cranky old man who seems to enjoy punching me in the face a little too much.

"What?" Ajax asks, smiling because I'm smiling.

"Just thinking."

I'm holding so still I must look like a deer on the freeway. He's not moving either, but somehow we're closer to each other than we were a moment ago.

"Jax," says Castor's voice on the other side of the door.

Ajax and I spring apart. I stand, quickly changing my face, and turn towards Castor as he comes into the room. He looks me over, narrowing his eyes.

"What're you doing?" he asks his brother.

"I was just leaving," I answer, and turn to Ajax. "Feel better," I say before fleeing from the room.

I have to squeeze past Castor to get out the door. He doesn't exactly block my way; he just uses the proximity as an opportunity to really look me over. I get past him before he calls out after me. He follows me out into the hallway, and I stop.

"Would you like to stay for dinner?" he asks. He isn't being polite. He's doing this so he can test me. See who his little brother is spending time with now that he's seen this face twice.

"Sure." *Um... what did I just say?*

"I'm Castor. I didn't get your name last night." He takes a few steps toward me. I notice he prowls when he walks, even though he isn't trying to be threatening or anything. It's like he can't help it. He puts his feet down like a predator—always balanced, always ready. Yeah, this guy is dangerous.

"Hye-Su. Just call me Sue," I reply.

"Jax, put some clothes on. We've got a dinner guest," Castor calls lazily over his shoulder.

He turns back to me. Still scanning me, trying to figure me out. I realize he's judging my stance, noticing just as I did with him a second ago that I stand like a fighter. *Crap.* I cock a hip like a normal teenaged girl would, throwing myself off balance, and smile at him nervously. Ten seconds is forever.

Ajax finally appears, fully dressed. He looks at me over his brother's shoulder with dread in his eyes. I hang back and let Castor lead the way so I can walk next to Ajax.

"I don't know why I said yes," I whisper to Ajax, feeling like a fool now for intruding. "I'm just making things worse for you, aren't I?"

"You make everything better." He pulls me closer until our shoulders are touching. I see Castor's head twitch back toward us in reaction to Ajax's words. He heard. I can't see his whole face, but he's definitely frowning.

Ajax lets go of my hand as we go downstairs to the ground level. I've never held a guy's hand before, never even close, but for some reason it feels wrong not to with Ajax. The lack of him is what I notice, like how sometimes you don't know how hungry you are until you start eating, and I hate that he's not touching me right now. He should always be touching me.

I follow him into the dining room and immediately feel underdressed. The men (except for Ajax who probably doesn't own anything that isn't paint-stained) are wearing button-down shirts and the girls, even little Pandora, are wearing dresses. They're not so dressed up that it looks ridiculous, but there is a ritual here—a nod to traditions that are long gone for the rest of the world.

Ajax pulls out my chair for me, his hand brushing my shoulder as I sit. My breath stutters. I feel like we're breaking some kind of rule, and all he did was touch the fraction of bare skin along the hem of my sleeve.

"Who is our guest?" an older woman asks. Maybe his mom?

"This is Sue," Ajax says. "Sue, this is my aunt Jordana."

"Pleased to meet you," I say around the lump in my throat. Jordana Lycian. She's sister to Paris Delos, Head of the House of Thebes.

And then it hits me. Ajax's father is Paris Delos, the prince and general of the largest House, and the famous slaughterer of dozens of Scions. Including my mother, supposedly. I mean, I knew that. But I still can't believe he's Ajax's dad.

I'm about to have dinner with a tableful of people who would cheerfully cut off my head.

"Do you go to school with Ajax?" Jordana asks with stiff civility.

Ajax and I look at each other. We have absolutely no script yet. "Yes," I say. "I'm new."

Her eyes flick up to mine and I have to remind myself to drop my gaze demurely. Don't challenge anyone. Just play dumb. Play normal. What the hell is normal?

Noel enters the dining room with a smile on her face and a gargantuan bag over her shoulder. She sees me and her expression changes.

"Oh, you did stay," she says, and then she turns around and goes back the way she came to account for me, the bag riding her more than being carried. Does she play ice hockey? That girl's either got a lot of hobbies, or more than one job to need a bag that big.

"Sorry," I mumble to no one in particular.

Castor sits across from me. He's staring after Noel, his eyes lingering on her trail as though the air had become special now that she'd moved through it.

I feel Ajax's knee press against mine under the table and I glance at him out of the corner of my eye. He's ignoring me, turning to Dora sitting on his other side to tease her, but his leg presses right against mine, and I can feel the heat of him seeping through my skin. My face is on fire with a raging blush.

"So how did you two meet?" asks another big blond guy about Castor's age. He's prettier than Castor, almost too pretty for my taste, and he has a playful glint in his eye. His clothes and hair are perfectly cut, and I can smell his cologne from across the table. Even his hands look manicured. If Castor looks like he'd be trouble in a fight, this other Delos brother looks like he'd be trouble anywhere women are.

"That's my brother Pallas," Ajax tells me.

"We met in art class." I tell Pallas.

"What do you think of Ajax's work?" Pallas asks me.

"I think it's amazing,"

"Of course you do." He says, with a hint of sarcasm.

"They don't share our appreciation for street art." Ajax says to me. "My father, he's an art dealer. So, you know, they're experts." He continues, with the same tone of sarcasm.

"What does *your* family do?" asks Castor.

Shit, shit, shit. Too many questions. Too many stories to keep straight. I've been able to change the way I look since my mother gave me my half of the Cestus when I was eleven, but I've never had to come up with alter egos because I've never actually used it to meet a whole family before. I figure I look Korean, so I may as well run with that.

"My dad works for a tech company," I say. "I'm not really sure what exactly he does for them to be honest."

That seems to placate Castor for the moment, but every time his eyes land on me, they narrow in suspicion. He hasn't figured me out yet. I smile at my folded hands, reminding myself that they will never see through my disguise. The other Scions have no idea that the Cestus of Aphrodite still exists. He's never going to figure me out.

Pallas launches into a story about a woman who came into the gallery that afternoon while he pours wine for himself, his aunt, and his brother Castor. The clock strikes six and an older woman in an apron starts bringing out the food.

Just as she finishes laying the table, a man walks to the head of the table and takes the vacant chair. I feel Ajax stiffen as soon as he enters the room. No one has to tell me that this is Paris Delos.

He wears his blond hair in waves that brush his collar. A streak of gray brightens the right temple. His shoulders are thick and rounded and his hands are enormous. He doesn't seem to be in a hurry, but his long legs eat up the room in a couple of strides.

He looks like a lion, a tawny, slit-eyed lion overlooking his pride, and in his presence the big Delos boys look like what they are. *Cubs.*

The Furies may be gone, but I size him up him anyway. I can't help but wonder what it would be like to face him with a sword in my hand. A shiver goes up my spine and I clench my fists to keep my lightning from crackling across the surface of my skin. Old lions are the most dangerous, they say.

I wonder if he uses the gladiolus—probably not. Those hulking shoulders look like they're more used to swinging a broadsword. Or a war hammer. *Gods, he's huge.* I can imagine this brute killing half of the thugs in the House of Athens, as the stories say. I wonder what he looked like when he came for my mother?

"Sue?"

Ajax is elbowing me, and I realize he's trying to get my attention. "Yes?" I reply.

I see that he's holding a plate of food out to me. I take it and serve myself. Paris doesn't look at me. He doesn't even acknowledge that he has a guest, he just starts lifting platters and putting food on his plate. Kind of rude, actually.

"Tantalus called, said the excavation is going as planned," Castor says in Paris' general direction.

Tantalus. The eldest of the Delos brothers. Heir to the House of Thebes, and the reason Deuce has been training me so hard every day of my life. I am in over my head.

"What are you excavating?" I ask as brightly as I can. I take a bite and chew, only sort of tasting the roasted chicken and herbs. Some part of my brain knows it's good, but the rest of my brain it too busy freaking out to notice.

Paris turns to me for the first time. I can tell he's used to scaring the crap out of humans with just a look. I can't meet his gaze with anything like a challenge, so I do the only thing I can. I act recklessly cheerful and hope like crazy he thinks I'm a dimwit.

"Our family has made an archaeological discovery off the coast of Bulgaria," he says. His voice is surprisingly soft, and the room quiets to match him. "A cache of relics from ancient Colchis that was moved there after—" Pallas continues for him.

"Well, we don't know when it was moved," Castor cuts in smoothly. "And we don't know exactly where the cache originated from."

"What's in the cache?" I ask. I feel Ajax press his leg against mine, and I remember I'm supposed to be a silly girl. "Is it, like, a buried treasure?"

"Kind of," Paris replies. My eyes go to Castor, looking broodingly into his wine.

Something about this archaeological find disturbs him. I wonder what it is. It hasn't escaped my attention that Colchis is the land of the Golden Fleece, and modern-day Bulgaria was Thrace in antiquity, but of course I can't say any of that or dig any deeper, because what teenaged girl would know those kinds of things offhand?

"Cool," I say. "You'll have to show me whatever it is when you bring it back. Especially if it turns out to be treasure."

I feel Ajax's laugh. When I look at him, he's watching me in that peculiar way. A little detached but missing nothing. The artist's eye.

Rather than wait for Castor to start grilling me again, I ask more questions about the family business and the galleries they own. Pallas loves to talk. The conversation goes from art to music in a moment and I forget I'm supposed to be uncomfortable. How can anyone be uncomfortable when they're talking about their favorite songs? The Delos family seems to love all music. Except, of course, Ajax's particular favorite—hip-hop.

"You like hip-hop?" I ask, readjusting my image of him to fit with this new information.

"Black Sheep. De La Soul. Dr. Dre. NWA," he replies, looking down.

I grin at him, loving that I have so much to learn about him, but I notice his brothers rolling their eyes.

"It's just recycled riffs, stolen from Funk and Soul," Castor argues, frustrated by his little brother's taste in music.

Ajax shakes his head. "It's not stolen or recycled any more than Jasper Johns stole the American flag. It's art," he says decisively, inciting a round a groans from the rest of the table. They've obviously had this argument many times before.

"Figures you'd like a band called Black Sheep," Paris grouses.

It's almost like Paris can't help but admire how different Ajax is from all his other sons. I don't think Ajax sees that, though. All he hears is disapproval. He deflates a little, and my heart sinks with his.

"What kind of doctor is he?" Pandora asks after having mulled this over for some time.

"Dr. Dre? He's for grown-ups." Ajax smiles at her and ruffles her crooked bangs. She gives him a jack-o-lantern grin, all adoration.

A girl glides silently into the room and takes a seat at the other end of the table, across from Paris. It's then I realize that Paris isn't at the head of the table, but at the end. This girl outranks him. Who outranks the Head of a House?

She's younger than me, but I can't tell if she's ten or fifteen because she's so painfully thin and small. She doesn't look like a sunny Delos. Her eyes are dark and shadowed with lack of sleep and her skin is pale enough that blue veins show through on her neck and hands. There's a slight pause in the conversation, and in that silence, I can feel it like I can feel electricity coursing through copper—this girl isn't alone. Not even in her own body. Others are with her. They pull at her and whisper to her. The hairs on the back of my neck stand on end. There's only one thing she can be.

The Oracle.

I have to stop myself from gasping, and not just because she is extremely creepy. My mother told me that the House of Thebes was the House of the Oracle—the most sacred of our kind. No other House has an Oracle. No other House knows the future.

I glance at Ajax and see a sad smile on his face as he watches the girl sit stock straight, twisting her hands, her rail-thin body swamped in her giant chair. Poor thing looks terrified. Like she's walking on a tightrope and one wrong move will send her spiraling down. *Gods, she's just a kid.* I smile at her.

"Hi," she says, smiling back nervously. For some reason her being nervous makes me relax.

"Hi," I reply. "I'm Sue."

"I'm Antigone."

"My cousin," Ajax adds.

"Nice to meet you," I say cheerfully.

"You too."

The table is silent. I try to think up something normal to follow with. "Do you go to school with Ajax... and me." I remember just in time that I'm supposed to be his classmate.

"No," Antigone replies. "I'm homeschooled."

"She's sick a lot." Pandora whispers to me.

Antigone looks panicked for a second. "Nothing contagious," she says.

"Oh good. Catching the plague would be inconvenient right now. I have a test next week." She laughs at my joke uncertainly, so surprised to be laughing it makes me wonder how lonely she is.

"Are you going to senior prom with Jax?" she asks.

Ajax chokes on his chicken. I thump him on the back as he goes beet red.

"Let's put a pin in that for now," I say to Antigone. She smiles.

Pallas deftly changes the subject and steals the show for a bit. He's got a way with words, and he's an entertaining storyteller— part poet, part used car salesman. Ajax takes my hand under the table as we listen and laugh at the nonsense story of miscommunication and poor timing.

It doesn't matter what Pallas is saying. I can't hear much of anything with my heart thumping so loudly. Ajax is taking slow breaths, like he's starving a flame, making sure it doesn't grow too big too fast. I don't look at him. I don't have to. Every molecule in me is attuned to him. Every now and again his hand tightens, like we're on a rollercoaster only the two of us can feel.

Antigone withdraws first. She detaches from the conversation and slowly sinks into herself. Fear starts to show on her face and she excuses herself from the table. For just a second, I think I see a shadow chasing after her. I think I hear the flapping of wings.

Jordana, her mother, goes to see if she's okay, and dinner doesn't survive their departure. Pandora and Paris both excuse themselves, and Pallas soon follows. Only Castor lingers. Ajax stares at his brother pointedly, but Castor doesn't leave the table.

"Aren't you going to walk your guest out?" he asks. His tone is polite, but his meaning is clear. I'm not welcome any longer.

Ajax stands, still holding my hand. Of course Castor sees it, and narrows his eyes. He trails behind us to the door. Ajax comes outside onto the stoop with me, shutting the door behind us.

"He's probably going to be peeking out from behind the curtains," Ajax says with a groan. He leads me down the steps, and across the street to Washington Square Park.

"Why is he freaking out?" I ask as Ajax pulls me around the NYU arch and out of sight.

"Just a sec. I'm dying to do this," he says. He stands against me and moves me back into a shadow. His fingertips brush against my jaw. "Your face. I want your real face," he whispers.

I change back to myself, and his eyes soften with relief. Then he kisses me. Kissing Ajax is like kissing someone in a dream. It's absolutely perfect and not nearly enough. I want to climb into him, but I can't get close enough. My hands slide under his shirt, trying to press him closer to me.

"Wait," he gasps, pulling back.

My laugh is so shaky it sounds like a sob. We're practically devouring each other in public. NYU students pass, eyebrows raised, but they're generally tolerant of our display. It's a pretty liberal school, I gather.

I let my face fall against his chest. He wraps his arms around me and puts his chin on the top of my head. We cling to each other for a long time.

"What are we going to do?" he asks, partly to me, but mostly to himself.

"I don't know," I whisper back. "We'll just have to keep it a secret. You'll never bring me home again, not as Sue. I'll be someone else next time. And the time after that."

He hugs me again. "So long as when we're alone, I want you to be you."

I melt against him. "Deal."

Tal

I watch them eating.

The Atreus Heir breaking bread with the Head of the House of Thebes. How could my plans have gone so spectacularly wrong? For over three thousand years I've managed to stop a romantic union between any of the Houses, even though nearly every generation has had its star-crossed lovers. The only possible explanation is that the Fates are working especially hard against me this Cycle. Against us all.

I've dealt with this before, though. Occasionally, the lovers have managed to appease the Furies by paying the blood debt. Daphne saved Ajax's life, and now she can be around any member of his House without inciting the Furies. Not so for him, though. Ajax still owes his blood debt to Atreus, although he doesn't seem to know it. If he is ever around anyone else in the House of Atreus, he will feel the Furies. That might still work to my advantage.

I see Daphne and Ajax join hands under the table as she laughs and jokes with the Princes of Thebes. She's tempered the old man's anger. He even smiles at his most wayward son. She doesn't know how charming she is. The Cestus can melt even the hardest heart until it's pliable enough to wrap around the bearer's little finger, but it's her innocence that makes them enjoy it. Even wearing the disguise of a regular young woman, and not the heart-stopping beauty she usually is, she is a marvel to watch. Looks don't really matter, though, when it comes to charm, and not even Medea's magic charms were this effective.

I see all this from close quarters, for I have snuck into their house and shrunk my body down to the size of a Tinkertoy. I stand in their entryway, disguised as one of their many bronze sculptures as they mention Medea's kingdom. And a discovery they've made. They don't say what it is, only that the Heir to Thebes is there retrieving it.

Tantalus. The one who was born with a prophecy spoken on the morning of his birth.

I must investigate. If the zealot Tantalus has found the dragon teeth, this one illicit union between Atreus and Thebes won't matter. If he uses them, there will be no other Houses left. And not much of a world left, either.

But I find myself torn. Daphne is the Heir to her House. And so, uniting with Ajax would unite the two Houses, leaving only Rome and Athens to stop the release of the gods. That's far too close to utter destruction to be allowed.

The dragon teeth first. They have become a priority. There will be time to decide about the star-crossed lovers after I deal with Tantalus.

I slip out of the house with ease and pass Daphne and Ajax hiding in the shadows. They hold each other like sailors clinging to the deck of a sinking ship. Unfortunately, I can't let the girl go down with him.

She must live. She must have a daughter or Aphrodite will exact her punishment on the world. And a terrible punishment it will be. I doubt humanity would survive it. So many things could go wrong—all in the name of love. I've never understood it.

They don't see me. They don't see anything but each other.

Why didn't I kill him? A knife at the base of the skull, and so many lives would be spared.

A gear in my chest grinds.

I turn back to do what I should have done, but the lovers have parted. Ajax is already climbing the stairs to join his brothers.

Chapter 12

"You never called me. How'd it go?" Harlow asks, leaning on my locker.

I pause, really thinking about it. Obviously, I can't say that my dad had Ajax beat to a pulp, shot, and left for dead in a lake. But I don't want to lie, either. "Everything that could go wrong did." I grin. "And it was still wonderful."

"Are you ever going to tell me how he managed to paint your face on top of the Empire State building?"

I don't reply. I just shuffle my books in and out of my locker, trying not to smile too smugly. Harlow makes a frustrated sound, but she doesn't press any further. That isn't like her. Something's up.

"Is it Tal?" I ask, taking a guess.

She groans. "How would I know? I haven't heard from him. He said he was going to be gone for a few days, and when I asked him where he was going, he hung up on me."

She's really upset, so I touch her arm in consolation. I frown again. Should I be worried? I make a mental note to talk about it with Ajax, and it occurs to me that he and I have never really discussed Tal, or what someone who was so obviously not what he seems doing in my life. In our lives.

The day drags until the final bell rings, and I see Ajax waiting for me outside school. He's wearing a red and gold tie, a tight button-down shirt, and khakis. It's a school uniform, and therefore destined to be dorky, but he manages to look like a Calvin Klein model, just before he takes his clothes off to get down to those famous tighty-whities. He smiles as I rush to him. Is it appropriate to throw myself into his arms? Probably not. I barely manage to stop myself in time.

"Hi," I say, stopping in front of him. What do I do with my books? No idea. I hug them to my chest rather than toss them to the ground and hurl myself at him.

"Hi," he replies, a little breathy, a lot sexy. How can one word be sexy?

I'm grinning like the village idiot. Can't stop. "What are you doing here?"

"I wanted to check out those interesting women you met in the park the other night," he says pointedly. His eyes dart over my shoulder and he smiles. "Hey, Harlow. What's up?"

"Ajax. You're looking edible, as always. Come to see your lady love?" she drawls playfully.

"Something like that," he replies, looking at me.

Ajax blushes. I blush. *Crap, what's next?* Are we going to kick pebbles with the toes of our shoes and say "Aw, shucks"?

"Okay, okay," I say, trying to quash my grin. "We're going to go," I tell her, taking his hand and edging away. "But I'll call you later?"

Someone tries to plow into Ajax, blindsiding him. But he shifts his weight deftly and Flynn goes stumbling past. His attempt at intimidating Ajax fell short, and so he steps to Ajax to cover his embarrassment. "You got a problem?"

"Not really," Ajax says quietly. He smiles like they're old friends, but I can see the tightness in his eyes. "Just walk away, man."

"Or what?" Flynn challenges. He can't let it go now.

I don't know what the human equivalent of the Furies is, but something has Flynn in its grip—anger, and a sense of wounded pride that is surely big and damaging enough to have its own personification, we just haven't named it yet. And Ajax is responding. He's not macho, and he has nothing to prove, but while I'm here, watching, he can't help himself. Flynn is trying to claim me, and Ajax can't have that.

I step between them and very pointedly take Ajax's hand and lead him away.

"You can have her," Flynn snarls after us. Like I'm his to give. I stop in my tracks and pivot.

"Easy, tiger," Ajax says, taking my arm, trying to guide me back. "Too many witnesses," he whispers.

I let Ajax pull me away, even though I really, really want to beat Flynn's face inside out.

I see Ajax smiling knowingly at me and I let it go with a shaky exhale. He pulls me into a hug while we're still moving away and we monster walk, laughing and hugging and turning around each other. Ajax eventually faces front and tucks me under an arm.

"Where are your books?" I ask, still juggling mine.

"No idea," he replies, shrugging. Free hand in his pocket. Tie pulled a little loose at his throat. I could just die right now. What has happened to me? He starts taking my books, reading the spines as he does so. "AP Physics. AP Calculus. AP Civics.... Tell the truth. Are you a geek?"

I blush furiously and try to snatch my books back, but he won't let go. "I've been locked in my room for seventeen years. What else is there to do besides homework? And don't try to tell me you don't do well in school. I see those books you have around your bed. Rilke. Kierkegaard. Feynman's lectures. Janson's *History of Art*. You're a closet geek. Admit it."

"Those aren't for school."

"What are they for, then?"

He smiles at the moving pavement and shifts my books. "This is going to sound really unflattering," he laughs self-deprecatingly, "but pretty much everything I do is for me. I'm trying to get as much as I can out of it all. Maybe I can leave something of value behind. We'll see. But I read for me, because there's no test at the end."

I watch him for half a block, letting what he said and how he said it sink in. "What happened to your mother?" I ask, taking a guess about him.

He looks at me, surprised but not displeased that I made that connection. "She died giving birth to Pandora."

I nod. Even with modern medical help, delivering a demigod is dangerous for mortals. Scion babies are strong, even before they're born, and some human mothers don't even survive carrying them. The fact that the Delos family is so large is surprising. Their mom must have been one tough lady.

"Do you remember her?"

He nods slowly, seeing a dozen things behind his eyes that I can't. "Oh yeah. I remember her very well. My dad and I have never really clicked, but my mom always understood me. Before I did, half the time."

"I'm sorry," I say. I don't have to ask if he misses her. The arm he has over my shoulder tightens.

"Let's get these back to your place," he says, indicating my books, "and then we can go to the park from there."

I don't say anything because, seriously? If he were to suggest we walk barefoot over a pile of rusty hypodermic needles, I'd go along with it just to stay near him.

A block before we go inside my building, I alter my face to look like one of my neighbors in the building. Ajax startles when he feels me shape-shift under his arm.

"I don't know if I'll ever get used to that," he says, looking dubiously at my altered appearance. I'm an average woman, early twenties, dark hair and eyes. Kind of a big nose.

"I can't walk in there as myself. Not with you," I say, shrugging a shoulder. "My dad still has someone posted downstairs to watch me come and go."

Ajax's expression freezes somewhere between disbelief and disgust. "Are you serious?" he asks.

"It's not the same guys from the park," I say hurriedly. "My father hired completely new staff. They won't recognize you."

"That's not what I mean, Daphne." He stops and takes my hand. "Is your dad hurting you?"

"No." I cross my arms over my chest and look down.

I pull away, ostensibly to push through the door, but mostly to get away from that look. If he knew how screwed up everything in my life really was, he'd probably run screaming. I wave to the security guard, and he lets us pass.

"Hey," he says, chasing me to the elevators. He grabs my hand and pulls me alongside him. "Don't do that."

"He doesn't hurt me. Physically, that is." I say.

I press the elevator button, stealing a quick glance of a huge guy with neck tattoos who's obviously not reading the edition of *Publisher's Weekly* that he has propped up in front of him.

Ajax jiggles my hand to get me to look at him. I glance at him and give him a limp smile, letting my eyes wander back to the goon. We get on the elevator and wait for the doors to close, even though he isn't paying us any attention.

"Hang on," Ajax says, turning to me as we ascend. "What's going on?"

I change my face back to my own and shake my head. "I don't know how all this looks to you and I can't do anything about it. So, it's weird and gross, and if that's too much for you then I don't know what to say—"

"Are you breaking up with me?" he asks. I look up at him and he's grinning. I don't know why—none of this is funny—but I start grinning too. "Cuz if you're going to break up with me, it can't be over some guy with neck tattoos."

I smother a laugh and lean back against the opposite side of the elevator, crossing my arms protectively in front of me. "I'm serious, Ajax. If you can't handle what's going on with me, just tell me now."

"I don't really know what's going on with you. We haven't known each other long enough and I've never met your dad," he says earnestly. "But don't just assume that I can't handle it. That's not fair."

He's right. I watch him from the other side of the elevator, mirroring smiles building on our faces. The doors open. "Okay," I say, and I go through the doors.

"Okay," he replies, and follows me.

We get to my uncle's door, and I put out a hand. "Maybe you should wait here?"

He shrugs. "I don't feel the Furies."

"Yeah, but if Deuce is in there and he sees you, he'll know what you are even without the Furies. You look very Scion-y."

Ajax chuckles and leans up against the wall to wait. I go inside and call out for my uncle, but he's not home. I poke my head back out into the hallway and wave Ajax inside.

"It's okay. He's not here," I say. Ajax enters, and I suddenly regret inviting him in.

"Wow," he says, eyes gaping at the huge fight cage and padded sparring arena set right in the living room. "And I thought my family focused a little too much on warfare."

"Deuce can't help it," I say, shrugging. "There are only three of us left. He takes my training very seriously."

"Polydeuces Atreus," Ajax says, frowning in thought. He looks up at me. "Bearer of the Aegis?" I nod and he takes a breath to steady himself. "Is it here?" he asks.

I nod again. "He probably keeps it under his bed. Or in it, most likely," I reply. Ajax and I share a weak laugh.

"Have you seen it?"

"Just for a moment." I shiver at the memory of when I accidentally saw Deuce's magical shield, given to my ancestors by Zeus himself. It had the same effect on me it has on anyone it's turned toward, anyone but the official bearer. "I had nightmares for a week."

"That's what it's for, right? To strike terror into the heart of the enemy?"

"Well, it works," I grumble.

He looks around at the ancient furniture, the dim lighting, and the general sense of dismay oozing from the walls. No fancy address or obscenely large apartment can hide the fact that this isn't a home. It's a place where a couple of sad people wait for another disappointing day to end.

"Let's get out of here?"

"Yeah," I agree, bolting for the door. My cheeks feel hot. "I told you my family was weird."

"Let's make a deal." He takes my hand in the hallway and pulls me to his side. It takes a moment for our strides to match, but once they do, it feels like we've done this a million times before.

"Okay," I reply cautiously.

"Let's stop saying things like weird and messed up when we're talking about our families." He hits the elevator button and smiles at me out of the corner of his eye. "I can fly. You think that's not weird?"

"Actually, I think it's pretty awesome."

"Of course it's awesome," he says, like that's a given. "But still not technically normal. We don't need to do the whole 'oh my god, you think I'm a freak thing.' Not with each other."

I look away as I get on the elevator. It's uncomfortable to have him name the things I want to hide about myself, even if he's ready to accept them. Because I don't know if I am.

"What?" he asks, sensing I'm still uneasy.

"I'm just thinking," I reply. "Trying to sort this out."

"Okay."

I can tell he wants to ask more questions, but he doesn't. He just backs up and lets me decide for myself what I can and can't do. We watch each other from opposite sides of the elevator car. Something weaving between us.

The elevator opens. I change back into the girl with a big nose, and Ajax and I sail past Neck Tattoo. On second thought, maybe he is reading *Publisher's Weekly*. *Odd*.

We get outside and walk toward Central Park. I wait until we pass behind the shadow of one of those horse-drawn carriages to change back into myself. I'm getting better at timing my transformations. I barely have to think about it anymore. Ajax shakes his head.

"That's a really scary ability," he says under his breath. "But I think I could figure out it was you no matter what face you were wearing. You always smell the same." He groans. "That sounded really creepy."

"Yes, it did." I laugh. He laughs. We forget about everything for a moment and just stare at each other, learning the sound of each other's laughter.

"So, the dryads," he begins.

"This way." I lead him to the grove of oak trees. It's farther from the lake than I'd thought. But I don't mind. Walking through the park with Ajax is something close to a normal date, right? Minus for the whole "mission to the mythological beings who we may or may not owe a life debt to" stuff, that is. We take our time. We talk about small things.

Central Park is full of old growth trees, but the oak grove we arrive at just before sunset feels different from the rest. It lies in a low grotto. I hadn't noticed them when I dragged Ajax here in the dark, but enormous granite boulders, kicked into a disturbingly regular circle by the glaciers of the last ice age, surround the ridge. The dappled light plays tricks on my eyes and the air feels dead, even though you can hear the branches at the tops of the trees moving with the breeze. There are no birds. No insects. No ground scrubs. Just trees and earth that looks as if it's been brushed clean.

"You brought me here?" Ajax asks. I nod. "I don't remember any of that."

"Well, that's because I think you were mostly dead," I say.

He takes a moment to recall. "I remember being in a dry land, like a desert. You were there. You told me to get up," he whispers.

"This was the tree," I say, stepping toward a stately oak. "No, wait." I spin around. "It wasn't there, was it?" I go to another big oak tree and walk around it. "It wasn't like this." I do a circuit of the grove. It doesn't look like it did the other night.

"Did the dryads say anything else to you?" he asks.

I shrug, not wanting to tell him all the stuff they said about him being better off without me. How our union would never bear fruit, only blood. I look at him, and I decide to keep that to myself.

"Only that there were more of their kind above and below the ground than ours," I answer.

Ajax looked around. "Does that mean we dig?" he asks reluctantly.

I recall chittering things, cold air, and weighty darkness from when I peered down the old service tunnel, right after retrieving Ajax's first letter. I shiver convulsively. He runs a hand down the bare skin of my arm to smooth away my goosebumps. His touch only makes them worse, though.

I take his hand. "Come on. I know where we need to go."

Running is faster than the subway or a cab at this time of day. It's rush hour, and Manhattan's buildings exude bodies like baby turtles bursting from a sandy beach. They scuttle frantically in all directions for a bit before they join up in a mad dash for the shores. Ajax and I run, but don't run as we could. The city's baby turtles are too fragile and they'd never survive a collision.

We get to the subway station on West Fourth Street—our subway station, as I now think of this particular stop—and it's predictably crowded, which works in our favor. We wait at the end of the platform. A train rushes into the station with a gust of ozone air, zapped stale by the third rail. The doors open, and in the scrum that follows, Ajax and I hop down behind the last car and onto the tracks. We race to the niche and press ourselves tightly to the wall. Ajax peeks around the edge. The curve of his neck and the strong edge of his jaw catch the light, and I'm struck.

"No one saw us," he says. He doesn't need to whisper. The subway is noisy enough to drown our conversation. He looks back at me. I'm standing here staring at him stupidly, and he smiles. "What?"

"Help me with this thing before the train pulls out," I say, forcing myself to focus. As soon as the train is gone there will undoubtedly be dozens of impatient faces peering our way, already looking down the tracks for the next train.

There's a padlock on the door that wasn't there when I was last here. Ajax grabs hold of it and twists. The padlock doesn't break, but the bolt it's attached with does, and the door swings open into darkness.

"You first?" Ajax says. I cock an eyebrow at him. "I'm kidding!" he says. He looks warily into the dark. "Kind of."

"Hurry," I say, shoving him into the service tunnel as the train pulls out. We close the door behind us and are swallowed by the darkness.

"Stand back," I say, making sure Ajax isn't touching me. I call up a spark and concentrate it in the palm of my hand. It glows blue, illuminating Ajax's awed face.

"Amazing," he whispers.

"Expensive," I correct. "See if you can find a light bulb anywhere. It takes way less energy for me to power a bulb than it does to keep a spark this bright going."

There are light fixtures about ten feet up the wall, but the bulbs are caged.

"I got this," Ajax says. And then he just floats up, weightless.

"Wow," I sigh. I hear him chuckling to himself as he pulls apart the mesh cage and unscrews the bulb.

He touches down gracefully and hands me the bulb. I take it and give it the tiny jolt of juice it needs to glow.

"You have to take me flying one day."

"It doesn't work like that." He says. "It isn't like birds flying.

"How does it work?"

"I change gravity. Gravity is everywhere, not just the earth, but it's between objects, too. Everything is falling toward everything else, so when I release the earth's pull on me, I float. Then I increase the gravity between myself and the air at the front of me, release the gravity behind, and that both pulls and pushes me along. So, I don't fly, really. It's more like... slipping through space."

I nod, thinking of how elegant he looks in the air. There's no silly arm flapping or superman fist thrust forward. A thought occurs to me.

"But you can only do it to your body, not to other things," I guess. "You can make yourself weightless or really heavy, like when we fought that time, but you can't change the gravity pulling on me."

"Right," he replies. "I can carry up to a certain weight when I fly—my clothes, small objects—but a full-grown person is too much. Believe me, I've tried. I've dropped my brothers dozens of times."

"We should get going," I say, making a move toward a metal ladder stretching down deeper into the darkness.

"Wait until I get to the bottom," I tell him. I point to my rubber-soled boots. "When I'm standing on metal in these, you're safe." I hold up a bare hand, palm facing him, fingers spread. "But when my skin touches metal, don't let your skin touch it. Not while I'm generating a charge."

"Got it," he replies. He watches as I climb down to the next platform. "How long can you keep a charge going?"

"Depends," I reply, stepping a safe distance away from the ladder and watching him descend. "On how many volts I'm putting out, how much water I've had."

"Water?" he asks, reaching the bottom and turning to me with a puzzled face.

"Water molecules are positive on one side, negative on the other. I can line them up and dismantle some to make a circuit inside me, and voila. Lightning."

"Right. Like a battery," he muses. "That so cool."

We go down a metal gangplank into the rock. Even with the glowing bulb, we can barely see more than fifteen feet in front of us.

"Are those scratch marks?" he asks. I hold the bulb closer to deep gouges raking the hewn walls and ceiling. I study them with mounting unease. The gouges are about three inches wide, two inches deep, and four feet long in some places.

"Claws?" he guesses. I purse my lips together grimly, hoping both he and my eyes are wrong. They sure look like claw marks to me. Enormous claw marks.

Conversation stops and tension builds as we travel deeper. The metal gangplank ends, but the tunnel into bare rock continues. I hear Ajax's breathing speed up to match mine. A smell—part rot, part animal musk—tinges the earthy air. Something scuttles away from us in the dark. We stop short and stare after it. It had too many feet to be a rat.

"You mentioned monsters..." he begins leadingly.

"How are your slaying skills?" I ask.

"Did I mention I'm an artist?" he says, raising an eyebrow. This makes me laugh, and I realize that's why he's doing it.

We see a faint glimmer of light up ahead. His voice drops. "Put out the bulb," he says. I do. "Do you have enough energy left to throw a lightning bolt if it comes to a fight?"

"Too risky," I whisper back in the near pitch-black. "It could strike you."

"Don't worry about me." I feel his hand on my shoulder and realize he's moving me behind him.

"That's not how this works," I reply, trying to stay level with him. I can't move him. I tug on his arm, but I can't pull him beside me. He's become so heavy. "You're doing your gravity thing, aren't you?"

"Stay behind me and get ready to throw a bolt and run." he says, focused on the growing light ahead.

Arguing would be ridiculous considering the circumstance, so I stow my ego and concentrate on placing my feet silently. We edge toward the light, keeping close to the wall. The ceiling begins to slope upward, and the tunnel widens abruptly into a cavern. We pause before the mouth.

Ajax stiffens and pivots to his left. He lowers his stance and plants a foot behind him, digging in. Over his shoulder I see something crawling toward us on the wall.

It's a head. Just a head, with a thick-browed, primitive-looking face. It reminds me of a Neanderthal. A dead Neanderthal. The skin is gray and scabrous. On the bottom of the head, beneath the chin and throat, are hundreds of tiny appendages, like starfish feet, that keep it stuck to the wall and propel it forward. Each foot waggles as it reaches forward, as if individually seeking a path, and more alive looking than the head itself.

I feel Ajax cringe away from it reflexively. He reaches his right arm back to hold me against him. The motion brings my attention to the wall behind me and I spin, getting into a crouch back to back with Ajax. Coming toward us across the other wall are more heads, and scuttling quickly around the heads are claw-like hands with ten fingers. The fingers pick their way forward like spider legs.

Ajax looks down. More of the hand and head things are making their way toward us, both in front and behind. I look up and see them clutching the ceiling as well.

We're surrounded.

CHAPTER 13

Tal

I crest the ridge and look down the rim of shrunken mountains that have been weathered into rolling hills. In the near distance, the Black Sea yawns in the night. Across the water is, or rather was, Colchis.

I wasn't there when the Argonauts landed here in what was, back then, ancient Thrace. I didn't become a part of the story until later on in that same quest, but the battle that happened here against Medea's brother, Apsyrtus, became known to me. Apsyrtus lost to his sister's treachery, but Jason and his Argonauts also lost much that they had stolen from Colchis.

Not the Fleece. If it were the Golden Fleece that Tantalus sought, I would not be concerned. The Fleece can only heal, not hurt.

It's basically useless.

What Jason and the Argonauts left behind were the dragon teeth. Once sowed in the ground like evil seeds, the dragon teeth rise up, changed, and become a terrifying weapon. In the wrong hands, those could be used to destroy the world and, with it, my island.

I hike down the hillside in the cover of darkness and make my way to a smudge halfway to the water's edge. The turned earth of their excavation will leave only a slight scar on the landscape, easily forgotten in this remote and abandoned area.

No one has dug here before, despite the many archaeological sites dotting this shore. No one has dug on this particular site because there is no ancient city to find. No grand ruins, crumbling colonnades, or shell-shaped amphitheaters. Just a ship (albeit a famous one) that was abandoned when its captain and crew had to hike across Thrace to get to the Aegean Sea on the other side.

As I approach the excavation site I can't help but recall Medea and Jason. Yet another love story I never understood. She was a learned woman, a bright and beautiful sorceress. Jason was an opportunist. A pirate, really.

I've yet to discover what she ever saw in him. She was gifted enough to defeat me for her average lover, Jason, and then raise me from the bottom of the sea after he had finished with her.

And I am Talus, the last of the bronze men. I can be a colossus that hurls giant stones the size of mountains if needed, but Medea knew my one weakness—one godly vein of ichor and one human vein of blood that flows through my ankle. She called up her hellhounds as I hurled rocks at the Argos so that Jason and his men would not land on Crete, my island, and pillage it of its riches.

She fought me and defeated me. In fact, she fought all of Jason's battles for him on the quest for the Golden Fleece. He was nothing without her, either before or after, and yet she loved him. And then she threw everything away when he threw her away.

After she murdered her own sons, she came back for me and took me to foster. She said it was because bronze was better than flesh. Her clockwork boy, she'd called me. I was the one she could bring back from the dead, and I often stayed in my smaller size so that she might hold me on her lap as she did her sons. She wept often. To wash the clouded judgment from her eyes, she'd said. I gathered her tears and use them still to cloud the judgment of others. She promised I would never run out of tears. Her folly was endless, she'd said.

I think of that turn of phrase often because it doesn't make sense to me. She died, so surely her folly ended. Or does her folly —the benighted love she had for one unworthy man—spiral down time, like a stone kicked off a cliff? Is life nothing more than a moment of impact, and your mistakes the only thing that makes it down the mountainside?

I asked. She never answered.

My gears click and slip. More and more often lately, I feel as if I'm standing on the top of her mountain. I hear my voice yelling after her, asking for answers, but I only get an echo in response. Do humans have someone who answers these questions for them, or do they only hear the sound of themselves reverberating back across the gulf?

I don't like these thoughts. I don't want to think them anymore.

I locate the camp and find the resting place of the Heir to the House of Thebes easily enough. His tent is the only one with the lights still ablaze. There are no guards. This wilderness is not filled with roving bandits as it once was, and Tantalus can more than take care of himself. Against humans, that is. I shrink myself even farther until I am no bigger than a rat and glide through the darkness, making no sound, leaving no trail, until I am looking right inside his tent.

I see him at his desk. He peers through a magnifying glass while he painstakingly brushes a small black object pinched between calipers. He's completely focused on his task and not on the alert for an intruder. It's not surprising how overconfident the prince and Heir is. Menelaus was the same. I see his face again in Tantalus.

It used to disturb me. Every few generations a face that is a little too familiar, a little too close to that of an ancient character from the Fates' Great Play will return and I'll feel as if I am haunted. They come in cycles, like a crop of ghosts waiting for the Fates' harvest.

I don't dare creep into the tent until after Tantalus has retired for the night. Then I expand my form back to human size in order to reach the desk and gather the small ebony bits from the jeweler's envelope. Dragon teeth are black, not white. They are sharp, even after millennia. They are poisonous, even to my bronze body. I carefully wrap them in a leather pouch and take them all. Now Crete is safe from the dead army. I spare a glance for the prince in his bed before I leave.

Should I kill him? I set down the pouch and silently move to the bed, considering. I waver, questioning how best to fulfill my duty.

He does not threaten Crete. He sleeps, as innocent as the dawning sun.

I stand down and return to the desk. When I pick up the pouch of dragon teeth, I see what they had been resting atop: a leather bound journal. I see these words engraved in gold on the cover:

> *The Tyrant Rises...*
> *Now a wave swelling far from shore*
> *Soon a world's birthing with unbreakable doors*
> *When the spawn or'step their parents' might*
> *An end to death will be their right*
> *Rise up, young Heir, and undying be*
> *A god for all eternity.*
>
> *Ismene Delos*

Ismene was the previous Oracle. Dead now. I puzzle over the words until I realize that this must be the secret prophecy whispered about amongst the Houses; the one that was made on the morning of Tantalus Delos's birth.

I'd often wondered at that name, Tantalus. It is an uncommon choice, considering Tantalus was a Scion who killed his own children, cooked them, and fed them to the gods to show his contempt for them, but the choice of name makes sense to me now. Paris heard this prophecy on the day of his Heir's birth. The prophecy promises immortality to the Scions who challenge the gods.

That's what the Hundred Cousins want. Immortality. Paris

heard this, knew it was unavoidable, and molded his son into a weapon to fight the gods. This is Thebes' battle cry. This is their bid for godhead.

But in that battle for immortality, how many fragile humans and defenseless lands will burn? My island could be clapped in chains. Surely, I should kill Tantalus before his crusade destroys this tattered, patchwork world, and with it my heart of soil and stone. My one purpose since the rest of my race was eradicated. Protecting my island, Crete.

Medea once asked me why I needed to protect it. She asked if I loved my island. I gave her the only answer I could. I was made to protect Crete. That is why I exist. Therefore, as long as I exist, I must protect it. She had laughed and promised to teach me about love. I think she tried. I think I almost loved her.

Yet it's neither love nor pity that stays my hand from slaying the Heir to the House of Thebes, but luck—or fate, depending on your perspective. A mechanical alarm sounds from the camp perimeter.

The dragon teeth are old magic and cannot be destroyed or altered in any way by my peculiar nature. If I change my size, they will stay the same. But I cannot allow myself to be discovered. I barely have time to drop the dragon teeth back onto the desk and shrink down to the size of a figurine before the prince is launching himself out of bed.

Machete in hand, he stops at the desk to gather up a pistol. He does not notice the small bronze figure of a kouros lying on its side on top of his desk like a toppled chess piece, but he does notice the pouch of dragon teeth.

He does not hesitate. If he did, I would have had time to swell to human size and kill him, but the prince sweeps up the pouch and moves at supernatural speed out of the tent.

Enlarging myself a moment too late, I chase the prince into the night. I run to the source of the disturbance, my bronze hair easily blending into the sea of blond spawn of Apollo. They call themselves the Hundred Cousins, and they do not overestimate their numbers. With that many rushing out of their tents to answer the alarm, it's conceivable that most do not know each other even though they are related. In the chaos, no one stops to question me.

I hope to find Tantalus at the perimeter. I circle once, locating the source of the alarm. An animal wandered too close and tripped a mechanical sensor. A false alarm. I crane my head in all directions, searching.

Tantalus is not here. The mechanical gears in my brain whir quickly, deducing one fact after another. He must have seen the misplaced pouch, realized an intruder had infiltrated, and fled with the dragon teeth. He was unwilling to take any chances with them even though he was among family. Those he should trust. The thought is like radio static that I'm trying to piece together into coherent speech.

A Theban—the Heir of Paris Delos—is willing to run out on his family in order to protect a weapon? He is not like the others, but why? Why does this one act as the others do not? I do not understand.

I slink off into the darkness knowing I have missed my chance. Inside my bronze mind that looks and feels like flesh, I yell from the peak of Medea's mountain. I hear nothing but echoes.

The creepy-crawly heads with their spidery hands stop in unison, leaving a ring of space around me and Ajax. I feel his back against mine. Heat radiates off of him as his muscles bunch and tense.

"What are they waiting for?" I growl.

"I don't know."

"Maybe we should ask?" I say sarcastically.

He takes me literally and straightens up out of his crouch. "What do you want?" he says, addressing the monstrosities.

Dead eyes roll inside the disembodied heads. Black tongues loll from between gray-blue lips. They click their broken teeth together and cluck their swollen tongues. I shrink against Ajax, revolted.

"I don't think they can speak," Ajax says, tilting his head in an attempt to see under one while still keeping his distance. "No throats or larynxes."

I don't say the obvious, like no bodies. Basic physiology has gone out the window here. The corners of my mouth tic up in a smile, charmed even in the midst of this nightmare that he's even trying to come up with a logical explanation for this.

The heads and hands move apart in a synchronized motion and a path opens up between them, leading deeper into the cavern. Ajax looks at me questioningly, silently asking what I want to do. I shrug as if to say that we don't have much of a choice. We follow the path.

The gloom steadily brightens, although I can find no light source. The deeper we go, the brighter it gets. Blue-silver light, like watery moonlight, radiates from the walls, from the ground, and traces through the air in will-o-the-wisps. Clawed things scuttle away. Something slithers away from us, its scales flashing in the luminescent dark. Ajax squeezes my hand. The heads and hands travel with us, leaving a space around us and leading us on in a gruesome swarm. Sometimes the hands scamper too close to my feet in an effort to direct me. I hop away from them, trying not to shriek.

We come to a chamber that disappears up and out into the gloom. Boulders form benches in a semicircle around a bowl, almost like an amphitheater, but with only one level of seats. The heads and hands lead us into the center of the bowl, and then scatter off in all directions like rats bursting from a sack.

"Well, child of Zeus. What have you gotten yourself into now?" asks a voice as thick and bittersweet as chocolate.

A woman, neither old nor young, steps into the bowl. She is tall and broad. Her long robes are dark blue, nearly black, and spangled with threads of silver, like spider webs. She has a long, aquiline nose that would mar a face less sculpted, but on her it looks more like a proud figurehead parting the waves before an elegant ship. There is something heavy about her presence. Something that makes both Ajax and I stand perfectly still, holding our breath.

I realize she's asked me a question, but I have no idea how to answer her, or if I'm even supposed to. Instead, I ask a question of my own.

"Who are you?"

She turns to the right and begins pacing around the edge of the bowl. Her face is always to us, though she doesn't crane her neck. There is no back to her head. She has many faces that wrap prism like around her head. As her body turns, her head doesn't. But rather than seeing the side of her face, we still see the front of it. I think this means she sees in all directions at once.

The ceiling above us rattles and the old brick gives off puffs of dust. The subway lines must be overhead.

"Hecate is one of my names," she replies.

"The witch goddess." I remember from my lessons.

Hecate is only supposed to appear at a crossroads where three roads intersect. Supposedly, the crossroads are where she bargains for the souls of humans in return for a favor. I look up at this century-old bit of construction to see three different arches, each supporting different tracks right above the very place where Hecate stands. *Crossroads*.

"Whatever deal she offers you, don't take it," I whisper to Ajax.

"Do you know what you're doing here?" she asks us.

Ajax and I share a look. At this point, I think both he and I have forgotten. He recovers his wits first.

"The dryads helped Daphne save my life, and now the Furies are gone—" he begins, and Hecate interrupts him.

"Gone for her when she paid her debt to the House of Thebes by saving your life. You still owe the House of Atreus," she corrected.

Ajax and I share a look. I raise an eyebrow.

"So, if I'm around anyone else from her House, I'll feel the Furies?" Ajax asks.

"Correct," Hecate replies.

Good thing Deuce wasn't home when I took him back to my place after school.

"What I want to know is if the dryads want something in return for my life," he finishes.

Hecate laughs. "Every gift has a price."

"What's yours?"

She lifts an eyebrow at him, amused. "The first one's free. You owe the dryads nothing." She looks at me. "What kind of tree were they in?"

I'm not a botanist. "Ah—oaks?" I guess.

Hecate nods. "Zeus's tree. Wherever there is an old stand of oaks, the dryads within those oaks belong to you. They must come to your aid in your time of need. They can heal you, hide you, and sustain you. You called on them to heal Ajax, and they were compelled to do as you say. By doing that, you saved his life."

Ajax gives me a sidelong glance. "They did seem to know a lot about me," I admit.

"Your mother should have told you about them." Hecate's voice is rebuking.

"She's not the nurturing type."

"Your problem is much bigger than dryads," she continues, looking now at Ajax. "The Fates have you in their sights. Unlike the Weaving Three who tug on every thread, I can only see partway down a few roads, yet every which way I turn, I see death." Her face flashes across many different sides of her prismatic head, as if looking in many directions at once. "What I need is someone who can escape fate," she decides.

"And that's not me?" Ajax asks, crestfallen.

"Do you know where your ancestor, Oedipus's father, King Laius of Thebes, went wrong?" she asks in return.

Ajax and I share another questioning look at the seeming non sequitur. We both shrug, unable to come up with anything.

"After hearing the prophecy that his son would kill him and take his queen and his throne, Laius decided to kill the son instead of the mother. By then it was too late." Hecate completes her circle around the bowl and comes to a stop in front of me. "The only way to beat fate is to be a generation early. Kill the mother before she can bear the child. Before she can bear the Tyrant."

"Who's the Tyrant?" I ask.

"My brother. Tantalus," Ajax replies in a subdued voice.

"Your brother is not the Tyrant, though his belief that he is will be the death of you all," Hecate says.

"Can we stop it from happening?" I ask.

"If you want to beat fate, you must throw the dice and leave it to chance." She smiles at me in a way that's warm. I think. "Not having the answer is the answer," she says to me quietly.

I have no idea what she's talking about.

"Every Cycle is a little different. So much magic in this one. So many potions." She looks me up and down. Then she turns to Ajax and folds her hands in front of her in a formal way. "You stand at a crossroads, Son of Apollo." Hecate's lips pull up in a knowing half smile. "So, I must help you. If you want the help I have to give, that is."

Ajax looks at me. I shake my head in a definite no.

"All you have to do is complete a task for me—what it is yet, I don't know, but do this for me with no questions asked and I will help you get what you really want. Maybe you'll even manage to escape fate. But you must do exactly as I say. No mistakes."

"I'm listening," Ajax replies.

"Come closer," she commands.

We both step forward, and she holds up a hand, barring my way. "Not you," she says. "Just him."

I stop Ajax and pull him aside for a moment. "Don't take an open-ended deal. Please. You have no idea what she'll ask of you in the future."

"She's not trying to take advantage of me. She wants what's

best for us." He taps on his breastbone with his sensitive fingertips—the ones that can take chemicals and concrete and turn them into art. "I can feel it."

I sigh. I have never in my life taken a leap of faith, but I'll take one for him. Because I know he knows what trustworthy looks like, though I'm too broken to ever recognize it.

"Okay," I whisper, releasing him.

He kisses me softly before he goes to her. I'm left shifting from foot to foot as Hecate leads Ajax into the penumbra outside the bowl. The hands scurry forward, encircling me in case I get the idea to follow.

When Ajax comes back into the bowl, I scan his face. His brow is furrowed in thought. I catch his eye and he gives me a brave smile, shaking his head.

"Safe journey," is all the witch goddess says. Then she sinks back into the gloom with a rustle of midnight silk and a glimmer of moonlight silver.

Ajax takes my hand and pulls me along, practically running from the cavern.

"What happened? What'd she say to you?" I ask as we retrace our steps.

"We have to help someone steal something from my family."

"What?" I burst out, both as an exclamation and as a question.

He shrugs as we run. "Don't know who or what yet. But we can't ask any questions."

"What else happened?" I ask, knowing there was more of an exchange than that between them. "What did she say?"

Ajax shakes his head again, his lips pursed. "I have to figure something out on my own before I can talk to you about it," he says. I open my mouth to argue. He cuts me off. "Please, Daphne."

The look he gives me is so lost, so confused, I can only nod and say, "Okay."

We're quiet the rest of the way, only exchanging quick words of communication as we ascend the many levels of ladders and platforms on our way up to the subway station.

Out in the chilly night air, I hear Ajax breathe deeply. He takes my hand. I pop into a deli and buy a giant bottle of water. Using my lightning, even just to light a lightbulb, always dehydrates me. I sip my water while we stroll slowly back toward his house. I can practically hear his brain shouting inside him.

We stop at his stoop. He looks up at the door, his brow pinched with warring thoughts.

"Good night," I say sharply, turning away from him.

He catches my hand and tugs me back. A smile warms his face. "No, not like that," he says, and pulls me into a hug.

"Why won't you tell me what she said?" I say, stiff in his arms.

"I will when I'm ready," he replies. He tilts back and looks at me. "I have a choice to make, and I have to make it alone. I just need some time."

I narrow my eyes at him. Then I remember how he stood back in the elevator earlier today. How he gave me space.

"You're lucky you're worth it," I say, succumbing to his request with a grin.

He kisses me. We try to say goodbye three or four more times and end up kissing some more. A light goes on inside his house, and finally Ajax pulls away for real, but keeps ahold of my hand.

"Come by tomorrow?" he asks, still breathless.

I nod. He comes back for one more kiss. We hear his front

door open and I hastily change into another girl. Ajax shies back, his swollen lips twisting.

"Please don't do that when we're kissing," he whispers.

"Sorry," I say. "I had to."

Castor stands at the top of the steps, dressed as if he's going out for the evening. He eyes the two of us, flipping his keys in his hand in agitation.

"Good night," Ajax says before hurrying up the steps.

I wave as he disappears inside the house. Castor's eyes take me in and narrow distrustfully as he comes down the steps and passes me. A muscle in his jaw twitches, but he doesn't say a word.

CHAPTER 14

"Daphne. Are you home?" my father asks.

Deuce left at the crack of dawn this morning. I hold very still and debate answering no. I've been dodging my dad since he tried to have Ajax murdered. I just don't even want to deal with it. But I can't hide from him forever. "Yes, I'm here."

"Will you open the door?"

He doesn't sound angry. In fact, he sounds sad. I check the time. It's early. Eight o'clock.

"What do you want?" I ask, padding closer to Deuce's front door.

I hear my father sigh on the other side of the door. "Look, I'm sorry about taking your phone and about the basketball game." He does not say anything about the armed guards who are following me and who may—for all he knows—have killed my boyfriend. "I've been under a lot of pressure... Will you open the door?" I wonder if he realizes that his temper is getting shorter.

Why apologize to someone if you're just going to yell at them again?

But I don't want to fight, and I definitely don't want to bring up the boyfriend he thinks he killed. "Dad, it's fine," I say through the closed door. "Let's just forget it ever happened, okay?"

There's a long pause. I can hear my father put his hand on the door and I take a compulsive step back. "Please open?" he asks plaintively.

"I'm not dressed," I reply. I'm wearing shorts and a tank top, and I don't want him to see me like this. I hear him take a shaky breath.

He starts to walk away, and then he comes back. "Let me make it up to you," he says brightly.

"You don't have to—"

"Let me take you out for brunch. Just like we used to do on Sundays in Virginia, remember? It's gorgeous out."

I glance out the window. It is a bright, lovely day. Brunch with Dad used to be a bright spot in my long, lonely weeks when I was a little girl. It was our thing, actually.

"Come ooon," he goads, sensing I'm close to caving.

"All right." I capitulate. "Give me a second."

Maybe brunch can be our thing again—maybe what happened in the park scared him. Made him realize that he'd gone too far, and now he's trying to come back. I realize that I really want my dad back. The way he used to be. Even if that wasn't really all that great, either. I know I'll never have a close-knit family like Ajax's, but can't I just have one family member who isn't broken?

I skip the punk rock makeup and jewelry and put on a very

pretty but conservative skirt and blouse. When I meet my dad out in the front room he frowns in disappointment.

"Oh. I thought you'd wear that new dress," he says. "You know the one..."

The one I wouldn't put on for him. Is that why he wanted me to dress up? To see me in it? "It's too formal for brunch," I reply, deflating.

"Never mind," he says, brushing it aside and smiling. I smile back in relief. "Let's go!" He actually races me to the door.

I figured he'd take me to the restaurant in Central Park, seeing as how it's just a quick walk from us, but instead he has the car brought around and we get in the back. As the street numbers get lower and lower, I start to worry.

"Where are we going?" I ask when we pass below 24th Street and head west.

"Downtown," my dad replies, still gazing out the window. "There's this great place I know with a view of the Statue of Liberty."

Oh, gods. That's past the territory belonging to the House of Thebes, and into the Athenian's territory.

I squirm in my seat and try to come up with an excuse for the driver to stop the car. If the Hundred Cousins are like an army, the House of Athens are little more than a savage clan. They have actual beasts in their lineage and my mother once told me they defy the gods by eating human flesh. I haven't considered going lower than Canal Street since I got here, not even when I first went looking for Ajax. Even though I never sat down and had a talk with myself about it, subconsciously I knew that if Ajax was a Son of Poseidon, I didn't want to find him.

"I hear there's this great coffee shop in Union Square," I say, hoping to appeal to my father's love of all things exclusive. Anything to keep us from getting closer to the monstrous Athenians. "I read about it in *Time Out*," I continue when he doesn't reply. "It's really trendy right now. Only models work there."

My dad swings his head in my direction and smirks. "Why would I need that when I've got my best girl right here?"

He takes my hand and gives the back of it a quick peck of a kiss. It's cute. My dad is being his most charming dad-self, the one I remember from when I was a little girl, the one who brought flowers to my kindergarten graduation and taught me how to ride a bike.

But then he doesn't let go of my hand when he looks back out the window. I try to gently slacken my hold, but he doesn't take the hint and he keeps my hand the whole way down the West Side Highway.

He takes me to a restaurant in the World Trade Center. This is the heart of Athenian territory. The ports. The two rivers coming together. Water, water everywhere and across the Hudson is the Statue of Liberty.

When we get out of the car, I take a few deep breaths. But I don't feel the Furies at all.

As my father and I sit at our white linen-clothed table and servers push in our heavy, padded chairs for us, we look out of the floor-to-ceiling glass windows at Lady Liberty. I actually haven't seen her in person yet, draped in her near-Greek robes and wearing a crown of light that makes her look like a classical goddess. She takes my breath away.

"First time?" my dad asks, noticing my adoring expression.

I nod and put my cloth napkin across my lap. "Yes, I've never been downtown. Mother told me to avoid it."

I shouldn't have mentioned her. I don't know why I did. It slipped out. Dad's eyes narrow at the thought of Elara and he hails a server imperiously.

"Champagne," he snaps, and the server hustles off without even asking what kind. He'll bring the best.

My dad has a glass set in front of me, too. He tells me I have to drink it. It's rude not to drink to a toast. I don't want it.

"What are we toasting?" I ask, holding my champagne flute self-consciously.

"Our move to New York, of course!" he says. Too abrasively. "I tried to get Elara to move here for years, but she wouldn't hear of it."

He throws back his whole glass and waits impatiently. A server refills for him, eyeing me the whole time. I take a sip and put my glass down.

"Don't you like it?" he asks, leaning forward. Getting closer to me.

"No," I reply.

"If you're anything like your mother, you will." He laughs bitterly. "And you are exactly like her. It's uncanny." His eyes unfocus. He reaches under the table, putting his hand on my thigh. "Elara," he whispers.

I'm shaking all over. I stand up abruptly and twist my leg out of his hand, smoothing down my skirt. I think I'm going to throw up. People are looking at us. Our age difference is enough to earn disapproving looks. If they knew I was his daughter they'd be disgusted. As I am. I turn to leave.

"Where are you going?" he demands.

"The ladies' room," I lie.

I go in that general direction and then bolt for the elevators. His goon waiting at the bar sees me leaving, but he doesn't chase me. As the elevator doors close, I think I even see him nod at me.

There are too many people on the street for me to break into a run yet. I quick-walk to Battery Park. It's nothing but a thin strip of green right along the Hudson River, but there's more cover there than the street.

I feel so panicky and angry and ashamed I hardly notice the touch of the Furies rising in me. At least at first. A chittering sound and a flash of matted hair and blackened teeth flashes on the edge of my attention.

I spin around, feeling rage rise up inside me, whiting out the buildings and the traffic and leaving only the image of four big, black-haired people. Three men and one woman. They're crossing the street and heading straight for me. It's too late to change my face. They see me. And I see them.

Four enormous warriors. They are wearing long coats that are too warm for the weather, probably to conceal both their weapons and their unnatural size. *Gods, they're huge.* The House of Athens is full of brutes, just as my mother said.

I could kill them all right now with a bolt. Static crackles in my hair and I feel a gust of wind that smells like ozone swirling around me. But I can't. Too many witnesses, and I can't risk the Athenians knowing that a bolt-thrower exists, or it won't take them long to figure out that the children of Zeus are still alive.

I swallow the hot spark of my greatest weapon and run for the park. I trusted Ajax with my secret, but unless I'm on the verge of dying, I cannot use my bolts and reveal that my House exists, or else it won't for much longer.

This park doesn't have the deep cover and old growth that Central Park has. Before I know it, I'm through the green and hemmed in by a paved bike path that is flowing with walking, biking, roller-blading mortals. Beyond that is a metal railing, and beneath the railing, the Hudson River. I've reached the edge of Manhattan.

I turn and face the four black-haired, blue-eyed bruisers. The Furies claw at my nerves.

"I mean no insult to the House of Athens," I growl. Gods, I want to fight these glorious savages. Their skin is pale like moonlight on water. Their lips are red like they're already bleeding.

"What do the Hundred Cousins want in Athenian territory?" snarls the woman. I notice she's thrown out an arm to keep one of her men back. He's younger than she is and he's spoiling for a fight. They all are, but she's more in control.

"I'm here by accident. I just want to go," I lie. I want to fight, but I can't. The chances of me getting out of this without dying or exposing my family are very small.

Still... the shorter, stocky one that the woman is holding back is just begging to be hit.

"She's lying," he hisses. "And she's not Theban, she's House of Rome. Only Romans can make you fall in love with them at first sight."

I zero in on him, my teeth itching to sink into his throat. While I'm distracted, the taller one on the left runs forward, his coat flapping like wings while he both unsheathes his weapon and keeps it concealed inside the billowing fabric. It surprises me for a moment. I've only ever practiced in skin-tight, modern workout gear or a chiton, and never in regular clothes that both conceal and confuse. I was trained in the classical way, not on the street. There is a difference, I realize. The Athenians know how to fight in the city, surrounded by the unknowing mortals. I don't, and he gets the drop on me.

But my opponent is hindered as well. He cannot kill me on the bike path with so many mortals about. He pulls me back into the green, angling me toward the shadows of the trees, thinking to hold off on his hidden death blow while I meekly take it.

Though I cannot use my lightning, that's not my only weapon.

His xiphos rebounds off my impervious skin. It feels like a punch in my liver, and it hurts, but seeing the shock in his ocean-blue eyes when he realizes that his sharp short sword is as useless as a rubber dummy against me is so satisfying, I can ignore the pain and wrench the weapon out of his jammed-up hand.

The Furies slip into my eyes and ears. They jitter in and out of my skin. I almost stab him in the heart. At the last second, I stop myself and lower the blade of his xiphos, turn it flat, and jab it between his ribs, puncturing a lung. He's out of the fight, but he shouldn't die.

That's another complication. If I kill any of them, the House of Athens will want revenge, and because of my blonde hair, they'll probably go to the House of Thebes to find it.

I can't kill any of them. It would start a war.

The woman is on me next. If she's got a weapon, she doesn't use it. She hits me so quickly I doubt a regular mortal could see the blows. She gets in a body blow, breaking a rib or two. I block the next one at my head, return the head shot and land it, and while she's still seeing stars, I take out her front leg with a vicious kick. She goes down, and she won't be getting back up again with a broken femur, but I'm not much better off. I can't take a deep breath, and one of my arms is pinned to my side.

The stocky one comes up behind me and puts me in a bear-hug, crushing my already broken bones. He puts his face against my neck, sniffing me, taking long inhales of my scent. My skin crawls.

The last Athenian stupidly walks right up to me like it's safe because I'm in a bear hug, and I kick him so hard in the nuts he keels over.

"All to myself then," the stocky one snuffles in my ear.

I throw myself back with all of my strength, knocking my head into his face. I hear the crunch of cartilage in his nose, and we fall down, but he doesn't let me go. We roll out onto the bike path and people scream. He tries to keep my back and put me in a headlock, but I turn in his arms and get control from the bottom. I wrap him up with my legs and I'm just about to break his arm when he pushes us under the railing, right off the side, and down to the water and rocks below.

I scream and twist in the air like a feral cat. My enemy is grinning like this is the best thing that's ever happened to him. The water is his element, but... there's more than water down there. *What an idiot.*

I manage to get above him in my mad scramble, and just before we hit the rocks that lie mere inches below the surface, he realizes his mistake. He absorbs the majority of the impact.

I don't know if he's dead or just unconscious. I don't know if he can drown or if that's impossible for an Athenian. I don't know much of anything about his condition, and I don't give a shit right now because I am sinking, and I am utterly terrified.

The rocks are slippery, and the water is so cold. It's agony to lift my arm on my injured side, but I need both hands to pull myself along the rocks to get away from the Athenians and away from the crowds of people who are looking down at us and shouting. The water covers my head with every lapping wave, and I sputter and gasp. I'm slow in the water. I don't float, and all it does is drag me down.

I grit my teeth and pull myself up a bit higher until I am a few feet up the wall. People will see. I'll have to move fast as soon as I'm back up to street level, though running will be like daggers in my side. I climb up the wall, swing myself back up onto the bike path and then push off the hands of bystanders.

"Oh my god," someone gasps.

"How did you...?" murmurs another.

"Someone call an ambulance!"

I stagger for the park. I need to find a place, any place away from these well-meaning people before they get me killed. I lope into the shade of a small cove of trees and then force myself to break into a run. Pain explodes in my body, but I have no choice. I must move so fast no full mortal can see me or I will never get away from this.

I make it back to my building and lean against Deuce's door while I pound on it. I don't have my keys or my phone. I've even lost my shoes. If he's not home, I'll just break it down and hide in there until he comes back.

The door is pulled open and I fall into Deuce's arms. He picks me up and closes the door with his foot. I close my eyes and go limp, relieved.

"What happened!?" he asks gruffly. He lays me out on his bed.

"My father took me for breakfast," I say ruefully. "Downtown."

Deuce curses under his breath and gingerly touches my ribs. I try not to make too much noise as he prods and feels for where the breaks are.

"How many of them were there?"

"Four. They think I'm House of Thebes."

He pauses and looks at me. "Did you kill anyone?" he asks gently.

I shake my head. "I don't know."

He starts winding a bandage around my broken ribs. "Did your father see the fight?"

"No," I grunt. "I left him at the table when he tried to put his hand up my skirt."

Deuce stops what he's doing and looks up at me, his eyes blazing with anger. After a beat he calms down and starts wrapping me again.

"I'm sorry," he says quietly. He looks old and tired all of a sudden. "Here," he says, handing me a jar of honey.

I pour it directly into my mouth and swallow. He watches me intently. The honey helps a little.

"You did good, kid," he says, proud of me. "You controlled yourself and you were smart."

I don't know what to say. Thanks doesn't seem appropriate.

"You keep eating that honey," he says. "I'm going to go upstairs and talk to your stepmom."

I nod and drop my head, knowing that he's going to tell her

that my dad isn't allowed to see me anymore. Not that she can do anything about it.

I feel Deuce's hand on my hair, trying to comfort me. Just for a moment. Then he goes upstairs.

I have only a few minutes to call Ajax. I haul myself to Deuce's rotary phone and dial, one ear listening to the phone ring and the other listening for Deuce's return.

"Hello...?" He sounds confused. *Gods.* I wish I could see him right now.

"I only have a few moments," I say. "My father took me downtown. I got in a fight with the Athenians. I'm okay, but they think I'm House of Thebes. I can't see you for a few days."

"Wait... are you hurt?" he asks.

"I'll be okay," I whisper. "I have to go."

"Come and see me as soon as you can."

I hang up and make it back to bed before Deuce returns. If I look guilty to him, he doesn't mention it.

Tal

I arrive back in New York before Tantalus. He did not come straight home as I'd hoped, but rather went a circuitous route, in case someone was following him. Which of course, I was.

There is much that I missed. A summit among the three known Scion bloodlines has been called.

The second highest-ranking members of the Houses are demanded by Athens. Heads of Houses are excluded for safety's sake, but Heirs are required to attend, or the Sons of Poseidon will declare war.

I learn of this through a conversation I overhear between Ladon and Daedelus Attica mere hours after I've given up the chase for the dragon teeth and arrive back at my subterranean lair. My vigilance had proven useful yet again.

Daedelus informs his brother that an unknown young woman has bested four great warriors from the House of Athens after invading their territory. No one was killed, but Nilus—one of Bellerophon's younger sons—was badly injured in the attack. Neither Daedelus nor Ladon care much for Nilus, but they do care about keeping the peace. Their father, Bellerophon, does not, and he would send them all to war for this insult. That would be very bad for my island.

As sunset approaches I hurry aboveground to the small amphitheater in Central Park that the Scions use for these inter-House meetings. Here, the Furies are lessened due to the blessing of Dionysus. That, coupled with the help of emotion-controlling abilities of some members of the House of Rome, allows the Scions to meet without fear of killing each other on sight.

Well, without too much fear.

I shrink myself down and hold still. They will think I am one of the sculptures.

The two members from the House of Rome are there first as per arrangement. Leda Tiber, Heir to the House, and her younger brother Adonis wait for Athens and Thebes so that they may temper everyone's emotions as they arrive. A powerful daughter of Aphrodite, Leda can sway hearts quite well, but it is said that her younger brother Adonis can control them completely. The other Houses would be terrified of him if he weren't also something called an Empath. As such, they write him off as weak, though I find no weakness in him. In fact, he is the perfect specimen of athletic manhood as it has been explained to me.

"Daedelus doesn't want war. I know that for a fact." Leda is saying to her younger brother.

"But the rest of his House does," Adonis reminds her gently. "And he does not lead them. Yet."

She looks sharply at her brother. "Taking out Bellerophon isn't an option. Yet." Her brother represses a smile. Leda can't help smiling back at him. "The question is how, and when," she continues.

"Something tells me you already have something in mind." he says.

"Nothing concrete."

He stays on her, admiringly. "Old bastard doesn't stand a chance, does he?"

She laughs.

"What's the saying?" Daedelus drawls as the House of Athens joins them. "When Rome laughs the rest of us weep?"

Leda flips her long, auburn hair behind her shoulder and tilts her chin up at the tall, dark Athenian. "Only because none of you mules know how to take a joke," she replies.

"This is no laughing matter," snaps Lelix, younger son of Bellerophon. "Where is Thebes?"

"Here," Castor calls.

Both Athens and Rome subtly change their stance and ease their hands toward the absent swords at their hips. No weapons are allowed on sacred ground, but they all wish they had them when Thebes arrives.

Castor, Pallas, and Ajax form a line across from Daedelus and

Lelix. Leda and Adonis stand between them, forming three sides of a box. Atreus is missing, of course, but the place is left for them still.

"Where's Tantalus?" Daedelus demands. "This is a matter for the Heirs, Castor."

Castor grits his teeth, eyes blazing. He and Daedelus do not need the Furies to hate each other. Adonis steps between them, raising his hands and lowering their tempers.

"I'm sure there's a reason Paris risks all three of his younger sons," Adonis points out to Athens, and then gestures for Castor to continue.

"We mean Athens no insult," Castor forces himself to say. "Tantalus is out of the country, and you called this meeting two hours ago. Wanna tell us why?"

"One of you trespassed on our territory and attacked Nilus!" Lelix yells.

Daedelus grabs his younger half-brother and shoves him back into place, annoyed, and then proceeds to explain what happened in Battery Park. As he speaks, Ajax become more and more agitated, and Adonis becomes more interested in him.

"The girl didn't declare her House, but she was fast and strong and blonde... just like the members of the House of Thebes." Daedelus finishes, looking right at the three blond Thebans.

Castor looks troubled for a moment, and he glances at his two brothers.

"Anyone can color their hair blond. It's called hair dye," Ajax says to his brothers to avoid insulting Daedelus to his face, but his voice is loud enough for all to hear.

Daedelus is not amused by Ajax's disrespectful tone.

"I assure you that no one from my House was in your territory today," Castor says. He looks at Adonis and Leda for confirmation. "I swear to it."

Though members of the House of Rome cannot hear a lie as some members of the House of Thebes can, they can read emotions. It's clear to both Leda and Adonis that Castor is speaking in all earnestness.

"What else can you tell us about this girl?" Adonis continues curiously.

"Nilus said she was the most beautiful girl he'd ever seen, and that he's in love with her," Lelix snarls back at him. "Which means that she can affect emotion. Which could make her Roman." Lelix continues brashly.

"The girl was far too strong to be Roman." Daedelus looks at Leda. "No offense."

"Oh, none taken," Leda replies with what I believe to be sarcasm. "Who else from your House was there?"

"That's our business," he replies, unwilling to give away any more information.

"So curious," Adonis muses, still watching Ajax, who is doing an admirable job of ignoring him. "Who is this mystery warrior girl who makes young men fall madly in love with her at first sight? I'd certainly like to meet her."

A combination of fear and anger is rising in Ajax, but he stays calm and addresses Adonis respectfully. "Whatever may have happened with Nilus, love at first sight is not one of the talents of the House of Thebes," Ajax says.

"This is a load of bullshit," Pallas whispers to Castor.

"Daedelus, with all due respect, you've got to come to a meeting with more than just speculation if you expect us to believe your brother was in a fight with a Scion," Castor says impatiently.

"Castor's right," she says. "No one from the House of Rome was downtown today. And I believe Castor when he says no one from his House is responsible, either." She shrugs a shoulder. "Are you sure your brother didn't just get blackout drunk again, and now he's trying to cover up the fact that he got rolled by a couple of humans by pinning it on us? He's done it before."

"I move that the House of Athens has insufficient evidence that its territory was invaded," Adonis says.

"Seconded," Castor agrees.

"Daedelus Attica, you have no claim for just retribution for whatever damage was done to your brother, Nilus Attica," Leda finishes.

"This is bullshit—!" Lelix begins, but Daedelus grabs the foolish young man by the scruff of his neck and hauls him away, furious.

Thebes and Rome face each other with a tentative familiarity.

"Castor. You're looking well," Leda says. A feline smile spreads across her face and her voluptuous body curves ever so slightly more in his direction.

Castor shakes his head, mutters a curse and turns away, leaving the meeting with his two brothers in tow.

"You don't have to torture him, you know. He tortures himself plenty," Adonis teases his sister. "They all do."

I leave the Tibers and catch up to the Delos brothers. They complain about the House of Athens, and tease Castor about Leda. They behave as if they have evaded some kind of conflict without ever once discussing why they were called to the meeting in the first place.

That's Ajax's doing. If ever the conversation starts to veer back in Daphne's direction, he deftly maneuvers his brothers away from all talk of her. He is protecting her. While that serves my purposes for now, it speaks to a deeper problem.

Ajax is betraying his family for her.

CHAPTER 15

"Is Ajax home?"

Pallas Delos stares blankly at the gorgeous dark-eyed girl standing on his doorstep. I smile. The girl I am today has a really pretty smile.

"Ah—and you are?" he asks. He's wearing workout gear, and he's taping up one of his wrists.

"Abigail. I'm here to see Ajax." Pallas is supremely nonplussed. After an uncomfortably long silence, he hits a button on an intercom.

"Jax. Abigail is here to see you." Pallas watches me with narrowed eyes while Ajax comes into the entryway. He doesn't look disapproving, just curious and a tad confused. He's all sweaty and there's a slight graze at the top of his cheek. "Hi," he says. The word rumbles deep in his chest.

He reaches out and squeezes my hand and leads me into the house. He looks me over anxiously while Pallas trails behind. We haven't seen each other since my fight with the Athenians.

"I'm okay," I whisper to him. He touches me briefly, his fingers brushing the underside of my wrist.

"Want something to drink?" Ajax asks, acting normal.

"Water, please." I reply.

Ajax brings me into the kitchen and takes a pitcher of water from the refrigerator. While he's pouring, Castor saunters in. He's even sweatier than Ajax. He's pulling a torn and bloody shirt up over his head, which he throws into the garbage bin under the sink. I get the feeling the Delos boys don't wear a lot of clothes when they're home. I want to make a crack about that, but I can't because this is supposed to be the first time I've ever been in their home.

I see some pretty big welts over Castor's kidneys, and there's some swelling under his left eye. How much would your average teenaged girl know about fighting? Would she know, for example, that it looks like Ajax just beat the crap out of his big brother?

Castor pulls out a large glass bottle of lemonade from the fridge and downs it.

"Let's go up to my room." Ajax says to me, already taking my hand and pulling me with him.

We head out of the kitchen, edging past Pallas who's standing in the doorway. *Man, can these guys loom.* Castor strolls along behind us. He stops at the bottom of the stairs, watching us go up. He doesn't say anything, but he's glaring at Ajax.

Ajax closes his bedroom door behind me, and I change back to my face. He takes two long strides and catches me up against him. He moves his lips into the hollow of my neck.

"I was worried about you," he whispers.

I feel guilty for making him upset, and stupid for getting into that situation to begin with. I start babbling. "I didn't mean to go downtown. It was my dad. He wanted to take me out for brunch, and I couldn't jump out of the car. I was trying to get back uptown... and..."

He pulls back and looks at me. "All that matters is that you're okay."

After holding me for a few moments and staring into my eyes, something shifts in him, and his hand starts to move upwards. His knee slides between mine.

"Ajax..." I start saying, trying to turn my mouth to his. He pushes off of me and spins me around.

"Sit," he says, leading me to his bed. "I need a quick shower."

He puts on some music. A woman's voice, dusky and full of stories, flows out of hidden speakers. A jazz trumpet reaches over her throwaway brilliance, bright but slow, like the low summer sun. This song is working a hot room. It was recorded in a venue, not a studio, and I can almost hear the audience sweating.

"Who's this?" I ask, sitting on the edge of his mattress.

"Billie Holiday." he replies as he heads into the bathroom.

I roll over and curl up on my side, staring at a mural in progress, lost in the music, the slight hiss of the shower in the adjoining bathroom. I can smell Ajax in the sheets, on the pillow. This is one of those moments where nothing in particular is happening, but that I know I'll remember in perfect detail no matter how many years go by. The way the light is. The song. The spicy scent of his bed. The changing sounds of his body moving under the spray of the shower. I let everything sink in. I just am, and that's just fine.

I hear a soft sound, like a breath snatched back from the edge of a sigh. I nearly turn my head around, but Ajax stops me.

"Don't move," he whispers from somewhere behind me.

Paper rustles. The stool in front of the easel gets dragged across the floor. Then I hear the sound of sketching.

"You shouldn't draw me," I say, reluctantly turning my head to look at him and ruin the pose. He's got his sketchpad on his lap, a stump of charcoal in his left hand. Hair wet. No shirt.

"I won't draw your face. I promise," he pleads. His voice is soft, as are his eyes, as his hand hovers over the drawing like it's a living animal sitting in his lap. I can practically see the ache in his chest.

"Okay," I relent and let my head fall back down on his pillow.

I can feel his hands making me on the page. His fingers brushing me into being.

I hear the doorknob of Ajax's bedroom turning and switch back into Abigail just in time. Castor pushes into the room. Ajax and I stare at him as he takes in the unexpected scene.

Castor wavers in the doorway.

Ajax takes a deep breath. "Do you mind?"

Castor takes an insolent moment.

"Close the door behind you." Ajax demands.

Castor looks at me, concerned. Almost as if worried for my safety. But in the end, he does as Ajax asks.

I turn back into myself. "What was *that* about?" I say, keeping my voice down in case Castor's still listening. Ajax keeps his eyes on his drawing as he shades a line with the edge of his thumb.

"What it's always about. Keeping Scions a secret. Making sure there are no... accidents," he says bitterly. I wait. He scratches a few more lines onto the page, his cheeks flushing. It takes me a while to figure out why he's so embarrassed.

"Right," I say, frowning.

Our god blood is eternal, and it doesn't dilute over the generations. I've always known this, but I never really considered what the implications would be for a male Scion because, well, I've never been a male, so I didn't have to. If Ajax were to accidentally get a human girl pregnant, the baby would be a Scion, and it would be stronger than the mother from day one. Our kind could easily be exposed by something like that.

"So, what do you do if, you know... if something like that were to happen. It must happen right?" I ask.

He looks down at the drawing again. "We have two choices. Marry the mother and bring her into all this," he waves a frustrated hand, "or take the baby away from her as soon as it's born."

"You mean steal a baby? Like, right from the hospital?"

He doesn't elaborate. It's not something he's proud of. We're quiet for a while. He keeps his eyes on the drawing as he works. I wish he'd look at me.

"Is that why you pull away from me?"

He doesn't answer. I can see his pulse pounding in his throat and I feel like something terrible is about to happen.

"After you called me and told me about the incident, I thought I was going to lose my mind. The thought of you hurt, in danger..." He meets my eyes, and the look he gives me is so angry it makes my breath catch. "It's not fair. I mean, it was just the thought of it all. I mean... what's gonna happen when we have to end this?"

My voice thickens. "What do you mean, end this?"

"Daphne—" he breaks off.

"What?" I wish he'd just say it. Rip off the Band-Aid. The image of him blurs. *Oh, hell no. I am not going to cry.*

"We can't unite our Houses, so someday... it has to come to an end." He says, defeated now.

"Is this the choice Hecate gave you?"

His face goes blank. "It's our problem no matter what I decide. We can't get around this."

I know he's right. Of course he's right. In a few years my mom is going to marry me off to some guy and I'll never see Ajax again. That is if we don't start a war first. I've known all of this from the start—I've ignored all of this from the start. Willfully. Hopefully. Hearing him say we can't be together takes both my will and my hope away. I guess I can only lie to myself for as long as he lies with me.

I stand up and scramble for an exit, tears already fighting to crawl out of my eyes. He's behind me, his hand flat against the door to keep it closed. He nuzzles his face into the back of my head.

"Don't go," he whispers.

"Why?" I ask, confused. Didn't he just try to end it? "Why should I stay?"

His other arm wraps around my waist and he turns me around to face him. "There is no reason. Nothing that makes any sense. Just don't go."

His kiss is slow and heavy. He is solid under my hands. He leans into me, pressing me back against the door, and something in me uncoils. As I loosen, he tightens. The door is suddenly gone and there are sheets under me. Now it's a race. Who can touch more of the other? Who can get closer? It feels like laughing and crying at the same time.

"Wait," he gasps. He pushes himself off me and sits back on his heels. I sit up, my thighs still gripping his hips, and shove him onto his back. I slide his hands over his head like he did to me and look down on him.

"Wait for what? For you to break up with me?"

He laughs. It's a painful, grating laugh that's more like groaning. "Just slow down."

I let my head fall onto his bare chest. He shifts me to the side and tucks me under his arm, pulling the sheet up to cover me. I have no idea where my shirt went.

"Why?" I ask, looking up at him. "If it's all going to end."

He swallows hard but doesn't answer. I know I'm putting him in a terrible position. He's trying to be the responsible one and do what's best. I don't care about that anymore. I don't care about anything but this and I want this for as long as I can have it.

"A few weeks ago, you thought my House was extinct. How is us being together any different from that?" I ask, looking for some way to convince him that we can make it. If I can convince him, maybe I can convince myself.

Ajax tilts his head back to look at me. "Because this would be our choice. The uniting of our Houses would be on us."

I sit up, confused. "But isn't that exactly what your family wants? Isn't that the goal of the Hundred Cousins?"

"One House—one way or the other," he recites. I'm not familiar with the phrase, but I gather it's something the House of Thebes says often. "That's what my dad and my brother Tantalus want," Ajax says. He sits up and runs a frustrated hand through his hair. "There was a prophecy about my brother..."

"I know, my uncle told me," I reply.

"The Tyrant Rises. Now a wave swelling far from shore/Soon a world's birthing with unbreakable doors. When the spawn or'step their parents' might/An end to death will be their right. Rise up, young Heir, and undying be/A god for all eternity," he quotes in a flat voice. "My dad and Tantalus believe releasing the gods will make Scions immortal. Tantalus wants us to take the gods' places. He thinks Scions will do a better job because we were mortal once, and we have compassion. He really believes he's doing the right thing. He talks about an end to suffering, to injustice..." he trails off, shaking his head. "He's very persuasive."

My eyes search the sheets, like I'm going to find the answers there. "But didn't Hecate say it won't work?" I reply. "She said he's not the Tyrant. He can't fight the gods. He'll lose." And the world will lose with him, I finish silently.

"So, I just call up my brother and tell him a goddess told me everything he's ever believed in is wrong—and by the way, I went to see that goddess because I'm dating the Heir to the House of Atreus?" He swipes a hand down his face, torn in two. "I know he's wrong. But how do I stop him without telling my family about you?"

"Lie your ass off?" I say, incredulous.

"Tantalus is a Falsefinder," Ajax admits. "I can't lie to him, and trust me, he never stops asking questions until he's heard the whole story."

"Shit," I say. Falsefinders are unique to the House of Thebes. They can hear a lie. If Ajax says anything about Hecate, that's it. The Hundred Cousins will be at my door.

"Shit is right." He sighs. "I'm still trying to figure it out, but it's like every morning I wake up to another obstacle between us." Ajax sees the goosebumps blooming across my skin and his eyes darken with hunger. "I won't put you in danger. No matter what," he says, running the back of his fingers down my arm. He looks away and goes back to his sketchpad, picks it up and starts a new sketch. Then another. He draws parts of me—my shoulder, my leg, my hand, but never my face—until the light dies. I watch him. I'm just happy. It's weird. And it almost hurts.

When he walks me out, we have to go by the third level, which is the family room. His brothers are playing a game with their little sister that apparently consists of throwing her up into the air and seeing how many times they can get her to flip before they have to catch her. Pandora is squealing like it's the best thing that ever happened to her.

She sees Ajax and shouts for him. "Come and play with us!" she begs.

"Let me walk my friend out," he replies.

As we continue down the stairs, I hear Pandora's piping voice asking loudly, "How many girlfriends does he have?"

At the door I'm slow to cross the threshold. I want to stay. "Bye," I say sadly.

"Tomorrow?" he asks, refusing to say goodbye.

"Tomorrow," I promise.

I've crossed the street and changed back into myself to cut across the park when I hear him behind me.

"That wasn't enough," he says, breathless, as he catches me, still shirtless.

We kiss until I feel him shiver. I chaff his big shoulders and bare arms with my hands to warm him.

"You should go back inside before you freeze to death" I laugh, pushing him away.

He kisses me one last time and runs back home.

🦋

Parry. Thrust. Cross. Don't get cornered, move your feet. Push him back. Watch that overextension. Crescent moon your steps, pushing forward with your toes first. Slip inside his guard. Here comes the flurry to get you to back off. Block, block, block, and counter. Push him into the cage. That's right. Fall back, old man. I've got you.

My sword twists out my grip. *Crap.* Deuce grabs me by the throat with one hand and brings his gladiolus down with the other, stopping a millimeter from bare skin.

"Aaaand you're dead," he says. "Or you would be if weapons could kill you. But you're still without a sword and whoever you're fighting could take you hostage."

I sigh. "Grip too tight?" I hazard, scrunching up my face.

"Yup." He lets me go and backs up a step.

"I could have just electrocuted you," I say. He grunts disapprovingly.

"You'll never face a lone combatant, Daphne—you know this. You fought off four Athenians, but when the Hundred Cousins come for you, they'll come in a pack. Electrocute one, and another brother will step forward and not make the same mistake." Deuce stoops down to pick up my sword. "Don't drop it again." He pushes the hilt of my gladiolus into my palm.

I stare at it, but all I can see are their faces. Castor. Pallas. Ajax. Kill one and another brother steps forward. I shrivel up inside.

"How can you be so sure it will be the Hundred Cousins? It could be Athens or Rome," I argue.

Deuce shakes his head. "If you're ever found, it will be Paris Delos and his sons who come for you. They're starting a war, girl. Since your fight with the Athenians they've been pushing against the edges of everyone else's territories, looking for trouble. They're coming for all of us."

"Because they want immortality, or because Elara killed Perseus?" *Oops. Probably shouldn't have said that.*

Deuce rounds on me, eyes narrowed. "How did you know that?" he asks.

"What happened between them?" I ask, deflecting. He's wound up enough to fall for it. All he can see is the past, not the fact that I know more than I should.

"She couldn't stay away from him," he says quietly, looking at his hands. "She chased him and chased him. It was an obsession. Elara killed Perseus in front of Paris and then just... gave herself up. Like she'd lost. It was the strangest thing I'd ever seen."

"Paris thinks he killed her." I press gently.

"He struck a dozen killing blows. And she let him." He pauses for a moment, sifting the incredulous memory through his head. He can't understand why Elara was obsessed with Perseus to begin with. I can, though.

"If it weren't for the Cestus—" he continues, trailing off with a shrug. I nod. We both know the Cestus makes my mother and me impervious to all weapons. "She was already covered in Perseus's blood and Paris was so swept up in the Furies that he never checked to see if she was really dead or not. We decided to use it and pretend she had died."

I've heard this part of the story many times. How they tricked the other Scions. Deuce and my mother are proud of it, even though it was no victory. There were only a handful of us left at that point. Now there are only three.

"She was never the same after," he says pensively.

I look down at my sword. "Again," I say.

Deuce laughs. "School," he counters. "We'll work some more tomorrow."

I go to school. But all day I'm just waiting for the final bell so I can run to Ajax's house.

"Is Ajax home?"

Pandora scowls at me resentfully. "Who are you?" she asks, pulling her ten-gallon hat down over her eyes and rocking back on her red cowgirl boots.

"I'm Patricia," I say. I was feeling sassy when I picked this bod. Today I'm a super curvy brunette straight out of a pinup magazine.

"You can't come in," Pandora says. She tries to slam the door in my face.

Ajax comes running up behind her, shirtless, wearing a cowboy hat and a pair of jeans. His fingernails are painted yellow and he's wearing glitter lip gloss.

"Whoa, Squire," he says, catching the knob and pulling the door open. "I think it's time you went back to the O.K. Corral and rustled up some grub," he tells her sternly.

Pandora reaches for her six-shooter but changes her mind when Ajax stares her down. She stomps all the way to the kitchen.

"Hi," he says to me, his eyes gobbling up the abundance of cleavage aimed at him. "Wow."

"Thought you'd like it," I say, laughing. "Your sister doesn't, though."

"She's used to having all of my attention," he says, sweeping me inside.

"Nice hat," I say.

He takes my hand and pulls me toward the steps. I hear

acoustic guitar wafting down the stairwell. Whoever is playing is damn good.

"Let me go change," he says, pulling me upstairs with him.

When we get to the third floor, I see Castor and Pallas are sitting on the rug of the living room across from each other, both of them with guitars in their laps.

I turn to his brothers and wave with just the tips of my fingers. "Hiya, fellas."

Pallas waves back uncertainly, as Ajax drags me upstairs.

I catch Castor saying, "What the f---?" as we go, and I burst out laughing.

We get to Ajax's room, practically running, and he shuts the door behind me. I lean against it. He pulls off the hat and stands an inch away from me, eyes narrowed.

"I appreciate the extra effort," he says, gesturing to my smoking hot body, "but you know what I like."

"You're not even curious?" I tease, cocking a hip and leaning into him.

He takes a step back and shakes his head. "Anything more than a handful and you're risking a sprained thumb." I laugh and change into myself. "Much better," he whispers, and pulls me into a hug. He lets me go after only a few seconds and heads to his bathroom.

"Where are we going?" I call after him.

"I know what we're supposed to steal."

I stand there, thrown, while he comes back, wiping the glitter off his face with a hand towel.

"Did you go back to see Hecate?" I ask.

"No. Someone came to me." He looks troubled about it but continues without giving me a chance to ask. "It shouldn't be too be hard to get what she wants," he says as he pulls on a shirt.

"What is it?"

Ajax looks around on the floor for something. "A rock."

"A rock?" I repeat dubiously. "Like, jewels or a famous frieze?"

"Nope. Just a rock." He finds a pair of sneakers and puts them on. "We're supposed to meet someone in the park soon. Washington Square Park, I mean, not Central."

I change back into Patricia to leave Ajax's house, but when we cross the street, he frowns at me.

"I'd really like to hang out with you today," he says.

"Okay," I say, secretly happy he'd rather be with me than Patricia. I change back into myself as we cross the street to Washington Square Park.

At one end there's a concrete bowl that has tiered stone seats, making a small in-the-round theater. We sit down on the top level and Ajax cranes his head around, looking for someone.

"Who are we meeting?" I ask.

He looks at me, thinking where to start. "Okay, so last night right after you left two people came by—a guy and a girl. Both of them our age. The guy looks like a younger version of Daedelus Attica."

"The Heir to the House of Athens," I say automatically.

"Yeah. That guy."

"Are you sure?"

Ajax nods. "Swear this kid looked so much like him I thought it was Daedelus when I opened the door. But like I said, he's a teenager."

"And you didn't feel the Furies?"

"Nope."

"So, it couldn't be his son," I say, just to make sure.

Ajax shakes his head. "Not unless he had a kid when he was, like, eight."

I stare at the ground for a minute with my mouth hanging open. "What's his name?"

"Lucas."

I frown. "That's not a Scion name. And what about the girl?"

"Get this," he says. "Her name is Helen."

"No way."

No Scions name their daughters Helen. It would be like a Christian naming their son Lucifer.

"Anyway, they should be here soon." He turns his head and then stiffens. I look where he's looking.

Oh, they're definitely Scions. I've never seen Daedelus Attica, but if this is the teen version of him, *damn*. The boy has the black hair and the piercing blue eyes of the House of Athens. He's tall, muscled, and just gorgeous. He's holding the girl's hand. She's also tall with an athletic build, but I couldn't say what House she was from by her features or her coloring. She's got mousy light-brown hair, nondescript eyes, and regular features. Still, I can tell she's a Scion. There's something familiar about her.

"She's pretty," I grumble under my breath.

Ajax chuckles. "She's no you."

For some reason his turn of phrase sticks in my head. We stand as they approach. The girl shifts from foot to foot anxiously and doesn't know what to do with her long arms. She kind of looks like a baby giraffe, practically prancing in place, torn between wanting to catch my eye and wanting to hide.

The guy, Lucas, stands firmly and tips his chin up at Ajax in greeting. "Have you found it yet?"

Ajax shakes his head. "It's not in my house, so that means it's in one of my family's warehouses."

"Or the gallery," Lucas says in an offhand way, his eyes scanning the park.

"Why would it be in the gallery?" Ajax argues. "You said it's a rock."

"It's the Omphalos," Lucas corrects, still looking around, distracted. He seems like kind of a dick, actually. "The gallery has better security."

Then I hear what's caught his attention. He must have sharp senses. Better than mine. I wonder if they really are Scions, or something else.

"Ajax! Daphne!" a girl is yelling. *Oh no.* It's Harlow.

She comes running over to us and grabs my hands. "I'm so glad I found you! I went to your house but your stepmom—not very nice, is she?—said you weren't there, and she didn't know where you were. Then I remembered you were staying with your uncle now, but he wasn't home, so I thought you were probably with Ajax."

"Is something wrong?" I ask, worried because it seems like she's been searching for me everywhere.

"Nah. Just bored." She turns to Lucas and Helen, still chattering excitedly. "Hi, I'm Harlow! Who are you? Are you, like, related to Ajax?"

She's eyeing Lucas like she's Oliver Twist and he's a second bowl of gruel.

"I'm Helen, this is Lucas. Nice to meet you, Harlow," Helen says enthusiastically, either completely oblivious or completely not bothered by the fact that Harlow wants to wear her boyfriend like a wetsuit. *Okay*. So, Helen is a sweetie. Why do I feel like I know her?

Lucas doesn't seem too thrilled about Harlow's presence, but Helen doesn't notice what a wrench Harlow could be in our plans.

"I like your skirt," Helen says to Harlow.

"Thanks! It's vintage!" Harlow beams. "What are you guys up to?"

"We're going to Ajax's art gallery," Helen answers immediately before Lucas can stop her.

"It's not mine, it's my family's," Ajax explains, but Harlow doesn't care.

"Can I come along?"

"Sure!" Helen says. "That'd be great!"

Holy crap. Where'd they find this girl?

Lucas laughs and rubs his forehead, like inviting an innocent bystander to come along while we go case a joint for robbery is just one of the many charming things only this girl Helen would do.

"Sure. Why not?" Lucas says, throwing up his hands.

Harlow and Helen walk in front, already acting like old friends.

"What school do you go to?" Harlow asks.

"Oh, I'm not from around here. But I've been thinking of applying to NYU, though. Do you go to school with my— Daphne?" Helen asks awkwardly.

That's strange. I never told her my name, but Harlow had shouted it, so maybe that's how she knows it. Helen keeps glancing back at me and then quickly away. I think she's hoping that I'll come up and join them.

Lucas and Ajax fall into step next to each other, matching each other's strides like they've done it a million times.

"You sure she's up for this?" Ajax says quietly to Lucas, gesturing to Helen.

"Oh, yeah," Lucas replies.

"Is she a Scion?"

Lucas thinks for a minute before shaking his head. "She's her own thing. One of a kind."

"And you?"

"Sorry, I'm not allowed to tell you anything," he replies regretfully. "But nothing Helen and I are doing here is going to hurt you or your family." He glances at me, as if including me in Ajax's family. "I promise you that."

I take it back. He's not a dick. But he isn't exactly a bundle of sunshine like his girl, either. I guess he's more like me. Guarded.

"What's the Omphalos?" Ajax asks quietly.

"You know the story about Cronus swallowing his children, and how Rhea switched Zeus for a stone?"

"No way," Ajax says, surprised. "The same one?"

"Uh-huh," Lucas replies.

"There used to be a whole line of priests who were charged with anointing it with oil every day," I add.

Lucas looks across Ajax at me and smiles approvingly. He's obviously a Greek geek.

"Lucas!" Helen calls. We see her and Harlow standing at a hotdog vendor. She waves us up while Harlow is giving her order. When we get there, Helen whispers something to Lucas. He laughs with her and steals a kiss, then he steals her hotdog. The way they look at each other. If he were anymore in love with her, cupids would start falling from the sky.

"Want one?" Ajax asks me, already ordering a hotdog.

We walk and eat our dirty water dogs and wonder aloud if we're all going to get tapeworm—or more likely, different parts of the same tapeworm. A couple of times I catch Helen looking at me, but not in a creepy or covetous way like I'm used to. She seems surprised or intrigued or a combination of both. When I catch her staring, she smiles shyly, dropping her eyes.

Lucas has his arm draped over Helen's shoulders. Ajax and I share a ginseng flavored Arizona Iced Tea. I don't think I've ever felt this comfortable in my life.

Harlow sighs heavily, looking at the four of us. "Guess, I'm the fifth wheel," she whines, but in that charming way of hers that is not at all annoying.

"So? The fifth wheel is the fun one on the back of the Jeep," Helen says with a shrug.

Despite my best efforts, I really like Helen.

"This is it," Lucas calls. He pauses and looks up at the outside of the building. He notices a video camera mounted above the door. I stay well out of its range.

"How did you know this was my family's gallery?" Ajax asks.

There is one discreet sign, and no other indication that there is a gallery in this SoHo loft.

Lucas smiles at him and shakes his head. "Can't tell you."

"Oh, mystery," Harlow drawls. "Who are we stalking?" She pops her eyes meaningfully at me as she enters.

I enter alongside Ajax, so his big body conceals me. I shouldn't have worn my face here, but I can't change in front of Harlow.

"It's okay," Ajax whispers to me, as if he understands my hesitation. "That's the only one out front."

I feel through the room for all the electrical outlets, focusing on the corners and high spots. Before I'm done, I hear Helen whisper to Lucas, "No cameras in here, but lots of motion detectors."

Huh. Maybe she's not just an adorable idiot.

The Delos gallery is white-walled and brightly lit with the latest track lighting. Wide floorboards, probably from the Soho loft's original warehouse, have been sanded and lacquered to imperfect perfection. Display cases with smaller objects break up the center space of the room, and simple clean-planked wooden benches are scattered about opposite some of the larger and more ambitious works. There is an intriguing mix of both modern art—off the bat I see two Basquiats and a Schnabel—and classical Greek works of sculpture and painted pottery that are interspersed throughout.

"Ajax." A groomed man in a gray suit with a pink silk handkerchief in the front pocket comes forward to greet us. He's smiling warmly at Ajax, definitely smitten. "I didn't know you were coming in today."

"Hi, Jeremy," Ajax says to him. "Is my dad here?"

"I'm sorry, he isn't. Is there anything I can do for you?" Jeremy replies, obviously upset to have to say no to Ajax about anything.

"Just showing my friends around. They're visiting from out of town."

"Let me know if I can help you with anything," Jeremy says, rushing off to attend to a customer, an elderly gentleman.

Lucas and Helen do a quick turn around the room. "Do you see it?" Lucas asks Ajax.

Ajax shakes his head. "Let's check the storeroom."

"Can you get in there?" Helen asks.

Ajax shrugs. "Key is in the office."

"Wait—what are we doing?" Harlow asks, sensing something is off.

"Come on," I say, turning Harlow and steering her to the back of the gallery.

"Aren't we going to look at the—nope," Harlow says, pointing at a Jackson Pollock as I push her along.

"I have to pick up something in the office," Ajax says as we pass Jeremy. He touches his shoulder and gives it a light squeeze, and Jeremy practically explodes with happiness. "That's a beautiful etching," Ajax comments to the elderly gentleman as we breeze past.

"Is that him?" the gentleman asks.

"We haven't staged an opening for him yet, but he is a singular talent." Jeremy practically flounces.

I look at Ajax. No one has ever spoken about my abilities with hushed fervor. I'm proud of him.

Ajax opens the office door. He goes behind the desk and opens the lockbox mounted on the wall, I notice Helen nudging Lucas. She meets his gaze regretfully and shakes her head. He nods in reply, as if he knows he's gone too far.

"Does anyone have a disguise?" Ajax asks, glancing meaningfully at me. "There are video cameras in there."

Harlow gasps. "Are we doing something... illegal?"

"'Course not," Helen answers, like that's completely out of the question. "Just sneaky."

Lucas steps forward, holding out his hand to Ajax. "I'll go."

"You sure?" Ajax warns.

Lucas takes the keys and whispers in Helen's ear, "Take them back out front."

Helen nods. "Come on," she says, flapping her arms to herd us out. "It'll look weird if we're all here for too long, just loitering in the office for no reason."

"Maybe I should leave a tag," Ajax says, shrugging.

"No!" I say before Ajax can get any ideas. "Your dad will kill you."

He gets that look in his eyes. "You guys go," he says, urging us on.

"Ajax," I start to say, but Helen and Harlow drag me away.

"What else would he be doing here today? And why would he need to go into the office?" Helen asks.

She's right. I have to let him deface the office and probably get into a ton of trouble for there to be a reason for this unexpected visit, or his family might start asking questions. Castor is the type to dig. But how would she know that?

Not thirty seconds later Lucas joins us as we walk toward the front. He is fast. Scary fast.

"It's there," Lucas tells Helen. Her eyes widen.

"Really, really?" she asks.

He nods. "Really, really."

She breathes a sigh of relief.

"Where's Ajax?" Jeremy asks us as we stand and wait for him in the main room of the gallery.

"Jeremy, could I trouble you for some water?" Lucas asks, deflecting. I notice he looks especially pouty.

"Flat or sparkling?" Jeremy asks, horrified that someone is thirsty in his presence.

"Sparkling." Lucas asks, his blue eyes as bubbly as the water he wants.

Jeremy hustles off to the refreshment station behind the front desk to get Lucas a San Pellegrino that's chilling in a silver ice bucket.

Helen rolls her eyes at Lucas. "You kiss one guy and now you're flirting with all of them?" she remarks good-naturedly.

"What can I say, it was a good kiss," he replies.

Ajax rushes toward us, his cheeks flushed, wiping his hands on a rag. "Go, go, go." He literally pushes us out of the gallery before Jeremy is done fussing with the lemon for Lucas's glass of mineral water.

"What did you do?" Harlow shrieks at him as we run sideways to face each other across the uneven cobblestones.

"I'm so screwed," says Ajax.

"You shouldn't have done it." I say, worried.

"But it's a GREAT TAG!!!" he says, laughing. "My dad will paint over it before tomorrow," Ajax says, like it's no big deal.

He's howling up the cavern of New York and it's infectious. Ajax's laughter, his happiness. We're all breathless. We sprint toward the Prince Street station, throw our tokens down the slots, and make it onto the N/R just as the doors close.

Ajax gathers me into his arms as the train pulls out and pushes me against the door to kiss me.

The track thunders *ka-klunk ka-klunk* under us, but I swear my heart is beating louder.

Chapter 16

I know I shouldn't be surprised that I can't see Ajax today. But still.

"He a... got himself into a bit of trouble. That's all I know." Noel says, keeping the front door partially closed.

"How long do you think before he's allowed to have friends over?" I ask.

Noel shrugs. "Not sure," she says.

"Okay," I say, walking away. "Well, thank you."

"Sorry," Noel calls after me, sounding like she really means it.

I start to wander down the block, not really knowing where I want to go. I feel someone come up beside me. It's Helen.

"Hi," she says. "I know it's you, Daphne, even if you look different."

I stop. How could she know it was me? I'm wearing the young version of Hye-Su's face. *Who is this girl? What is she?*

"How did you know?" I ask her, assuming she won't give me a good answer.

"The less you know the better." She's doing that baby giraffe thing again, where she doesn't know where to put her arms. Something about her seems so familiar to me, but I can't put my finger on it.

"Did you get the Omphalos last night?" I ask, rather than continue a line of questioning I know will not get me anywhere.

She nods. "It'll be a while before they notice it's gone."

"Where's Lucas?" I ask.

"With Ajax. He had something to give him."

I look up to Ajax' window. It's open, but it's still daytime. There's no way he could have climbed up there without being seen, and Noel is the acting bouncer at the door today.

"How'd he get in?"

Helen shakes her head. "Can't tell you."

I breathe a laugh. "Of course."

While Ajax was kissing me on the train yesterday, she and Lucas must have gotten off at the next stop, so I didn't get to say goodbye. It's strange. A part of me was sad to think that I'd never see her again.

"What kind of music do you listen to?" Helen asks out of the blue.

Wasn't expecting that. "Lately, hip-hop. It's what Ajax likes. I'm trying to catch up."

"I'm asking about you."

I can't figure her out. I stare at her for a moment, wondering what she wants from me.

"Forget it," she says, looking down. "It's stupid."

I've spent my whole life being a bitch to people preemptively. I'm so sick of it.

"I like The Cure and The Pixies and Nine Inch Nails."

"Favorite place. Like, where do you go when you want to sit by yourself for a while and think?" She asks, intrigued.

I can't figure out why she's asking me all these questions. What does she want with me? "I don't know. I've always been alone, so I don't really have to go anywhere to be by myself and think," I answer.

She smiles. "Not alone anymore, are you?" She glances up at Ajax's window, which we are just passing under, and then back at me. "I get it, you know."

"What—me and Ajax?" I ask.

"All of it. What you're willing to do for him," she replies. "He really is special. Not just to you, because you love him, but because he's got a gift. And it would be a shame for everyone, the whole world, really... um... if he couldn't share it."

I stare at her because I'm wondering how old she is. When I first met her, I thought she was younger than me. Now I'm not so sure.

"I don't get you," I admit, "but you seem like a good person. Whatever it is you're doing here, I hope it works out for you."

"Thanks," she whispers.

Lucas appears out of nowhere, just calmly standing beside us. Not even a fast-moving Scion can appear out of thin air.

"We should go," Lucas says.

The front door to Ajax's house opens and Noel sticks her head out.

"Shit," Lucas looks like he's seen a ghost.

Noel waves at me to come to her. I start toward her, but Lucas and Helen stay back.

"We can't," Lucas says, moving away and shaking his head.

I hold up a finger to Noel, asking for one second, and turn to them. "Should I ask if I'm going to see you again, or are you just going to say you can't tell me?"

Helen smiles widely at me. "Bye, Daphne," she says.

"Bye," I say and then go to Noel, who is waiting impatiently.

"Who were they?" Noel asks curiously.

"Um—college kids, I think." I look back at Helen and Lucas, but they're already gone.

Noel gives me a mischievous look. "Okay, so I'm leaving, and Ajax is the only one home right now." She picks up a duffel bag and slings it over her shoulder. "If you were to just walk in as I walked out..."

I trade places with her in the doorway. "Are you sure?" I ask. "You won't get into trouble?"

"Not if you don't get caught. So don't get caught." She smiles at me and says, "Have fun," over her shoulder as she goes.

I go upstairs and knock on Ajax' door.

"I'm not hungry, Noel," he answers.

I'm nervous. Why am I so nervous?

"Not Noel," I say.

I hear a thump and then Ajax pulls open his door. He stares at me.

Sometimes when Ajax looks at me it's like he's seeing me for the first time. He really sees me as I am in the world, not as I am in relation to him. It's unique. And I think of what Helen said. About how he is important apart from how I feel about him. He is important, and not just to me or to his House.

"How'd you get in?" he asks, still surprised.

"Noel. But this is a bad idea. I should go before anyone gets home," I say, turning.

He grabs my arms, drawing me into his room and into a hug.

And it's impossible for me to keep thinking about what he could mean to the world, when he means more than the world to me.

We stay in a hug like that for a long time, but instead of kissing me he lets me go.

"How much trouble are you in?" I ask, trying not to feel hurt that he didn't kiss me.

"My dad will forget about it by tomorrow," he says, as he pulls the stool away from his easel and sits on it. "I promised him I would never tag again."

My eyes widen. "But you love it."

Ajax nods, looking down. "I told him that was my last tag. And I can't go back on that." He looks sad, but he smiles at me. "Totally worth it, by the way."

"No, Ajax," I say, feeling horrible. "You can't."

"It's done," he says, twisting left and right on his stool.

"Was it really worth it?" I ask him, wondering what Lucas gave him.

He nods but doesn't offer any more information. I guess he's still not ready to tell me.

"Anyway," I continue, "Harlow wants us to all hang out again."

"She won't tell, will she?"

"No. She's too upset because Tal is still MIA—" and then it hits me. "By the way, what do you make of Tal?"

"I keep meaning to ask you about that guy." Ajax says, like he's trying to remember something.

"But you forget, right?"

"Yeah." He scowls. "There's something not right about him."

"He can do stuff, too," I say, and tell him about how Harlow and I tried to follow him home and how he lost us.

"So, he can move as fast as a Scion," Ajax says.

"Faster than me," I reply.

Ajax grimaces ruefully. "I think Lucas would have told me if Tal was with them. No idea where he went?"

"He just disappeared. *Poof.*"

"Maybe that's a good thing."

"Maybe. I definitely want him to stay away from Harlow, but I can't tell her that." I say and flop onto my back on his bed.

"Why not?" he asks.

"Tal picked her. That's kind of a big deal when you always feel like a runner-up—which she totally isn't, by the way. She's just been made to feel that way by a series of unfortunate friends." I don't want to think about Tal anymore. Or what an unfortunate friend I am. I glare at the ceiling. "What's that?" I say, pointing up. There's scribbling up there.

Ajax' gaze follows my gesture, completely forgetting Tal. "Oh. I realized one day that I always look up when I'm trying to figure something out, so I use it to work out problems."

I squint, trying to make out the minuscule handwriting up there. "The sum of the parts is not equal to the whole?" I read.

"It's gotta be the answer to something," he replies, shrugging. *Damn, he's adorable.*

"Come here," I say, patting the sheets.

"Yeah," he replies. He grips the edges of his stool and takes a shaky breath. "I want to."

"But?" I ask.

"But everything." He wavers for another few moments, and then something changes in him.

He isn't playful when he comes toward me and sits on the bed. He's completely serious. I'm lying on my back, looking up at him. Still sitting up, he strokes my face, my hair, and then my body. He slides his hands under my clothes and touches me more boldly than he ever has before. A sound comes out of me, a sound I've never made before. His bright eyes darken.

"Kiss me," I whisper.

"I will," he whispers back, but he doesn't. "Take off your clothes." He stands, leaving me in bed. "Change into the girl you were yesterday," he says before I have a chance to be shocked. He grabs his sketchpad and regards me coolly.

"Patricia? Why?" I ask, still shaking and strangely shy now that he's turning that artist eye on me again.

"I'm going to draw her," he says, like it's obvious. "Please?" He turns his back politely.

I oblige and change into the pin-up girl before I start peeling off my clothes. "Okay," I say when I'm ready.

He regards me dispassionately. "Face away from me. No, towards the light. Look over your shoulder," he orders, distracted. More than distracted. Caught up. Seeing something I can't.

I feel him arranging the sheets around my waist, strategically covering my bare lower half.

"You want to draw Patricia topless?" I ask, giggling to let off some of the tension when his hands brush up against me.

"No, I want to draw you naked, but I'll settle for drawing Patricia topless. For now."

Out of the corner of my eye I see his hand sweeping over the sketchpad. I hear the sound of the charcoal whisking across the page. I feel proud and beautiful. It doesn't matter that he's drawing a form that technically isn't mine because Ajax draws more than the outside of a person. Somehow, he's still drawing me, no matter what I look like. That's why he's as good as he is.

No. Not good. He's one of the greats, or will be one day. I get to be a small part of that just by sitting here.

We hear some of his family come home. Feet shuffling, jackets coming off, keys being dropped. I stiffen and try to cover myself.

"Don't move," Ajax tells me. "I'm almost done."

"But—" I start to argue.

"Stay still," Ajax orders. "I'm losing the light." I notice the sun is setting. He keeps working. We hear someone come to his door and I nearly panic. Is he insane?

"Jax?" says Castor on the other side of it.

"I'm working." His tone is curt. Preoccupied. Even though I'm freaking out, I love the whole temperamental and demanding artist thing he's got going on right now, and I smile secretly. We are so close to getting caught, but he doesn't seem worried.

"Can I come in?"

"No." Ajax makes some strong strokes across the page. He isn't worried because he knows Castor won't come into his room without his permission.

After a few more moments Castor leaves. I think about Ajax' mother. How he told me she always understood him. It must have been really hard for him to lose that.

We're silent while Ajax fixes the last few strokes in a hurry, and then tosses his sketchpad aside like it no longer matters to him. He dives toward me with a dangerous glint in his eye.

"You. I want you now," he whispers. I turn back into myself, and he tackles me, but he doesn't kiss me. He pulls me close and lies on top of me with the sheet between us, just hugging me. He turns his head to the side, placing his cheek on my shoulder. I stroke his hair. It's nearly dark in his bedroom. Lights from outside begin to glow. I don't know why, but I start to feel sad.

"Can you really be any woman in the world?" he asks.

"Uh-huh," I say, threading my fingers in his curls. "Any woman, any age."

"How does it work?"

"I just get a picture in my head, and it happens." I move so I can see his face. "Magic." I waggle my eyebrows and grin.

He laughs under his breath. "This is going to be great for my art." He snuggles into me, trying to get closer. "I can have any model I need."

I don't want this afternoon to end, but it already has. Soon I'm going to have to go home to my uncle's depressing apartment. I didn't know how depressing it was until I spent some time in the Delos house. You can almost always make out the muffled sound of laughing or talking on the other side of the walls here, smell cooked food, not boxed calories molecularly spasmed to lava in a microwave, sense busy people going up and down the stairs. Even when they're fighting with each other, like now, you can feel that that's okay. It's safe to fight. People don't walk out the front door here and never come back.

Ajax pushes himself up onto his elbows above me. "Are you okay?" he whispers. The bossiness and impatience from earlier is gone. Like he sketched it out of his system or something. He's wide open to me. Because he's never had to shut himself off, I realize. I touch his tender mouth.

"Yeah," I say. I want to keep him like this forever.

"Was I too rough on you?"

I shake my head, holding his eyes. "You're perfect."

He smiles. "Are you hungry? I could sneak some food up."

I shrug because I don't know what I am anymore—hungry, full, happy, sad? I'm a little bit of everything right now.

I look out the window. It's already dark. I can climb out without being seen if I'm careful. "I should go."

He nods and rolls off me. He puts his charcoals away while I search for my shirt. We turn our backs to each other while I dress, which is ridiculous in a way, but totally makes sense in another. There's something about tidying up after being intimate that requires a little privacy, I guess. I definitely need to start putting some space between us or I'll never be able to leave.

I look at the drawing he did of Patricia. I'll never understand art, or how he makes it. How can dry charcoal appear to be lush skin? It doesn't make sense to me, but I feel it. I feel whatever he wants me to feel.

"Wow," I whisper. He's watching me in that way he does, like he's learning something about me. "Just wow."

He takes the sketchpad out of my hands and tosses it on the floor.

"Don't," I say, trying to catch it before it's damaged.

"It doesn't matter anymore," he says, taking my hands. "Here and gone. Put up a mural, someone paints over it. It's not meant to last."

"Then why do it?"

He thinks for a moment, and he looks old and young at the same time. "For the few who see it. They really see it, because they know it's not permanent," he says.

"Like we're not permanent," I whisper, putting another piece into the Ajax puzzle. "So that's why your art is so good. You don't want it to be pretty or eternal, like the gods. You want it to be alive. A little messy. And precious. Like people are." I look at him, and I really see him even if I don't have an artist's eye. "That's why your dad doesn't get you or your art. He wants you to be like the gods. You just want to be a good person."

His smile vanishes. He tilts his head down and finally kisses me, like what I've said has unlocked some door in him. This kiss is different. This kiss scares me. When he lifts his head I can see fear in his eyes, too. He hugs me, and I feel both of us shaking against the other.

He asks, "What are we going to do?" He rubs his hands up and down my spine.

I cling to his narrow hipbones, to the indents in the small of his back. "I don't know," I reply.

Up at five a.m. Train with Deuce. Shower, change, eat, and it's off to school. Only eight more hours and I'll be standing on Ajax' stoop, waiting for one of his clan to pull open the door. Just eight hours. Like sleeping, it can be over in the blink of an eye.

I get to my locker and see Flynn loitering at his. For a while there we had a system all figured out, so we didn't run into each other. I'm here first thing in the morning, and he doesn't come until second hour. And then between third and fourth hour it's my turn again, and so on. It was a silent agreement that we never discussed, but that had been working out nicely, or at least I thought so. My feet slow, but stalling isn't going to prevent an encounter. I step up to my locker and get it over with.

"Good morning, Flynn," I say pleasantly. I avoid his eyes.

He doesn't say anything. He just stares into his locker, occasionally shifting a book listlessly from the top of one pile to the top of another. His face is flushed and frozen. I hurry up and trade out my books. Just as I'm about to shut my locker and go, he speaks.

"You know he's cheating on you?" he snarls as he rounds on me.

"What are you talking about?" I'm completely bewildered.

"That kid from downtown. Ajax." Flynn says the name with loathing.

I'm not just furious to hear him say "Ajax" in that taunting tone, I'm also terrified. "How do you know his name?"

His throat works when he swallows. "He's totally using you. I've seen him with, like, three other girls this week. They go by his house and they're there for hours."

I'm so blown away by this I don't know where to start.

"Hang on. How do you know where Ajax lives? Have you been following me?" I start to mentally list all the things that Flynn could have seen over the past seven days. Sparks glide under my skin and I have to breathe to keep them from raining down out of my fingertips. I feel Harlow at my elbow.

"Daphne?" she asks uncertainly. "Are you okay?"

Flynn ignores her. I realize people are starting to stare at us. "Every day a different girl shows up at his house," Flynn continues, trying to talk over my question.

"Flynn. Have you been following me?" I ask, my voice rising dangerously. I don't care how many people gawk.

Flynn looks down, ashamed. "Him," he admits reluctantly. "I followed him from his stupid school. You know he has no friends? Probably because he screws, like, five different girls a week."

I press my fingertips into my eyelids, trying to calm down. I don't think Flynn has seen anything that would give us away, or he would have said something.

"Flynn." My voice is like ice. "You can't follow Ajax or me ever again. Do you understand?"

"He's making a fool of you," he says with enough venom to make me shy back.

"Those girls are models. He's an artist. He draws them."

"Yeah, right," Flynn scoffs. "Is that what he told you?"

"Whatever," I say. "It's none of your business. I'm none of your business."

"Come on, Daphne," Harlow says. She takes my elbow and leads me away. She's shaken. "What the hell?" she whispers under her breath.

"He's cheating on you!" Flynn screams after me. Everyone in the school hallway stops dead.

"Stop following us, Flynn!" I shout back. "I will seriously call the police if you don't quit stalking!"

I won't. I can't involve the police, or they'll start poking around my family. They'll see my strange uncle who comes after me with swords on a daily basis. They'll see my sick father who may or may not have killed a teenaged boy because he's obsessed with me.

I wasn't paying attention and the situation with Flynn got way out of control. Now I can't even tell Deuce, or it'll be Virginia all over again.

Just like that, I'm back in Virginia. A hole opens up in my head. And I can't fill it up because it's the size of a dead boy.

"Daphne. It's okay," Harlow coos repeatedly. I realize we're in the girls' bathroom and she's running cold water over my wrists.

I look into the mirror and nearly gag when I see my Face with a capital F.

"Some people just don't know how to stalk. They gotta make it creepy. It's embarrassing to us normal stalkers." Harlow's trying to joke. I love her so much. I look up at her and see a wobbly smile on her lips. "Welcome back," she says. "I thought I lost you there for a second."

She looks so scared. I hug her. "I'm right here," I say. But that's the problem, isn't it? I'm a menace.

"What the hell is wrong with Flynn?" she asks, and I can tell she knows this is deeper than infatuation. "I'm not blaming you," she clarifies. She leans back, crossing her arms so she can see me squarely. "But I've known him since the third grade. This isn't him."

I nod and bite my lower lip. "What do you think is going on?" I ask.

She narrows her eyes at me. "Okay. I've watched people stop dead when they see you walking down the street. They stare at you, and this darkness comes out of them. And then there's all that stuff with your dad putting guards on you—it's not to protect you. It's to keep you." She looks down, embarrassed. "Sometimes I ask myself why I'm working so hard to be your friend, and I know it's because at least I think I'm your best friend. At least I get to 'own' that part of you. And I hate that I think like that. That's not me! Any more than Flynn screaming in the hallway is him. There's something going on that you haven't told me."

I swallow down tears, but they're going to happen no matter how tightly I squeeze myself shut.

She's willing to tell me the not-so-great truths about herself.

That's courage. I'm a coward. I could tell her everything and she'd believe me. She'd never tell anyone, either.

But I'm crying now and here's the thing I'm left with, and it's the only thing I can say. "If you knew, really knew, someone would come after you. They'd kill you, Harlow."

Her eyes unfocus for a second, and then she takes a bracing breath and nods. "That bad, huh?"

"That bad." I wipe my tears away and get a hold of myself.

Something occurs to her. "It was better when Tal was here." She's not talking about missing him.

"You're right. It was better," I realize.

"He's like you, isn't he?"

"I don't know what he is," I say honestly. "But he did make it easier on everyone. Even if he turned you into robots."

"Better that than this. As soon as Tal went away Flynn got the crazies again. Kayla went back to bitchy. I started getting jealous of Ajax just because you're spending time with him." She gives me a half smile, realizing. "Ajax is like you, too, isn't he? And like Helen and Lucas?"

I give her a watery smile back, but I don't answer. "I shouldn't be friends with you anymore," I say. I'm such a weakling. Leaving the door open like that. She leans her forehead against mine.

"Don't make me wait outside your building with Flynn," she says, grinning. "I could teach a tiger how to stalk."

I laugh. I should be pushing her away, but I won't. I'm too selfish. I give her hug, imagining that I could somehow tuck her inside my impervious skin and keep her safe. Then we walk to class together, like best friends do.

"Is Ajax home?"

Ajax stands on the other side of the door, looking deeply confused.

"Oh. It's just, whenever I come here, someone else always seems to answer the door and I say..."

"Is Ajax home," he finishes for me as he draws me inside. Jokes are never funny if you have to explain them.

He's half-dressed and flushed. His hair is sticking up, and although messy hair is nothing new for Ajax, I can tell he just woke up. The particular mussiness of a paralyzing evening nap still hangs heavily on him.

"Why aren't you someone else?" he mumbles.

"I'm Gina today," I say, fluffing my dark curls.

He pulls me toward him and shutting the door quickly. "You really shouldn't come here as yourself, Daphne, even if my family is gone."

He's dragging me into the nearest room—the antique parlor —as he talks, holding me, kissing me, pushing off my purse and my jacket and letting everything fall to the floor. I shy away when I realize he's kissing me while I'm still disguised. That's not like him.

"Wait. What do you see right now?" I ask as he eases me back onto the nearest couch. It's viciously uncomfortable, and obviously just here for decoration.

"I see you," he murmurs, his mouth on my neck, my shoulder, and any other part of skin he can find around my clothes.

He's really out of it. I look down at my arms, just to make sure. Nope, I'm definitely not me. I push back on his shoulders and make him look at me.

"Ajax, I'm not me right now," I say.

His mouth quirks up in a confused smile. "Yes, you are," he replies. His eyes are clear and sincere. I change back into myself, and he gasps. "I... wait a sec," he pushes himself up and holds himself over me. "I swear, you looked like you," he says, disturbed now.

"It's okay," I murmur, guiding him back down on top of me. "You were half asleep."

"No," he says, stopping me and shaking his head. We sit up. "Do it again. Change into someone else." I do. He sits there, expressionless. "Go ahead."

"I just did," I say. "I'm... wearing Gina again."

He buries his face in his hands. "This is so weird." He rubs his eyes and looks at me, bemused. "You're still you. To me, anyway." He squints. "I guess I see something hovering right around you, like your edges are blurry, but that's it."

I turn back into myself.

He takes a sharp breath. "I see something in the air shift when you drop it. But still, you're always you."

"Good." I smile at him, wondering what it means. I can't hide from him or pretend to be someone else around him. That should scare me, but it doesn't. It just makes me happy. We sit beside each other, holding hands, fidgeting uncomfortably on the horrid couch, the cushions getting harder and lumpier every second. The house is completely silent. The room we're in has a single lamp on, but the rest of the house is dark.

"Where is everyone?" I ask.

"Out. I dunno."

"So, we're alone?"

"Uh-huh."

"How was that nap?" I ask.

"Interesting. I had a dream about you."

"Yeah? Tell me about it." I say, sliding closer to him.

"You were in bed with me," he whispers, then pauses for effect. "I told you that I loved you." He meets my eyes. Everything spirals down to this sphere of lamplight, this diabolical couch, and him.

"Do you?" I ask. My voice is shaking so badly it almost sounds like I'm crying.

"I do. Do you?"

"Yeah," I whisper. Then I raise my voice, wanting to say it out loud and see how it feels because I've never said it before, not to anyone. "I love you, Ajax." It feels right.

"I love you, Daphne," he replies, just as clearly. It's more than words. It's a vow.

We hear the sound of a bag being dropped heavily on the floor and we both bolt up from the couch and spin toward the entry hallway. It's too late to change my appearance. A man stands right at the edge of light and dark. I couldn't say how long he's been there watching us, but it's obvious he's heard what we just said.

For a moment, I think it's Castor, but I know it's not. He's bigger than Castor, rumpled, and travel-stained with the scruff of a beard on his chin. There's a sad, shocked look on his face, like there's a landslide happening inside of him. As I'm taking in every detail about him, he's doing the same. His sharp blue eyes rake over every inch of me.

He knows what I am. *She's a Scion*, the landslide inside of him roars. *She's a Scion from an enemy House.*

"Oh, Jax," the man says heavily. "What have you done?"

Ajax takes a step toward his eldest brother and puts his body between us, shielding me. "Don't," he warns. His voice softens. "Please, don't."

Tantalus Delos drops his head and sighs. He takes a moment to think things through. When he looks up at his youngest brother his hurt is obvious.

"Do you really think I'd harm her after hearing what you said?" he asks in a surprisingly gentle voice. He holds out his arms. "Come here," he says. Ajax goes to him, and they wrap up each other. I am forgotten, only a witness to something wonderful. Something I've never experienced, but it makes me smile.

Tantalus pulls away and puts a hand on the back of Ajax' neck. "So, you went and fell in love." he says, smiling. "I'm happy for you."

Ajax reaches back for my hand and draws me forward. "This is Daphne," he says.

Without hesitation, Tantalus gathers me to him. I stiffen for one moment, and then relax into his chest. I feel enveloped by this big man.

"Welcome, Daphne." he whispers in my ear. His warm breath makes me shiver. He stands back a little to look at Ajax on one side and me on the other, both of us loosely held in the broad circle of his arms.

Ajax and I follow him into the kitchen, but I'm glancing back at the door. Should I just run?

"What House are you?" Tantalus asks. He yanks open the fridge and pulls out a beer. He twists the top open and drinks deeply, waiting for me to respond.

I stop at the entrance to the kitchen. I try to concoct a cover story, but what's the point? May as well dive all the way in, now that I'm already wet. Besides, Ajax said he's a Falsefinder. I can't lie to him. Knowing that is distinctly unnerving, like he can see inside my head.

"I'm Daphne Atreus. Daughter of Elara. Daughter of Zeus. Heir to the House of Atreus," I say in a surprisingly commanding voice. "You're Tantalus," I add.

Tantalus nods once and his eyes get a faraway look in them. He gestures to the table. "Sit, Daughter of Zeus," he says.

I hesitate, calculating the distance between him and me and between me and the door. He cocks an eyebrow as if he knows what I'm doing. Again, that hurt look.

"I already said you were welcome here," he says. "I would never break the laws of hospitality."

Okay. That I believe. The Greeks were funny about hospitality. It was sacred to them, and everything about Tantalus screams family and honor. He would never risk both just to kill me. I perch on the edge of one of the kitchen chairs and Ajax takes the place next to me. He gathers my hand in his and squeezes my fingers under the table, his brother watching carefully.

"So, how come I don't feel Furies?" Tantalus asks with genuine curiosity.

Ajax glances at me before he begins. "We used to feel them. But they went away," he says. Tantalus leans closer, consumed, as Ajax tells him our not-so-cute-meet story, ending with how my human father nearly had him killed.

"She saved me," Ajax finishes, giving me a conspiratorial smile. "She walked right out into the middle of a lake, even though she sinks like a rock in water, and pulled me out."

Tantalus says, raising an eyebrow at me. "You can't swim?"

"No," I admit reluctantly. Inside my head, Deuce is rolling his eyes and telling me to just go ahead and tell my enemy all of my weaknesses while I'm at it.

"Well, you'll never have to worry about that around any one of us." He tells me. "A great-grandmother of ours was a water nymph. I'm telling you because I thought you would like to know some hidden detail about our skills, seeing as how I had just learned one about yours."

I frown in surprise.

"I'm not trying to outmaneuver you, Daphne," he says in that gentle voice of his. Like his father's, it's quieter than you'd think. "I'm trying to understand you." He speaks carefully as he picks the label off his beer bottle. "I've fought the Furies my whole life. I've killed because of them. Sitting here with you..." he exhales slowly and rubs his eyes. "It's a game changer." His gaze lands on me and sticks. "You're the one who fought the Athenians?" he guesses.

I nod.

"And you're the girl Jax painted on the Empire State Building," he says. This time, it's not a question.

I nod again.

"Our father hasn't seen you in person yet, has he?"

Ajax and I share a look. He's silently asking me for permission. "He's seen me, and he hasn't," I prevaricate.

"Explain," Tantalus says.

"I'd rather not," I say.

Tantalus sighs heavily. He's tired. I wonder how long he's been traveling.

"I can't help you if I don't know the details," he says simply.

"Why do you want to help me?" I ask, failing to keep the mistrust out of my voice.

"Because I love my brother," he replies.

"Well, we have one thing in common then."

Deuce is screaming in my head, but what choice do I have? Ajax and I will never make it without Tantalus's help. I don't know if I trust him, but Ajax does.

I change into Gina and back.

Tantalus curses under his breath.

"I've been coming here as other girls for a while now." I say.

Tantalus manages a grin through his shock. "So, I've heard," he says wryly. He looks at Ajax. "Castor giving you hell?"

Ajax groans. "You have no idea."

Tantalus looks at me. "Pick one girl to be while you're here. Our father doesn't approve of that kind of behavior and Ajax has enough on his plate right now as it is."

"Okay," I reply, casting my eyes downward. Ajax squeezes my hand. He never liked that his family thought he was fooling around, and I understand why now. It lessened him in his father's eyes. I look at him and whisper, "Sorry."

"It's okay," he whispers back.

"And speaking of our father, he has a tricky history with the House of Atreus, so we'll have to keep your true identity to ourselves for now. But I'll make it known that I accept Ajax's new girlfriend, and the rest of the family will too," Tantalus continues.

He's so certain. I see Ajax nod with relief. Can anyone do that? Just swoop in and make everything better?

"Why do you accept me?" I ask, still unable to believe it.

Tantalus leans back in his chair. "You belong here with us, Daphne. I can feel it." He shakes himself. "So, what's this new girl going to look like?" he asks.

I look at Ajax and we laugh. "Any requests?" I ask him.

"Up to you," he replies, shrugging a shoulder. "I can't see the illusion anymore anyway."

"What do you mean?" Tantalus asks, a worried crease between his brows. "Does it wear off?"

"No, it just started tonight," I say. Ajax and I stare at each other. "All of a sudden he sees me no matter what face I wear. He's the only who ever has."

Tantalus breaks the long silence. His voice is rough. "Choose a face and body close to the real you. Change just enough so my father won't suspect you're a Scion, or more importantly, so that you don't remind him of your mother. I gather from his reaction to Ajax' mural that you look a lot like Elara." He thinks for a moment and his voice softens. "Keep your name. Daphne's common enough not to raise suspicion."

"But it's so Greek," I protest.

Tantalus shakes his head. "Pick another name and one day Ajax will call you Daphne by mistake in front of everyone." Tantalus is deadly serious. "Because if you really love her, her name will always be on the tip of your tongue and someday it will fall off." He looks down at his empty beer, his eyes hazy with fatigue, and whispers something too softly for Ajax and I to hear. He shakes himself and looks up at us apologetically. "I need to sleep," he says. "You should probably go home for now, Daphne."

He stands up and we follow him out of the kitchen. His feet seem to drag, and I notice a weight on his shoulders that wasn't there before. Tantalus glances at me and then looks away quickly. It takes him a moment to gather the strength to get himself up the stairs.

Ajax helps me pick my jacket and purse off the floor. We stand in front of the door, shy with each other.

"I wasn't expecting that," I say.

"My brother?" Ajax asks, distracted. "I'm not surprised. He's always been there for me." Ajax falls to brooding again.

"What is it?" I ask.

Ajax shakes his head and smiles. "I don't have to choose," is all he'll say.

He reaches out and I go to him. Our kiss is broken by his smile. His happiness passes to me, and we giggle and hold each other. All I can think is that this is exactly what love is supposed to feel like.

Tal

I pace outside the Delos house, waiting for the sounds of a struggle. Tantalus arrived ahead of me, but I made it in time to see him confront them in the parlor.

He hugged them.

It must be a ruse. There is no way the leader of the Hundred Cousins would let her live, and if he attacks, I must intervene. The Face must survive to have another look-alike daughter or love itself will leave this world, as decreed by Aphrodite. I've never understood love, but one thing I do understand is that it is the one thing that seems to keep humanity from blowing the whole world to bits.

I shrink down to toy soldier-size and press myself against the window. The three go back into the kitchen to talk. Ten minutes pass. Then a few more. And then Tantalus goes upstairs (with the dragon teeth on his person) and leaves the star-crossed lovers to linger in the doorway, kissing and laughing.

The Face eventually leaves, brimming with the sweet sorrow of parting, as another son of Apollo once called it.

I have no idea what to do next.

Usually at this point the poor boy would be dead by his love's hand, or by mine in protection of The Face. Why is this generation different?

I don't want to kill the boy, but it seems I have no choice. I've already waited too long.

The time is now. I start to scale the outside of the building, but I must stop when I hear commotion inside. Lights blaze on. The sons of Paris shout greetings to each other. Feet pound downstairs.

In my small form, I cling to the wall in the darkness, waiting for the reunion to end and for the brothers to break off to their separate rooms so I can slit Ajax's throat.

But it doesn't happen. The brothers never leave each other's sides.

The four of them stay up talking until the sun rises. They discuss tightening security around the house. Tantalus tells them about the near theft of the "artifacts" he recovered from the site, and how someone was able to get into his tent without being detected. The brothers are put on high alert, and they are told to stick together. But that's something they do naturally. Then one by one they drift off to sleep—together, in the family room, sprawled on couches and pillows on the floor. Never parting.

I cannot wipe out all the sons of Paris. There would be no surer way to start the final war.

I peer in the window to see them scattered haphazardly across the couches. Their thick chests rise and fall in unison. Their huge hands lay open and slack.

I feel grinding in me. A slipped gear. A loose spoke. Heat builds.

Am I breaking?

Chapter 17

"Let's try something different tonight," Ajax suggests.

"Like what?"

I step down off the wooden box that I've been standing on for about two hours. Ajax has discovered that if he concentrates and thinks of me as a model, he can see the illusion again. But if he thinks of me as me, he sees me, and right now me is naked.

He looks away as I slip into the button-down shirt he offers. It's his. Soft and faded and huge. The tails trail down to mid-thigh in the front, but flash plenty of skin at the sides. Strange how a little bit of clothes can actually make you feel sexier than nothing at all.

Ajax stands back and looks. I know he's considering starting a sketch of me—the real me—just like this, which we agreed was off-limits. My cursed face will never be immortalized, not if I have anything to say about it. I rub the kink in my neck and make a pouty face.

"No more modeling," I plead. "I'm starting to feel like furniture." The irony of being his model is not lost on me, considering how many times I've derided the profession.

"Fine," he agrees. I take a step toward him, and he moves away. He goes to his easel and starts cleaning his brushes. "We should do something tonight."

"Like what?" I ask.

"I dunno. Go out with your friends?"

I pause, a little thrown. "Really?" I ask.

He shrugs, rubbing oil paint from his fingers with a rag. "It's Friday night. It's what people do."

I eye him, confused. "Yesterday you told me we'd catch up later when I said I was with Harlow, like you didn't want to be around her or something."

He runs a hand through his hair, smearing oil paint everywhere. "I'm sorry. I like Harlow. It's just… I kinda feel like I make you choose between spending time with your friends or me. I don't want to be that guy."

"You're not."

"Do you think I smother you?" he asks.

"What? No," I say, laughing at the absurdity of it. "Where did you even get that idea?"

He's still fiddling with his brushes, not looking at me. "Tanny," he says quietly. "I've never been… in love before. Not sure what the proper etiquette is. He said I needed to back off a bit, give you some space."

"That's crazy," I say.

I come toward him. I move to put my hair behind my ear with my pinkie—a useless gesture with my hair so short—and I let my hand flop down awkwardly. We've only been together for a week, so I don't know if this is a fight or not.

"Why are you so anxious about this?" I ask.

"I'm not good at small talk."

"Harlow can talk enough for all of us. Believe me, she doesn't need help holding a conversation," I joke. He's still anxious, though.

He dabs at his palette and pours more of his noxious turpentine and does chemist stuff with his metallic tubes of precious oil paints that I don't understand, and I watch every second of it, loving how precise he is with his tools and how deftly his hands move, even if he is using his art to shut me out. He's inscrutable and otherworldly and he's touched by the Muses and gifted in a way I'll never be. And even with me here, he's a little lonely because he is set apart. He has a greater calling and he'll always have a purpose outside of me. But the best part about loving him is knowing that I'm strong enough for that. I don't have to be the center of his world. Being a part of it is enough.

I'll protect it. I'll protect him, and his art. I will do whatever I have to do to keep Ajax exactly the way he is. Because I know I am strong enough to do whatever needs to be done.

"Alright then, a night out it is." He says.

"I'll call Harlow."

I use Ajax's phone. Harlow squeals, completely overjoyed. Ajax digs through his closet to find something that either isn't a school uniform or covered in paint. After ten minutes, we decide it's a useless gesture, and besides, I like that his clothes are always covered in paint.

We go downstairs and find his father and brothers are dressed up for a formal dinner, having drinks together in the dining area. They are hosting guests.

My neck prickles when I see who they are entertaining—my father and Rebecca.

My hand tightens around Ajax's, and he looks at me, confused.

"My father and stepmother," I whisper in his ear.

"Ajax, Daphne. Come in," Paris calls when he sees us. My father whirls around at my name. I don't look like me, but I look a lot like me. His eyes narrow in confusion. "Mitch, Rebecca," Paris says jovially, "this is my youngest son, Ajax, and his girlfriend Daphne."

"My daughter's name is Daphne," my father says stiffly.

"Really?" I reply quietly. "What a coincidence."

"We're going out to meet some friends," Ajax tells Paris, but my dad ignores him.

"Your school uniform..." my dad says, pointing to my kilt. "What school do you go to?"

I have no choice but to play along. "I think I know your daughter," I say in an offhand way, but how would I know who she is when he hasn't told me his last name? "There's another girl named Daphne in my grade," I amend quickly.

He steps closer to me. "Brown eyes, blonde hair, and you're beautiful, just like her," he mumbles. He's spooked now, like he's looking at a ghost. "It's an uncommon combination. Uncommon name, too."

My eyes dart over his shoulder to Tantalus. They beg for help. He steps forward to intercede.

"In my graduating class, there were four guys named Ryan," Tantalus says.

Castor picks up Tantalus's cue. "My year it was the Kyles," he says with a bemused look on his face. "There were two. One would have been plenty."

"How does that happen anyway?" Pallas asks, as if they'd rehearsed this. "Do moms get together and decide they're going to make an obscure name popular? Everyone I know wants to name their daughter Taylor all of a sudden."

Given so many explanations, my father has no choice but to give up his questioning. Ajax bustles me out of the house with a "You all have a great night. Really nice to meet you." I thank Tantalus with a smile. He nods once and smiles back at me.

As we jog down his front steps Ajax locks eyes with a big man, dressed all in black, standing near a town car. One of my father's goons. And not just any goon, but Nameless. Nameless' eyes widen in recognition and disbelief. Ajax turns his face away, but Nameless is already stepping forward.

"Hey," he says, trying to get Ajax to stop.

We hurry away and leave the guy shuffling his feet in indecision. He stays at his post rather than come after us, but when I glance back, I see him speaking into the wire at his wrist.

"Run," I tell Ajax. And we disappear.

A block away from Harlow's we stop at a pay phone so Ajax can call the house. He asks for Tantalus and waits for his brother to come on the line. "Tanny," he says briskly. "We have a situation with one of the bodyguards." He explains quickly, describes Nameless, and hangs up.

"What'd he say?" I ask.

"Don't worry," Ajax says. "He'll take care of it."

"He takes care of everything?" I say, cocking an eyebrow.

"That's what he does." Ajax visibly relaxes and takes my hand.

"It's nice to have brothers like that." I'd gotten used to living in a state of low-grade panic that someone would discover me, and I'd have to deal with it alone. Ajax makes one phone call and the problem's solved.

"Come on. Let's go have some fun." He says.

I grin as we go up Harlow's steps. She rips open the front door before we can knock.

We go down to her rec room and play pool. Her parents join us before they go out again for their weekly date night. Ajax and Harlow's dad talk about drafting and architecture. Ajax gets so engrossed in the conversation I have to kick his ankle to make him miss a shot, so he doesn't have a perfect game.

"I'd just like to point out that I think you might be having a good time," I tease him. He smiles.

Flynn and Kayla show up bearing alcohol, flanked by Flynn's wingmen Parkman and David and some of Kayla's friends. Kayla greets Ajax with a smile, but Flynn won't even look at him.

Two of Kayla's friends, Coco and Brenda, corner Ajax, walling me out, and Coco asks Ajax so many questions you'd think she was a game show host. Brenda just whispers in Coco's ear while she humps Ajax with her eyes.

"So, you're an artist?" Coco says to him. "What kind of art?"

"I haven't done much sculpture yet. Takes too much space, but everything else. Oil, charcoal, pen and ink, graffiti," he says with a shy smile. He's inadvertently charming, but even still. Could he try to be just a little less adorable right now?

"Do you draw nudes?" Coco asks, skipping the bread and going right for the meat.

Ajax laughs. "All the time," he replies. "I paint them, too."

Frantic whispers from Brenda. Coco asks, "Is it hard?"

I have to take a deep breath or I'm going to punch her. But Ajax handles it. He raises an eyebrow. "I could do it all day."

Both the girls make *woo* noises, like it's the most audacious thing they've ever heard.

"Does Daphne model for you?" Brenda asks, the words flying out of her. Ajax looks at me.

"I'm trying to get her to," he replies, his eyes warming.

"I'd model for you," Coco says with a note of desperation in her voice.

"Me too," Brenda says breathlessly.

Should I punch them?

"I appreciate that," Ajax replies politely, but without accepting. He notices Parkman and David circling him with mounting anger and tries to break away, but the lusty girls just won't let Ajax go. Each of them grabs a wrist and they force him to stay. I'm trying to think of how to interject when I feel someone touch my elbow.

"Drink?" Flynn asks, holding out a red cup.

"Thanks," I say. I take the cup and wave the drink around my lips, but don't sip it. *Yikes.* It smells like syrup and battery acid. "Potent," I say.

"It'll get you messed up," Flynn says, like that's something to be proud of. His face falls. "About the other day, in the hallway —" he begins.

"Don't worry about it," I say, taking a step back. He's edging closer to me and cutting me off from Ajax.

"But I am worried about it," Flynn persists. "I acted like a jerk, and I get that, but it's only because I really care about you."

Oh perfect. I wonder if he knows he's one sweaty white tank top away from being that "I really love you, that's why I hit you guy" in a TV movie.

"You don't know me, Flynn," I say as gently as I can.

"I *want* to know you," he says, eyes flashing with more passion than they should. "I just wish you'd give me a chance."

Now I'm getting angry. "Please stop."

I feel Ajax put a hand on the small of my back and relief rinses through me.

"Hey," Ajax says, his eyes flinty. "Is there a problem?"

Flynn walks away. I turn to Ajax apologetically. "I don't know what I was thinking. I shouldn't have told Harlow to invite them over."

"I thought it'd be worse," Ajax replies, smiling. He thinks better of it. "But the night's still young."

"You want to go?" I ask.

"No." He rests his hands on my hips and pulls me closer to him. My breathing stutters. "I want people to see us together. Because they're going to have to get used to it."

I slide my hands up over his shoulders and wrap my arms around his neck. He brushes his lips against mine, and I don't care where we are or who's watching because anything that isn't him is just static.

"You realize what will come of this," someone hisses in my ear. Ajax and I spring apart to find Tal standing too close. He's back—and no one seems to notice that he was gone at all. "And yet you still insist on it. Why?"

He's so close that I realize something's missing. I can't hear him breathing. I can't hear a heartbeat, either.

"What are you?" I ask Tal, trying to seem as normal as possible.

Tal starts to pace in a circle. His skin glimmers. In the lowered mood lighting, I notice it's a little too smooth, a little too reflective. Has it always been like that?

"Every Face is a temptation. Every generation, the world teeters on the brink. This is as it always has been."

"Tal?" Harlow interrupts.

He points a finger at Ajax. "You should be dead by now."

That gets everyone's attention. The party stops to focus on us.

Ajax puts himself between me and Tal and plasters on a smile. "Why don't we go outside. I think you need some fresh air."

Tal's eyes are serpent flat. "Yes." he says.

I don't know how I know this, but something in me says that if Ajax fights Tal, he'll lose.

"You'll have to go through me first," I threaten Tal.

His face twitches in a violent, alien motion that scares me.

"Walk away, Atreus." He steps back and gestures about him with a careless hand. "Or all of this human life... gone. And all for love. Sound familiar?"

"I think you should go," Harlow tells Tal shakily.

His head whips around to her, like he can't believe she said that.

"You heard her," I say. There's nothing shaky about my voice.

Tal looks between Ajax and me and another one of those violent twitches seizes up half his face. Then he leaves. But I doubt this is over.

The room is silent. Harlow stares at me, her expression frozen like a tragic mask. "Why did he call you Daphne Atreus? That's not your name."

"Harlow. Remember what I said in the bathroom?" I ask.

She nods, looking devastated. "Do I need to stay away from him?" she asks calmly.

"Please." I whisper.

Harlow nods, looking devastated. I give her a hug. I know she's giving up a lot, and she's doing it without any explanation.

"I'm sorry," I say, squeezing her tight before I have to let her go.

I latch on to Ajax's hand and lead him upstairs. I say thank you and goodbye to Harlow's parents on our way out the door.

"I'll walk you home," he says when we get outside.

"No. I'm walking *you* home," I tell him. Anxiety hums under my skin. I strike out south toward his house, shedding sparks from my hands.

He gives me a puzzled look, and then understanding dawns on him. "You don't think I stand a chance against Tal?" he asks quietly.

"I don't know *what* he is. Do *you*?" I ask. My voice skips a little as my stomach flutters. I realize I'm terrified, but not for me. I struggle to get myself under control.

Ajax is silent for a while, looking at his feet as we swift-walk downtown. "If you don't know what he is, then why are you so sure that *you* can protect me?" he asks.

"The Cestus makes me impervious to all weapons and I'm naturally impervious to heat and fire because of my lightning," I say. "You could shoot me, stab me, hit me with a flame thrower— nothing will happen to me. I'm pretty unkillable in a fight."

After another long pause, Ajax says, "That's good to know."

"I don't want you going anywhere without me or one of your brothers from now on," I tell him.

"I'm not nine, Daphne. I can look out for myself."

I'm shaking my head before he finishes. "Tal's targeted you. I think he means to keep the Houses separate."

Ajax stops and turns to me. "Then he's targeted *us*."

"He can't kill me. Killing me would defeat the whole purpose of keeping the Houses separate to begin with." We've reached his stoop. I go up the stairs and knock on the door. "We've got to tell Tantalus."

"I'll tell him," he says, frustrated. "You go home."

The chill in his eyes scares me. "Are you angry with me?" I ask, my voice shrinking.

He comes up the stairs and glares at me as he passes. "I'll see you later."

"Ajax," I say, stopping him.

"Don't," he says, shrugging me off.

Castor opens the door. I remember just in time to change my face to other-Daphne—or at least I hope it was in time. Castor does a double take when he sees me and blinks as if to clear his eyes. Then he looks between the two of us, sensing the tension. I don't hang around. When I'm around the corner, I run. This is definitely a fight, and it's horrible.

It's almost dawn when he shows up at the oak hollow in Central Park. The place where we stopped hating each other. I don't know how he knew I'd be here, but he's strange like that.

I hear a whoosh and see Ajax alight a few feet away from me. *Gods, he's beautiful.*

"I'm sorry about last night," he says.

Tears start leaking out of my eyes. *Dammit.* I had just stopped crying, too. I dash them off my cheeks and stare at him, waiting.

"I'm supposed to be the one protecting *you*."

I nod and sniff, still waiting.

"I don't like it when people assume that since I'm the youngest of my brothers, and since I'm the artist, I'm the weak one. I can't tell you how many of my cousins I've had to prove myself to." He takes a breath, lets it out slowly, and looks at me. "And it's not easy for a guy to swallow that his girlfriend could probably beat the crap out of him."

I laugh through my tears, and he takes a step toward me, smiling now with relief. "But you were right about the danger I'm in. I told Tanny. He agreed with you. He's going to have a cousin follow Tal. And I'm being safe."

"And?" I ask.

"And what?" he says, searching for a response.

"Are we over?"

He rushes forward and sits next to me. "Of course not," he says.

I look at him and swallow. I have to force myself to say it. "Should we be?"

He looks down, frowning. He's really thinking it through, and it's killing me that he's actually considering it. He looks back up at me.

"Probably?"

I stand up. I have to go somewhere else. I don't know where, but somewhere far. He grabs my arm frantically and stands up and faces me.

"You asked if we should end this, and the answer is, yes. But I'm not going to do it, so *you'll* have to. The only way I'll stay away from you is if you tell me to do so."

"I can't," I whisper.

"Good," he says.

We stare at each other.

He holds me as the sun rises.

🦋

"Don't put your weight on your front foot," Tantalus warns his little brother.

I grin at him and take Ajax down. He hits the mat with a meaty, *thunk*.

"Too late," Tantalus says, grinning back at me.

As soon as we're down on the mat in the Delos's subterranean fight cage, Ajax spills under me like water, so fluid and elegant I'm starstruck for a moment, just watching his body. He's doing something I can't understand. He's closed his eyes. His weight changes from light to heavy and then he's on top, eyes open, pressing me into the mat. His knees pry my thighs apart. His hips grind into mine. I am well and truly pinned. I'm having a hard time being upset about it, though.

Ajax taunts cheerfully. "Do you yield?"

I look at Tantalus, who's lounging on the mats outside the cage and watching us spar. "Any suggestions?" I ask.

"I got nothing," Tantalus replies, shrugging apologetically.

"You've gotten much better, Jax. See what I mean about closing your eyes?"

"Yeah," he replies. "I have a better sense of where she is and where she's going to be. Like I'm just feeling the field of gravity around her."

"It only works when you're really close in, though. You have to be right up against your opponent to feel it," says Tantalus.

Fascinating as this is, Ajax is distracted, and I haven't yielded. Time to salvage some dignity. I flip our positions and get him into an arm bar. There's nothing fluid or elegant here, just brute force. I'm stronger than he is—stronger than all of them, I think.

"Do you yield?" I ask him, pressing his elbow in exactly the wrong direction.

Ajax sucks in a breath, his face a grimace. He taps. I release him and he flops off of me, rubbing his elbow.

"Brutal," Tantalus howls appreciatively.

I mount Ajax, my face hovering above his. "Ha," I say.

"Sneaky," Ajax grumbles. He attacks my sides with his fingers and tickles me until I squeal. We roll across the mat.

"Who's the boss?" he taunts. "Are you the boss?" His tickle torture is relentless.

"No!" I scream.

"Then who is?"

"I'll electrocute you!"

"Say it!"

"You're the boss!"

"That's right," he says, and the tickling mercifully stops. We lie next to each other, exhausted and smiling. Our breathing starts to settle, but we stay on our backs, our faces turned toward each other.

"You're a bolt-thrower?" Tantalus asks quietly from outside the cage.

I sit up and look at Tantalus through the extra thick chicken wire. "Yeah," I admit.

Tantalus looks down at his hands. "Wow," he mumbles. He chuckles quietly. "Ajax?"

"What?" Ajax replies.

"*She's* the boss."

The three of us share a laugh until we hear the crackle of the intercom that links the vault-like lower levels of the house to the upstairs.

"Tanny, get up here, now." Castor says in a grim voice.

Ajax and Tantalus bolt to the elevator. I follow and as we ascend to the ground level it dawns on me. We were just supposed to be down on the lowest level looking at the ancient weapon's room, which happens to be right next to the fight cage. The other Daphne wouldn't be sparring with a Scion. I change my face and we step off the elevator and into the kitchen, hoping no one notices we're all wearing sparring gear.

It's chaos. Castor and five other big blond men crowd around the kitchen table covered in blood. Tantalus surges forward. As he does the bodies blocking my view part just enough for me to see Pallas stretched out in a puddle of blood on the kitchen table, clutching his stomach, moaning.

"What happened?" asks Tantalus.

"Athenians." Castor replies.

"Where's Ceyx?"

"On his way," Castor says as he spots me standing behind Ajax. "Get her out of here!"

I feel Ajax wrap his arm around my waist and pull me out of the kitchen. He takes me up to his room and shuts the door.

"What's happening?" I ask.

"Fucking idiots!" he yells.

"Who?" I shove my face into his, so he sees me through his anger.

"My brothers! My father!"

"Ajax. What's going on?"

"They're starting a war. Ever since your fight with the Athenians they've been purposely infringing on other Houses' territories, saying if Athens is going to blame us anyway, we might as well."

I then remember what Deuce told me when he said that the House of Thebes was coming for us all. "This is all my fault." I admit.

"No," Ajax says firmly. "It was going to happen no matter what."

I sit back and watch him. Every twenty years or so the Houses go at it until everyone has lost someone they shouldn't, and then it settles down again; but to go looking for a fight like this is different somehow. This isn't accidental run-ins or Fury-blind revenge killing. It's strangely dispassionate. It's not like a Scion war at all.

Tantalus knocks and pops his head in.

"Ceyx is here. Pallas is going to be fine."

"Who's Ceyx?" I ask quietly.

"He's a healer," Ajax mumbles before facing his brother. "You're going to keep at it, aren't you? Even though sending Pallas into Athenian territory almost got him killed."

"One House, Jax. One House, one way or another. The prophecy will be fulfilled no matter what we do."

I look back and forth between the brothers. "Ajax. You have to tell him what Hecate told us."

"I've told him," Ajax says.

"Ajax, please give us a moment." Tantalus orders his younger brother. Ajax debates it, but in the end does what Tantalus asks.

"I'm going to go check on Pallas," he says as he leaves the room.

I turn to Tantalus. "You're not the Tyrant," I say bluntly.

Tantalus locks eyes with me. He's so intense, but gentle at the same time. "Does it really matter?"

"If you're the Tyrant or not?" I ask, incredulous. "Of course, it does."

Tantalus shakes his head, smiling. "It doesn't. All that matters is whether or not you believe the prophecy is true. Do you believe the Fates are real?"

"It's not a question of belief," I reply, frustrated. "I know they're real. My face is proof enough that I'm fated."

"Then who cares if I'm the Tyrant or not?" Tantalus pins me with a look. "All that matters is that the prophecy is going to happen, and someday soon 'the children will or'step their parents' might.' The war with the gods is coming. That means they will be released from Olympus. There's only one way I know of to bring that about."

"When only one Scion House is left, the gods will be released," I repeat hollowly.

"No matter how we try to avoid that, it's going to happen."

"And you intend to be the last House standing."

For a second, he seems younger. Or maybe he just seems his

age. It strikes me that Tantalus is only in his mid to late twenties, although he always seems so much older. "The Fates are going to get what they want. All I want is to protect my family."

"So, strike first. Kill everyone who isn't you?" I ask accusingly.

"To protect Castor, Pallas, Pandora, and Ajax?" Tantalus's eyes narrow to slits. "Count on it."

"Every generation thinks they'll be the last," I scoff. "The end is always here."

Tantalus doesn't accept my derision. He shakes his head patiently. "You feel it, don't you? The war. You feel it coming." His keen eyes are urging me. I can't lie to those eyes. I can't pretend I don't know what he's talking about.

"Yes," I whisper. I think of Deuce and how hard he pushes me. And how hard he pushes me away. Like he knows he's going to lose me. "We all feel it coming."

"The prophecy was made at my birth—that's not a coincidence. It will come to pass in my lifetime. That could be years from now, or it could be tomorrow," Tantalus says. He runs a hand through his hair, messing it up. It makes him look like Ajax. "Do you think I like any of this? I don't. But I'm not going to stick my head in the sand and pretend that it isn't going to happen, either. Because it will. Even if I try to avoid it."

I nod and look down. "'You meet your fate on the road you take to escape it,'" I say, unenthusiastically quoting Oedipus Rex.

"The one thing I can do is act first. Act now. And maybe with a head start my family will be the one that makes it in the end."

I breathe a laugh, lightning crackling across my scalp, fluffing my hair. "Over my dead body?"

Tantalus looks up at me, shocked. "I could never do that to Ajax. Never."

We're silent. His intense eyes are pushing and pulling at me, asking questions I can't quite understand. I shift under the weight of his gaze, but neither of us break the silence. He stares at my face.

"Your eyes," he says. "I can't decide if they're amber or golden."

"They're brown," I say, annoyed as to why it should matter.

He smiles at me. "Do you have to do that a lot?"

"What?" I ask.

"Deflect, so men don't start inflicting poetry on you."

I laugh, and then decide to answer him honestly. "Yes."

"It must be tiring."

He isn't being facetious. We lapse into silence again. For some reason I feel like he understands me, and I never have to explain anything to him.

When Ajax comes back he looks relieved.

"How is he?" I ask.

"Eating already," Ajax replies as he takes my hand, rubbing the back of it with his thumb.

"You should go now," Tantalus tells me. "I'm supposed to be in here interrogating you to make sure you don't know anything."

I nod and the three of us go downstairs. Tantalus stops with us in front of the door.

"Can you give us a minute?" Ajax says pointedly.

Tantalus's brow furrows, but he eventually leaves us.

"The Delos monastery," Ajax mutters as his brother disappears.

"I think I've actually had less time alone with you since he got back," I say quietly. I get the feeling Tantalus is hovering just inside the kitchen entrance, listening.

"Yeah," Ajax replies, frowning. "He's worse than Castor in some ways. Always preaching purity and honorable action."

"It's ironic," I remark. "The hottest guys in the city, and they're all celibate."

"Not all of us," he says, sliding his hands down my back and pulling me against him. His kiss flutters across my lips at first, then flares and deepens. He backs me into the parlor. I know he needs me right now, but I eye the dreaded couch and shake my head.

"Oh, please, no."

Ajax buries his face in my neck and the breath of his laughter lights up my skin. "I'm going to burn that couch," he growls.

"Jax!" Tantalus calls down the hallway. "Say goodbye."

Our laughter dissolves and we give each other suffering looks.

"Tomorrow?" Ajax asks as he leads me to the front door.

"Tomorrow," I promise, dragging my feet as I go through it.

The next day is Saturday. I go by Harlow's in the morning, but she tells me she doesn't feel like getting a coffee or going shopping.

I tell her I get it. I ruined her relationship with Tal, and that I'd be mad at me too if I were her.

Then I go to the deli around the corner and buy a can of Diet Coke and a package of Twizzlers. I leave them on her doorstep, ring her doorbell a half dozen times and go before she opens it. I hear her calling down the block.

"You're not forgiven! But you left Twizzlers and Diet Coke, so maybe I'll forgive you tomorrow!" she yells.

I laugh as I run, turning the corner to head downtown.

About half a block away I can smell the spray paint fumes. There's always a whiff of them clinging to Ajax's clothes, but this is on an industrial level. He must be really caught up in something. At least, that's what I'm hoping. He didn't call me last night, though I thought he would. I went to sleep, staring at my phone.

I see all his windows are open on this crisp afternoon. Rattling, swooping bass thumps from inside his room, and on top of the bass a brassy DJ is telling all of Washington Square Park a little story about his horsey named Paul Revere. I knock and wait, nodding my head when a second DJ named Mike D, who gets respect, lets me know that my cash and my jewelry are what he expects. The door bursts open.

Tantalus stands there wearing a chef's hat, a pink and white striped apron, a lobster-shaped potholder on his right hand, and a desperate look on his face.

"I think this tops the cowboy hat," I say.

"What do you mean?" he asks blankly.

"Never mind." It would take me too long to explain.

He grabs my wrist and hauls me inside. "Get in here and please tell me you can cook."

"Wait. Why? Where's Noel?" I ask.

Tantalus shakes his head and waves an impatient hand. It's the hand with the lobster on it so I'm having a hard time keeping a straight face. "She took a personal day," he says, loading the words with tons of undercurrents.

In the kitchen, a completely healed Pallas is sitting on a stool with Pandora on his lap. The directions to a food processor are spread in front of him. Said food processor is in pieces on the counter. Something's boiling on the stove and an egg timer is beeping. Pallas looks up at me with the same desperate look Tantalus just gave me at the door.

"Please say you can cook," Pallas begs.

"I can't even boil water," I say, gesturing to the pot. "You guys already have me beat."

"Dammit," Pallas says. He tilts his head back and hollers, "Jax, get down here and suffer with the rest of us!"

"No, that bit goes in this thingy, and that other bit over there goes on top," Pandora says as she takes apart the pieces that Pallas just put together.

I shut off the egg timer. "Just order take out," I say, unable to believe they didn't think of this themselves.

"Not tonight," Pallas says. He ruffles Pandora's hair.

"It's a special night," Tantalus says. He forces a smile.

"It's my birthday!" Pandora says, grinning her jack-o-lantern grin.

"Oh," I say, shrinking for a moment before I smile at her as brightly as I can. Pandora's birthday is also their mother's death day. "Happy birthday," I say. I look up and see that Tantalus is watching me carefully.

"Ajax told you?" he asks quietly.

"Briefly," I say, looking away from both of the brothers' intense stares. I feel like I'm intruding now. "I didn't know it was today. Should I go?"

"No," Pallas says. "Ajax will want to see you. He was up all night painting and won't come down." He manages to keep Pandora tucked under one arm as he takes a bottle out of the fridge. "He won't eat, but maybe you can get him to drink some water?"

"Tell him he can have the first piece of cake if he wants it. I'll even let him blow out the candles!" Pandora adds, worry shining in her eyes. "Maybe then he'll come down. Of course, we still have to bake the cake first." She frowns, rethinking her strategy.

"I'll tell him," I say, and make my way up the stairs. I knock once, then knock more loudly while a rapper with enviable elocution insists that everyone fuck the police.

"Ajax, it's me. Daphne."

The music stops and the door swings open. Ajax is wearing a gas mask and goggles. He quickly closes the door behind him and joins me in the hallway but not before a wall of fumes hits me and makes me cough.

"Sorry," he says, pulling the stuff off his face. He stares at me, holding his breath like he's dumbfounded. My eyes sting as I look him over. He's a mess, and not just disheveled as usual. He looks pale and his eyes burn with a feverish light.

"You didn't call." I shuffle my feet nervously. "Why didn't you tell me it was today?"

He kisses me in response. He feels wild and shaky in my arms. His skin is chilled with perspiration and his chin is stubbly. We stumble back across the hallway and crash into the wall opposite Ajax's door. As much as I would usually enjoy this, I'm too worried about him to let it continue.

"Stop," I say, pushing against his shoulders. He steps back. Confused. Hurt. I pick up the water bottle I just dropped and give it to him. "Drink this."

Ajax takes a trial sip, then starts to chug it in long pulls like he just crossed a desert. He finishes the bottle and stands in front of me, gasping for air. I wonder how long it's been since he's taken a break. I put the bottle on the floor.

"Now. Why didn't you tell me?" I ask gently.

His eyes are jumping everywhere, his thoughts darting like fish behind them.

"I didn't not tell you," he says once he gets himself to focus. "Yesterday, Caz asked me what I made Pandora for her birthday." He looks at me. "I forgot. I forgot what day it was, what month. I forgot my mother. And I needed to remember." A shiver shakes him from head to toe. His windows have probably been open all night and he's just wearing a thin shirt and jeans to keep the worst of the spray paint off his skin. "Put these on," he says, picking up the goggles and mask. "I'm almost done."

As I strap the gear on, he takes off his paint-dusted shirt and ties it around his mouth and nose. He leads me into his room.

The walls are covered in a new mural. It starts to the left of the door and begins with a sequence that look like dream images. Everything is big, disjointed, and seen from below like small eyes looking up on the world. One pair of eyes looks down. Sweet, adoring eyes. They're a shade or two darker than my amber eyes. Warm and brown. I know that they are his mother's. As we wrap around the room the perspective changes, growing taller. There are beaches and fireworks and dancing and laughing and always those eyes. Pivoting around in a circle, the images progress from dreamlike to snapshot reality and the perspective grows until it is that of tall man, like him, looking down on a patch of grass. Her grave, it must be.

I don't know what to say so I just stand there, looking at the inside of Ajax's head. He shakes another spray can and attacks the last sliver of bare wall. His strokes are huge but so precise. He uses his whole body when he paints like this. There are no mistakes. No second-guesses. It's just him and the thought that is so overwhelming it takes a canvas this big to work it out.

He finishes and stands next to me. I sniffle loudly and Ajax pulls me from the room.

"The fumes," he apologizes, shutting the door and taking off my mask.

But it's not the fumes. I'm just trying not to cry. He pulls the shirt off his mouth and nose and watches me with a longing look.

"I'm not sad," he tells me. "I'm... I don't know what I am." He's like a little boy lost. "I had to paint it. I had to make it," he waves a hand in front of his forehead, "go elsewhere."

"Come here," I whisper. He does, and I hold him. His heart is tapping against my chest. He breathes out in one long gust, and I feel him sink back from the manic edge he'd been riding.

There are stories about the Muses, and what it's like to be beloved by them. I've never seen it firsthand before, though.

"I'm not sad, really," he whispers again. He lets out a long breath and I feel his body settle into mine. And I know he's going to be okay. I hold him until he's calm.

When we get downstairs, Pallas gives me a shocked look. "You got him," he says.

Ajax looks over at me, smiling another meaning into the words.

Castor comes home and joins us in the kitchen. He's sullen and withdrawn from everyone but Pandora. For her he acts like they're on their way to a carnival.

Ajax's father joins us with his aunt Jordana and Antigone. They've brought stacks of beautifully wrapped presents. I try to talk to Antigone, but she connected with Sue, not Daphne, and she only smiles at me nervously when I ask her about school. I've only met her twice, but something in her has changed. She's pulled even farther away from the world.

We make what is probably the worst dinner ever. If it doesn't get burnt, it's raw. Even the mashed potatoes end up gritty, like there's sand in them, and I don't know if I'll ever figure out how we managed that. Not that anyone cares. Oh, there are a few jokes about the meal, but the food is just the excuse for why they're really here.

When everyone has given up trying to choke down a few forkfuls of our hell hash, Paris tells a story about Tantalus trying to feed Castor a half rotten starfish that he pulled out of a tide pool when they were little. Castor and Tantalus both watch their father, enraptured, as he talks about that summer and the cottage on the beach in Nantucket. Neither of them remembers the place, but Paris does. Fondly, too, from the way he keeps smiling long after he's done talking.

The elder brothers trade a few stories about their mother, the kind that start really happy, crescendos with a big laugh from everyone, then crumbles a little around the corners when everyone gets a chance to really feel how big a hole she left in their lives. But even that seems okay. Even the disgusting food tastes good because it's just another memory in the making. Another anecdote that will begin, "Remember that time we tried to cook Pandora's birthday dinner?"

The brothers could do this all night, but Paris, Jordana, and a sickly-looking Antigone, excuse themselves right after Pandora opens their gifts. I watch Antigone try to connect with everyone else at least once as she leaves the room, and I try to think of something to say to make her feel included, but the magic words elude me.

I mumble, "See you soon," as she goes, and reach to touch her hand. But she shakes her head, like she's sorry she won't be able to make it. Like she knows for certain she won't see me again. I gnaw anxiously on my lower lip as she leaves.

Tantalus, who's sitting on my left, leans over and brushes my arm with his fingertips. "No cake," he says out of the corner of his mouth.

My eyes pop. "We gotta go get one," I whisper back. "Pandora's gotta have cake."

"Come on," Tantalus says, standing and pulling me up after him.

I look at Ajax on my right. He's practically falling asleep in his chair, and I nod at Tantalus that we should leave him here. We *blah-blah* some excuse and bolt out the front door before Pandora can suspect that the cake part isn't taken care of yet.

"You can wear your true face now," Tantalus tells me when we get a few steps away from his house. I watch him uncertainly. "Be yourself," he urges.

I smile and change into myself. He glances away.

"Is it hard?" he asks. Off my look he adds, "To keep up the illusion."

I shake my head. "Everyone wears a mask." I think about that. "Correction. Everyone wears a different mask for every single person they know." He looks at me. "That's way harder than what I do."

"It'll suck you dry," he whispers.

"Yeah," I say, arrested by his passion. I wonder how many masks Tantalus has to wear, and I wonder which one he's wearing for me.

"Here," he says, grabbing my arm and pulling me toward a street vendor. "I'm starving."

"I couldn't get myself to eat anything either," I admit, laughing. "Not brave enough." We buy two packets of roasted nuts and munch as we walk.

"So, where're we going?" I mumble around my cashews.

"Bakery up a few blocks," he mumbles back. He helps himself to a few of my cashews and reciprocates by shaking a few of his almonds into my hand. "Yours are better," he declares, and steals more of mine.

I'm grinning. I'm happy. I'm sharing nuts with Tantalus Delos. "This is so weird," I say, grimacing at him.

He chuckles softly. "Maybe not. Maybe the way we were before was the weird part, and this is the way we're supposed to be."

I'm struck. "Maybe," I say with more hope than I've ever felt before.

Maybe what the Scions have always needed was a leader. That's who he is, after all. A leader, not a Tyrant. What the hell does Hecate know? Since the moment I met Tantalus, every single thing he's done has been to better understand me, help me, and even rescue me when I needed it.

"I'm glad I've gotten to know you," I say, smiling at him. "I believe in you, you know." I laugh at myself. "Wow. That sounded really cheesy."

"It didn't," he says quietly. "It means a lot to me." Tantalus balls up both our empty wrappers and chucks them into a garbage bin. "I want you to become a part of our family."

No fanfare, no segue. He just casually suggests we unite our Houses and break an oath made thousands of years ago. I look down at my feet and the pavement scrolling under them. I've always been the Heir to Atreus. I don't even know how to start to become part of the House of Thebes.

"What does that mean, exactly?" I ask.

He stops and looks at me. "There are two ways. You can marry a Delos in the old way or bear one of us a child."

A startled laugh flies out of me and my cheeks flame. "Ajax and I are only seventeen." I'm so nervous I try to tuck my hair behind my ear with my pinkie, forgetting that it's still not long enough. "Do we have to get fully married or is going steady enough for right now?"

Tantalus makes a frustrated noise and puts his hands on his hips. "Married. Consummated. You have to share a fire, a meal, and a bed with family present to witness. The whole thing, Daphne." He pauses for effect. "And you have to do it soon."

The old way—the fire, meal, bed thing—is how ancient Greeks got married before there were things like marriage contracts.

I cross my arms over my chest and look anywhere but at him. "So, this was your plan for me?"

"Yes," he replies unapologetically.

I spin away from him and stride faster down the street, as if I could run away from it. I feel like the Fates are pushing me around, and I hate it. Every time they get their way, someone with my face suffers for it. Hecate said that this time Ajax would suffer with me.

"Daphne," he says. He grabs my arm and stops me, turning me back to face him. His eyes plead with me. "One House—one way or another." His voice drops to a whisper. "Don't make me do it."

I can't believe he said that. "Would you really try to kill me?" I ask, not even attempting to conceal how much he just hurt me.

He shakes his head. "I honestly don't think I could. Please don't make me find out."

"But we're only seventeen," I repeat in a small voice. "What about Ajax? Shouldn't he have a say in this?"

Tantalus takes a breath. "If he won't marry you, I will," he says.

At first, I tell myself I'm not hearing him right. But I know I am. I stare at him with my mouth open.

"What?" I whisper.

Tantalus scrubs his hands down his face and starts pacing in a tight circle. "You're the Heir to your House, I'm the Heir to mine. It makes sense." He stops and stares at me, breathing hard. "I know I'm older than you. But ten years isn't that big a deal when you're talking about a whole life together."

"What!?" I shout, earning looks from people passing by. I lower my voice. "As if our age difference was the main issue here."

He swallows hard. "I've never met anyone I wanted to bring into all this," he gestures around himself amorphously, as if being a Scion hung in the air, "but you're the one. You fit in my life. And... Daphne..."

"Don't say it," I interrupt harshly before he can profess his love. "I'm going to forget this conversation ever happened. You should too."

I turn away from him and push my way into the bakery. I'm standing at the counter, staring unseeingly at the cakes behind the glass. He comes and stands next to me. His body runs hot like Ajax's does, and I can feel the heat radiating off his skin.

"I love my brother," Tantalus says.

I round on him. "I know you do! And that's what's real—your love for your brother. Not what you think you feel for me." I catch a glimpse of my face reflected in the mirror behind the counter, and I remember. I remember my entire life. "None of this is your fault," I tell him. "It's mine."

He shakes his head, brimming with regret. "You haven't done anything wrong here. I'm the jerk." He starts to sigh, and it turns into a growl. "Ajax can never find out I said any of this to you." I can feel how this is tearing him apart.

I reach out and touch his wrist. "It's not you," I say. "It's my face. Just think about this for a second. You laid eyes on me and, presto, you think you're in love. Do you really think love works that way?"

He isn't sure about anything right this moment.

"It's like a spell—don't give in to it."

He narrows his eyes, staring at me. "I see your face in my sleep, you know. It's all I see anymore. It's... blinding me."

"It's The Face," I correct. "Helen of Troy's face. You've got to let it go. I love Ajax. What you're feeling for me isn't love," I tell him. Inside I'm begging. *Please. Not him too.*

He rams his fists into his pockets and lowers his head. I have to keep reminding myself that he's a Falsefinder; he can hear the truth. And he's hearing it right now.

When he looks up, he gives me a wistful smile. "I'm sorry I put you in this position."

He wraps an arm around my shoulder, pulling me in for a brotherly hug, and he even kisses the top of my head like he does with Pandora. I'm so relieved that I lean into him, wanting desperately to be his little sister in truth. He's solid and loyal, and

I can tell he's strong enough to stay that way. He breaks away first and turns to the counter, peering through the glass.

"Which one are we going to get?" he asks, forcing himself to be upbeat.

"The one with the pony on it," I answer. "She'll love it," I say decisively.

And she does. But not for long, because the cake doesn't last ten minutes. Everyone is still so hungry from not eating the inedible dinner that they attack the pony cake like vultures.

Ajax has three pieces and then starts to pull me upstairs after his brothers. He's yawning the whole way. He leads me into the family-room level, where the brothers crash out on what seem to be their usual places. Throw blankets are tossed across the room and everyone snuggles in.

"Do you guys sleep here a lot?" I ask, trying not to tremble too much when Ajax pulls me under his blanket with him. Tantalus stretches out on the couch opposite us. Pandora curls up at the foot of Tantalus's couch like a cat and shuts her eyes.

"Every time Ajax fumigates the fourth floor," Pallas answers somewhere down past my feet. "So, pretty much every night." He chucks a pillow at Ajax's face. Ajax catches it and throws it to Castor. Castor takes the pillow and puts it under his head.

Ajax spoons into my back and wraps his arm across my stomach. There's a phone on the end table. Tantalus sees me looking at it.

"You should call home," he tells me. "You don't want your family to worry."

I sit up as much as Ajax will let me to call Deuce.

"I'm staying over at a friend's house," I say when he answers. Tantalus is watching me.

"Boy or girl?" Deuce asks.

"I'll see you tomorrow," I reply, chuckling.

"Have fun, kid," Deuce says, and then hangs up.

Ajax barely gives me a chance to put the receiver back in its cradle before he pulls me under the blanket again. His lips are against my neck. I feel him sigh deeply, breathing me in. He falls asleep in minutes, but I'm wide-awake.

They switch out the lights, and after a long silence, Pallas, Castor, and Tantalus start to whisper to each other. They must have either forgotten I'm here, or they think I'm asleep.

"Have you heard from Noel?" Pallas asks.

"No," Castor answers.

"Is she okay?" Tantalus asks.

"She apparently doesn't want anything to do with me." Castor replies.

Tantalus props himself up on an elbow. "She's just confused. You can fix that."

"You have to fix it," Pallas adds. "Or we'll all starve to death."

I hear grudging laughter. Then, one by one they eventually drop off to sleep. I try to stay awake, wanting to stay in this moment for as long as I can. This is what family is supposed to feel like.

I wake to feel Ajax moving behind me. The darkness has given way to the metallic, drowned light of predawn and I look nervously at his brothers lying scattered around us. They're still sleeping deeply. Ajax pulls my hips tightly to him and presses himself against me. He runs his lips along my neck, trying his best to breathe quietly. His fingers slip under my clothes, and I arch against his hand, stifling my sounds as he touches me.

I pull away. "Your brothers," I say in my softest whisper.

"*Shhh*," he breathes back, moving from behind me to get on top.

He rocks against me, swallowing up the soft, surprised noises I'm making with his kiss. He goes slowly, trying to lessen the sound of our scuffing clothes. The quiet around us hums with our shaking. At the same moment I bite my lips together to keep from screaming out his name, I feel him tense and shudder, and then collapse. In the aftermath, both of us are trying to calm our panting. I can feel his heart pounding against mine.

"I love you," he whispers against my cheek.

"I love you too." My voice catches.

He raises his head. "Was that okay?" he asks.

"Yes," I whisper.

He rolls under me, and I lay my head on his chest. I hear his heart slow, and I know he's fallen back to sleep. On the couch across from us Tantalus turns away, and with that movement I realize he'd been much too still. I stare at his back. He's awake. He's been awake. I just don't know for how long.

I sneak downstairs a few minutes later.

I'm nearly to the door when I see something move in the parlor with the heinous couch. I startle and turn, barely stifling a scream.

I see Antigone standing by the window in her nightgown. Her head is bent so her dark hair covers her face, and her body is uncannily still. The shadows crawl in the corners behind her. I can feel others are with her and I shiver and step back.

"Only blood will join the Houses. The spilt blood of Thebes, Athens, and Rome will mix in your daughter." Antigone's head snaps up and she looks at me. Her eyes are not her own and her mouth is a perfect O of fear. "And the Tyrant will rise."

Antigone crumples to the ground. I can't move. I don't want to go to her. Don't want to touch her. I see her stir and hear her make a soft sound of pain and I force myself to help her. She's pale and shaking with exhaustion and a thin sheen of sweat covers her body.

"What did I say?" she asks me in a plaintive voice.

Only blood will join the Houses? Spilt blood? If I tell her that, she's sure to tell Tantalus. I saw the resolve in his eyes when Pallas was injured and nearly killed. Not even the death of a brother will stop him. He'll never stop. And with this new prophecy his war will become a slaughter. I'm not going to let the Fates win this one. I'm not going to let them use me to start a war. Like they did with the first Helen.

"I couldn't make it out," I lie. "You were whispering something, but I couldn't hear."

She sighs with relief. "Good." She bites her lower lip. "I have a fever, okay? I get sick a lot. Promise me you won't tell anyone you saw that. It'll be our secret."

"I promise," I say quickly. She smiles at me. She trusts me and I don't know why. Maybe she's never had a reason not to trust people.

I help her to the couch.

"You should go," she tells me as she tries and fails to find a comfortable seat.

"Let me get you back to bed," I say, but she shakes her head.

"Go. I might get sick again." She squeezes my hand. "Really. Go."

I creep out the front door, leaving her looking small and frightened in the dark.

I get back to Deuce's, still tender inside and out.

There's too much blood in our future for happiness. But you know what? I refuse to accept that this prophecy is the whole story. The Fates always tell you the end, but they leave out all the details, and the details are what make the story happy or sad. Maybe the blood of Thebes will mix with Atreus in my daughter without violence somehow.

I could have Ajax's child, and our blood would be mixed then, wouldn't it? I am going to have a daughter someday. I have to. It's been foretold. Why not his? I blush and glow at the thought.

I miss him already. I started missing him before I crept out his front door. Am I grasping at straws? These excuses I'm conjuring in my head suddenly feel hollow. Hollowness is supposed to feel light, but this gouged-out feeling is so heavy I can barely lift my arms to turn the key in the deadbolt on Deuce's apartment door. It's like my arms knew what was waiting for me inside.

"You'd better have said your goodbyes," says my mother.

My mother. Sitting at Deuce's woefully small Formica table. I walk to her, not completely certain my legs are going to make it, and sit down before I do something stupid, childish, or most likely both.

"You're back," I say stupidly, childishly.

My mother raises a disdainful eyebrow as if to say "obviously." She looks me over. "You're in love." It isn't a question. I don't respond, but she can see right through me. She sighs. "Well, that's unfortunate. Is that where you spent the night?"

"Yes," I say dully. "But not like that. We're not..."

"Having sex? Then I'm *really* sorry for you," she says, eyes and voice dropping. I think she might actually mean that.

She takes a sip from a chipped mug that says, "I Hate Mondays." Deuce's favorite, although technically inaccurate. Deuce hates every day equally, and he's told me as much many times. She takes another sip, her throat working. I don't know what's in there, but it isn't cocoa. Even though it's seven a.m. on a Sunday.

"Why did you come back?" I'm asking, but I already know.

Deuce told me what she was planning, and if there's one thing I know about my mother it's that she never misses an opportunity to hurt me. She gives me that raised eyebrow again. This time it's telling me that I shouldn't need to ask.

"Arrangements have been made," she says.

She's going to have to say it to my face. "What kind of arrangements?" I ask.

She looks me in the eye. Our identical amber eyes—mine blank, hers hard. "Pack your things, Daphne. You're getting married."

CHAPTER 18

I know I argued with her. I remember yelling.

I used words like antiquated and absurd. She responded in kind, yelling back that I was the one who was absurd. Did I really think that I would be allowed to choose? Did I think I was the special one to escape the fate she'd suffered, that her mother had suffered, and on and on back to when Helen of Troy was given to Menelaus?

"You've known your whole life that we don't get to choose who owns us, but someone always does," she'd said. "You are property. You are just going to have to accept it."

"I won't," I say, shaking my head. *May as well stamp my foot and pout while I'm at it.*

Elara sighs. "Am I going to have to find this boy you're in love with and kill him? Is that what you want?" She waits, watching me freeze solid. "I've made a very advantageous match for the House of Atreus. He's cute too, in a reedy sort of way." She pauses to inspect her manicure. "Marry who I tell you to marry, or your lover boy dies. It's up to you."

How she hates me. It's a stunningly perfect emotion, unclouded by pity or objectivity. It is as fully and completely formed as another living being, like a sibling I had my whole life without knowing it. I am the daughter Elara owed the Goddess of Love, and my twin is Hate.

I shut my mouth. I have already been pushed off the cliff and there's no arguing with gravity.

She looks surprised when I just stop talking. Stop fighting. Then she tells me to go to my room and pack my things. And I do because I am leaving tonight. I just don't know exactly where I'm going yet.

Hours pass. I sit on the thin mattress of my bed, staring at my bag. Is it pathetic that everything I value fits in a backpack? I'm looking at the phone my uncle Deuce put in my room for me. I'm trying to picture what I should say to Ajax, but every time I try to shape the words in my mind, they dribble away.

I look up at the ceiling. Maybe the answers are up there. They aren't because Ajax has never been in my bedroom.

What's worse, I can't say to my mother, "If you marry me to this mortal you've picked, Tantalus Delos will murder us all." Because my mother has no idea that the Delos family knows we exist, and if she did know, she'd kill all of them. Including Ajax.

I can't tell if this is irony, or just a mess. A mess I made.

My phone's been ringing all day. I haven't picked up because I know it's Ajax and I can't talk to him until I'm sure about what I'm going to say.

I won't force him to marry me. I can't even believe I'm thinking about marriage to begin with, let alone thinking about saying to him, "Marry me or your brother's going to kill me and Deuce. Oh, and my mom, but whatever about her." That way I'd never know. Did he marry me because he loved me, or because he had to?

And if Ajax won't marry me willingly, happily, and without reservations then I won't marry anybody—I'm certainly not going to marry the mortal my mother picked for me. So, I'll have to run.

Tantalus said that he didn't know if he could go through with killing me, but I know better. He's willing to let everyone in his family fight and die. Pallas almost died already, and the war hasn't even started yet.

He'll feel tortured about it, but in the end, Tantalus won't let me live if I don't unite our Houses, either by marrying him or Ajax; and if Ajax won't, I don't think I could marry Tantalus, not even to save my life.

Just to test it, I try to imagine what it would be like to let Tantalus kiss me. Touch me. Take me to bed. I picture his face—so close to Ajax's—above mine, and I shiver at the wrongness of it. I couldn't do it.

Mostly, I couldn't wake up the next morning and see Ajax across the breakfast table. I couldn't sit there every subsequent morning, watching him bring other girls home until he found that special someone that I wasn't and married her. I know what a day is worth. I know that every day for next sixty years or so will be the sum total of my life, and it isn't worth that. I'd honestly rather die.

There's a knock at the door. I don't say anything.

"Daphne?" Deuce says. "Can I come in?"

"Sure," I answer.

He cracks open the door and stares at me for a while. He looks like a spooked horse. Finally, he comes in and sits down next to me. Deuce perches on the edge of the mattress a foot away from me. He has to lean to put an arm around me. It's not comfortable, but it is comforting in an awkward way, and it's the best he can do. I used to fault him for that, but I don't anymore. He's been as good to me as he knows how.

In a flash of weakness, I consider telling him about the deal I've made with the House of Thebes. How they'll kill us if I let Elara marry me off to a human. Deuce would die for me, even though I was so unforgivably stupid. Even though I told Tantalus things about our House. Gave away our secrets. Let him know exactly how to wipe us out.

Yes, Deuce would die for me. But he'd never let me join the House of Thebes. He'd never let me threaten the pact with the gods. He'd try to kill every last one of the Delos brothers before he'd let that happen. Deuce is not on my side. No one's on my side—not anymore. Because I'm a traitor, and traitors don't have allies.

So, this is how Helen of Troy felt.

"Your mother's upstairs talking to your father. Sorting things out with him," he says. I quash a smile and try to figure out how I can get Deuce out of the way too. "Your father's the main reason she's set up this marriage, you know, but we talked about this," he continues. "You're seventeen now, and that's a big year for you. It's the year Helen of Troy—well, you've hit that age where things need to be settled for you so the men around you don't start fighting. It'll help your father most of all. It's how it's been done since the start. You knew this would eventually happen."

I turn my face to his. "You didn't tell me it was happening now."

He has the decency to look ashamed. "I had to tell her about your father. You weren't safe with him anymore. I tried to tell her that we'd sorted it out. You were going to stay with me and there was no sense marrying you off just yet, but next time we spoke she already knew you had a fella too, and that made her quite angry. She didn't get to choose." He looks tired. "She'd started vetting husbands for you. I should've told you then, but I didn't want to spoil what time you had left with him." He takes a deep breath. "You looked so happy."

I put my hand over his because I know this isn't his fault. And he did give me precious time with Ajax. Might be the only time I get with him.

"How did she know I was seeing someone?"

Deuce shrugs. "She's your mother," he says, like that explains it, but it doesn't.

"Looks like everyone wants me to get married," I mumble, struck by the irony of it.

"I don't," Deuce says.

I act like I don't believe him, but I do. I have to push him away. "Am I allowed to pick my own maid of honor at least?" I ask.

He frowns. "That girl from school? The one you go shopping with?"

I laugh, realizing something. "You don't even know her name, do you?"

He can't look at me. "Ask your mother."

"I'm not asking for this. I'm taking it." I stand up. Deuce opens his mouth to argue, but I stop him. "I deserve to have one person at my wedding who actually cares about me."

That hurt him like I knew it would. Deuce is the only one who ever cared about me before Ajax, even if it was a crooked, broken kind of caring. He's my last bridge, the only bridge I have to burn to get away.

I leave my stuff behind because taking it would look too suspicious. Doesn't matter. I'll get different stuff. I walk out, knowing this is my only chance.

"Daphne?" Deuce says. And I know he knows what I'm doing. Funny how we can know each other so well without ever being close. Am I going to have to fight him to get away? Could I do that?

My hand tightens on the doorknob. The too-dim lights buzz. The naked walls contract. This isn't a home. The empty space that should be filled up with stories and throw blankets and pony cake presses down around us. Presses us apart.

"What?"

"I was hoping it would be different for you. I always wanted you to be happy," he says.

I turn and look at him.

"So go." He clears his throat. Biologically, clearing the throat stops you from crying. I hate that I know that now more than ever, because it means Deuce is about to do something I've never seen him do. "Run," he says.

And I do.

I'm crying when I get to Ajax's house.

He pulls the door open, and I fall against him. "What is it? What happened?" he asks with concern in his eyes.

"Is anyone home?" I ask, glancing around.

"My dad's in his office," Ajax says, keeping his voice down. "Caz and Pallas are in Rhode Island. Tantalus is at a meeting." By the way he says that last part, tight-lipped and disapproving, I know he means with the Hundred Cousins, and I wonder fleetingly what it is they're doing. "We can talk in my room."

His room still smells like paint, but the fumes have dispersed enough to be tolerable. It's freezing, though. All the windows are open and now that the sun has set it's getting cold out. He sees me shiver and pulls me close.

"Tell me what happened," he whispers, putting his chin on the top of my head. I want to stay like this, wrapped up in him, but I can't. When I'm calm, I pull away.

"Sit down," I tell him. His eyes widen with trepidation. He sits down on his stool, every muscle taut. I pace, thinking about what to tell him and what to keep hidden.

"You're freaking me out," he says.

I stop and look at him. "I'll just say it, then." I take a breath and give him the part of the truth that matters right now. "My mother came back. She's arranged for me to be married."

"What?" Ajax says, the word gusting out of him.

"In my House, the Heir is married at seventeen. Her husband is always chosen for her by her parents. To protect other people."

"From what?" He looks horrified.

I look away. "Themselves, mostly. People like my father who feel something inappropriate toward me and can't control it." I almost say and people like your brother, but I can't bring myself to tell him anything about Tantalus. "If I'm married, it makes it easier on them. If I don't marry the fighting will start."

"Let them fight." Ajax stands up urgently. "Tell her you won't do it," he says. "Tell her you're seeing someone."

"She knows. She doesn't care. She doesn't want me to be happy. She wants me to suffer as much as she did. Like that's going to make what she went through worth it or something because it's just the way things are. And if I don't marry the guy she's picked for me, she told me she's going to come find you and kill you."

"She can try," he replies.

My face falls. He's not getting it. "She can be anyone at any time. She can be me. She can be Pandora. She can be your mother, miraculously returned from the grave. Any female you ever meet for the rest of your life could be her."

Now he gets it. He goes to his phone and starts dialing. "There won't be any reason for her to kill me if it's too late."

"Who are you calling?" I ask, confused.

"Tanny." He talks into the receiver. "Daphne is here. She said yes. We need a witness." He smiles gently, his eyes drifting away. "I will."

He hangs up and looks up at me, realizing something. "Oh shit," he says. He takes my hand and gets down on one knee. His voice shakes a little when he asks, "Will you marry me?"

I almost scream yes, but I manage to control myself. I slip my hand out of his and step back. "You haven't really thought this through."

He bounds up and comes toward me, smiling. "I don't need to think it through." He catches my arms and leans down to kiss me. I stop him.

"Are you just doing this so Elara doesn't come after you?"

"She could still try to kill me," he replies. "But if we're married and our Houses are joined it'll be too late. The less incentive I give her the better."

I narrow my eyes at him.

"Look, I don't want to die," he admits. "I don't want to join our Houses, either, but if I had to choose between that and thinking about you with another man?" He shakes his head, like he can't deal with it. "And to be completely honest, my brother and I have been talking about this since the night he came back. He told me then that I had to marry you. So, yeah. I've thought about it. I've been thinking about it nonstop."

I almost tell him about the prophecy Antigone made this morning when I was leaving his house. Simply getting married isn't going to join our Houses. Only bloodshed will. But if I tell him, will he tell his brother?

I don't think he would—not on purpose—but Tantalus is a Falsefinder. The only way to lie to him is to not know the truth. And it isn't like not knowing is going to harm Ajax in any way that I can see. I don't have to tell him.

I can do this. I'm going to make this work because I can't just lie down and accept a bloody end. The Fates, Hecate, even the damn dryads who moaned about me being nothing more than a bringer of blood and more blood are trying to maneuver me. They're trying to make me the bad guy, but I'm not going to let them. I'm going find a happy ending for us somehow. All of us.

If the Houses must be joined in blood, then let it be with love. Antigone says only blood will do it, and marriage isn't enough? Fine. I'm going to have Ajax's baby as soon as possible, and I'll figure out how to get the blood of the other two Houses into her later if that's what it takes to stop Tantalus and his war. Maybe my daughter will come to love someone like her, someone with the blood of the other two Houses in him and they'll have their own daughter together. That would be perfect. I could make that happen. Better than everyone dying.

Fate is unavoidable, I know that. But the ending never tells you the whole story. I'm going to make this story about love and not death.

I look up at him. I realize I've been quiet for too long. I'm going to have to get faster at deciding what Ajax knows and doesn't know if I'm going to have Tantalus for a brother-in-law.

"Ajax, I want you more than anything," I say seriously as I step closer to him. "I just need you to be sure."

"I am." He gives me a tentative smile. "So, is that a yes-yes?"

"That's a yes-yes."

He wraps his arms around me, and I can finally relax enough to let it hit me. I pull away so I can see him.

"We're getting married," I say. It's too good to be true. But I'm going to make it true somehow.

"As soon as my brother gets here to witness." He runs his thumb along my lower lip. "What do you want for our wedding meal?"

I laugh and tip my head back, thinking. What's the happiest food in the world? "S'mores."

He hugs me, burying his face in that place in my neck he loves so much. "We can roast them over the fire."

"Two birds."

"That'll definitely get us to bed quicker."

Our laughter dies and my stomach flips. I can feel his body heating up and I see his eyelids grow heavy.

"Ajax, do you really want this?"

"Oh yeah," he says, his voice low and rocky. "More than anything."

Our kisses used to scare me, but I'm not afraid anymore. Right now, I'm not afraid of anything.

Waiting for Tantalus to get here turns out to be a huge problem.

My mouth aches from kissing Ajax. He lies on top of me, trying to press closer, and he's so heavy I can barely breathe. My shirt and bra are gone, and my hand wants to slip under the waistband of his jeans. At first, I'm shy to touch him there, but then I think he's going to be my husband in an hour or so. So, I do.

"Waitwaitwaitwait," he says, sitting back onto his heels. He's shaking but even in this freezing room his skin is burning. "We've got to wait for my brother."

"Right," I say, panting. I prop myself up on my elbows. He looks at me like he's drowning and climbs back on top of me. I giggle. "Going backward, here," I remind him.

"Do something really unsexy," he says, and lowers his head to my chest. I start to say okay, but it turns into a purring sound when he kisses me there. "That was the opposite of what I just said," he mumbles around a mouthful of my skin, which tickles like crazy. I push him off me.

"Okay. This is unsexy." I tilt his chin up so he looks me in the eye. "What are we going to do about your father?" I ask. "He hates my family. He might actually try to murder my mother. Again. What's he going to think about you and me?"

Ajax rolls one of his big, bare shoulders. "When it's done, he won't be able to undo it," he replies quietly. "And it's not like he can be more disappointed in me than he already is."

"You don't mean that. He loves you."

"I know he loves me. I also know I disappoint him." He's not being self-pitying. He's telling the truth.

"Why?" I ask, unable to understand how anyone could be disappointed in Ajax. "You're perfect."

He smiles and looks down. "Because I'm the strongest and the fastest, I'm the only flier in decades, and I'm actually better at combat than anyone else in my family." He looks up at my baffled face. "And I hate it. I love to train, but a real fight is different. Killing is different. I won't kill Scions to satisfy my father's ambitions and he thinks that means I'm a coward. That I don't love my family." He breathes a bitter laugh. "Maybe I am a coward. I'm still not going to kill for him."

"You're not a coward. And killing isn't bravery." I swallow and blink, trying to push Virginia back down into the hole in my head. Ajax cranes his neck to catch my eye.

"Are you okay?" he asks.

I nod. Then I shake my head when I think better of it. If we're really going to be together, he has to know.

"Ajax, there's something I need to tell you." I take a moment to reconsider what I'm about to tell him. But it's too late now. If we are to marry, he needs to know. "I've killed someone," I whisper. "A human boy in Virginia. He was obsessed with me. He used to follow me around and corner me... try to touch me. He was sixteen. I was only twelve. He stalked me, peeking through my windows at night. He somehow found out what I am and followed me inside the girls' bathroom at school. I tried to get him to stop. But he forced himself upon me. Tried to rape me. I had no choice. I killed him."

I look up at Ajax, expecting him to hate me. But he touches my cheek instead.

"How did you do it?" he asks.

"I broke his neck. Made it look like he slipped," I whisper. "I didn't want him to suffer, I just wanted it over with." My voice breaks. "But it's still not over. Sometimes I feel like it'll never be over."

He sees me shiver and he lies down and pulls me on top of him. He drapes his arms around me for warmth and stares up at the ceiling.

"He deserved it."

I feel him grinding his teeth so I reach up and smooth my hand across his jaw. "I've never spoken about it," I say, feeling a sense of relief I've never felt before.

"I'd have killed him much more slowly," Ajax snarls, but with lessening anger. He squeezes me. "That's always going to be a problem, isn't it? Men will always chase you?" I nod. "Good thing I'm not the jealous type."

We both laugh, and just like that, the hole in me is filled.

"How do you do that?" I ask suspiciously.

He tilts his head to look at me. "Do what?"

"Make everything better. Make everything beautiful."

"It's what you do when you love someone."

And then he's kissing me.

Tantalus had better get here soon.

Tal

I come up from underground for the first time in days and blink my eyes at the brightness of it all. It's night, but still my eyes shy away from the garish city lights.

Hiding from Tantalus's foot soldiers with the Hecatonchires was less than comfortable. I've never been fond of flesh, and the half rotten hands and heads that are all that's left of the Hundred Handers make for strange bedfellows. But Hecate, their half-sister and commander, wants my actions watched. She has lost faith in me. Even now, she sends a hand along to trail me. Her audacity is astounding. She has no authority over me, but I have no way to stop her. Hecate has the power to open Tartarus and put me in it, forever separating me from my one purpose.

I must not be swayed by the brotherhood that so starkly reminds me that I am the last of my race. That I am alone.

My eye spasms shut, and my lip pulls up in a leer. Gears grind. Small tendrils of smoke rise from a seam in my side. It's getting worse.

I check the lump of metal at my heel. The cauterized veins, one of ichor and one of blood, are still tightly sealed shut. Medea patched me up perfectly. I can't think why so many of my cogs are set against each other. Why one spins as it should while another skips and halts and wants to turn the other way.

I must rid myself of this malfunction. I must end this Cycle so I may rest before the next Cycle begins in another twenty years or so. I'm left with no other option but to reveal myself to the one person who can stop this.

I knock and wait.

She pulls open the door and stares at me, stuck inside her head as her senses go to war with her logic.

"It's me, Elara," I admit. "Tal." She still doesn't move. "Talus, actually, although I never told you that." Still nothing. "May I come in?"

Her eyes fade into a memory, and I wonder if she's seeing our old high school. How buddy-buddy we got. How I goaded her into that meeting, which turned into that fight, which turned out to be the end of Perseus.

"I'll just get to the point, then. Your daughter is about to marry a Delos. Ajax Delos, nephew to your Perseus, as fate and irony would have it. You need to stop her."

"What are you?" she whispers.

"I'm the last of the race of bronze men."

"How long have you been interfering in our lives?"

"Since the start."

"Why?" she asks, and she seems so much younger suddenly. She is the girl I knew decades ago.

"To keep the Houses separate, and the gods imprisoned. To protect my island," I say.

She takes an uneven breath. "Then we work toward the same goal," she says concisely. "But afterward? I'm going to kill you."

🦋

I hear Ajax's phone ringing on the floor next to our heads.

"Ajax," I mumble around his lips.

"*Hmm,*" he says, still intent on kissing me.

"Phone," I say, giggling and pushing against his chest, but he only doubles his pursuit. I flip him over onto his back, straddle him, and pick up his phone, but the caller has already hung up.

Ajax's mood changes abruptly. I see him narrow his eyes and motion with his head like he's listening to something.

"What is it?" I ask.

"I felt—" he breaks off and shakes his head. "It felt like the Furies."

I hear Ajax's bedroom door boom and splinter. We both spring up onto our knees as the door sails through the air and comes apart when it hits the opposite wall.

Elara strides into the room, her body crackling with lightning.

"Mother," I gasp. I'm utterly frozen as she steps forward and grabs me by the hair. It's too short for her to get much purchase, and I slip free and throw myself between her and Ajax.

She slaps me across the face, knocking me halfway off the bed. "Get dressed," she snarls.

I hear Ajax make an animal sound. "Don't touch her," he growls.

Neon blue light from my mother's bolts surrounds her hands like a halo. "Move and you're dead, boy," she tells him. "You can hear that through the wailing of Furies, can't you?" she taunts.

"Furies?" I ask, confused. I sit up, rubbing my jaw.

"I feel them," Ajax says, his voice louder than it needs to be.

Elara looks at me and her teeth grind together. She hears them too. "Daphne. Get dressed quick, or watch him burn."

"Don't hurt him," I say, whispering it like a prayer as I dig through the sheets. "Please don't hurt him."

I pull my shirt over my head, and she grabs me by the neck and pushes me in front of her. She throws me down the stairs. I pick myself up and try to turn and face her, but she shoves me again so I can't get my numb feet under me.

"This has to be a mistake. Please listen to me, Mother," I beg.

"Hurry!" she snarls at me.

I'm facing up a staircase and tripping my way down it backward. I see Ajax following behind us. My mother keeps a crackling hand held up toward him, and he maintains his distance while searching for an angle. She's gritting her teeth with the effort to stay in control of her bloodlust. On the landing behind me, I hear a familiar voice that is completely out of context.

"Control yourself, Elara, there's no time for a fight! Tantalus is nearly here," Tal says. I whirl around to face him. He glitters faintly in the light and his face twitches horribly.

My mouth hangs open for a moment before my mother shoves me down the next flight of stairs. She looks over me.

"Clear?" my mother calls out to someone on the ground floor.

"Clear," Deuce answers. I see Deuce at the bottom of the stairs, wielding the Aegis. Paris cowers in front of him, his sword tossed to the ground.

"Dad!" Ajax yells. He soars over us to get to his father. I hear my mother gasp when she sees Ajax take flight.

Deuce loses what little control he had been exerting over the Furies and he moves to strike Ajax and Paris.

"Deuce, no!" I scream, pitching myself forward and grabbing his shield arm.

The front door bursts open. Tantalus and three blond and burly Cousins pile inside. Deuce throws me to Elara and Tal, and together they wrestle me into a chokehold.

"Get her out of here!" Deuce yells, and then he charges the sons of Thebes, Aegis first.

The Cousins run from the magical shield that strikes utter panic into anyone who looks at it. Tantalus is the only one who stays. He stands firm, eyes shut, but Deuce easily plows him down and knocks him unconscious with the Aegis. He's about to cut Tantalus in half with his gladiolus when Ajax tackles him from behind.

They roll, and Ajax gets to his feet first. He barely manages to step out of the way as Deuce makes a sweeping cut with his blade, and he stumbles over his father's prone body. Given a new target, Deuce is about to chop off Paris's head. Ajax snatches up his father's sword and blocks Deuce's killing blow. Deuce brings the Aegis around to throw the full brunt of its panic-inducing power at Ajax and Paris.

Ajax closes his eyes. Deuce smiles and goes in for the kill.

A "No!" fumbles its way out of my mouth. It's a weak and useless syllable that has no hope of being heeded. I watch as Ajax deftly parries with his eyes still closed. He's moving with that flowing grace that tells me he is feeling his opponent's gravity.

He brings his sword around and sinks his father's blade into Deuce's chest all the way up to the hilt.

Ajax opens his eyes. He looks first at Deuce, dying an inch away. Then he looks at me. For one brief second the Furies haven't found me yet. I see his eyes, as wide as the ocean. The only eyes that have ever seen past my face and into heart. And then the Furies reawaken our blood debt.

It was paid when I saved his life, but now by killing someone of my blood, Ajax has put us back in the red. There's just one second when he and I can look at each other without hate. Then, as Deuce dies, the Furies take me.

I'm screaming. Tearing at Elara and Tal to get to Ajax. To kill him.

"Elara," Paris says, and there's more than hate in him when he says that name. There's longing.

Finally left with a clear shot, my mother fires a bolt at them, leaving Ajax and Paris senseless on the floor. She hauls me over Tantalus as he struggles to get up and hurls us both out the front door. I don't know what I'm shrieking anymore, but I scream so hard I taste blood in the back of my throat.

Tantalus has dragged himself to the top of the stoop. "Daphne," he calls weakly. Blood gushes down his face. He reaches toward me with one hand and almost tumbles down the steps.

My mother spins me around. "You'll thank me later," she says. She hits me so hard I see stars. Then nothing at all.

CHAPTER 19

I come around to the smell of earth and leaves. I open my eyes and see the night sky peeking out from behind a canopy of trees. The treetops move, but I feel no wind.

I know where I am before I sit up. I know a lot of things before I'm ready to rise and face them. The first thing I know is how perfectly the term "broken heart" describes what it feels like. Like the shards of something once precious were left to rattle around inside of me. I don't want to move for fear of sharp edges.

"You're awake," Elara says. "Don't just lie there. It'll only get worse unless you get going."

I sit up, after a fashion. My body curls forward, my shoulders hunched like I've been mule-kicked in the chest. I pull my knees up to keep myself braced and look around the dryad's hollow. I hear voices outside the hollow calling my name. The dryads sit cross-legged on the ground in front of their trees. They are silent. Elara and I sit across from each other on the ground.

"Drink this," she tells me. She hands me a wooden bowl with

some murky liquid in it. I swallow without tasting anything. Without caring, really.

"Tal made it. He's got the old magic—witch's magic—from Medea of all people. He told me it'll keep you calm while Ajax and his brothers are still looking for us. I wasn't fast enough to get out of Manhattan with you over my shoulder, so we're stuck here for a bit," she tells me. I ignore her but she continues anyway. "You will feel the Furies toward them again, although they won't feel them for you because your debt is still paid. But I don't want you running out to try and slaughter them. We'll lose."

I look at the woman I once thought of as my mother. "I didn't ask you to explain, Elara," I reply.

"I tried to spare your feelings. I could have just killed him."

"You didn't kill him because you needed me to come quietly." I think of Deuce and it's like falling. "Keeping him alive is the only way to get me to do what you want." I look her in the eyes.

She gives me the eyebrow and I know I'm right.

"These oaks belong to Zeus," she says merrily, almost as if she knows how much I hate the sound of her voice. "The dryads must do as we say because they belong to us. Right now, they're hiding us. No one can find a way in without our consent."

Found that out on my own. No thanks to her.

"Again," I say, handing back the bowl. "I didn't ask you to explain."

I hear stumbling that comes closer to us than any sounds have yet. Leaves rustle and twigs snap as someone falls to the ground. "Daphne!" Ajax cries into the dark. "I know you're here!"

I look at Elara. She takes a breath, feeling an echo of the Furies but managing to stay calm. "He can't see us or hear us." She watches me. "We'll wait until he and his brothers leave. Then we'll go."

I feel a hint of the Furies rising in me until the brew she gave me oozes through my muscles, leaving them warm and tingling. I stay motionless. I see Ajax through a blanched wash of moonlight. He's still covered in blood—Deuce's blood—and his face is wild and stark in the cutting light.

"I know you can hear me!" Ajax shouts to the rustling treetops. "What was I supposed to do!?

I never should have gone back to that subway station. I should have left that origami swan in the dirt. Deuce is dead. Ajax is a killer. Because I was too selfish to understand that I don't get to love anyone. I fill my lungs with cold air, fill them to bursting, and let them empty with a gusty sigh.

"Don't do this," he pleads. "Don't let it end like this!"

"Jax?" a familiar voice calls. A figure runs into the clearing. It's Castor. "Jax, you've got to come home now," he says gently.

He reaches for his brother's shoulders. Ajax knocks his hands away violently.

"These trees belong to her. They're hiding her. She's here!" Ajax shouts. "She's hiding somewhere!"

"Okay. Fine. I believe you," Castor says. But the sun's coming up. The park will be opening soon, and we have to go."

Ajax whirls away from his brother. "You can't run from me, Daphne!" he screams to the treetops.

Castor tackles his little brother and holds him in a bear hug. "Please, Jax. Don't do this," he murmurs desperately.

Ajax struggles and hits his brother, but Castor weathers it patiently until Ajax wilts in his arms. "It's okay," Castor says over and over.

Ajax breaks free. "It'll never be okay," he says, and then launches himself into the sky.

Castor's chest flutters with unshed tears. He looks around the clearing, feeling how different this space is from the rest of the park. He looks up at the ever-moving treetops and notices the still air.

"You're here, aren't you?" he says softly. "I don't know what happened tonight, but I know you've got a reason to come after my family. So, let's make a deal. I promise to give Polydeuces Atreus the proper funeral rites if you'll stay away from my brother." He puts out his hands in a surrendering gesture and pivots in a circle so anyone hiding in any of the bushes can see him. "If you still need vengeance, take it out on me."

He completes his circle and faces me blindly. "If you have to come for someone, come for me." Castor's voice is low and dangerous. "I'll give you the fight you're looking for."

He nods at the silence and the darkness that are his only answer. Then he does something I've never seen anyone do before. His body twists and cracks and changes.

Castor Delos turns into a wolf before my eyes.

"An avatar of Apollo," Elara whispers with awe. "Quite the range of talents in this brood."

Castor sniffs around the perimeter of the hollow and stops, catching my scent. In this form, he can smell me. Recognize me. Luckily, he couldn't do that as a human. He stares at me through the barrier of the sacred hollow, almost like he sees me, and he growls. Then he's gone.

"That Castor is something special," Elara muses. "It's not every day a Scion can become one of the animal forms of their parent-god."

"They're all special," I reply. "But you know that. You were in love with Perseus, their uncle."

Elara nods, her eyes drifting away. "You know when I realized it?" she asks.

I shrug.

"The moment I cut off his head." She looks at me with that perfect hatred again. I look back at her with the same. It's comforting to have at least one untainted thing in my life. "You got weeks with Ajax. Do you have any idea how lucky you are?"

Then she lies down and shuts her eyes.

I don't sleep so much as play a game with myself. The game goes like this: I close my eyes and images burn through my head. I have to figure out if I'm asleep and having a nightmare, or if I'm awake and recalling things from my actual life.

The part that shakes me right down to the ground is that while I'm on the edge of sleep I honestly have no idea which is which anymore.

We get to Boston a few hours later.

My mother has a suite of rooms for us at the Boston Harbor Hotel under an unfamiliar last name. She's still taking precautions in case the Delos come looking for us. She's got to know registering under a fake name won't keep them at bay for long. Tantalus is coming for me, one way or another.

I'm going along with this because I know I'm not getting married. Tantalus will make sure I'm dead before I become another man's wife. I'm counting on it.

Sandwich boards down in the lobby of the hotel announce

the wedding party of Jonathan Hardwick and Daphne James. So, I guess my fiancé's name is Jonathan.

In my room stands a mannequin wearing a wedding dress. I look it over, noticing the simple yet elegant cut. Cold white crystals—maybe they're diamonds—seed the trim and scatter across the veil.

Of course, there's a veil. To cover my face.

"It'll fit," Elara says behind me.

I don't turn around. I go to the bathroom and fill the tub. Time to get ready to meet the man who bought me.

I wear what's hanging in the closet. Designer labels keep choosing outfits easy—same name, same outfit. The proper shoes are waiting underneath. The matching handbag is on the shelf above. When I open the bag, I see a compact and lip gloss. I powder my nose and slick my lips. I look in the tiny round mirror and I realize I left my jacket and purse on the floor of Ajax's bedroom. I left my bra in his bed.

I start to laugh even though it's not funny. The laugh threatens to turn into something else—some crazed hybrid of bawling and cackling. I blow all the air out of my lungs and keep exhaling until I see black blobs. I hold my breath and count. When there's nothing left but the instinct to breathe, I know it's passed. Something in me still wants to live, so there's no point in blubbering away in a hotel closet about how much I want to die.

I've fallen to my knees. I stand up. I brush out the wrinkles in my expensive outfit and join Elara in the sitting room.

The dinner tonight is a meet-the-relatives ordeal. Since Elara and I have only my dad and stepmother on our side, it's a mercifully small event with only a few tables. Everyone gawks when we enter. Elara has altered her face ever so slightly so as not to freak out everyone with our uncanny resemblance. I can tell she's more relaxed when she's not wearing The Face. That's my job, now. I keep my eyes down and trail behind Elara.

I hear the whispers. Is she even legal? *No, actually, I'm not.* Right now, I'm skipping school, and I'll never finish my senior year. But none of that matters anymore. I won't be going to college.

Elara leads me to the head table where my father and Rebecca are waiting. They sit with a pair of middle-aged people who regard me with an unsettling combination of resentment and possessiveness. With them is a young woman, maybe early twenties, who looks down her beaky nose at me. Her teeth grind behind her red lipstick. Next to her stands a young man, maybe mid-twenties. He has the same razor thin nose as his sister, and the doughy pallor of someone who's spent a lot of years shut up in boarding school. He stares at me in disbelief.

Elara elbows me. "Your intended," she informs me.

"Hello, Jonathan," I say, tipping my head at him.

"Hiiii," he says, dragging it out until it becomes a sigh. He collects himself and holds out his hand. "It's wonderful to meet you," he says.

I shake hands with him. His palm is swampy. "You're British," I say, marking his accent.

He looks disconcerted. "Your mother didn't tell you?" he asks with a nervous laugh. I shake my head. "What did she tell you, then?"

"The date and place," I reply.

Hurt pools in his eyes. I guess he was expecting me to have

asked about him. To have gazed at his picture. Imagining us together. Maybe he did that about me.

My intended is thrown by my apparent lack of interest in him, but he soldiers on. He introduces me to his sister, Mildred, and his parents, Jonathan and Margery. I like that I only have to remember three names.

I nod at them and sit in the chair Jonathan Junior pulls out for me. My father's lips are pursed, and he glares at my husband-to-be. Rebecca starts hissing in his ear immediately. Elara sits on the other side of table, as far away from me as she can, with Jonathan's parents.

"You're the most beautiful girl I've ever seen," Jonathan says, his voice breaking. He shakes his head and laughs at himself when I don't react to the compliment. "May I start over?" I nod. "Hi. I'm Jonathan. I'm twenty-six. I went to Oxford. I like cars." He takes an unsteady breath. "Your turn."

I give him a confused smile. "You seem nice," I say.

"I am nice." He grins hopefully.

"It's unfortunate," I say, frowning. "Because every single thing I'm going to tell you from this point on will be a lie." His face pales. "Do you want me to keep talking?"

The silence rings. He looks at his empty plate, and then quickly over to my father and stepmother to make sure they're out of earshot, and then back at me.

"We know," he whispers. "My parents, my sister, and I. We know what you are. I know who you are, Daphne Atreus. My father has been following clues his whole life. He learned about the existence of..." he breaks off and looks around to make sure no one is listening. "The existence of Scions. He taught me all about your history and your..." he gestures to my face and grows misty-eyed, "your lineage. I've studied your kind my whole life and, well, I may be just a mortal, but I can protect you. Your secret. It would be my honor to protect you."

He really believes that. He and his family believe they've solved an ancient mystery and dug up buried treasure all in one. To his parents this is a contest. Proof that their family is not just richer, but better than everyone else here even if everyone else doesn't know it. They're getting gods for in-laws and demigods for grandchildren. Top that, peasants.

I look around at the other tables and briefly listen in on the whispering. They don't know why Jonathan has agreed to an arranged marriage. Half of them think I must be pregnant. I look at his sister. She hates me, but I have a feeling it's because she can't marry me herself. With this wedding, I'm making her brother the favorite in their parents' eyes.

None of this is Jonathan's fault. His father raised him to believe in unicorns, and now he thinks he gets to keep one. I'm trying to feel sympathy toward him, but whenever I reach inside to pull out a genuine emotion, it feels like I'm snatching at thin air.

"Daphne?" Jonathan prompts. His face works as he thinks of something to say. He's trying really hard here. "I just want you to know you don't have to lie or pretend to be something you're not. Not around me."

He tentatively puts just his fingers on top of mine in what I'm sure he thinks is a bonding gesture. I look down at our hands, feeling nothing, and glad for that at least.

We aren't getting married in Boston. The wedding is set on Martha's Vineyard, even though it's off-season and the island is half empty and starting to get cold. Probably another dodge and feint to throw off the Delos. We set out well before dawn and I have the feeling I'm being spirited away.

Whatever Elara is doing to stay one step ahead of Tantalus is working. She's good at this. But I know it's only a matter of time. Before the wedding, after the wedding—it doesn't matter. Tantalus is going to find me.

I sit outside at the front of the ferry. Jonathan tries to talk to me over the sound of the wind, but his voice keeps getting snatched away. He gives up and goes inside when his chattering teeth overpower his ability to form words. I see him through the windows of the cabin, pacing frantically while his learned parents coach him on how to win me over.

Elara appears next to me. She places a hand on the railing to steady herself, sparing one terrified glance at the waves, before she leans close and whispers in my ear.

"I went through a lot of trouble to make sure I picked someone kind, someone who knew what you are so you wouldn't have to be hiding from him all the time. That's more than my mother did for me," she hisses warningly. "Blow it, and my next choice will be a mean son of a bitch."

I look her in the eye.

"You didn't pick him. You had to buy his family's silence," I say impatiently. "And you know that after a few months of being married to someone who can't love him, Jonathan won't be so kind to me anymore."

She gives me a knowing smile. "You're getting smarter," she says.

"Why not just kill them?" I ask.

"The Hardwicks are an important family, aristocrats or minor royalty, and they were thorough. Safety deposit boxes squirreled away all over world with teams of lawyers ready to sift through the contents if any of them suffer an untimely death." She heaves a belabored sigh. "I probably could have sorted it out if I had to. I've done it before to protect the secret of Scions. But. You are seventeen, which is our lucky year. You need a husband. They have a son who's the right age, and they are desperate for a union with any Scion line. It's just easier this way. That, and I fortuitously came back for a day to check on you and right away heard about this mysterious boy you were seeing."

"How?" I swivel my head to look at her. "How did you hear that? You weren't in New York."

For a split second she transforms just her face into Kayla's. I turn away from her, feeling the tightness of betrayal in my throat, although I don't know why I should. At least she didn't try to be Harlow. Probably because she doesn't know me well enough to pretend to be my best friend.

"Don't you know I can never really leave?" She touches my hair. I wait for it, because I know it's coming, and she doesn't disappoint me. Elara leans close again and whispers my ear. "Because if you die, I'll have to have another brat while I still can, and I'm not doing this again. When you have your daughter, then I'll be free. Finally, I can give your daughter the other half, my half of the Cestus and the burden of carrying on the line will be yours." Her voice trembles. "If you ruin it with the Hardwicks and make me wait one day longer than I have to... I'll make you pay for it."

I can feel her smiling behind my back as she watches me. I stifle a smile and pretend to sink into bitterness. Like I'm actually going to be married off to someone the same way she was.

"Don't stay out here too long," she calls loudly so everyone can hear and think she's a concerned mother. But I know she hates me just as much as she hates herself. That's our real curse. "We don't want you catching a cold." She goes back inside.

I look at the water. Like Elara, I've always feared it. The fear is still there, but now something else is, too. Fascination. The ocean seems so clean.

Eventually, I join the wedding party with an approximation of a smile smeared on my lips. Not because I'm afraid of what Elara will do to me—there's nothing left for her to do—but because deep down I know I deserve this. I was selfish, and now Deuce is dead.

It won't matter for much longer. Not to me, at least. Tantalus will find me and kill me.

The Hardwicks have a summer home on the beach, "home" being a relative term. It's more like a compound, nestled between the peculiar striped bluffs of Martha's Vineyard.

When the wedding party drives up the long, private road in caravan style I see that a white pavilion is set up and ready to go. There are only about twenty chairs unfolded around the silk-draped stage. The Hardwicks are keeping it a relatively hush-hush affair, as much as they can and still avoid scandal in their high society circles. Probably so as few people as possible can note that the bride is a bit too young and apparently dead inside.

Elara and I are given a room in the boathouse, which is closest to the pavilion and will serve as a staging area for my launch down the aisle. Our room is nestled into the roof of the boathouse, many stories away from the lapping water just underneath half of the building. Three sailboats are docked beneath my attic suite.

The room is luxurious, and it has a beautiful view. Of course. The Hardwicks don't do ugly.

Elara leaves to meet with Mildred, my de facto maid of honor, to hassle her about the bridesmaids' choice of hairstyle.

"I better not see one flower garland. This isn't a Renaissance Fair," Elara sneers as she heads out the door.

I look through the picture window. A wooden dock stretches into the water and then just ends. It makes me think of sleep.

There's a knock at the door. "Come in," I say without bothering to ask who it is. There are so many people hired to dress me and paint me and do my hair before the sunset ceremony that I may as well just keep the door open.

"Daphne?" Jonathan says.

I turn around, a little surprised.

"I know I'm not supposed to see you before the wedding tonight," he says sheepishly as his eyes dart down to my robe.

"It's fine," I say, wrapping the front more securely over my cleavage. Ridiculous, considering he's going to be seeing more than just my cleavage in a few hours. But I'm not his property yet. "Come in."

"I have something for you," he says. He comes toward me and holds out a small velvet box. "Your mother knew your ring size. It just came back from the jewelers." He opens the box to reveal a giant blue stone. I notice his hands shake a little. "It's a blue diamond," he tells me. "A rare one. Like you."

He thinks I'm a blue diamond, I say silently to myself. I almost laugh, but again, he's really nervous and trying so hard, so I smile at him and put it on.

"I couldn't have chosen better for myself," I tell him truthfully. Because I don't really care for jewelry. I omit that to spare him.

"Really?" He beams. He shifts awkwardly from foot to foot and then leans forward. At first, I don't get it, and then I realize he's trying to kiss me.

I lean forward at the waist and allow him to press his lips to mine. He tastes like a tube of toothpaste. He must have scrubbed the inside of his mouth like he was preparing it for surgery. I wonder if he's going to scour his entire body this ruthlessly before he tries to have sex with me tonight. That won't be happening. I'll put him off with an excuse, like, let's get to know each other. I just need to stall him long enough so that Tantalus has a chance to find me.

He pulls back and looks at me. His gaze keeps shifting left to right, like he can't decide which of my eyeballs to focus on. I pat him on the forearm. He looks down at the gesture and I realize too late that I couldn't have picked a more condescending thing to do to him.

"I have a surprise," he says, forcing a bright smile.

"The ring wasn't enough?" I reply, worried now. I realize I'm waiting for him to turn cruel on me. Bracing myself for the inevitable.

"You seem a little lonely," he says. Then he rolls his eyes at his understatement. "I happened to be talking with security when we had some arrivals. I brought them here because I think it might cheer you to see some friendly faces." He goes to the door and calls out, "Do come in."

Harlow appears. I stop and stare at her with my mouth open. And then I'm hugging her.

"What are you doing here?" I ask. I can feel how tense she is. She squeezes me tightly.

"Are you okay?" she whispers.

I pull back and see she's not alone. Tal steps toward me with a dazed Flynn and a dreamy-looking Kayla trailing behind him.

"Hi, Daphne," Tal says. He physically takes Harlow away from me and puts one of his arms over her shoulders. "Hope it's okay we just showed up, but we were so happy for you we had to come and see it for ourselves."

Flynn and Kayla look like they're on autopilot, but Harlow doesn't. Her smile is brittle and she's trying to edge away from Tal. He tightens his grip on her and fear sweeps through me. I look at Harlow's narrow shoulders, rounded under the weight of Tal's arm, and I lock eyes with her.

All those times Deuce warned me that humans would only be used against me, and I didn't listen. *Selfish again.*

I swallow and look pleadingly at Harlow. "Want to see my dress?"

Tal releases her with a warning look at me, and I drag her to the white-gowned mannequin that's haunting a corner of the suite. Harlow's round, panicked eyes are begging me to explain.

Behind us, I hear poor Jonathan trying to make conversation with Tal, Flynn, and Kayla: "So, you're all schoolmates, then?" he asks uncomfortably.

I turn to Harlow. "Don't worry," I whisper. I take her hand and squeeze it like that's going to protect her somehow. "Tal just wants to make sure I get married. If I do that, he won't hurt you or Flynn and Kayla."

"This is insane," she whispers back. Her eyes fill with tears. "You love Ajax," she insists angrily.

"Don't say his name," I snap, as the Furies whisper and moan in my head. The first stab of sadness I've allowed myself to feel comes quickly on the heels of the anger.

I can't hear his name without feeling anger. Even that has been taken from me.

"He's looking for you, you know. He's called me about a thousand times. He loves you and I know you love him."

I'm baffled as to how this conversation has unfolded. She's essentially been kidnapped, and this is what concerns her?

I put my hands on her shoulders. "Listen to me. Tal is dangerous, but I'm not going to let anything bad happen to you."

"I know that." She says, convinced of it. "And I'm not going to let anything bad happen to you."

I hear Deuce's voice in my head and all those warnings he gave me about humans and their brave hearts and fragile bodies.

"Harlow, promise me you won't do anything brave," I demand.

My hairdresser and makeup artist arrive and start fluttering around me like moths. I have no choice but to end our conversation before I can explain anything about my true situation. I give her one tight hug before my beauty staff descends on me, and Tal swoops in to collect Harlow. She suffers Tal's arm on her shoulder, and we share one last look of solidarity before she's taken away from me.

I get primped and perfumed and eventually stuffed into my wedding gown. Elara returns to inspect me. My father comes with her. I hear them arguing before they come in.

"You're not the only parent here, Elara," my father says peevishly. "She isn't eighteen yet. I'm going to put a stop to this whole thing."

Elara sweeps into the room and glares at my staff. "Out," she barks at them. They scatter and she turns to my father. "This 'whole thing,'" Elara mocks coldly with her fingers in air quotes, "is because of how you lust after your own daughter. So keep your mouth shut, or I'll make sure everyone knows it."

He chokes on his own frustration because he can't even deny it. Especially not now, seeing me in my gown. Elara gestures at me tauntingly while he swallows and sweats.

"Say goodbye to her, Mitch." She glances at her watch. "You've got five minutes and then you're going to walk her down the aisle." She stops and looks me over from head to toe. "Don't you look beautiful?" she says.

Elara sweeps out of the room, happier than I've ever seen her. My father stands about ten feet away from me. When he finally speaks, his voice crackles like his throat is dry.

"Do you want out?" he asks. "Tell me, and I'll get you out."

Wouldn't that be great? My dad rushes in at the last moment and saves me. I'm a princess, and my dad gets to be the best version of himself. And then Elara kills him, and Tal kills Harlow, just to make me suffer.

"It's okay, Dad," I reply. "Thank you for offering, though." I smile at him, and I realize it's been a long time since I've done that.

"Elara," he sighs.

I shouldn't have smiled I realize too late. He crosses the gap between us and reaches for me. I duck away from him and stumble on the train of my gown, and for a moment he's just my father, trying to catch me when I fall.

When I was a little girl, I pretended I didn't know how to tie my shoes so he would do it for me. I pretended I couldn't ride a bike so he would run along next to me, holding the handlebars, and shouting encouragement. And then for years I pretended I didn't notice that he had changed. But he had.

I hear fabric tear as I regain my footing. He has my shoulders and he's trying to pull me closer. I can't bring myself to hurt him. I turn my face away, willing this not to be happening. It's so strange. I'm a warrior, born and bred. I could dismantle an army of men just like him. But he's my father, and with him I'm powerless.

And then he's flying away from me. I see him land and tumble across the floor.

Ajax nearly goes after him as my father moans in a heap in the corner but stops himself and stares at me. He looks me up and down.

He looks flushed and windswept. I can feel and smell cold ocean air coming off him. We reach for each other at the same time, and at the same time we stop.

The Furies wail, but only I hear them.

I let my hand drop and I start to back away from him. Blood-lust rises, and I realize I simply can't do this anymore. I'm too tired and I'm sick with hatred and I've lost too much, and I know I'll just go on losing. The Furies whisper in my head, and I squeeze my eyes shut.

"Daphne," he whispers. "I'm sorry."

"Get away from me, Ajax!" I beg, still backing away and fighting the Furies. But I'm going to lose. "I don't want to hurt you!"

"I can't. I love you! I won't let them do this to you!" he chokes. He takes another step toward me, and the Furies scream.

Lightning builds under my skin until it is a bolt big enough to kill him. I have to get out.

I force myself to turn and fire the thunderbolt at the window instead of him. I hear Ajax shout my name as I hurl myself through the smoking crater in the wall, but it's too late. I've already jumped.

The sunset-gilded ocean sucks me down in my heavy wedding dress like it has been hungering for me for millennia.

The water closes over my head, and I feel clean again.

CHAPTER 20

The strangest thing about drowning is how much it burns.

Saltwater scalds my lungs, my nose, my eyes, even my skin is on fire in the "it's-so-frigging-cold-somehow-it-feels-like-hot water." But I'm free. I can sink to the bottom and stop.

I'm setting all of us free, actually. Harlow will be free of Tal. My dad will be free of Elara, and Ajax can be anything now that I'm gone, and he never has to kill again. At least, he won't have to kill because of me.

I'd rather die than hate him for one more second. I suck in, and water fills my lungs.

So I die.

The water is gone. Grit and sand replace it. I feel unrelenting heat radiating off the parched ground. The sun is a white-blue ball in an otherwise empty sky. I stand up and walk across this dry land.

There is a tree in the distance. I take one step, or I take a thousand, I'm not sure. I feel like I've been walking for half my life. The tree is in front of me, and I can go no farther.

I dare not look up into the branches that loom overhead. I hear teeth clacking and claws scraping. I hear weeping.

A tall young man stands beneath the tree. He wears a black chiton tied around his lower body, but his broad chest is bare. Shadows crowd close to him like cats begging to be petted. He removes his black helmet.

He is beautiful.

"Ajax won't let you die," the beauty tells me. His voice is kind and sad. "It's his life I must claim first. Not yours."

I smile at him. "And yet here I am." I take a guess in naming both the man and the location. "Hades."

Hades smiles back at me. "You have a life left to live."

And then I'm cold and wet. And someone's pounding on my chest. And I'm puking buckets of salt water. And I'm alive.

Ajax lifts me into his arms and holds me so tightly it hurts. "Why would you do that?" he's asking. His voice is high and thin with fear. "Why would you try to kill yourself?"

I push against his arms and put some space between us. I wait. I wait for the Furies. I hear water instead of wailing.

"They're gone," I croak. I then wrap my arms around his neck and let my head fall onto his shoulder.

I feel us bobbing up and down. We're on the dock that reminds me of sleep. Somewhere not too far away people are shouting and running, but as always, everything that isn't Ajax is just static.

He holds my face between his hands. "Don't you ever, ever,

give up on us again," he says. He's doing his best to look fierce. I touch his trembling lips.

"I won't," I promise. "I'll climb out of Hades a hundred times if I have to, but I'll never give up on us again. I swear it."

He kisses me. This is what home is supposed to feel like.

Tal

I see them kissing. They've escaped the Furies once again. Impossible.

There is an order to things, a pattern that the rest of the natural world adheres to. Night and day don't fill the sky at the same time. Spring does not turn back into winter. And Scions from different Houses do not escape the Furies twice.

Harlow rejoices at the sight of her alive. She moves to run toward them as others of the wedding party are doing. I see Tantalus Delos appear from the water and pound down the dock toward his brother and Daphne. I hold out a hand to stop Harlow.

And then Tantalus, Heir to the House of Thebes, embraces the star-crossed lovers. He kisses the Heir to the House of Atreus on her forehead as if in benediction. As if their Houses have already been united.

I have failed.

"Impossible," I say. I hear my laughter through the sound of screeching bronze and hissing steam.

One of the remnants of the Hundred Handers skitters out of

my joints and over my shoulder like an insect. Harlow squeals and claws at my arms and face in an attempt to escape. I flick the rotting hand away, and it dashes to the water. But I don't relinquish my grip on her.

I feel Flynn and Kayla attack me from behind as they fight their way through Medea's Folly and my weakening control over their minds. Kayla bites and Flynn punches. They valiantly try to tear Harlow from me to no avail. They are dead before they hit the ground.

The panicking humans around me have no answer. They look at me with awe and terror as I start to grow to my true size.

The grinding gear finally slips free, and all is suddenly made clear.

Everyone here has seen. Everyone here must die.

"Jax! Daphne!" Tantalus yells.

Ajax and I break apart. I feel the dock swaying under Tantalus as he runs down it toward us. He's going to kill me, I think, and then he throws his arms around both of us.

"What were you thinking?" Tantalus whispers in my ear. He pulls back and searches my eyes, looking for an answer. He's soaking wet and his eyelashes are spiky with saltwater. He must have swum here. "Don't you ever—" he starts to scold me and stops, as if he can't even get himself to think the words. He clutches me to him in another crushing hug and kisses my forehead.

"I won't," I say, shock keeping my answers brief, not sure if I'm more stunned about having just died a little or the fact that, apparently, Tantalus Delos is not going to kill me.

We hear a deafening, un-human roar. In front of the pavilion something is causing a commotion. It takes my paralyzed brain a moment to register what's happening.

Tal is swelling into a colossus. His glinting skin turns completely into bronze as he balloons to a height of over a hundred and fifty feet.

There is a moment of collective awe. Every face is turned up to watch the enlarging bronze statue, burnished by the last glimmers of the setting sun. Then the colossus takes one thundering step, and panic erupts.

Ajax hauls me to my feet. "Can you run?" he asks. I look at him and then up at Tal.

Tal has something in his hand.

"Harlow," I whisper.

Ajax and Tantalus exchange a look. "We fight," Tantalus decides.

"Stay here," Ajax orders me.

"No way." I say, determined to save my friend.

Ajax realizes he doesn't have a choice, drops down to a knee and starts ripping the skirt off my gown. I roll down my stockings and chuck them on the pile of discarded silk as the colossus takes another earthshaking step.

My lungs are still burning, but I run down the dock. Tantalus dives into the water and swims straight for Tal. Ajax leaps into the air and gets to him first.

Holding Harlow in one of his gigantic hands, the colossus stoops down and swipes his other hand at the people frantically trying to run away from him. Bodies arc through the air. Ajax flies after them so fast I can barely see him. He grabs onto the nearest falling bodies he can reach and slows their descent. He can't carry anyone, but he does manage to deposit a few people on the ground with little more than jarring *thuds*. Those Ajax doesn't catch land on the sand in pulpy heaps.

Tal swipes his free hand down again at the scampering humans and comes up against resistance. Elara has charged him and managed to stop his hand from sending a small family soaring through the air. Her efforts only slow his hand, though, and she is knocked violently aside. The family is demolished, despite her efforts.

As I charge toward her to help, I see lightning begin to crackle across her skin and I scream, "Mother, don't!

She squints into the tricky light of sunset and notices the thrashing girl clutched in Tal's hand. "Please don't kill her," I beg her.

Tantalus pulls himself from the water and makes it to Elara's side just as Tal is about to stomp on her. He throws himself over Elara's body and tumbles across the sand with her under him. Tal's foot comes down, narrowly missing killing both of them.

I reach them in time to see their eyes meet. Something changes between them.

"Why?" Elara ask him disbelievingly.

Tantalus is just as confused by his actions and by the lack of rage towards my mother. By saving her, he has driven away the Furies.

Above us, Tal roars in frustration and we all look up to see him taking a swipe at Ajax, who is harrying Tal's eyes. Tal rubs his eyes with the back of his free hand. His stumbling feet send more screaming people scattering in different directions.

"We have to get him to put down the girl so we can hit him with our bolts," my mother says to me.

"Will that even affect him?" Tantalus asks.

"He's bronze. Our lightning is hot enough to melt him if we work together." Ajax and Tantalus's eyes widen at this bit of information. In the momentary lull while Tal regains his vision, we hear Harlow screaming blazing obscenities at him.

"What a mouth on that girl," Elara mumbles at me.

"It's part of her charm," I say.

The barrage continues. Tal wheels his free arm over his shoulder and the four of us are forced to scramble in different directions as he drops a hammer fist. I leap away as a shower of sand displaced by Tal's blow nearly buries me. Ajax is at my side in a moment, hauling me to my feet.

We're forced to jump away again as Tal tries to stomp on us. Ajax and I roll together, past broken bodies that are now littering the sand.

I come face to face with Rebecca's dead eyes. I don't think about the triumphant look on her face when she sent me to finishing school. All I can remember is her standing in front of me protectively, shielding me from my father's anger.

I close her eyes. Ajax pulls me away and we have to run as Tal brings his foot down yet again.

"Tanny!" Ajax shouts as we thunder toward him up and over a dune. "I'm going for Harlow. Keep him busy down here."

Ajax jets into the air and disappears in the darkness of falling night. I scream something useless after him and latch onto Tantalus's arm, pulling him close to me.

"Do you have anything? If you have any secret strength or talent that you're holding back, now would be the time to use it," I tell him.

He sets his jaw and pulls up his shirt. Wrapped around his

waist is a security wallet. He unzips the flat pouch and carefully takes out five shiny black things that look like fangs. He crouches down and buries them in the sand, rises, and takes me by the shoulders.

"Get as far away as you can," he tells me. For a moment I think he's going to kiss me, but he shoves me away from him. "Run!" he yells.

The sand all around starts to vibrate and jump, like a giant subwoofer is buried deep down. I look to see if Tal is causing the strange phenomenon, but his back is to me as he rips up the pavilion tent to reveal hiding humans who, discovered, scatter like ants from under a lifted rock.

I see a pale hand reach up from the vibrating sand. It braces itself on the edge, then presses down. I kick my way back as a bloodless body rises up from the beach. The sand spills away and I can see that it's dressed in ancient leather and bronze armor—a breastplate, greaves, and Corinthian helmet—and it carries a spear.

"The Dragon's teeth," Elara whispers to herself in awe.

Four more undead hoplites grown from the black fangs follow behind the first and make a beeline for Tantalus. I raise a hand, just about to shout a warning to Tantalus, when he turns and orders them to attack Tal. They charge across the beach and vault up the legs of the colossus.

Tal rears back as the undead hoplites climb up him, and the people cowering under broken folding chairs in the demolished pavilion see their chance and make a run for the main house.

Tal roars as one of the hoplites drives his spear into Tal's groin. He drops Harlow.

I hear her scream, my heart in my throat, and start running to catch her. I see Ajax dive for her. He grabs one of her arms and they tumble to the ground together. Tal bats at the attacking hoplites, swatting them from his body, and they fall to the sand, their limbs splayed out at impossible angles.

Ajax picks up Harlow and carries her away. She isn't moving.

The freed people from the pavilion run past me, and as they do, I see it's the Hardwicks. Jonathan spots me.

"Daphne, hurry! We have a panic room!" he screams, reaching a hand out beckoning me toward him.

I stand up. "Go lock yourselves in it," I tell him.

"Daphne!" I hear my mother call. I find her with my eyes. "Now!" she yells, already summoning a lightning bolt.

My hands glow blue as I loop charge upon charge. Jonathan backs away from me, his mouth hanging open like a carp's. And then I run into the fray.

I see my mother's blue-glowing hands bobbing down the beach as we converge on our target.

"Ready?" she calls out to me.

"Ready," I reply. "Everyone, get back!" I scream just in case, and then my mother and I fire neon veins of liquid electricity at Tal's heart and head.

Tal's bronze body sings. It's an eerie sound, almost like a woman's voice hitting a note meant to shatter crystal. The metal glows bright and drips fat yellow drops that sizzle in the sand. His chest and face melt like tallow. We spend every last bolt bringing him down.

I see the hoplites scattered around us starting to reanimate, and one by one they drag their broken bodies up again.

Tal falls to a knee, tips forward, and spills buckets of molten bronze onto one of the hoplites below. The intense heat eats away at the undead until there is nothing left to rise again. As the colossus falls onto his side and lands, hissing with steam in the cold Atlantic, the four remaining hoplites turn their attention to my mother and me.

I can't see their eyes through the small, almond-shaped opening of their Corinthian helmets, but I can feel the menace in their attitude. They suss out my mother and I, deeming us a threat. However indirectly, we killed one of their own.

"Daphne," my mother says, her expression frozen with fear. "Run!" As she starts to run toward the hoplites, charging them, waving her arms over her head, trying to distract them.

Despite my mother's frantic attempt, two hoplites break for her and two for me. I try to summon a bolt, but I'm spent. My mouth is so dry it's sore. I hear Tantalus shouting for the undead warriors to stop, but they don't.

I let their first spear hit me in the chest. I hear Ajax screaming something as I fall to my knees. The blow hurts, but it doesn't penetrate. I wrest the spear out of the hoplite's hands and turn it back on him. The spear is not my specialty, but I know how to use one. Thanks to Deuce. From my lowered position I aim up and under the armored breastplate. Before I can lose the element of surprise, I run the disarmed hoplite through with his own spear and pin him to the sand with it. I can't kill him since he's already dead, but I might be able to keep him out of the fight.

I sink the spearhead as deeply into the sand as I can, and the added effort gives the other hoplite a chance to attack. He doesn't use his spear on me—whatever they are, they learn fast. Instead, he drops his spear and wraps his cold, dead hands around my neck to cut off my air. We flop back onto the sand, kicking up rainbows of sand grains as we struggle.

Ajax touches down next to us, creating another shower of sand. He kicks up the discarded spear, hefts it, and puts it right through the hoplite's neck. He keeps driving the hoplite back, until the undead is pinned to the beach like his comrade.

Ajax pulls me into his arms.

"Harlow?" I gasp, throat still burning.

"Alive. I brought her inside," he answers. Tantalus reaches us and I realize they've both come to my aid.

"My mother," I say, breaking out of Ajax's arms and into a run.

One hoplite lays in pieces. My mother pulled it limb from limb, leaving the undead stump of a torso to flounder uselessly. But there's still one hoplite left.

We see two figures fighting ruthlessly in the ocean's shallows. A third person rushes in, screaming my mother's name.

"Dad!" I shout.

The hoplite doesn't even turn to look at him but spins his spear so the point sticks out behind him and my father runs himself through on it.

I reach them a moment too late. My mother goes to my father's side as if transfixed, and the hoplite seizes her head and wrenches it around. She's dead before her knees touch the foamy seam of the surf.

My knees buckle with hers. I lunge forward to catch her. "Mom!" I scream. But her eyes are empty and her face, The Face, is a blank mask.

Tantalus and Ajax make short work of the final hoplite, their battle rage spurring them to choose my mother's tactic of dismemberment.

Ajax and Tantalus fall panting to their knees beside me. I lay my mother next to my father. The ocean she no longer fears nudges her along one side in gently lapping waves. I take off her necklace and put it on with mine. The two hearts link together on their own and make an interlocking design.

During the fight she'd tried to save me—to distract Tal from me, even if it meant her own life. And my dad tried to save her, even though he didn't stand a chance. I don't cry. I don't know how to feel about either of them, and even less about how to feel now that I've lost them.

"Let's get them inside for now," Tantalus says quietly.

As I gather up my mother, I see something moving under the water. I startle back. There are thousands of things down there. It looks like an army of crabs. We move my parents' bodies up the beach as hundreds of scuttling things make their way up from the water. But they're not crabs.

"It's the hands!" I say to Ajax.

"Look," he replies, pointing at Tal's hulking ruin. It starts to move.

The hands swarm up the beach and gather the bits and pieces of the torn hoplites. Still more of them wrest the two pinned hoplites from the ground and drag the struggling, undead warriors into the water.

"Get back!" Tantalus orders as Tal's bronze body suddenly sinks with a wrenching sound.

A giant wave swells onto shore as the colossus gets towed out to sea. In moments, anything that isn't human or Scion has been removed from the beach.

Ajax holds my hand as a woman rises up from the water as if lifted on a platform from below. She strides across the surface of the ocean toward us. The moon glows behind her, but I can still see her face.

"Hecate," I whisper.

The goddess stands in front of us, completely dry. We incline our heads respectfully.

"She died a hero and so passed through to the Elysian Fields." Hecate gestures to my mother's body. "Elara Atreus drinks from the River of Joy."

And now the tears decide to come, running in hot little streams down my cheeks. I drop my head and nod, unable to speak, and wonder where my father is now. I feel Ajax's hand run across my back and he pulls me closer.

Hecate looks at Ajax. "Have you decided?" she asks him.

"I have," he replies. I feel his arm tighten against my shoulder, wondering what he's decided on.

Hecate looks at Tantalus. "You stand at a crossroads, Son of Apollo," she informs him. She gestures to the ocean, and it takes me a moment. They may be liquid, but there are many roads here. "Have you ever wondered why the Fates give prophecy?"

Tantalus shakes his head, too wary to speak.

"Better to ask yourself this, then," she continues. "If the future is truly set, why tell anyone about it?"

Tantalus frowns deeply. "But they *have* told me," he replies. "How can I unknow what I already know, even if it is meant to manipulate me?"

Hecate glances at Ajax although she still speaks to Tantalus. "The Fates want mortals to believe there is only one way, but there's always a choice. The right one is usually the hardest."

We are silent. Hecate walks down the beach, strewn with dead humans, and disappears over a dune.

We carry my parents' bodies inside the boathouse and wrap them in spare blankets that we find in my mother's room. We leave them on the bed and go up to the main house.

Harlow emerges from the panic room with the few survivors from the wedding party. Jonathan junior and senior made it, as did Mildred. The mother, however, is missing. Only four human survivors. We didn't save many at all.

Harlow and I hug. She's shaking with shock. I make sure she's sitting before I join the discussion.

Mr. Hardwick paces back and forth, eyeing the three Scions in his den with a combination of fear and anticipation.

"We can't explain this away," Jonathan argues. "We'll have to tell the truth."

Tantalus shakes his head. "I can't let you do that."

The threat is clear. The room grows unnaturally quiet.

"May I?" Tantalus asks gesturing to Mr. Hardwick's scotch.

Mr. Hardwick nods. He narrows his eyes. "Who are you?"

"Tantalus Delos," he replies, pouring several glasses of sticky amber liquid. "Son of Paris, Son of Apollo, Heir to the House of Thebes." He hands a glass to Mr. Hardwick. "That's my brother Ajax." He brings a glass to Jonathan who stares at Ajax and me. We're holding hands.

Mr. Hardwick manages a smile. "It's an honor."

Tantalus brings a glass to Mildred. She takes it, eyeing him with blunt appreciation. "We're going to have to come up with something to tell the police," she says in a surprisingly levelheaded tone for someone who just witnessed what she did.

Tantalus looks out a set of glass French doors at the deck, and beyond that in the dark, the carnage on the beach. He spins a new version of events.

"You set the pavilion up on one of the bluffs," he says. "Close to the edge so the view would be beautiful. You didn't know it was unstable. Just before the groom and most of the immediate family took their places, there was a disaster. The cliff gave way. Everyone fell to their deaths."

There's a long silence. Mildred speaks first. "You can knock down one of the bluffs?" she asks.

Tantalus looks at Ajax and me. "Enough of one. If we work together."

"So, we're just supposed to lie?" Jonathan asks bitterly. His voice begins to rise with hysteria. "And the three of you are off the hook even though you've killed my mother and my closest friends?"

"We didn't kill anyone. We tried to save people. Daphne's own mother and father died fighting," Ajax counters angrily. "Where were you?"

Jonathan scowls at the floor.

I twist off the ring he gave me and hold it out to him. "You were very kind to me, and I'm sorry."

Jonathan takes the ring and stares at it.

"Hang on just a bloody moment," Mr. Hardwick replies. "We were promised a union between our family and a Scion." He shakes his head, guffawing. "We've got a lot to answer for here. We're not taking on this much risk without some kind of compensation."

I glare at the scheming old man. "I'm not compensation."

"Daddy, it's no use. Those two are obviously in love," Mildred says, flipping a disdainful hand at Ajax and me. "But she's not the only Scion in the room."

She eyes Tantalus with nothing short of lust as her meaning sinks in.

Tantalus doesn't object.

"Tanny," Ajax says. "You don't have to do this."

"It's okay, Jax," he says. "Dad's been after me for years to pick a bride. It's time I settled down." He turns to Mildred and offers his hand. "Tantalus Delos."

"Mildred Hardwick." She replies, taking his hand.

This isn't right.

"Wait. Come with me for a sec," I say, stepping forward. I pull Tantalus outside onto the deck.

We're both still drained and humming from our battle against Tal and the hoplites, and the air feels good. We take a deep breath at the same time. And we look at each other.

"Are you sure about this?" I ask him. "You don't know anything about them. She's in there horse-trading when her mother just died. Is that the woman you want to marry?"

He rolls his eyes. "You were about to marry her brother."

"Not by choice. They are very well protected, and they were going to reveal us," I say. "They basically blackmailed my mother."

"At least my future wife knows what she's getting—dead bodies on the beach and all." He smiles at me and raises his hand to touch my face, but lets it drop. "It doesn't matter who she is. Whoever I marry will never be you."

My mouth opens and nothing comes out.

"It's okay. You don't have to say anything. And I'm happy for Ajax." He kisses me on the forehead and goes back inside.

Ajax motions me over. I go to him, and he whispers, "What was that about?"

"Just making sure he knows what he's marrying into," I say, watching Mildred salivate over her catch.

"So protective of my brother," he says carefully.

"He's my brother now, too," I reply quietly.

Ajax gives me a strange little smile. "Not quite yet." The look he gives me sends shivers down my spine. He lets an irreverent finger flick one of the clasps of the garter belt still dangling against my thighs. I smile.

The look on his face changes. "Harlow..."

I turn to find her downing scotch, staring wide-eyed at the carpet. We head over.

"Hi," she says. "You can fly," She turns to me. "And you can apparently shoot lightning out of your hands." She barks a weird laugh, and it threatens to turn weepy. She pinches the bridge of her nose and calms down. "Sorry. I'm okay. Don't worry. I won't freak out."

The three of us spend a few moments standing there awkwardly. We all feel like freaking out.

"I really wanted to tell you," I say, grabbing her hand.

"But, you know, then you'd have to kill me. Ha!" The weird laugh happens again and stops abruptly. "Um. You're not going to, are you?"

"No," Ajax and I say at the same time.

"You just can't ever say anything, Harlow," I tell her. "To anyone. Ever."

"Right," she says. She's nodding an awful lot. "I'm going to need more scotch."

"Good idea," I say. "Take Jonathan with you?" He's sitting on the couch, sulking.

Harlow salutes me and turns, but I stop her. "Did I mention

that you're probably the most amazing girl I've ever met in my entire life, and I don't deserve you as a friend?"

"Yeah, yeah." Harlow hugs me. "You still owe me, like, gallons of Diet Coke and cases of Twizzlers. You know that, right?"

"Anything you want," I whisper, returning her hug.

Harlow lets me go and scoops up Jonathan on her way to the wet bar. "So, my boyfriend turned into a thousand-foot psychopath tonight. How're you doing?" she asks him.

The only thing I want is to be back in New York in Ajax's bed listening to his music and wondering which member of his family is going to barge in on us next. Instead, I spend the next few hours hauling bodies up a bluff and setting them up on chairs.

Some of the bodies I can't even look at. Some are children. Entire families. My family. We decide it's best to let Elara, Rebecca, my father, and Mrs. Hardwick be found with the others. Less conspicuous if the survivors have suffered losses too.

Every time he sees me crying, Tantalus tells Ajax and me to take a break. Me, because I can't see through my own tears to stand any longer, and Ajax because Tantalus knows I need him to hold me up. By the time the three of us are set to knock down the cliff, I'm convinced Tantalus did most of the dirty work himself.

I drink a ton of water to recharge my lightning. Then I hit a few of the natural fissures with my bolts, opening them up wide enough for us to fit inside. Ajax, Tantalus, and I wedge ourselves between the cracks and push.

It isn't easy. But it works. The cliff collapses, the bodies tumble down the crumbling earth, and the ocean immediately begins to scrub away any remaining incriminating evidence.

An urgent 911 phone call to the police is made, and then we wait for the cavalry to come and buy our lie.

And of course, they buy it. Humans can't control lightning. Humans could never push over a cliff. It has to be a natural disaster. The police murmur about reports of powerful lightning strikes and strange booming sounds on this side of the island, despite a lack of clouds. They shake their heads and curse New England weather, bad luck and El Niño, and anything else they can think of to explain away the impossible.

It's nearly dawn by the time the police leave. As Mildred assigns spare rooms in the Hardwicks' mansion to Harlow and Tantalus, Ajax and I slip out and run to the boathouse.

I bathe and cry and let the water rinse everything down the drain. They were terrible parents. Really, the worst. But they were mine.

I put on the only nightgown I have. It's a fancy, silky white, one meant for my wedding night. Ajax sits on the end of the bed, his hair wet from a shower and just a towel wrapped around his waist. One of his legs is bouncing.

"Nervous?" I ask.

He stands up and comes to me. "I'm ready to tell you what Hecate told me," he says.

"Okay," I say, my voice small. I'm not sure I can handle another shock tonight, but I let him lead me back to the end of the bed and we sit down next to each other.

"She told me the Fates shouldn't rule the universe. She said I should have a choice. But the choice was between you and my family. I can't have both."

"But she's wrong," I argue.

Ajax shakes his head. "No. She's right. Tantalus accepts you, but the fact is my father never will, and my father is still Head of our House. I thought it would be okay eventually, but after the other night, seeing your mother again... It did something to him. His feelings aren't completely—" He searches for the right word.

I remember how Paris looked at Elara. How he said her name with so much longing.

"My father has ordered the Hundred Cousins to find you and kill you." He finally says.

"My mother is dead. It's over," I insist.

Ajax shakes his head again, his eyes empty. "After you left, he went on and on about how you were a cancer, just like your mother. That you'd destroy our House from the inside." He pauses, and finally says it. "That Tanny and I would fight over you."

I take a startled breath. Ajax glances at me and smiles ruefully. "I see how he looks at you," he says. There's no blame in his voice. Just regret.

"I love *you*," I say. I stand up and come to him. "I don't want your brother."

"I believe you," Ajax replies quietly. "And I know Tanny feels horrible about it. That's why he's agreed to marry —to punish himself." Ajax grimaces. "But marriage won't change anything. The more he sees you the more he'll want you. I still have to choose."

I nod and look down. "I understand," I say. "You're right. We should have ended this a long time ago."

He tilts up my face, a bemused look on his face. "I choose you," he says.

He kisses me gently, wiping the tears off my face.

"You can't give up your family," I say.

"I've made up my mind."

I shake my head as if to clear it. "Your family won't just let you disappear. They'll look for you, and they'll keep hunting me."

Ajax drops his towel and climbs into bed, pulling me in with him. "Not if they think we're dead."

He kisses me deeply and grabs a handful of my nightgown, pushing it up my thighs.

"But," I murmur, trying to hang on to the thread of the conversation as his mouth moves down my neck, "how are we going to fake our deaths?"

He props himself up on an elbow.

"Lucas. Before he and Helen left, he gave me a potion that would make me appear dead. He told me to use it and disappear with you. If you were what I really wanted."

"How Shakespearean."

"He was House of Thebes," he says.

I'm not surprised, actually.

"A potion, huh?" I frown, thinking of Tal. "More witch's magic."

"It's from Hecate, and she is the Witch Titan," Ajax says. He swallows and continues. "I wasn't ready then, but I am now." He looks away. "Tanny will help us. We'll stage a fight between us so my family will have no doubt. You'll pretend to kill me, and Tantalus will pretend to kill you. We take the potion, and Tantalus will take care of our bodies. In three days, you and I will wake up... and then we run."

"What makes you think Tantalus will help us?"

"Because he loves you and he'd do anything to keep you alive."

I take his face between my hands. "It will destroy your other brothers... and Pandora."

Ajax's eyes round with pain. "It took me this long to decide because I thought I had to choose who I was going to hurt. You or them. But that's not it. That's not my choice. I'm choosing how I want to be dead."

I frown, not understanding.

"I can appear dead on the outside to my family, or be dead on the inside without you. Which do you think they'd choose for me?"

I think of Castor offering himself up in place of Ajax in the dryads' hollow, and I nod.

He slides my nightgown over my head and carefully climbs on top me. Talking becomes impossible for a while. We kiss and hold each other, desperately gentle. He closes his eyes and gives himself up, ready to bury himself in me, but I won't be his grave, so I stop him.

"Are you sure?" I ask.

"You are my whole family now, and I'm yours."

It hurts like crazy for exactly ten seconds. Then we are incandescent.

EPILOGUE

I wake in Tantalus's arms.

"It's okay," he whispers when I spasm against him.

"Where's Ajax?" I slur. My mouth doesn't work very well yet. Neither do my eyes. I can't see anything but Tantalus' face and shoulders above me. I hear the sound of water. Waves. A seagull.

"He's right beside you," Tantalus says, holding me up. He places the rim of a cup against my lips. I'm so thirsty. I want to gulp it, but Tantalus won't let me. "Easy," he coos soothingly. I can't move my arms.

Tantalus props me up on some pillows and I can see Ajax lying next to me in bed. The same bed where he told me about this plan over a month ago.

"What's wrong with him?" I ask. He looks dead. Not sleeping, not unconscious, but gray and shrunken and dead.

Tantalus takes my shoulders and makes me look at him. I'm starting to panic. Ajax should have woken first, but hasn't.

"He'll be okay," he says, his eyes locked sternly with mine.

"But he went first." I say, confused.

"It hasn't been three days yet. Give it time. You're stronger than he is," he says.

We set it up perfectly. Ajax and Tantalus pretended to hunt me down. They made sure Castor and Pallas were there as witnesses when they "found" me. Ajax and I fought. I stabbed him, and he took the potion.

He really did look dead.

All the Delos men chased me. Even Paris. I made sure Tantalus got to me first, before the rest of his brothers could notice that what they felt was just rage and pain and not the Furies at all. I slipped him the Cestus for safekeeping, and he slit my throat. As he watched me bleed out in his arms, he poured the potion into my mouth. The last thing I remember is seeing Paris, Castor and Pallas standing over my "dead" body.

I look around what was once my bridal suite at the Hardwick's summer home. There are duffel bags full of clothes, storage containers, boxed survival equipment—just piles and piles of stuff for us to use on the run.

I look at Ajax, cleaned and wearing a burial chiton. They had a funeral for him, and buried him.

I look at Tantalus. He's a mess. His eyes are sunken, and his cheeks are pale. He looks thinner, like he hasn't eaten in weeks. I can see the suffering he must have witnessed, even if he didn't really feel it himself. He saw his family feel it.

I can move my arms again, so I reach out and cup his jaw in my hand.

"Thank you," I say.

He smiles at me and drops his head, removing my hand from his cheek. He stands to get something.

I notice I'm clean, too. Tantalus must have bathed and dressed me. I doubt the Delos family gave my body the proper funeral rites.

"Here," Tantalus says, sitting down next to me. He clasps the Cestus around my neck. "I'm going to start loading the sailboat," he says instead.

He gets up and starts bringing our gear down to the Argo IX —a gift from Tantalus' new bride, Mildred. I don't know whether Mildred knows that Ajax and I are faking our deaths or not, but I can't see any reason for her or her family to break their silence about it if they do. What other leverage do they have to keep Tantalus married to her?

It's another hour before I feel Ajax stir. Tantalus and I are both there to help him up, out of his deathly sleep. I prop him up on pillows, urging him to drink some water, rushing him back to life before he's ready. Sixty minutes is too long to stare at the lifeless body of the one you love, and it takes Tantalus reminding me to give him time to get me to back off. Even still, I can't stop kissing parts of him—his cheek, his forehead, the backs of his hands—like some fairy tale princess trying repeatedly to wake her prince.

It takes us two days before we're back to full health and ready to set sail. It's a good thing Ajax knows how to handle a boat. I've been reading a lot of books in preparation, but I've never even been on so much as a canoe before. Ajax used to have those idyllic summers where his family would vacation on Nantucket Island, all of them learning to sail so they could race each other. I don't tease him about it and call him a Kennedy, though. No need to remind him of what he's lost.

When the time comes to leave I give Tantalus a hug that he ends, pulling back and saying, "I'll see you in a year," like it's no big deal.

That's what Ajax and Tantalus decided. Once a year we'd see each other. I wanted to say no. Hecate's choice had been clear. It was supposed to be me or his entire family, but somehow Tantalus has talked Ajax into it. Ajax was giving up everything for me. I couldn't deny him this.

"A year," I agree. "By then I'll probably be wearing an eye-patch and a pirate's hat." I get a chuckle out of both of them.

I watch as Tantalus and Ajax hug goodbye. "Take care of each other," Tantalus says.

"We will," Ajax replies.

Tantalus looks at me while he holds his brother. "I love you," he says.

I know he's talking to me. But I look away and pretend he meant to say it to his brother. He stays on the dock, watching as we sail away. I can still feel him tugging at us, though, like an invisible anchor that we'll never truly be free of. If Ajax feels it, he doesn't speak of it. I have a feeling he will rarely speak of his family in the days to come.

"Where to?" Ajax asks me as he takes the helm.

And it hits me. We really could go wherever we want. There was so much fear and doubt and loss for so long that I forgot to consider the fact that we get to start over. Go anywhere. Do anything. I've never had that kind of freedom before. I never stopped to think that I might get what I want. But I did. I got Ajax.

"Do you know that spot on maps where they used to write, *Where There be Dragons*?" I ask, slipping under one of his arms.

Ajax holds me against him. "The edge of the world it is," he agrees, smiling at me.

We sail into the sunrise, not the sunset. I decide it's an auspicious omen. Our lives are just beginning.

TIMELESS EXCERPT

Please enjoy the following excerpt from TIMELESS, book five in the STARCROSSED saga.

The Titan Cronus, Lord of Time, opened his black eyes wide. Helen could see the whirling galaxy in the center of them as if they were drawing her near, and then there was darkness and cold...

...Helen and Lucas appeared across the street from the Delos's brownstone on Washington Square Park in Manhattan.

As they looked around, Lucas took a deep breath. "This is so weird," he said, letting his breath out in a gust. "Everything is just a little bit... different."

It was nighttime. There were still a few people about, but they were going somewhere else, and not there to linger. Helen and Lucas, frozen, looked at the Delos's front door.

"Is it just me, or is 1993 a little dirtier?" Helen asked.

"Grunge," Lucas said.

There were lights on inside the Delos's brownstone. Every floor blazed with activity. With their Scion hearing, Helen and Lucas could hear the low rumble of many male voices, and every now and again the high, piercing laughter of a young girl.

"Pandora," Lucas whispered, hearing his aunt's voice from when she was a little girl.

Helen turned her head to watch Lucas. He'd spoken of his aunt Pandora maybe once or twice since she'd died, but Helen knew he missed her deeply. The color of his heart was dull, bruised red.

"Do we wait for Ajax to come out?" she asked, mostly to give him something else to think about. Lucas operated best when he had a problem to solve.

He shook his head. "We'll probably be here until morning if we do," he replied.

Helen changed her face with the Cestus. "Ring the doorbell, then?"

Lucas's brow furrowed in thought. He looked up at the building's façade. He pointed at a window on the third floor. "That's Ajax's bedroom," he said. "We could fly up, hidden, and..."

"Freak him out when we suddenly appear in his bedroom, and either knock him unconscious or get into a giant fight that brings everyone running?" Helen asked sardonically.

"Good point," Lucas admitted, nodding.

Helen sighed. They both perked up when they noticed the door opening. Lucas quickly veiled them in invisibility.

"Oh my god," Helen gasped. It was her. And Hector. Only it wasn't either of them.

"Tomorrow?" Ajax asked.

"Tomorrow," Daphne said. She went down the steps, but Ajax didn't close the door. He watched her heading for the park.

"He's going to go after her," Lucas whispered, his eyes glued to Ajax.

He was right. Just as Daphne was alongside Helen and Lucas, Ajax followed her.

"That wasn't enough," Ajax said, as he turned Daphne around and kissed her.

Helen and Lucas stayed very still, though Ajax and Daphne could have been hit by a car without noticing. Helen couldn't take her eyes off of them. It really looked like her and Hector.

Ajax and Daphne kissed their last goodbye, and Ajax started back for his door. But as Daphne cut through the park, striding with New Yorker purpose, he stayed and watched her until she was all the way across, before he turned and slowly made his way back to the front door.

Lucas looked at Helen. "Disguise yourself," he whispered. She changed her face and he unveiled them.

"Ajax," Lucas called.

Ajax was at the base of his steps, and spun around quickly, immediately taking a fighter's stance. Lucas held up his hands in a placating gesture.

"Daedelus," Ajax growled, then he looked closer, confused. "Wait. Who are you?"

Helen could see Ajax's heart racing and his hot blood fanning out to his muscles, ready for a fight. Lucas was reacting too, even though he didn't mean to, it was just too engrained in him to stand his ground when facing aggression. Helen stepped forward before things got out of hand.

"I'm Helen, this is Lucas. Hecate should have told you by now that you're supposed to help us steal something," she told Ajax.

It was disorienting to be talking to someone who looked so much like Hector, but certain details were different, like his hands and the sound of his voice. Speaking to Ajax was akin to being on this street in another decade. Ajax was close, but not exactly what Helen knew. And Daphne had been an exact copy of Helen physically, except for her cropped hair. Helen didn't know what to do with that yet.

Ajax dropped his stance and cursed under his breath, taking a few calming breaths. "Your name is Helen?" he asked, his face twisted into a grimace. He glanced anxiously up at his door. "My brothers are going to notice I left the door open soon, so talk fast. What do you need?"

"The Omphalos. It's a rock," Lucas replied, glancing up at the door with dread. Helen knew he was picturing seeing his dad come through it and squaring off with him as Ajax had done. Lucas looked like he was from the House of Athens. His father or uncles would attack him on sight.

Ajax shook his head. He had no idea what they were talking about.

"It's about this big. It's mostly round. It just looks like a plain ol' stone," Lucas said, describing it quickly with his hands. "Check around the house. It could be there."

"And if it isn't?" Ajax asked, his eyes darted to the door. Someone was coming. "Meet me in the park after school tomorrow," he said, and then he flew up to his bedroom window so quickly a human couldn't see him do it in the dark.

Lucas veiled them just as his parents came to the door.

Helen took Lucas' hand as they watched an early twenty-something Noel and Castor come outside, in the middle of what seemed to be an argument.

Helen and Lucas weren't stunned simply because Noel and Castor looked so young. It was how raw they both were, emotionally, that came as the greatest shock. Neither Helen nor Lucas was used to seeing either of these people so tangled up in their feelings.

Noel was carrying a large bag. A look of determination was fixed on her face. Castor chased after her. Noel paused when she noticed the front door open, giving Castor a chance to take her arm and turn her around.

"You don't have to go," Castor said. "Just quit."

"I'm not quitting my other job!" she told him angrily, knocking away his hand. She tried to go down the steps, but Castor reached for her again, like he couldn't stop himself.

"We'll pay you whatever you're making at Lush, and then some," he promised.

She tilted back her head for a moment, like she was asking the stars for help. Then she looked directly at Castor and said, "So this can be my only job, and then I'm screwed if the Delos family decides to fire me? No, thank you."

"Where does this mistrust even come from, Noel?"

"Practice!" she shouted back at him. "I've been taking care of myself and my dad my whole life and the one thing I know for sure is that you can never rely on anyone." She poked him right in the middle of his chest. "Especially not the people who promise you that you can."

She tried to leave again, and he followed her, stopping her at the bottom of the steps right next to Helen and Lucas. Helen could feel Lucas's heart thrumming. She could also see the wildfire of longing and fear in Castor. And she could see the hurt, the want, and rage boiling away in Noel. Lucas's mother had been an angry young woman, and Helen never would have guessed that.

"Adonis and Leda Tiber are dangerous, Noel," Castor said, gripping her by the shoulders and nearly growling at her. "The only reason they hired you was because of me."

Noel laughed in that way people do when they want to scream. "That's just... unbelievable," she said coldly. "I've been slinging drinks since I was sixteen, and you think I got my job at the hottest nightclub in town because of you?"

Castor let her go and grabbed his hair, spinning around in a circle because he was so frustrated. "I have history with the Tiber family," he admitted.

"Which one? Leda or Don?" she asked suggestively.

"Our *families* have history," he clarified.

Noel made a dismissive gesture. "Look, I've never talked to them about you, and they've never asked questions about you, so you don't have to worry about me telling them private things about your family, if that's what this is about."

"It's not," Castor replied. "I'm not worried about you saying anything. I'm just worried about you."

"I can take care of myself. And I barely know you," Noel shot back. "What do you care where I go to work when I leave here?"

He threw his arms wide, like he was giving up. "I've never cared about anyone outside my family, but I care about you—and they know that."

Knowing the situation had deepened, Noel didn't attempt a sassy comeback. She stood there, staring at him, like she could nearly figure him out, but not quite.

"*Flaca!*" called a young woman. She came striding up to

them, wearing lace-up platform combat boots, torn fishnets, a tiny miniskirt that puckered around her bodacious backside, and a cropped leather motorcycle jacket. She snapped her gum behind her deep wine-colored matte lipstick that was lined in black.

"Hey, Castor," she said, her full lips sliding apart in a knowing smile.

"Aileen," Castor said, tipping his chin up at her in greeting.

Helen had to cover her mouth to keep herself from gasping aloud. Aileen was Pallas's wife—and Hector, Jason, and Ariadne's mother. She'd died years ago. The firecracker in front of her was not what Helen had imagined.

"*Mami*," Aileen scolded, taking Noel's hand. "You better have something else to wear in that bag," she said, her voice sliding up and down and all around with her New Nuyorican accent. "We're working the same well. No tits, no tips," she said, pulling Noel away. "'Bye," she singsonged over her shoulder to Castor. "Oh and tell your brother he can kiss my ass."

Aileen's laugher floated through the air, as Castor went inside, his eyes hungrily following Noel's every step, like his worry for both of them was dragging him down.

Helen and Lucas waited until the door closed. Then Lucas let out a held breath.

"That was so bizarre," Helen said, turning to Lucas, stupefied. "Are you okay?" she asked.

Lucas shrugged. Then shook his head. And then laughed. "I don't know what I am. It's so strange to see all of them like this."

Helen curved her hand over his bicep and leaned her head against his shoulder. But they didn't get much of a chance to process what they had just seen. Not three minutes after Castor had closed the front door, it opened again.

"It's like Grand Central," Lucas complained.

Still veiled, he and Helen turned to see a black-haired, blue-eyed, painfully skinny girl tiptoe out of the brownstone and close the door silently behind her.

The girl, who resembled Cassandra and had the same haunted look, rested her hand flat against the door.

"Goodbye," she whispered, and then she tiptoed down the front steps. Helen noticed the girl was wearing slippers, and underneath the black wool overcoat that was several sizes too large for her, Helen saw the hem of a white nightgown.

Helen felt Lucas's hand tense around hers so tightly it was painful.

"Pandora?" Helen whispered, though she knew it couldn't be her. She just couldn't think of any other young girl in the Delos family at this time.

Lucas shook his head, his eyes wild. "Antigone. The Oracle before Cass," Lucas whispered back. "We have to follow her."

Helen nodded even though she knew they should probably leave. Something was terribly wrong, and there was no way they weren't going to see where Antigone led them.

Helen and Lucas stayed veiled as they followed Antigone to the 8th Street N/R subway station. They stood near her while she sat, curled tight inside the enormous man's overcoat she wore. Her eyes were hollow, and her face was gaunt, like she was used to staring down demons, but her legs were too short to reach the ground. Her little white bedroom slippers with pink bows on them dangled childishly beneath her. The whole ride downtown Lucas never took his eyes off her.

Antigone got off at South Ferry, the very bottom of

Manhattan Island, and the territory of the House of Athens. In 1993, Athens and Thebes were bitter enemies. If Antigone were to encounter anyone from the House of Athens, the Furies would take them, and the girl, who was no warrior, would surely be killed.

Helen could hear Lucas's breath rasping in and out with fear as they followed Antigone to the water. She stayed small as she made her way through the station so no one would see her. She crept closer to the long wooden pylons that stretched out into the water and demarcated where the ferries made berth at South Ferry Station. She made sure no one was looking. She squeezed through a fence and hid, waiting. Then she started to walk out onto the pylons that made the slips for the ferries. The wind snatched at her frail body. Her huge black overcoat flapped around her girlish white nightgown.

Lucas strained to chase her down and grab her, but Helen stopped him.

"She's planned this," Helen whispered to Lucas.

He nodded and squeezed his eyes shut for a moment. When he opened them again he looked at Helen.

"So, we have to stand here and let her kill herself?" he asked, his throat working like the words were too bitter to say.

"I don't know," she replied.

Helen knew why this hurt him so much. Instead of Antigone, this could easily be his sister. Helen searched her mind, looking for anything that would comfort him. "When did Antigone die?" she asked.

Lucas brightened. "After Ajax," he said.

"That means she doesn't die tonight," Helen said optimistically.

Lucas's eyes scanned around. No one was anywhere near them. "Who saved her, then? Did we do it?" he asked desperately.

Helen shrugged and shook her head at the same time. She didn't know. But she did know that Cronus had told them to get the Omphalos. And nothing else.

"I don't think so," she replied.

Antigone had reached the end of the pylons. She held out her arms like she was going to hug that famous, sparkling skyline. And then she toppled forward, into the cold, black water.

Lucas charged down the pylons and Helen followed. She caught him before he could dive off the end, holding him back.

"Wait," Helen hissed in his ear. She clamped her arms around him, stopping him from saving Antigone, and hoping he didn't hate her for this. "Please, Lucas. Just trust that this is exactly what's supposed to happen."

Lucas went slack in her arms as they watched Antigone's white nightgown get sucked beneath the surface, her pale face sinking like the moon into the sea. Suddenly, they saw the flash of iridescent scales, and an enormous creature with triangular spikes sticking out of his back breach the surface and dive down after her. The creature took Antigone in his arms and darted down beneath the waves with her.

Helen and Lucas shared one shocked look, and then—without thinking—they both dove into the water.

Helen's lungs instantly closed. She couldn't breathe water—she couldn't even swim. She flailed as she sank. There was an iridescent flash of scales in front of them. Lucas's hand gripped tightly around her forearm, and he pulled her along with him, swimming for the both of them, as they sped through the water.

They almost couldn't keep up, but as they chased the sea

monster and the girl he had stolen from death, Helen recognized him. It was Ladon, First Born to the House of Athens, Disowned Son of Bellerophon, Spawn of Poseidon and Gaia. It wasn't long before they were swimming through old brick tunnels and sunken supports—the flooded bones buried under New York— and they breached in one of those forgotten chambers.

Helen gasped for air as soon as her head was above water. Lucas's worried eyes, spiked with wet black lashes, begged her not to make a noise as he swam with her to the other side of the subterranean cove from Ladon and Antigone. Luckily, Antigone was gasping and sputtering enough to cover for Helen while Lucas kept them veiled. He silently swam with her to the shore and then eased her gently out of the water.

"Are you okay?" Lucas whispered frantically as he pushed Helen's wet hair out of her eyes. "I forgot—I forgot you can't breathe water anymore," he said, guilt eating him up inside.

"I forgot too," Helen replied, stroking his shoulders and his face to soothe him. "I'm okay now."

He kissed her, squeezing her, touching her everywhere to make sure she was whole.

They heard Antigone scream and turned to see her skittering away from Ladon on the heels of her hands and kicking at him with her tiny feet.

Ladon cringed away from her, trying to tuck the most monstrous bits of him out of sight so as not to scare her.

"Please—I won't hurt you," he begged. "But you must stay still, or you could injure yourself. Some of my scales are as sharp as knives and if you flail about, you may cut yourself on me."

Antigone rolled over and, bracing herself on her thin, shaking arms, she wretched several times to clear her lungs. Ladon slithered closer, the human torso and head of him hovering above her anxiously, but not touching her.

"I will bring you a blanket," he said, his long, draconian lower body undulating across the brick floor toward what appeared to be a very refined living room, right in the middle of a sunken 1900's subway station.

Helen and Lucas moved closer, dodging crumbled bricks and loose black and white subway tiles as they made their way around the edge of the subterranean cove that was Ladon's lair and closer to the living space that he had amassed for himself.

While Helen and Lucas inched closer, Ladon gathered blankets and lit lamps for Antigone. He paused briefly to put on clothing. From the waist up Ladon was very much a man in his late twenties. He looked like Lucas. They had the same black hair and blue eyes of the House of Athens, and most of him was covered in the same smooth skin. But there were patches of iridescent scales on his handsome face and torso. From the waist down and all across his back, Ladon was a dragon. He had crooked legs, talons, and a tail. His spine had a row of wicked-looking spikes sticking out of his fiery-blue hide, and his tail seemed to snake about on its own.

He was monstrous. And beautiful.

He had a problem dressing himself. His dragon scales seemed to slice his clothes to shreds. He tried to cover his bare chest and his lower half, but it was a losing battle. Finally, he gave up and went back to Antigone, cringing in on himself so he didn't frighten her with his huge body.

Antigone had pulled her knees up to her chest. She was shivering and crying quietly.

"Why didn't you just let me die?" she sobbed.

Ladon laid a blanket near her and backed away quickly. "Why would someone as perfect as you want to die?" he asked.

Antigone heaved a sob that was almost a laugh. Tears slipped in curtains down her cheeks, and she brushed them away heedlessly with the back of her hand.

Ladon nudged the blanket closer to her, his hind talons prancing with worry because she hadn't put it around her yet.

"You're cold," he offered. "The blanket will help."

She pulled the blanket up over her pale skin. "Are you House of Athens?" she asked, sniffling.

Ladon nodded. Then shook his head. "I am Disowned."

Antigone hiccuped as she stared at him. "Why don't we feel the Furies?" she asked.

Ladon backed away from her and curled his lower body in a coil. He rested his human torso on top of his dragon half.

"I don't think I could ever look at you and feel anything close to fury," he replied.

Antigone took a deep, shuddering breath and snuggled down into her blanket. "I'm so tired," she said. "The Fates haven't let me sleep in weeks."

"And why not?" Ladon asked.

She yawned hugely and lowered her head. "They've been punishing me for disobeying them. They want me to say something, but I won't."

"It must be very hard to fight them," Ladon said, sympathizing.

Antigone nodded and yawned again. "But they're not here with you. What's your name?" she mumbled, her eyes closing.

"Ladon," he replied.

"Ladon. My dragon," she sighed, as she closed her eyes, and fell asleep.

Ladon watched the girl carefully for a few moments until he was satisfied that she was sleeping deeply. Then he uncoiled himself and came right for Helen and Lucas. He moved surprisingly fast, darting forward to corral them against the wall of the cavern. His sharp scales flared out from his skin, creating a gleaming ruff.

"Though I cannot see you, I can smell you and I can feel the heat of your body. Reveal yourselves," Ladon called quietly, looming above them. "I do not need to see you to kill you."

Helen and Lucas didn't have a choice. Helen used the Cestus to change her face and Lucas unveiled them.

Slated for release October 2023

For more information visit Josephineangelini.com

Also by Josephine Angelini

Starcrossed Series

Starcrossed

Dreamless

Goddess

Worldwalker Series

Trial by Fire

Firewalker

Witch's Pyre

Thriller

What She Found in the Woods

Middle Grade

Snow Lane